Any good Thing

Any *good* Thing

JOY E. RANCATORE

LOGOS & MYTHOS PRESS
SLIDELL, LA, USA

ISBN 13: 978-1-7331387-0-3 (Print)

ISBN 13: 978-1-7331387-2-7 (Epub Ebook)

ISBN 13: 978-1-7331387-1-0 (Kindle Ebook)

Library of Congress Control Number:2019947250

Logos & Mythos Press LLC

Slidell, LA, USA

For Jane who said I would;
For Mea who said I could;
For Tony who said I should.

OTHER WORKS

FICTION

Carolina's Legacy Collection:
Any Good Thing: A Novel
This Good Thing: A Novella
Every Good Thing: A Short Story Collection
One Good Thing: An Epistolary

The Crux Anthology
"Ealiverel Awakened"
Edited & Compiled by Rachael Ritchey

NONFICTION

*Finders Keepers: A Practical Approach to Find and Keep
Your Writing Critique Partner*
Joy E. Rancatore and Meagan Smith

None of us deserves any good thing.
So, when one does come—it's a gift.

CONTENTS

ACT IV: INSTAURATION

ACT V: INQUEST

Act I
Impetus

I

Grief & Capital Letters

June 22, 2016

"**L**ooking back on life provides clarity of vision and the ability to sight in on a key choice—a split second that transforms the future.

"I look out at your faces and see pasts littered with pain, tainted by addiction and scarred with battle wounds from the split-second choices you've made. Choices that altered your futures. You're not alone. You can glance around and see that. Today I'm here to share the story of a guy who once sat where you now do.

"Our paths crisscrossed his whole life. He was born twelve days before my daughter, and they became best buddies in their playpens. They grew up together and away from God until the day a tragedy sent them in opposite directions. Her on her knees; him to the bottle. That impetus struck on his fifteenth birthday, March 20, 1999, in his nearby hometown.

"I drove him into this mission. I held his hand as the poison fought to keep its grip on his body. I prayed over him from the moment he came to me for help and through each battle he faced after he walked out those doors.

"See ... the choices won't stop. The destructive ones often wear disguises, but they have one intent. To destroy. To stop you from being more, having more. More peace, joy, hope. That's exactly how it happened for him.

"Across from these choices lie lessons. Some come easier than others. And some ... well, some are never fully learned. The ones that kept eluding him were true sacrifice and acceptance of forgiveness. Trouble is, they're the most important of all.

"This is the story of Jack Calhoun."

* * *

March 20-21, 1999
Some places and times demand capital letters for their importance to life's grand scheme. When spoken, the words' importance passes through the speaker's tone to the knowing listener's ears. The Clearing was one of those places. It had long witnessed parties, fights, loves and losses. This field stood as a rite of passage for every Bellum-born teen.

Bellum, Georgia, exemplified Smalltown, U.S.A. Native teens knew the art of amusing themselves. They had big-tired trucks with hunting rifles hanging in the rear windows and mud pits to spin out in. Vices came in the forms of tobacco—along with enough peppermints and spritz to hide it from parents' disapproval—and magically-appearing liquid courage in all its forms from Boone's and Bud on up to Jim and

Jack. Late nights in nature made for early mornings of hiding from damnation in straight-backed pews.

Leading into one of these twilight trysts, the sun wafted away for its mysterious nightly Brigadoon, washing its conscience of the night ahead in the horizon's sea. Far below, thick clouds of dust whirled around a rusty pickup. As of that day, Jack officially shared the ancient vehicle with his mom, though he'd been driving since his feet could reach the pedals. The hardship license he'd get in a couple weeks was a formality. No one blinked at a pre-license boy driving a truck.

Old Mr. Cloud's hay fields rolled past. Dirt settled on the rutted and hole-laden road behind Jack. The Clearing lay ahead on the left, and the teen slowed to turn into this evergreen field. Usually bare, the field resembled a used car lot. Dotted across it rested a mixture of shiny vehicles, hand-me-down clunkers and more trucks than you could shake a stick at.

Jerry and Steven rushed him before he'd even parked.

"Jack-O!"

The party had already started for the brothers. Of course, determining when they officially reached two sheets to the wind was easier said than done. They were juniors looking for a fountain of youth to avoid adulthood.

"We got ourselves a birthday boy! Birthday boy's here, ladies!"

Jerry, beer can dangling from his hand, tossed an arm across Jack's shoulders. "You're drinkin' with us tonight, man."

"No sayin' 'no' this time," Steven commanded with a couple of oddly-placed slurs. His jet-black hair hung in a signature bowl cut.

"Y'all have each other to drink with; I'd only leave you less anyway."

As the Goodtime—a last name they chose to live up to—brothers howled at what was to them a great joke, a group of girls sashayed over, led by Leslee McKay, Bellum High's cheer captain. They each wore the official Bellum belles' uniform: skintight jeans and V-necks. In a few weeks, they'd switch to halter tops and daisy dukes.

"Happy birthday, Jack!" Rachael Burns had been friends with him from birth. It was an inevitable bond since their mothers were best friends until Carolina Burns' death when the kids were only twelve. Their relationship had been heating up since the winter formal when they spent a little alone time in a supply closet while a medley of Bon Jovi ballads set the mood.

Rachael planted a not-so-subtle sign of possession on Jack's lips as she wrapped her arms around his neck. She slid her hands down his chest and stomach until her fingers latched onto a couple of his belt loops. Preacher's daughter in pearls and curls on Sunday morning, Rachael was all heathen on Saturday nights. Jack had leaned in for a deeper kiss when Jerry and Steven pulled the couple apart. They ushered Jack past the makeshift parking lot toward a raging bonfire at the edge of the mud pit.

"Pick your poison, brother." Jerry pointed to a massive ice chest, no doubt stocked by the brothers' dad. Jack had always said no, but he'd tasted the alcohol on Rachael's tongue and decided it was time to say yes. To heck with his old man. Maybe he died drunk in a ditch, or maybe he just ran off with a shorter skirt and Jack's mom spun him a tale she could live with. Even if his dad were a hopeless drunk, that didn't mean he'd be one.

Jack grabbed a beer, tapped it before pulling the tab and took a man-sized swig. The bitter taste slid down his throat as he fought off a coughing fit. Jerry slapped him on the back and bumped their cans together.

Mid-way through his first beer, Jack felt flushed and decided this could be the best birthday ever. Mid-way through the third, he was invincible; and the world was his for the taking.

"I'm Master of my Sea, y'all! I'm gonna' get the hell out of this dead end as soon as I can." Philosophy flowed as quickly as the drink for Jack; and he proclaimed a new order, flipping the dirty blond pseudo bangs out of his eyes for the umpteenth time.

Rebel yells of agreement—a redneck version of the "Hallelujah Chorus"—rose up around him. Someone tossed more broken furniture on the bonfire followed by the rest of the lighter fluid. Flames shot straight up, higher than the surrounding pines. Curses issued from a couple of girls standing too close. They pushed on the chests of the guys who fed the fire. Stumbles and laughter. Another round for everyone.

Out of a dense cloud rising on the road near the Clearing, a rumble emerged.

"State Line's here." Jerry needed no further words. Everyone knew the guys from the neighboring town even smaller than theirs. Sworn rivals on the football field, kids from opposing sides continued the grudge away from the uprights.

Ryan Newsome spun his straight-from-the-assembly-line Camaro around before parking. Tall with a slender build and stringy hair brushing his chin, Ryan ruled his town and dreamt of a county-wide takeover. His daddy was certainly rich enough. That's what happens when you make a deal with the Devil and acquire every gas station in a fifty-mile radius.

Ryan was the kind of kid everyone feared but longed to be closest to.

Four more vehicles rolled up after him; their passengers dutifully following their master. Once he unfolded himself from his new ride, Ryan sauntered over, a derisive grin lifting one corner of his mouth. "So, this is how you 'big town' hicks live it up, huh?"

He snatched a bottle out of a girl's hand, drained it and tossed the container to the flames before dipping its previous owner backward for a forceful kiss. The muddied mixture of repugnance and incredulity on her face summed up everyone's reaction to Ryan.

Everyone but Steven Goodtime.

There was a lot Steven didn't have going for him. He wasn't much for academics; his brain couldn't seem to wrap itself around facts and dates. The football field was where he shone. He was the best center Bellum High's football team had ever boasted. The last grade he'd failed was fourth. As long as the state required a passing GPA for athletes, Steven's teachers made sure he obtained it. As great as Steven was on the field, he was even better with one other thing—cars.

Mechanics came as naturally to Steven as playing dead to a possum. His greatest pride was his car—a jet black '67 Charger. It was a machine meant for one thing only ... dragging. Steven got it as a steel shell. After a couple years of tweaking and wrenching, he had produced a hybrid monster no one could touch—though many had tried.

Ryan certainly had. Not only did he lack Steven's mechanical skills; he also couldn't touch his rival's finesse for coaxing extra power and speed from a machine. Each time they had dragged in the past, State Line's crown prince found himself a few seconds behind. And Ryan wasn't one to drop a grudge.

Now, Anna Claire, the girl Ryan had planted his mark on, happened to be Steven's sweetheart. They'd been together five years, and he'd tucked away a tiny diamond in his drawer for her. He'd set aside half his drag winnings over the past year and a half and planned to slide it on her finger after the junior/senior prom in a few months.

When he saw Ryan force himself on his girl, Steven morphed into a linebacker and barreled toward the guy who thought he could take whatever—or whoever—he wanted. "Not my girl, you asshole!"

Ryan went down hard under every ounce of Steven's 220-pound frame. With their fall, every boy in sight converged for a free-for-all fist fight, overactive testosterone coursing through them and blocking logical processing.

Jerry inserted himself between Ryan and Steven until a couple of Ryan's bouncers pulled him away and ganged up on him. Jack tackled one—a tall kid with a ponytail. They rolled around in the dirt, swapping punches, until Jack pinned his opponent down, face in the dirt. Jack held him in a merciless chokehold, as a bottle rose to strike above his own head. Just then, a girl's voice rang out—commanding and clear.

"STOP IT!"

Whistles from the other girls joined Rachael's scream to demand the attention of the wild creatures before them. Fighters pushed and shoved themselves free of one another as they looked around for the source of the interruption.

"What the heck is wrong with you idiots? Get out of the dirt and act like normal human beings!" Rachael's fiery cheeks matched her hair as she spoke reason.

Ryan spit blood and spewed curses. "This isn't over. You boys can't hide behind your skirts when real men roll in." He turned to Steven who sported what would be an impressive black eye. "I'm sure as hell not done with you. We'll settle this behind the wheel. Winner gets the bitch tonight."

Anna Claire's eyes widened, and steam poured from Steven's entire head as his face reddened. Jerry pressed his whole weight into his brother. "Not tonight, man. He's not worth it. Settle this another time."

Steven swatted his kid brother aside, like a bothersome gnat. "My girl's not up for grabs. I'll race you—keys for keys. That overpriced heap of yours will be mine."

He pointed toward the cherry red car as Ryan tossed back his head and howled. "You're dumber than you look if you think that car's goin' home with you. I'll be taking your junker back for parts. You've got no idea what you're up against, Goodtime."

He drew out the name with a deep, greasy voice. Disdain dripped from each syllable.

"No! No dragging tonight! We'll set up a time and do it right ... at the strip." Jerry's mass made an imposing figure in the space between the opponents. His shoulder-length hair swayed around his head as he looked back and forth.

"Aww ... Little Brother doesn't want to walk home through the cornfields tonight. Must suck to have your own family not believe in you." Ryan shot the insults over his shoulder as he headed back to his car.

"Stay out of this, Jer. I'm finishin' him tonight." Steven's eyes pierced Ryan's back.

"Man, you're lit. Don't do this." Jerry fought for eye contact and pled with his brother to see reason. "Walk away."

"You know I can't do that. I got two things in this world—Anna Claire and cars."

"And, if you wreck, you'll lose 'em both." Jerry saw a flicker of hesitation in his brother's eyes.

"Steve, think it through. This road's the worst place to drag. Ryan ain't half the driver you are. He hits one of those giant holes, he's gonna lose his shit. You know you can trump him any day; set it up. Next weekend'll be perfect. Reggie would love to have you two square off at his strip."

"I ain't got all night, Goodtime. Kick your brother's fat ass to the curb and meet me on the dirt."

Jack stumbled into Steven's sightline and gestured toward the party crasher. "You got him, Steve! He hasn't beat you yet; and you know he doesn't stand a chance. Kick his ass and send him cryin' to his mommy."

Beer sloshed as Jack wildly waved his arms. The mass around them responded with cheers and shouts as they followed Jack's lead.

"Do it for Bellum. Teach these pricks they can't come in our house and have their way." With a nod toward the guy he'd had on the ground earlier, Jack urged harder as he felt the crowd's excitement and watched his words' effect on his friend.

The yelling he instigated sent Jack soaring higher than the alcohol had. He tossed back the remainder of another can before flattening it atop the beaten field. Faced with the chance of watching a race on his birthday, Jack was all for it. After all, he deserved a good thrill.

"Ste-ven! Ste-ven! Ste-ven!" Jack began a chant that soon spread around the spectators. The mob converged as several of the bigger guys hoisted Steven up, and Jack led the throng to deliver their champion to his car. The mob's cheers had won; no backing down this night.

"Steven!"

He turned toward his girl's voice, jumped down and pressed through the crowd to encircle her in his arms.

"Be safe," Anna Claire whispered.

"Always." With a wink, Steven turned his focus to the track.

Jerry spun and hit the dirt beside the raging fire to pray. Jack led everyone else to line the powdery road along the Clearing and cheer on their gladiators. Shouts greeted the engines as they revved into high gear and kicked up dust for the entertainment of the mob. Their course was simple—down and back. First to the turnoff at the Clearing won.

Steven charged into the lead, intuitively weaving around the road's craters. Dust and dirt billowed behind the powerful machines. The cloud blinded the crowd to some of the action, so they pressed closer into the course for a better view of the return trip.

At the turn, Ryan swung ahead. Steven recovered quickly; and they barreled toward the cheering crowd, bouncing back and forth on the pockmarked road—pinballs in an obstacle-laden playfield.

With the finish line in sight, Steven pushed his Charger into the red. Not to be outdone, State Line hit the floor and turned to watch the face of the guy he was sure to finally beat.

Ryan never saw the gaping hole waiting to flip his tire.

Cheers and shouts ceased. Silence swallowed the air along Bellum's countryside as the space filled with flying red and black blurs.

Like a pinball whose momentum collides with a slingshot, the Camaro flipped into the Charger, sending both soaring in opposite directions. The instantaneous slow motion pressed pause on the teens' lives and scrambled the tape before hitting fast forward.

Metal's scraping and grating shredded the deafening silence. A car slammed to the earth as easily as a ragdoll in a toddler's rage produces aftershocks guaranteed to reverberate long after the debris settles.

Jerry robotically drifted toward the sounds—across the field, up the rise, to the road strewn with tragedy. Drawn toward what he didn't want to see with a resolve he couldn't feel, Jerry reached the carnage. The scene he witnessed would never leave the minds of any who survived it.

Like a piece of aluminum foil folded around a corn cob at the state fair, a crumple of red molded to a giant pine. Ryan's body slumped against his seatbelt; his bloodied head pressed against the shattered window. The top half of Leslee's body splayed across the hood, arms outstretched to greet her end with a terror her eyes would forever hold.

Beyond that, pieces of Steven's handiwork littered the road, ditches, fields, trees. Its bulk perched off in Cloud's field, leaning awkwardly toward the driver's side.

Gasoline. Hot metal. Fear. Three odors permeating the air, joined by a fourth. Heavy and foul—but not quite—this scent invoked drowsiness, lured one in, then shot fear straight to the brain, heightening all awareness. When its reality hit him, Jerry retched where he stood; his eyes fixed on the few intact chunks of his brother's masterpiece. On the smears of blood and brains across the windows. On the still-emptying remains of the head dangling from the windowless door.

Steven had tossed around the steel can with every spin and rotation—no one could agree on how many. Reports varied from five to twenty-two. Everyone did agree he'd gone end over end and side over side.

Screams of terror and cries of pain mingled, indistinguishable. More injuries dotted the road. Car parts, like shrapnel, had filled the air, maiming onlookers lined up too close to a finish line that had sped up to greet its competitors. One of the few with a car phone put in the call for help.

The jagged edges of glass from someone's windshield had found the region near Jack's carotid artery. In the seconds after he felt the searing sting of its cut, but before he succumbed to darkness, he thought back to the taste of Rachael's lips, the sound of the beer tab popping and the invincibility the heavy liquid brought.

He needed more.

Rachael knelt in the road, uttering prayers of repentance for herself and intercession for the life in her hands as she attempted to keep the blood from spilling out on either side of the glistening chunk of glass. She breathed only when sirens released the dam on her tears.

EMTs took charge and rushed Jack away. Once Rachael comprehended that he was out of her care, she mechanically turned. She and Anna Claire locked eyes.

"I held his blood in. The cut was deep on his neck. That's bad, right? I mean, the neck ... that's bad?" Rachael held out bright red hands. The sticky air dried them to rust as the reality of the split-second alteration to their futures numbed her to her core.

"I was gonna tell him tonight." Anna Claire whispered her secret as shock dried up her tears. "I'm pregnant."

* * *

The race crowd's shell shock followed them to Bellum Medical Hospital. The church bells tolled midnight, though no one in the lobby heard them over the shrieking of grieving mothers and the profanities of Ryan's father. A tornado of hate and self-importance, he raised hell with every staff person he encountered before following a stretcher to a waiting chopper.

Silence settled as news spread through the waiting family and friends. The coroner brought back two kids who would never see adulthood—Steven and Leslee. Life over.

Bobby Lee had a jagged exhaust pipe sticking out of his gut. After three codes in the ambulance, he'd already bled out by the time they arrived. Two girls suffered head injuries from flying debris. Susan lingered in a coma for a few days after her transfer to Atlanta. A doctor there finally called her death at 9:03 Wednesday morning. Beth Anne endured stitches all over her face. Bellum Medical wasn't a tempting enough post for a plastic surgeon, so she would carry visible scars of that night.

And then there was Jack.

With blood seeping from his wound, Jack had been too unstable for a transfer. Dr. Harvey bowed over him for hours. He stopped the bleeding, irrigated the gash and painstakingly sewed up the giant wound, running diagonally from just beneath his chin to his chest. Most small-town surgeons didn't get the chance at a save like that. Of course, most hadn't stitched guys back together in battlefield conditions either. It wasn't pretty, but Jack would get his life back ... and a giant scar to remind him of what he lost.

As if he could ever forget.

Rachael cried on her dad's shoulder in the upstairs waiting room. She broke in the midst of the horror that night and reached for the only Absolute she knew—God. She preached her dad a sermon of God's forgiveness as she asked for his. She shared her fears for Jack and her resolve for a new life. Rev. Benjamin Burns felt his heart tighten at her words. When it comes to daddies whose daughters tend to choose the wrong boys, forgiveness doesn't come naturally—even for reverends.

Deep in the night, Rachael fell asleep against him, a single tear resting in the corner of her eye. Ben wiped it off with his thumb and kissed her head. He thought about how he'd failed her time and again since his wife had lost her battle with cancer, but he knew God hadn't. He breathed a prayer of thanks that his little girl had been spared and prayed God would do the same for all the kids who'd been out there. Salvation from death, of course; but, of higher importance, salvation for a life in Christ.

Jack's mother, Becky Calhoun, sat in a corner. A single mom for most of Jack's life, she was usually alone. The only close friend she'd ever had was Carolina Burns. The preacher's wife had extended friendship to Becky before they even knew they had little ones on the way. Their pregnancies sealed their bond.

Smeared mascara and red eyes evidenced the tears Becky had shed previously. She sat then, drawn into herself; eyes fixed on the clasped hands in her lap. Her face carried the resignation of one used to facing life's worst bullets one-on-one.

At 3:25, Becky expected the worst as Dr. Harvey stiffly strode toward her.

"He'll make it."

With those three words, Becky cried in public for the first time in her life. Her decades of holding in the pain of a husband who walked away, the loss of her only friend and the anxiety of raising a child alone got knocked loose; and it all flowed from her. Rachael woke to the news of Jack's survival and went to hold and comfort his mom. Becky had become a stand-in mama for Rachael over the years, and the girl willingly offered her a shoulder.

Bellum's entire population shifted as the cemetery's yawning earth embraced four new children. Without a doubt, the race spectators' lives would never be the same. Whenever anyone mentioned the old dirt Road or That Night, they were breathed with grief and capital letters.

II

Empty Bottles & an Open Door

Spring 1999 to March 20, 2001

Jack carried more from the tragedies than the scar on his neck. He staggered under the responsibility he felt for his role in the incident. The way he urged Steven on, straight into the driver's seat. The blame he caught in glances from Jerry and Beth Anne, along with many adults, reiterated his conviction that his words drove Steven to the deaths of That Night. Once he returned home following his recovery from surgery, he woke up screaming every night. No one knew but his mama—and the bottles he always found a way to get his hands on. Since his initial taste, he couldn't get enough alcohol. Like a parched man in a desert, he craved it, needed it, lusted after it. He sought company in the liquid and preferred solitude everywhere else, including the school cafeteria.

After a week of sitting in a corner by himself at lunch, Jack heard a familiar voice cut through his angry, hazy thoughts.

"Hey there, stranger!" Rachael lowered herself onto the bench across from him. She slid her food between them. It rested on the same type of brown tray they used back in elementary to fly down the giant hill between the school building and the gym.

He looked up, a mixture of longing, sadness and loss in his expression. It passed rapidly, though; and he met her cheerful gaze with a guarded glare.

"Go on back to your friends, Rach. I don't need to be your good deed for the day."

"Oh, get over yourself, Jack. I want to sit here. Can't you just let me sit with you one day?"

He stabbed at the ketchup with his fries, sending red splashes across the table.

"I miss my best friend and just want to see you more."

His downturned face gave her nothing to read. She casually took the top bun off her chicken sandwich. "You still like pickles?"

His head snapped up, and a flicker of the friend he used to be sparked far beneath the mask he'd donned. She smiled as he reached over and took them, popping them all in his mouth at once.

A rising memory brightened Rachael's expression. "Remember the time we went swimming in our underwear in Mr. Brown's pond? He caught us and said he was going to tell my daddy."

Jack's mouth rose in a half-grin. "Yeah, until I told him I'd be happy to tell your daddy what I saw him and the pianist doing in her car the weekend before."

Rachael's musical laughter caught him off guard. He'd missed that sound but hadn't realized how much. The pang within terrified him. When had she become his other half? The whole nightmare he pressed into motion could have killed her. That realization penetrated to the center of his being and stuck, sharp and severing.

"Remember the letters my mom left me when she died? I read one. It was all about finding ways to serve God in little things. So, I've been playing around with painting." Rachael slid a notecard toward him. On it was a watercolor painting of a foal with round cursive letters to one side. "This is my favorite Bible verse. I thought you might like it."

Jack glanced at it long enough to see something about *perfect peace* before he leapt from the bench. He gathered his trash and remaining burger pieces, back to his previous raging state.

"Look, Rach. I don't know why you really came over here." Jack turned, not quick enough for Rachael to miss the moisture welling in his eyes or the fuzziness in his tone with his next statement. "I'm not who I used to be. You need to stay the hell away from me."

Rachael grabbed his wrist. "My mom wrote something else in that letter. 'None of us deserves any good thing. So, when one does come—it's a gift. Accept it.'"

Her smile tugged at him even as he chose to leave. His words rose as he walked away, looking back with a parting sneer. "I don't need a tease like you in my life anyway."

That inner ache he'd experienced a moment earlier exploded into jagged pieces that sank into his heart, twisting deeper. Rachael was the only girl he'd ever deeply cared about, and he'd just discarded her care like his lunch remnants.

"I'll never stop being here for you, Jack. And neither will God."

Her words, softly spoken, paused his getaway for a split second. She recognized his hesitation as a sign he'd heard her and sighed, despite the clenching grip she felt around her heart. Jack stormed down the hall as he shook his head in a futile attempt to still the turbulent confusion inside. He couldn't deny the way his connection to Rachael had deepened in recent years, but he also knew he would only cast his pain onto her. He slammed his locker after retrieving books for the next class. She was just another reminder anyway.

For her part, Rachael kept the promise she made that day. She prayed for Jack, talked to him when he'd let her. And, she loved him. That, she never stopped doing, even long after he made it clear to her, repeatedly, that he'd left her behind with some part of his soul in the Clearing.

Jack ignored Rachael and buried his conflicted emotions by making the rounds of parties in the area. There was no shortage of parents willing to purchase libations for their children and friends. When Jack started filling a bag with bottles to get him through to the next throwdown, though, word got out. He found his name showed up less often on guest lists. On top of that, the new sheriff put his boot to underage drinking, so Jack found fewer parties to crash.

At the first party Jack had attended in months, an acquaintance shakily scrawled out the name of a cashier and the liquor store where she worked in Clemson. It was less than an hour away, and she never asked for identification if the buyer was young, handsome and willing to return her flirting. Jack had all three going for him and soon became one of Misty's favorite regulars.

Jack's grades remained steady through freshman year, despite the time he'd missed following his surgery; but they took a nosedive mid-way through his sophomore year. By his junior year, it was clear he wouldn't be graduating alongside classmates with whom he'd once shared nap mats.

A deeper blow came when he lost his spot on the football team. Grades could be managed; shaky hands after a day locked away without liquor? Lashing out at teammates when double vision caused dropped passes? Those made for a different story. Jack took the loss of a place on his team hard. Prior to That Night, he was on his way to being a team leader. He'd found a knack for teaching the junior high kids and leading even the senior players.

When the nightmares finally dissolved, the rage flared up. As the school days crept past, his fidgeting grew longer and his fuse shorter. Once the life of the party, Jack found himself more an outcast. His constant fluctuations between the rage and sullenness of sobriety and the soaring emotions infused through his veins with the liquor made him unstable and unpredictable. He drank to make himself social and then drank some more to handle the solitude that stuck beside him.

As his junior year dragged on, Jack started fights and even punched a dent in Marc Parker's locker when he called Jack a dumb drunk. Suspension after suspension resulted in expulsion.

His time to drink doubled, and he took to stealing to keep up with his demand. Within a few months of walking out of the doors of Bellum High for the last time, he'd stolen money and alcohol from nearly every person around. In a town of only 4,944—until a new fall when another group of lucky graduates flew like colorful leaves into the real world, never to return—residents talked about each neighbor and the business behind their front doors.

"Did you hear about Ruby Appleby? Poor dear!" Hester Lee, the town's queen gossip, could be overheard outside Taylor's Grocery.

"Why, no! Whatever's happened now? It's not that no-account granddaughter of hers who ran off with the mobster boy to New Orleans?" The look of distaste on Emma Jean Handy's face left no doubt as to her view of folks with Sicilian surnames.

"Not this time; though, I did hear she's havin' a baby. Due about a month or two before it should be for her to wear that white gown we saw in the Society section." Hester gave the second tidbit in appropriately hushed tones.

Emma Jean nodded knowingly. "I told you to remember that wedding date."

"If it weren't bad enough Ruby's lost her hussy granddaughter to that criminal, last night she got robbed."

"Robbed? Lord, have mercy!" Emma Jean gasped. Her eyes widened as she dropped wrinkled hands to her chest. "The Calhoun boy?"

Hester nodded. "Of course! Who else? Ruby's brother, Hyram, was spittin' mad when he found out this morning. You should have heard him outside the American Legion. Of course, that boy deserves to be under the jail, if you ask me; but we've got a Christian duty to his poor mama. I s'pose we'll all just keep feedin' his foul habits until he drinks himself to death."

"Disgusting! Of course, it's no wonder. She chose to marry that drunk. It's in the genes, they say."

"Do you think she hoped his leavin' would keep her boy from it?" Hester asked.

"If so, 'twere a fool's hope." Emma Jean shook her head as the two parted ways to carry their news on with them to the post office and beauty parlor.

They were right that no one wanted to press charges against Jack on account of his mom. Everyone knew Becky was doing the best she could. And, though Jack didn't notice, they all did—she had aged twenty years since the night her son took his first sip.

Becky loved Jack. His father had left her; her best friend had died. But, Jack … Jack was hers. The one person she thought wouldn't abandon her. She longed to hold him close to her heart like she did the night he was born, but she was terrified of smothering him and losing him that way, too. So, she clung to him from a distance as she fretted—all alone—over how to handle the mess he was creating. When she looked at him, she saw him for what he still was—despite his actions—a kid. Her kid. The one she had rocked and nursed and loved. The one whose skinned knees she'd healed with kisses. The one whose dreams she'd heard even as she prayed her own desires for his future.

With all those memories in mind, Becky prepared her son's favorite dinner and baked him a chocolate cake with chocolate chips. She wanted his seventeenth birthday to be more special than his sixteenth, when he'd skipped school to spend the day in a drunken stupor. He didn't want to feel the pain of the year before, he'd told her. She thought, perhaps, if she could remind him of happier times, he'd come back to her, be whole again. Not be his father and disappear into the night.

The afternoon evaporated into evening; the evening dissolved into darkness. It was nearly midnight when Jack stumbled in to the kitchen. Becky's immediate relief crumbled under her anger at his selfishness, at his lack of care for her. At him. She screamed at him through a rush of tears. "Where have you been? I've been scared out of my mind for you. You could've been dead in a ditch for all I knew. I fixed your favorite dinner … and the cake …" Becky gestured toward the carefully decorated cake on the table before continuing in a broken whisper. "It's your birthday, Jack. I just wanted it to be special. Tried to …."

His inner flame erupted. He spat out, "Stop caring about me! No one else in this God-forsaken hole does. Leave me the hell alone to be what I am." Those words sliced Becky's heart in half as Jack shoved his mom toward the stove, hard enough for her knees to buckle and her head to bounce off the corner of the oven's handle as she crumpled to the floor.

When she regained consciousness, Becky gingerly felt her throbbing head and brought back bloodied fingertips. She slowly stood and reached for the phone.

"Ben? It's Becky. I'm calling because ..."

She paused, surprise registering as she listened.

"Yes, I'm okay. I hear the siren now."

Closer and closer the wail drifted.

"And he came right to you?"

It turned on her street.

"How long is the program?"

Lights filled her house.

"And, this will help him? He'll be okay after ...?"

The silence after the siren ceased echoed in her head. Becky looked at the blood on the phone but didn't wipe it off. She shook her pounding head and grabbed her purse. Experience told her not to hope. She turned to the table and the layers of chocolate with the number candles—red, his favorite color. The thing about moms is they keep hoping, even when it makes no sense. She passed the paramedics as they rushed through the door her son had left ajar in his earlier escape. Her words beat any out of their open mouths.

"Sorry you were bothered, boys. I'm fine—just a little slip. I've got somewhere to be. Lock up for me?"

* * *

The rehabilitation dormitories of the Damascus Road Mission had been designed for comfort with all the feel of home. In contrast, the medical building was sterile, built for efficiency and survival. Bare hallways looked like the simplest of nursing homes without color or décor. Nowhere was there more gloom across the facility than within Jack. That day had been his worst drinking day. He wasn't sure how much he'd consumed, but he knew he'd never been in this much pain. He also knew he'd never desired the relief of death as he did right then. The hard tile floor couldn't cool the flaming liquid that still filled him. He released a barely audible moan and wondered how long such pain could last.

As Jack battled his inner beast, Ben strode down the eggshell hall toward Jack's room. On Sundays in the line that snaked out of Bellum Baptist's steepled door, he was Rev. Burns. At the mission, he was simply Ben. He had known many addicts over the years, and he also knew it often took multiple admissions before a person finally accepted help. With the first excruciating pangs of withdrawal, they'd hit the bricks and head straight for their surest supply. Ben had mentally lumped Jack in that group—the Repeaters.

His dad side grieved for his daughter's devotion to the boy who, for a while, had her going down his dangerous path and who still held her heart. The preacher side knew the beauty of redemption and forgiveness. The family friend side entertained a repeating mental slideshow of Jack growing up. He'd played catch with Jack, been at every ballgame and somewhat filled the dad gap. Ben was working on pulling all these sides together in hopes of counseling Jack on the path to a much brighter future. That day, he'd fill the father-figure role as he took Becky's place by Jack's side. She had left a few minutes before he arrived.

After knocking twice on the stark white door, Ben peered around it.

"Jack!"

Ben rushed to kneel beside Jack. He lay curled in the fetal position, trembling uncontrollably.

"Send Dr. Maives to the Calhoun boy's room immediately!" Ben clipped the walkie-talkie back to his belt loop and placed a hand on Jack's back.

Jack's widened eyes locked with Ben's and fed off the calm he found there as the pastor spoke. "It's okay, son; you're going to be okay. This is all part of the withdrawal process. You're going to make it through this. Doc Maives is on his way. I'm right here with you. I'm not going anywhere."

Finding Jack this way both encouraged and terrified Ben. The boy had made it through the night without bolting. If they could carry him through this initial nightmare of withdrawals, he may make it after all.

Bit by bit, the shaking subsided. Jack's heart slowed as Ben spoke softly to him. Before Ben had arrived, Jack feared his heart was going to explode inside his chest. The doctor arrived ahead of a nurse pushing a vitals' monitor. He listened as Ben updated him on how he had found the boy a few moments earlier.

"Good morning, Jack. I'm Dr. Maives. This is my nurse Hannah. Let's sit you up here; yep, right here in this chair. We're going to check your vitals and see what we can do to help you feel better. Jack, I want you to know all of this—as scary and painful as it is—means you're getting better. Your body is fighting hard to overcome your addiction. You've got a lot of poison to flush out. We won't win the war right away; but, one battle at a time, we'll get there."

As the doctor spoke, Hannah adjusted the blood pressure cuff on Jack's arm. She checked his temperature and jotted numbers on a clipboard she handed to Dr. Maives.

Jack brought his misty hazel eyes level with the doctor's as he focused on that final promise. His boyish gaze pled for release from the poison that enslaved him. All the pain, confusion, fear, grief, rage and dependence roiling within him raged for his attention. Every inch of his body screamed in pain. His insides flamed. Breathing required concentration he wasn't sure he could muster. For a moment, he wasn't convinced he even wanted to draw another breath.

* * *

During the later stages of his withdrawal, Jack experienced hallucinations as he revisited his final drunken hours and other memories. It became a mental motion picture he wouldn't forget.

The first image was Rachael. She bent over him, a slight smile on her face. She laughed and tossed back her shiny red hair. Man, he loved it when she laughed and when she wore her hair down. Down and silky straight. She looked back at him with her dark blue eyes, twinkling with a secret. A secret he had to know. Wanted to know. Wanted ... her.

His eyes retreated into the dark safety behind his eyelids. Slowly, more moments rose in his mind.

Smashing the empty bottle behind the church. *That was my last. Not enough.*

I need money. Mom's got money.

His mama. A birthday cake. Bright red candles. Red—his favorite color. The color of blood. His mama bleeding.

Bleeding because of him.

Walking. Darkness. Falling. Darkness.

And then a rush of understanding came as his eyes flew open despite the light.

I hurt her. Left her, bleeding and unconscious. I went to Rach. Her dad opened the door I beat on. Her dad, the preacher. The director of ... the mission for addicts. Rach's dad. He brought me here to get sober. To get back to how I was before …

Before the night he took his first sip. Before the night he urged one of his best friends to get behind the wheel of a suped up muscle car and drag, drunk. Before the night his friend's brains got beat out of his skull. Before the night he almost died. Before the night he longed for one thing—and one thing only—to drown the guilt and pain.

I'm an alcoholic.

Jack called on his core muscles to help him up; they screamed back at him with a searing wrench that made him cry out and sent tears spilling down his face. Both hands on his stomach, Jack didn't bother to wipe back his emotion. This is how he would die. On a rock for a bed. In a tiny oatmeal-colored room. All alone. An addict without his assuagement.

Another memory emerged from one of those usually locked compartments in the mind. His neck was warm, sticky. Rachael's face had never looked that way before. Terror. And, a smell … putrid, nauseating … rose from nearby with a sound … retching. Jerry's unearthly wail of "Steven!" cut through his other senses. A loud clang switched the rolling screen in Jack's brain to black. His arm hung off the bed, dangling above a cup that had fallen from his nightstand. Fallen … like Steven.

During the withdrawal process, Jack begged for sleep, for death, for release. But his eyes refused to close because, each time they did, he was back on the night he relinquished control to the alcohol. His mind wouldn't rest. And then something terrifying happened. His internal eyes widened and stuck; scenes flickered in and out, out and in.

Flying dust, candles, car exhaust, birthday cake, fire to the heavens, stove, flying glass, home.

The warm, sticky feeling on his neck. His mama crumpled against the stove, bleeding. Blood. On his neck. Mama bleeding. Mama's blood on his neck. Steven dead. Steven. Mama. He killed them. Both dead. Death. Never forget the smell of ... blood ... emptiness ... life spilling out ... death.

He did it.

Mama. *Mama, I'm sorry. Mama, I killed you. I didn't mean to.*

Sorry, Mama.

Mama.

A familiar voice soothed him as a soft, cool hand caressed his dripping forehead.

"Yes. I'm here." Becky lifted a rag out of ice water and rang out excess moisture before folding and resting it on Jack's brow. "I'm right here. I'm not gonna leave you. I won't ever leave you."

He looked up with an unspoken apology into the golden gaze of the woman who loved him, even after he tossed her the same brokenness his father had left behind—empty bottles and an open door.

III

Accept the Gift

March through June 2001

The hallucinations lasted nearly two days, off and on. Jack faded in and out of consciousness as his mom and Ben took turns watching over him.

Damascus Road Mission, near Bellum, was the only rehab facility in the area and the only Christian one in the region. Dr. Maives and other medical staff oversaw the withdrawal process. Next, the recovering residents found themselves ready to learn to live again. Counseling and discipleship with Ben and other leaders began, along with classes for career preparation. Jack found himself ready for that second stage a few days after the haze of his withdrawals. The realization of what he did to his mom convinced him he needed all the help they could give. He reflected on the mistakes of his past as he began to dream of a brighter future.

Jack leaned against the window casing. He stared out, not registering the signs of life beyond the panes. Ducks glided in for a landing on the pond across from him. The water cast off blinding shimmers that caught his eye until his door's creaking broke the spell of his introspection.

He turned to see his mom. She smiled, but her eyes held little joy.

"How're you feeling, sweetie?"

"Much better than last week around this time." Jack's grin only lifted a corner of his mouth. "How's your head?"

Her answer held a sincerity that went deeper than its words' complexity. "It's just fine."

Jack sat on the twin bed and Becky joined him. She took his hand in both of hers. "Jack. I've failed you. No, don't interrupt. I need you to listen. Instead of coming down hard on you when I saw what you were doing to yourself, I gave in to my own fear. Fear of pushing you away. Of losing you."

Tears marked her cheeks as she looked up from their hands. "I nearly lost you. Twice. Perhaps more than that. I turned my head and didn't pull you back where you needed to be. I didn't help you like a mother should."

She shook her head and brushed at her eyes with the back of one hand before continuing. "Now, you can get the help you need. Do not waste this. Ben can help you. Let him; because, Jack, I want you to have a future—a bright one, full of whatever possibilities you can dream up. That's all I've ever wanted for you." Becky placed a hand on her son's damp cheek.

"I'm so sorry. For everything. I do want help, and I want to make so many things right. I promise not to blow this. I've been thinking a lot about the future. About how Steven and the others, they don't get one. I don't want to screw this up because I want to take care of you for a change. You've put up with so much crap from me the past few years and taken such good care of me my whole life. All I want to do is find a way to provide for you for a change, help you quit the job you hate. I love you so much, Mama."

Her hands framed his face, as they rested their foreheads together. "I love you, too, Jack. Do not shut me out again. I promise not to let you slip back into the darkness of where you were ever again, if I can help it."

"I don't ever want to go back there."

***

On the final day of Jack's medical rehabilitation, Dr. Maives entered the boy's room. He patted Jack's leg and greeted him with a smile before sitting down on the bed beside him.

"You're a very lucky young man." The doctor's white hair set the stage for sage advice. "I realize I'm bordering on the preaching side of things right now, but this has to be said. The fact that you haven't killed yourself or someone else yet is the first amazing aspect of all this. The next two are that you got help and you've come this far."

Jack had never really considered how many times he could have killed someone else with his drinking. As Dr. Maives uttered cautionary words, Jack ran through the countless times he swerved home, more in the wrong lane than the right.

"You still have a long way to go. The mission will get you there, though, if you open yourself up and give it your all. Ben's here to help you in ways no medicine can." Dr. Maives' grandfatherly smile calmed the turmoil in Jack's heart. "From a medical standpoint, I can say you should be okay without any lasting effects. You've got youth on your side. However, I have to send you off with a stern warning. Don't ever drink again. Not even a single drop. One of the things you'll learn much more about in the mission is that you're an addict. Alcohol is your enemy. It wants to wield its power over you, so don't let down your guard. Not for a buddy's wedding, your twenty-first birthday, your own wedding—no event is special enough. Even one drop is too much for you because I know you don't want to repeat what you just went through, right?"

"You're right about that," Jack agreed.

"Good. Now, I'm done preaching." The doctor placed a hand on Jack's shoulder as he continued. "I also want to tell you how proud I am of you. You took the first giant leap— getting help. I believe God's got a special future for you."

Jack returned the man's smile but wondered how God could have any good thing in store for him. He didn't think God thought much of him at all.

* * *

When it came time for him to move over to the men's rehab dorm, Jack had plenty of help. Becky and Ben walked with him, talking about everything from the mission's reputation for great food to daily chapel services to the gym on campus. By the time they arrived at the room that would be Jack's home for the next several months, his head swam with their chatter. The room Jack walked into after Ben opened the door had walls only slightly darker than the oatmeal color he'd grown accustomed to, but throughout the space, splashes of color masked the neutral base. Directly across from the room's entrance, a watercolor painting filled the space between two windows. Dark purple flowers and greenery covered a cross. The artist had accentuated each wood grain, petal vein and stem variation with such skill that Jack thought he could feel the roughness of the cross or caress the silkiness of the flowers.

Someone to the right cleared his throat, and Jack's gaze was diverted from the painting. An older gentleman sat on the bed, a Bible opened on his knee. The initial expression he gave when he realized Jack would be his roommate was one of irritation and distrust, but—like a rogue storm cloud passes on a late spring day—it coasted across his face. In its place, Jack found a sympathy that surprised him.

The man closed the book in his lap and tucked it under an arm before rising to extend a hand to Jack. "I'm Pete."

"Jack." They nodded at one another, an awkward acknowledgement of the years between them. Introductions continued around the group. Jack wondered how old the man was. He certainly looked spry as he bent to scoop up a trucker hat he'd knocked off the bed when he stood. The tufts of gray remaining on his head gave away his age. It was in the bags under his eyes—bloodshot from too little sleep—and the defeated droop to his shoulders that Jack read the story of his years.

"I'll be headin' on down to the cafeteria now, get outta y'all's way. I hear they got good rolls. I do like rolls." Pete nodded as he passed them.

Ben and Becky made sure Jack had everything he needed, knew his schedule and understood what was expected of him. They chuckled at his declaration that the dorm beds were a "heckuva lot comfier" than the ones in the medical facility. Fifteen minutes later, Jack entered the cafeteria and located an empty spot next to Pete. They both enjoyed thirds on the rolls.

* * *

Jack's time at the mission settled into a routine after his orientation week. Every morning, right after breakfast, he met with Ben for individual counseling.

"You already look better than you did a couple weeks ago, that's for sure." During their first session, Ben leaned forward casually, forearms on his legs.

"I feel even better." Jack's response accompanied one of the first boyish grins he'd flashed in a while.

Ben nodded as he chose the right words. "This isn't going to be an easy three months. And, you're not going to exit these doors and have everything be simple. You're starting an uphill climb today. With the help of family and friends, it can be easier. But, only God can lighten our burdens."

Jack looked down when Ben mentioned God. He hated to break it to the man in front of him, but he just didn't buy the whole "God thing." How could some faceless, voiceless Being out there, somewhere help him with anything? Besides, he still didn't see how this God would have anything to do with him after all he'd done. He'd attended enough church to know how serious this deity was about people not doing bad stuff. And, he'd done plenty.

If Ben noticed Jack's unease, he didn't let on. "Let's talk a little about what you can expect as you continue through the program. We'll meet together one-on-one every weekday morning to talk about how you're doing, what questions you may have; really just make sure you're making progress and getting all the help you need. We'll do some group counseling sessions each afternoon as well. That'll start today."

Jack shifted. Meeting one-on-one with a man whose house he'd practically grown up in was one thing. Spilling innermost thoughts and feelings with a bunch of total strangers? That felt weird.

Ben continued, "Everyone's got to have a job around here, too. I thought Grounds Maintenance would be a good fit for you. What do you think?"

"I do like being outside." Jack's crooked grin held the uncertainty of a kid who'd never held a job.

"You'll also be able to take some classes, so let's look through what's available and find something that interests you." They scooted together as Ben opened a worn black binder. "You're welcome to look through all of these, but these first few pages hold some I thought you'd like. Career Preparation, Financial Math … Planning for Retirement. Anyway, give them a glance and see what grabs you."

Jack chuckled at Ben's attempt at humor and flipped through the pages until one caught his eye. "This. I want to get my GED. I told my mom I was gonna have a future, and I think this will start me toward one."

Ben looked where Jack was pointing and nodded his head as he made a note on his legal pad. "That's great. We'll add that. Now, you might not be able to take the tests until after your eighteenth birthday, but this will give you a great start at studying."

"Woodworking could be cool." Jack straightened in his seat as he read the course details and ran his fingers across pictures of some students' finished products.

Ben checked a schedule on his desk. "Looks like that conflicts with the GED classes. Which would you rather do?"

The teen considered his options for a moment before sighing. "GED. I need all the help I can get to prep for those tests."

"Wise choice." Ben smiled as he considered Jack's concentration on the opportunities in front of him. "If anything changes with the schedule, I'll let you know."

"Thanks." Jack's brow wrinkled with worry and concern beyond his years, but notes of hope dotted the melody of his words as he dared to dream further than ever. "I know I screwed up big time, getting kicked out of school. But, I want more than flipping burgers."

He cleared his throat and continued. "Plus, I don't want to waste the life I've still got. Too many friends ... they don't get that shot. So, I need a piece of paper to go on to the next stage and a fresh start—maybe college ... or the Marines. I've looked at them as the biggest heroes since I watched *Sands of Iwo Jima* every Saturday morning for about five years when I was a kid. The recruiter who came to school when we took the ASVAB test was a Marine. He was a cool guy—told me all the things you could do and learn in the Corps. Not many people were talking to me at that point, so I was pretty free to hang out and chat with him."

"Your past has no right to dictate your future when you're willing to change your present condition." Ben caught a watery reflection in Jack's eyes as his words hit home.

He broke the still solemnity and asked, "What else can we work on while you're here?"

Jack considered Ben's question as he returned the binder. "I'd really like to see about getting a job after. It's time I start helping my mom. She works too hard. And ... well ..." He paused and lowered colored cheeks as he leaned forward. "I want to pay back all the people I stole from. So, maybe I can make a list and plan that out?"

"I think we can make both of those things happen," Ben confirmed with a smile. "I'm proud of you for these requests. They show me you're maturing. Unless you have any questions for me, it's time to head to our morning chapel. Want to walk together?"

"Sure." Jack mirrored Ben's smile and found himself leaving with a lighter heart than when he'd entered.

That afternoon Jack got a rapid and personal introduction to each member of his counseling group. After lunch, he moseyed into their meeting room. Ben sat in one of the blue plastic chairs surrounded by Pete and two other residents.

"Hey Jack! Come on in." Ben's easy-going nature relaxed everyone around him. Jack sat next to Ben in the last empty chair and quickly surveyed the group before letting his bangs shade him from their glances.

Rounding out the circle were two women. One of them was about the same age as Jack and clearly pregnant. The other woman landed in the 30s range and had the kindest eyes and smile. Jack had a hard time picturing her addicted to anything but sweet tea.

As the first session began, Ben told them some of the same things he'd already told Jack. He talked about God and burdens and mountains. Though Jack thought he should be annoyed with all this preaching, he was surprised that it both comforted him and addressed some of his worries. The first concern Ben calmed for Jack was that he should magically and instantly be better.

"You've each started a lifelong war that won't end at graduation. You will face struggles when you return home." Ben made eye contact with each participant as he continued. "Every person on earth faces battles of some kind. For some, it's drugs or alcohol; for others, it's an incurable disease or life-stopping depression. Whatever it is, we each have to fight something.

"Y'all face a particularly challenging war. The first battle was admitting you have a problem. You've been drug addicts and alcoholics. Those were labels that defined your past. Once you accepted them, you were ready to approach the steps needed to come out as victors in the end. Yes, you'll struggle. No, every day isn't going to be better than the last. But, you know what? That's okay.

"Life isn't a steady course to some distant finish line. It's pitch black valleys, mountaintops too high to see and endless plains of nothing but grass. It's also majestic views of mountain skylines, peaceful valleys and unhindered sunrises. Take each day as it comes. Pick up your sword and fight when you have to, ask for help when you're too weak to lift your weapon and drink in the beauty around you every chance you get."

Ben addressed Jack's concern of sharing with a group of strangers through a request. "We're going to be spending a good deal of time with each other, so let's start off this first session with each of you sharing what led you here today."

The girl with track marks on her arms spoke first. "I'm Shannon. When I was thirteen, I started hanging out with older guys. I liked the attention and took all of it I could get. Before my next birthday, I hopped in a truck with one of them and disappeared."

Tears formed as she paused to chew a nail and sift through her memories. "My parents wouldn't stop searching. Some officers found me a couple years later in Memphis."

Shannon straightened in her chair and erased all spilled emotion on her face. "I'd been sold to pushers and kept in a rundown apartment building with some other girls. I spent most of my time passed out on the thin mattresses on the floor. When they found me, I had a needle dangling from my arm. I fought the help my parents got for me—fought it hard. Finally, it was Rachael—Ben's daughter—who helped me see my life can be more." She rubbed her growing belly and finished, "And that we can still have a future."

Silence blanketed them for a moment before a deep voice filled the room with another story of survival. "I'm Pete. I've been a truck driver all my life. Retirement had been chasin' me, but I wasn't ready to hang up the CB … even if my body was.

"I'd been ridin' a carousel of pills to either stay awake for runs longer than my logs showed or for sleep on demand. I'd also been fightin' double vision and leg numbness for months. There'd been a few close calls, but I kept on truckin' until the night I nearly killed a family of five on a late-night run across Arizona." Pete shook his head. "Those kids were the same ages as my grandbabies. I hit my knees that night."

The other woman reached out and squeezed Pete's hand before she spoke.

"I'm Jaida Masters. I'm a preacher's wife and mom to four precious kiddos." Her smile lit up the circle as she clutched a bright white Bible to her chest and tucked her long brown hair behind her ear. "I'm also a recovering alcoholic."

She smiled as she set the Bible in her lap and smoothed her skirt. "I grew up in church and surrendered my life early. I married Charles and followed him to seminary. I delivered four little blessings to him, baked bread from scratch, cleaned cloth diapers and counseled women at the local pregnancy support clinic—all while humming hymns."

The others chuckled with her as she finished her background. "The truth was I masked the loneliness, exhaustion and lost identity of my heart with a smile … because I thought I had to. By the time all four children were fully mobile (and all still under five years old), that mask began to crack. So, I patched it with a vodka veneer."

Sorrow dimmed Jaida's countenance. "For two years I sat in the pew—two little ones on either side—and beamed up at my husband, taking occasional sips from a water bottle. The clear liquid kept my smile intact … until the day I ran out. I took a spill in the aisle that set tongues to wagging, opened my husband's eyes and landed me at the altar."

As each shared pieces of their stories, Jack found himself sinking in to the group around him. His turn had come. He cleared his throat and shifted until the chair squeaked. "On my fifteenth birthday, I took my first sip of beer."

He raised his head and cleared his throat. "And then, I pushed my friend to drag race. He'd been drinking—a lot. We all had."

Jack leaned forward, the weight of the admission he had to make pressing down on his hunched shoulders.

"It didn't end well." He tugged at the neck of the T-shirt that had suddenly tightened on his scar as he spoke. "I lost four friends that night."

Jaida clutched his hand with a motherly squeeze that gave him courage to continue.

"I didn't handle it well and decided to drown my guilt in alcohol. It didn't help, of course. So, I'm here because I want to live a life worthy for them. Because they can't. Because I want to atone, I guess. And, I want to be better for my mom and the people who've stuck by me ... despite all I've done."

With the end of his explanation, Jack looked into Ben's clear blue eyes—the ones he'd passed down to Rachael. They and every other eye resting on Jack was watering by this point in their session. So much pain in every past around the circle. Ben smiled encouragement at the faces around him and prayed silently for each.

"Each of you came here from various backgrounds, but you've got two things in common. You slid down the slippery sides of the cavern of addiction to your rock bottoms. But, you also asked for help, for a rope to hoist you out, and now you're here; and we're holding your rope. People here will pull you up, back into the light of freedom from those beasts you've been battling on your own."

Realization dawned on Jack—he wasn't alone in all this. Other people had battled what he had. He thought back to the misery of his first week as the poison did its best to sink its claws in and stay. Each person there had been through that awful process. Jack saw them in a new light.

"The second thing you've got in common is a need for Jesus. Every person has it ... including me." Ben laughed as he brought himself into the conversation. "I've already told Jack and Pete in our one-on-one sessions, all the support in the world can't be as good as the strength and peace God's got for those who accept it."

Ben looked around the circle. "I believe each of you can flee your pasts for fresh futures, untarnished by addiction. There is one further challenge, though. We all serve something. If it's not a drug, it could just as easily be our work or our relationships or our hobbies. To lead lives of absolute freedom, you must surrender your life to the only Master whose 'yoke is easy, and burden is light.'"

Jack felt that pang from earlier return. He shifted in his seat as he wondered if they'd kick him out for not believing in Ben's God. He recalled the painted postcard Rachael had tried to give him and the two words he'd noticed before he ran from her—*perfect peace.* That may not be something he'd ever experience. Her voice rose in his mind. "Accept it." If Rachael thought she didn't deserve good, he knew he didn't.

Ben ended the session with a promise. "I am here for each of you. Any time, day or night. You've each got my phone number, if you have questions or just want to talk."

When Ben smiled at Jack, the boy felt confident not only in his recovery but also in the acceptance of the man before him—whether he could ultimately believe in his God or not.

***

Though Jack wasn't a huge fan of chapel, he came to accept it as part of his day and even listened now and then. Sometimes residents nearing their graduations spoke. Their stories held his interest. For most, this was a last-chance stop. They either came out victorious or became residents of the state. Or the cemetery.

As the weeks crawled past, Jack found he enjoyed his daily work with the grounds crew that Ben led. Jack learned to care for the lawn and trees and buildings across the twenty-acre property. Frequently he and Ben worked together on one task or another. Jack had been surprised to see the preacher eagerly tackle an unruly holly bush or go to war on runaway weeds.

Filled with classes, work, chapel and sessions, the days often sped forward. Jack usually collapsed into bed, exhausted not only from the physical exertion but also the mental and emotional tasking. One evening before his eyes could close, he heard a gentle tone from the man across from him.

"How you doin', son?" Pete sat much as he did that first day, his Bible spread across his legs.

Jack leaned on his elbow and contemplated an answer. "Really good, I think. I've got a future now. One I plan to protect."

Pete flashed one of the most joyful smiles Jack had ever seen. "Sure am glad to hear that. A future's a terrible thing to waste. You got much more of one than I do, but I sure don't plan to waste what's left of mine."

"What're you reading?" Jack surprised himself by asking.

"About David. Shepherd boy turned king. Boy howdy! Did he make some big mistakes." Pete chuckled and shook his head as if he were talking about a buddy. "Even with all those mistakes, though, God forgave him. Even called him a man 'after his own heart.' Imagine that! God gave him a big job to do—gather all the materials so his people could build him a house ... a church of sorts ... where God could live among his people. Some might think that wasn't such a big task, but it sure was. Took a lot of gathering, and David's son turned it all into one of the most amazing structures of the time. They knew and finished the purposes God gave 'em."

He closed his Bible and lifted it, one finger holding his place. "This book here's my new purpose. My wife, she went to church ev'ry Sunday since I've known her. Never understood why until I finally saw the miracle in Jesus' sacrifice on that cross. Now, thanks to that and David's story, I've got my plan for the rest of my days, too—share this message with as many folks as I can."

Jack glanced at the cross painting Pete pointed at and wondered again what he seemed to be missing about all this Jesus stuff. He didn't ponder long, though, because the man posed a question. "What d'you think's your purpose?"

At the excitement in the man's eyes, Jack longed to have an answer for him—a good one—but he couldn't seem to raise one. He'd always thought of life as a series of doing things. Schooling. Graduating. Taking a job. Making money. Paying the bills. Beyond that, he'd never given much consideration; but he didn't think any of those things fit in the "purpose" category. Jack shook his head. Pete noticed the droop to Jack's shoulders when he looked up without an answer.

"That's okay. You're young. Just don't take too long. Here I've finally got a purpose worth livin' for, but not a whole lotta time to live it."

That night, sleep came slowly for Jack.

* * *

In the final quarter of Jack's time at the mission, he and Ben took up the task of repainting the fence around the campus.

"Thank you."

Ben looked up from the task, surprise edging his expression. Jack rarely said much, but he'd been extra quiet as they worked together at the front of the property. Jack saw the question in the pastor's eyes.

"For answering the door that night and not kicking me out. Or calling Sheriff Pounds."

Ben grinned as he turned back to the brush. "I'll be honest with you, Jack. When I heard you banging on my door in the middle of the night and screaming for my girl to open up, I didn't want to call the Sheriff."

"You wanted to get your gun, huh?"

A genuine smile passed between them as Ben nodded.

Jack's brow furrowed. He studied the emerging gray around the man's temples, the tinge of sadness ringing the blue of his eyes. "Why didn't you?"

The preacher held his grin. He balanced his brush on the paint can before sitting back against a pine towering behind him. Ben twisted the gold band he'd never removed and finally spoke. "The father in me wants to hate you, Jack."

At the stunned expression on the boy's face, Ben chuckled. "Yeah, preachers are as far from perfect as the next guy. I wanted to knock you into the next state every time I saw the way you looked at my little girl; and I won't say what I wanted to do when I saw you put so much as a finger on her. Then, the alcohol took hold of you; and I watched my baby's heart crumble time and again under your boot. That really twisted my insides."

Jack shifted uneasily and lowered his head. He thought back over the way he had treated Rachael and realized only the stiffest punishment would suffice.

"That night when you came beating down the door, I bolted down those stairs in a bright-red rage; but God met me at the bottom and slapped me with peace, love and a reminder. See, Jack, I haven't always been a preacher or always followed Jesus. My beast was acid; and it nearly killed me.

"Marshall Winters. He was this crusty old Sheriff. He'd been with Noah on the ark and walked around glaring at everyone and everything in his path. I was off on a wild trip one night, convinced I was being chased by some thugs; so, I catapulted myself through a jewelry store window. Anyway, Marshall showed up right after they got me on the gurney. He gave me his normal glare and said something I'll never forget, 'This boy ain't dyin' on my watch; he's gonna amount to somethin', damn it.' That grumpy old man stayed on my backside from that day on—through rehab, college and seminary."

White paint dripped all over Jack's tennis shoes, but he didn't notice. He clung to every word the preacher said, like a shipwreck survivor to a lifebuoy.

"Marshall's words came back to me that night. You didn't die on my watch, Jack; and, sure as I believe in God above, you're going to amount to something, something great. I had someone believe in me; now I get to believe in you."

The man before Jack was the closest thing to a dad he'd ever known. He'd always thought of Ben as a saint—somehow above common struggles. Hearing this reality gave Jack a glimpse into the truth behind the grace thing he'd heard so often. He thought about the king Pete mentioned whenever they did talk at night. David was a killing man; he had also taken another man's wife and then had that man killed. Despite all of that, God wiped David's slate clean and gave him a purpose. Maybe—just maybe—God did forgive.

Jack's misty eyes said it all; but, for good measure, he whispered again, "Thank you."

* * *

The final week at the mission dawned with an early morning counseling group. Five days to graduation. Graduation back to the real world with real problems, real temptations. Consequences.

Every member of the group around Jack had changed in some way, including him.

At the end of her second full week, Shannon wept as Ben shared in chapel how Jesus accepted and forgave the adulterous woman. Jesus had dried the woman's tears and told her to go, live, sin no more. And, the woman did. Then she went and told everyone she knew or met what Jesus did for her. When Ben extended an invitation for anyone who wanted to pray or ask questions to come forward, Shannon walked straight and tall with purpose.

During their final Monday session, Shannon shared her plan to study photography. "Rachael and I have had lots of afternoon talks about our futures—something I'd never thought of before. Probably because I didn't think I could. Anyway, I realized I want to capture all the beauty of God's creation and the precious moments between people ... the ones we often take for granted. I want to hold on to those lovely things and teach my little girl to do the same in her life." She caressed the child she carried and beamed at the group.

Pete, too, had made a decision over the weeks. He would be an evangelist, traveling from church to church to share his story and the Bible. Jack noticed whenever Pete prayed, it really felt like he was having a conversation with the God of the universe.

Jaida wore a peace-filled smile. She finally understood that a Christian life didn't mean perfection. It was one of sin and forgiveness, stumbling and being picked back up by her heavenly Father.

"I'm ready to go home and get some hugs and kisses from my babies." She wiped away tears before running her hands along the sides of her legs and sharing her plans. "God's got a plan for everything, even the sinful choices we make. I will use my story to help other women like me who feel so lost and alone and tired and fed up, but don't think they can admit that. I want them to see that's normal. It's human. We're human, but God ... well, he's God! He'll carry us through when we turn all our cares over to him. I'm done with the mask; I'm ready to be open and honest. Real."

Jack found himself overwhelmed by the stories around him. Their purpose. Despite feeling like he was missing something compared to the rest of his group, he knew he could fight this battle. He and Ben had discussed with his mom a plan for staying away from the temptation to drink as well as ways to handle situations that may make him want to search for a bottle. They would dispose of any liquor he had remaining. Becky told him he would need to check in with her any time he decided to go somewhere other than work or church. That was another detail Ben insisted on—attending church was not an option. Jack didn't roll his eyes at their regulations. He wanted their accountability. And, he had another helper in Pete who lived about an hour away but told Jack he didn't sleep much and would be available to talk day or night. Of course, Ben's number was also safe in his mind. Jack may not have God to call on, but he had them.

Jaida and Shannon had formed a tight bond. They giggled over baby shower plans as they left that day's session. Jack knew Shannon had a friend in Rachael as well. She was the best kind of friend. A pang of loss hit him again like it had in the school cafeteria a couple of long years ago. He missed Rachael's friendship.

***

Ben opened their final session with honesty. "I'm not going to paint you a rosy picture and send you out to the world you came from with a pat on the head and a 'Good luck!' You've got a few more hours here at the mission, but you've got *us* for life.

"This is a long, hard road you're on. You're going to see the old road running alongside you, sometimes closer than other times. It'll look fantastic—easy, even—and you'll want to hop that fence. In those moments, remember the pain and hopelessness of your first week; focus on that until you can look forward again. When you find yourself stuck straddling that fence, call on us and—most importantly—call on God. He doesn't promise an easy life with him, but he does promise you'll never face your battles alone. When none of us are around, he is. Call on him."

Ben rested his ankle on his knee as he leaned back. "In your one-on-one sessions, you've each been identifying triggers and challenges that could send you reaching for your addictions when you return home. I'd like to spend the rest of our time together sharing those, so you can help each other prepare safeguards against them."

They shared their plans and who their support people would be once they got home. Jack and Shannon had parents; Pete and Jaida had spouses and children and friends. Shannon mentioned Rachael. Jack wondered if he could have her friendship waiting for him as well. After a closing prayer with the group, Ben asked Jack, "Wanna chat while we head out to the maintenance shed?"

"Sure."

Ben had been called that morning to the hospital to sit with a church member whose husband was dying, so he had missed his earlier session with Jack.

"I know you're not so sure about all this God stuff we've been talking about." Jack's pale face and widened eyes raised a chuckle from Ben. "It's not that hard to tell, especially since I've been doing this for a while. I just wondered if you have any questions."

Jack kicked at a rock as they followed the gravel driveway toward a metal building. "Not really. I know you want us to believe and all that, but I just can't." He turned to the man beside him with an apologetic face.

"Son, you don't need to apologize to me for that. The only thing I want you to do is talk to me and ask me your questions." Ben looked down at his feet as he considered his next statement. "Yes, I want you to believe in God because he is the only source of true joy and peace and I want to call you my brother in Christ. But that's something you have to decide. He's there, and the gift is free when you're ready to take it. I'm here, too, whenever you have questions."

Jack nodded as he looked off toward the pond. They had reached the shed but stopped outside. "I appreciate that. I have seen the difference in Shannon and Jaida and Mr. Pete. They're like you and Rach and Mama. I do see God makes a difference. I just can't put it all together in my head."

Ben waited for Jack's explanation. "I know God's supposed to be full of goodness and love and all, but ..."

Jack paused as he dug for the right words. "He made this world, right? Well, he didn't seem to put a whole lot of his good and love in it. I know he's pretty serious about the whole sin thing, and I've messed up bad. So, I don't see how he can forgive me. I'm pretty sure I'm a lost cause."

"God happens to specialize in lost causes." Ben's smile conveyed genuine care as he considered all that Jack had shared. "And, yes, this world God made is full of sin and evil. That's because he gave his people the chance to choose."

"But why? I don't get that. Could he not make them stay perfect?" Jack asked one of the questions that had bugged him through all the Bible stories he'd heard as a kid.

"He could." Ben nodded thoughtfully. "But, he didn't want an army of robots. He wanted people who choose to love and obey him, and he gets glory in taking a 'lost cause' and transforming him into a loved child."

Jack reflected on Ben's response as they watched a flock of ducks fly over the pond. Ben continued, "There's one more thing you should know. You can never do more bad than God can forgive."

That line became a token of hope for Jack; one he would carry for many years and mull over often, especially when he observed differences unique to Christians around him. Another that frequently came to mind was a paraphrase that replayed in Rachael's voice: *Accept the gift.*

IV

Straight & Narrow

June 22, 2001

Graduation morning stretched from beneath night's bedclothes, muggy and damp. A typical southern summer wake-up, where a deep breath floods a person's lungs with steam. Jack sat on the edge of his bed, looking out the window at the rising light. The sun glowed like a flaming phoenix, and Jack shifted his attention to save his eyes. The reflection in the mirror across from him highlighted his scar, dazzlingly white under a sunbeam's kiss.

Some things had changed over his time at the mission. His eyes shone more clearly than they had three months earlier. His skin held a healthy glow; his mind felt clearer; and even his lungs felt stronger. Jack inhaled deeply as he stood and stretched his arms to the heavens. Legs together, he bent over to grab his toes. Working out and playing basketball in the mission gym had wiped away the physical effects of too much alcohol and not enough motion. He'd taken up running and found himself looking forward to daily morning and evening runs. He never timed himself and wasn't even sure how far he went, but he knew he was going faster as he added a little distance every few days. Back upright, Jack pulled his elbow against his chest. He noticed his abs and biceps. The weights had done more good than he'd thought. Those muscles' strength would be tested next week when he started the construction job Ben had helped him find. He'd always heard roofing was rough, especially in the Georgia heat; but he was thankful for a job. An opportunity. An open door.

Ben had talked with him the night before about doors. He said his door would always be open to him and reminded him about the one Jesus opened to God the Father. That's something Jack understood—and didn't understand. He got that the world was full of evil—sin, Ben called it. He didn't have to look far to observe that; he was full of it. This was the point where his understanding wavered every time.

Jack finished stretching and walked out of his room for one final run at the mission. He jogged to the fence line. The dew from the grass splashed across his shins as he kicked his legs—and mind—into high gear. As he ran, he filed through all he'd learned about sacrifice and open doors.

With a world full of sin-filled people there was still this perfect—What was the word Ben always used?—this perfectly *holy* God who couldn't look on all these people he'd made. He had to make a way for those sins to get forgiven, but that required a sacrifice—a perfect one. So, he sent his son— that was Jesus Christ—to be this sacrifice.

And, that's where Jack lost the desire to understand. Too many *whys* popped in his head whenever he got to this part. *Why* would a father send his son to be killed? *Why* would the son willingly go? Jesus knew exactly what he had waiting for him on this messed-up planet he'd created. So, who in his right mind would do it?

Jack turned a corner as he met the property's east side fence. The cross overlooking the pond reminded him of one long-ago Easter. His mom had dragged him off to church after cinching him up in a tight, itchy suit with a gosh-awful tie—a real one—that choked him. He whined and cried and did his best to convince her he was choking to death. Jack rubbed his neck at the memory before swiping sweat off his forehead.

His mom had picked him up, plopped him in the car and ignored his gasps and wheezes the whole way to the red brick Baptist church on the corner of Main Street. She switched off the car, turned to him and promised a quick but painful death if he didn't shut up that instant. With that warning, she got out of the car and smiled at the Presbyterians strolling in the opposite direction toward their white wooden church.

He chuckled despite his heavy breathing. No matter how rough he made Sunday mornings, his mom always did her best to appear put together and draw as little attention to herself as possible. She also tried to make holidays special—despite his lack of appreciation.

That holiday morning had started off great with a basket of chocolate eggs, turned rotten with the suit and tie and bounced back to interesting once the sermon started and the visiting preacher began sharing all the gory details of how veins in Jesus' head burst and he sweated blood. He described Jesus' beating with a Roman torture device called a cat-o-nine-tails. Then the message blended together with nails pounded into appendages and darkness and lungs collapsing and dead people rising and swords piercing through Jesus' side.

For a little boy, all the blood and guts talk seemed pretty cool. For an adult trying to grasp the *whys*, though, those *hows* made it even harder. What kind of dad would do such a thing? He made Jack's deadbeat dad seem like an angel of mercy. At least he was never in the picture to send his son off to be beaten up for a bunch of rotten people who didn't deserve it.

Jack slowed to a jog and then a walk as he reentered the men's dorm. Sweat trickled down his neck and back as he stopped it from dripping into his eyes. He reached his room. *Doors.* Jesus' sacrifice, as inexplicable as it was, opened the door to God and heaven—eternal life; Ben had explained that more than once. Well, maybe Jack didn't want to live forever floating around on a fluffy cloud in his birthday suit with a halo on his head and a harp in his hands. Rachael would laugh if he shared that thought with her. He knew that wasn't the typical description of heaven; but, for some reason, that's always how he pictured it.

These were all thoughts for another day, though. He needed to clean himself up and walk back through that very real door before him. Its existence and symbolism suddenly terrified him. Today he'd pick up the red duffle bag he'd already packed and return home.

Home.

Home—where he could have killed his mom in his final drunken rage. Home—where the nightmares lurked in the corners of his room. Home—where the reminders dwelt. Home—where he had liquor hidden until he told Ben all his hiding places. The loose board on the porch. The hidden eaves in the unfinished attic. The plumbing access hole in his closet.

Did I remember them all? What if I forgot one?
Can I do this?

Jack wasn't certain. Ben's door was open. The mission's door was open. Jesus' door was open. As reality seeped into his core, Jack felt these doors were far too fictional in the face of his fears and inner foes. The questions flooded his mind.

What if all the nightmares return? What if I fail at this job? What if I can't catch up enough to get my GED? What if I can't get myself back on track and give up instead? What if I land back among the bottles? Why am I here anyway? What purpose does life even hold?

Jack flipped on the shower and stripped down. He shoved his head beneath the water, jerking his head back and forth, spraying drops all over.

No. He couldn't—wouldn't—do this again. That first week rushed back. The fear and anxiety that made his heart feel like it would explode. The hallucinations. The memories washed over him like the water under which he stood. He could still feel the despair. Those memories lived within him. Probably always would.

That wasn't for him. Moving forward was the only option for him from that point on. He'd made a promise to his mom. A promise to have a future. He would do that and find a way to care for her, no matter what.

Jack dried off vigorously before exiting the bathroom. He opened the closet door and pulled out his remaining clothes—khakis and a polo. Today was special—graduation day.

Maybe I should've asked mom to bring a suit instead. And maybe even a tie.

He smiled as he envisioned the shock on her face if he'd asked for those. As soon as he dressed, Jack inhaled to calm his nerves. He gave himself a final glance in the mirror. He had changed—maybe not exactly how Ben had hoped, but definitely for the better. He was better. Much better.

I will do this.

***

In the chapel, Jack surveyed his fellow graduates' dress choices. They ranged from cut-off shorts to dress slacks, but each person who crossed that stage sparkled. Their outward appearances matched their inner bodies—clean from the burden of addictions they'd carried when they entered.

Pete walked up to him and slapped him on the back. "Well, we made it! You ready for this, son?"

"I sure hope so," Jack answered candidly.

"You've got your support system. Your mom's a real gem; spoke with her for a few minutes." Pete nodded toward where Becky sat next to a trim little lady in a smart pantsuit. Jack knew from photos that was Pete's wife, Cynthia. "You'll have people enter your life that'll be more of a support than you might think. Some are there for a few minutes; others decades. Each has a reason for meeting you when they do. Look for those reasons and thank God for 'em."

Jack nodded at the man's wisdom.

Following the ceremony, Becky beamed at her son as Rachael took their photo in front of the mission chapel. Jack finally noticed the changes in his mom. Gray streaked her previously solid brown hair, and her worries and sadness—though invisible on this joyous occasion—marked her face. He knew the cause of those changes was him and, again, vowed never to go back to the bottle. His mom kissed his forehead; and, for a moment, he was a kid again. Not a care in the world. Mom kissed him and sent him out to play with his friends—Steven and Jerry, Rachael and Anna Claire, Bobby Lee and Beth Anne.

Friends. Two gone forever; the rest scarred. So much changed in the crack of a few can tabs. Jack smiled as his mom hugged and kissed Rachael. They would have both been seniors this year. He may have been considering a ring purchase. Who could say what would've been happening on this sweltering day if there hadn't been That Night?

The breeze stirred, running its lucky fingers through Rachael's thick red hair. It had gotten so long over the past couple of years. Jack longed to take it in his hands and pull Rachael into him. He missed her. Missed the smell of her, warmth of her, taste of her. She had been his first love. His first kiss.

All the horrible words he'd spoken to her and the countless ways he'd intentionally hurt her flew up in his face. The day in the cafeteria when he'd turned away from her precious gift was only the tip of the iceberg. He thought of the other girls he'd used to hurt her, and a mental image of betrayal on Rachael's face appeared. Jack had seen her walking toward him with a smile and two cartons of nachos. It was the basketball championship their sophomore year. She kept trying to reach out to him—to be his friend. All she really did, though, was remind him how far he'd slid. So, instead of accepting her gesture of friendship, he pulled Lindsay Philips in for a long, drawn-out kiss directly in front of Rachael.

He felt the color of shame rise in his cheeks and knew he needed to guard her from himself. She deserved more, better. Her smile—the widest he'd ever seen—embraced his emotions as she strode up to him. He felt his heart soften. He could be hers to control with one word from those soft, red lips.

"Hey you!" Her nose scrunched as she squinted in the sun to gaze up at him. He loved her face and how she looked at him.

Rachael raised up on her tiptoes to gently kiss his cheek. *Soft, so incredibly soft.* He tucked his emotions away and reminded himself he had a long way to go to be what she deserved. He may never get there; but, as he gazed down at her, he decided he'd really like to try.

"I'm proud of you, Jack."

Her sunshine smile turned his knees and heart to jelly. Those sapphire eyes sparkled up at him beneath endless lashes. She used to laugh at how they had that trait in common. Warmth rose in his chest as he recalled the day he told her their kids would have lashes so long they'd have to trim them with hedge clippers. She had thrown back her head and laughed. He had joined her until they ended up on their backs on the picnic blanket. That moment had ended in a pretty hot make-out session—one he wouldn't mind revisiting. Jack and Rachael had a connection that went deeper than the physical, though. It defied any descriptions. All he knew was he suddenly felt whole in her presence.

"I start my new job next week."

"Dad told me. Are you excited about it?"

Jack lowered his grin as he considered his response. "I sure am thankful for it. I've got to save up some money so I can take my GED tests in the spring and then—I don't know—maybe college?" His gaze shifted across the field to the pond where several families took portraits, some for the first time in decades. "I don't really want to hammer on shingles, but I like the idea of building. I went to the Pattersons' build site last week to meet Mr. Dickson. That's where we'll be working. Have you been out there?"

"Not since they cleared the land. Susan, Anna Claire and I used to go out and tiptoe through the stream that runs through their property. The water was always ice cold, so it was perfect on a steamy day. Dad says there's a natural spring somewhere that feeds it, and that's why it's freezing."

"I may want to dip my toes in there after standing in the sun for eight hours."

"You should. I'll come join you."

Jack's stomach took a rapid dip. Before he realized what he was asking, he heard, "How about you meet me there next Friday? We knock off around two. I'll bring a picnic, and you can introduce me to that magic water. Maybe we'll even go hunting for the spring together."

Damn it, Jack! Is that staying away from her, taking it slow and making sure you don't hurt her again?

His reprimanding thoughts vanished under the glow of a smile that lit up her face in a way he hadn't seen in too long.

"I'd like that, but you better leave the food up to me. We'll end up with burnt toast and beef jerky if you're in charge." The breeze caught her laughter and carried it to his ears. Their notes composed a magical symphony.

Jack brushed away a stray hair the wind had tossed across Rachael's forehead. "For the record, I happen to like beef jerky." Their eyes remained locked as he continued, "And a few burnt edges never hurt anybody." He winked and willed his hand to drop from her warm skin.

Nervous laughter followed as they strolled to a group of other graduates. In the center of the circle stood Ben. He smiled at his little girl and nodded toward Jack. "I don't know, guys. Not sure he'd be much of an asset. They think you should be on the mission softball team."

"Not an asset? C'mon, man! Did you never watch me run on the football field? I can run those bases twice before you even get up off the bench, old man."

"Big words! But, can you hit?" Ben's eyes twinkled at the banter. He'd played shortstop at Georgia Tech.

"Good enough to beat you. How many times did Tech get to the championships while you were there?"

"Low blow! I think I'll offer you up to the Methodists, so we can settle this on the diamond."

Rachael rolled her eyes at the exchange before she chimed in. "Is this your team? If so, you definitely want to keep him. Jack's got more speed than all of you put together." Her mischief matched her dad's as chuckles danced around the group. "Come on. I'm hungry."

Most of the softball hopefuls, along with Jack's group members and their families, joined Ben at the mission bus. Jack slid into the seat beside Rachael and asked, "Where are we eating?"

"Memaw's, of course!" Rachael grinned as she rubbed her rumbling stomach.

Jack shook his head as he warned, "Get ready to stand in line for a few hours."

Rachael surprised Jack with a laugh and head shake. "Don't worry. Dad's got us a reservation." In response to Jack's confused expression, she explained. "Daddy never waits at Memaw's. She loves him as much as any kid she's adopted over the years—actually, come to think of it, I'm pretty sure she loves him more. She doesn't give any of them reservations!"

The pair shared some laughter before she continued. "Memaw's husband was knockin' on death's door a while back. Daddy went in to pray with them. She wasn't interested in religion but told him to go right ahead. Mr. Haney made a full recovery; and, to this day, Memaw credits Daddy's praying. The Haneys have sat on the front row at church ever since, and Memaw dotes on Daddy every time we eat at her restaurant."

Jack looked up at Ben who had just parked the bus and turned to smile at his passengers. "Your dad does have a unique way about him. He's not your average preacher, is he?"

Rachael laughed as they filed out of the bus. "You got that right!"

Memaw made the best fried catfish anywhere. People drove for hours just to get some of that and her made-from-scratch hush puppies. They often waited for hours for a table—rain or shine.

When the mission bus passengers spilled through the door of the catfish house, Memaw pulled out all the stops for hospitality. There wasn't anything she wouldn't do for her Preacher Boy and his recovering souls.

As soon as Ben walked through the door, Memaw tossed her staff—adopted kids and grandkids—out of her way so she could greet him with a bear hug, a kiss on the cheek and a booming, "How's my Preacher Boy today? You get in here and sit in your booth. We got tables all ready for y'all. I'll be right back with your hushpuppies and sweet tea, baby." Memaw patted Ben's arm as she proceeded to wait hand and foot on her "Preacher Boy" and his guests.

Jack appreciated the special treatment as he popped a piping hot, cheese sauce-dipped hush puppy in his mouth a few minutes later. He watched Rachael talk and laugh with Shannon. He didn't know what open doors he may pass through one day, but he knew Rachael had opened one today that he was determined to enter. If he kept his focus on her beautiful face, no number of bottles could lure him off the straight and narrow.

V

The Weight of Guilt

Late June 2001 to April 20, 2002

J ack baked on rooftops in the blistering Georgia sun the rest of that summer. Bellum might be more pine trees than people, but their shade never seemed to touch the houses. His first week on the job, Jack began a routine. When he got home each day, he'd reach in the fridge for an ice-cold bottle of water and hit the books. He was determined to earn his GED by the time he should have accepted his diploma. He had plenty of time to study—and he wasn't going to take a single minute of it for granted.

He and Rachael kept their picnic date at the stream. The heat of the sun and the chilly stream, the burning desire between them and their frigid fear of it made for an afternoon of opposites. They headed straight for the refreshing water. Rachael shrieked and laughed as Jack kicked up an icy spray on her. They ran and played like they were back in elementary school. She jumped on his back, catching him by surprise. He lost his balance, twisting mid-air and tossing her off into the stream beside him. Jack splashed her face. More howls of laughter resulted in her straddling him to keep his hands from splashing. With her on top of him, staring deeply into his eyes and holding his wrists beneath the freezing currents, Jack wanted nothing in life but Rachael Burns. She was his life's dream. He wanted to earn her trust, walk worthy of her love and lasso every dream she desired.

His lips found hers. Seconds ceased. Nothing else mattered. Not past sins, present confusion, future uncertainty. Their hearts connected as they breathed together—inhale, exhale. Nothing could rend this connection between them. It was magnetic, life-giving, time-altering. Her hands found his face and framed it as his dove into the depths of her hair, pulling her closer, deeper into him—into them. She sank into his strength and promise. Their reserve drifted away like the fog on a muggy morning. They were Jack and Rach once more, but in a deeper way they hadn't been before. Lips interlocked; the frozen drops of spring water dripped down their hair to their cheeks and mingled with salty ones from their eyes.

Home.

In each other's arms they were *home*. Reality and reason, thrown high in the air above them, drifted back down upon them like a binding net. They reluctantly broke their embrace. A few more gentle kisses before, foreheads pressed together, they drank the dregs of uncertainty.

"I don't want to disappoint you, Rach. I'm terrified of screwing this up, of breaking your faith in me again. I just want to grow into the man you deserve."

"'None of us deserves any good thing.'"

"You told me that before—that day in the cafeteria when I was such a …"

"Jerk?" Rachael laughed and then lifted Jack's dropped chin. "My mom went on to explain in that letter that God chooses to gift us good things, but all things—even the bad—are part of his master plan for us. It's okay if we don't have it all figured out … because God does."

Her smile enveloped his fears and worries and shipped them far away. "Jack, I love you and I believe in you—in us. And that's a start."

They sat there, heads together, hearts beating in unison until they both shivered under the melting sun. Jack stood them both up, Rachael's legs wrapped around his waist. Back on the bank, his lips caressed hers as he whispered, "I love you, Rachael Jane Burns. I always will. And, that's why I'm going to take us slow. Slow, but steady."

As planned, they hunted for the stream's source, but it proved elusive. They ate. They talked. Dreams rose on their lips as they shared their secrets for the future. Rachael talked about her job in the hospital's new Wellness Center. She chattered on about the equipment and the classes and the opportunity to teach people about fitness. Jack smiled at her glowing countenance.

"Mama would have liked the center, I think." Rachael occasionally talked about her mom but thought about her constantly. That was another common bond—missing a parent.

"She had the greenest thumb and could grow anything. She clearly didn't pass that on … I actually killed a cactus." Rachael's admission made them both laugh. She continued to reminisce, her thoughts turning more serious. "I miss eating fresh veggies from her garden."

"Your mom's why I like green beans and peas."

Rachael smiled as she brushed aside Jack's unruly bangs. "She could make even the pickiest kids fall in love with veggies. She inspired me to want to eat healthy, and I want to do the same for others."

She rested her head on Jack's shoulder as they watched the sun set through the framing of the new construction.

"One day those boards and nails and concrete and pipes will be a family's home."

Rachael looked at Jack. His voice had broken a prolonged stillness and caught her off guard. She saw a wistfulness in his hazel eyes. "Do you always want to build houses?"

Jack turned to her. He hadn't even realized he was thinking aloud, and her question startled him. After a moment's reflection, he replied, "You know, I might. There's just something about helping someone reach their true home."

They smiled, and Rachael looped her arms around his bicep. They sat shoulder to shoulder until the sun disappeared beyond the horizon, leaving only a few ribbons of majestic color spanning their view.

***

That summer aged and died like a smoldering fire's slow burn. Jack and Rachael still found time to be together. They went to the movies with friends, took long drives on dusty country roads and even squeezed in a few more picnics.

One sultry Tuesday morning in September, time stood still across the nation. Rachael was walking into her history class when a buzz swarmed up and down the hall behind her. Marc pushed past her into the room.

"Mrs. Heath, turn on the TV right now! A plane crashed into the Towers!"

They turned on the news in time to witness another plane fireball into the second Tower.

"Dear God, Almighty ..." Rachael breathed the opening of a prayer without end as she crumpled beside the nearest desk to watch in horror as the nightmare developed live before them. People launched themselves from windows countless stories up to escape the inferno within the walls that had stood firm for three decades. Others passed cameras, expressionless, their emotions buried beneath gray soot.

Every classroom kept the TVs on that day. Algebraic equations, chemistry labs and history tests no longer mattered. Girls sobbed. Boys spoke in hushed tones about the recruiter in the next town. Teachers didn't even try to hide their grave faces. September 11, 2001, was the day the United States—and the young people who were old enough to understand its enormity—grew up. A shroud covered the window to the future, and everyone sought refuge in the arms of their loved ones.

All day Rachael longed for one pair of arms. She was the first out the doors with the final bell's ring and spotted Jack immediately. He was waiting under the canopy to the entrance. She ran full speed to weep against his chest. He buried his emotions in her vanilla-scented hair and breathed in her strength to steady himself. His crew had listened to the radio in disbelief all morning. By noon, two of the workers had left to enlist. Jack almost joined them.

"I thought about joining the Marines."

Rachael focused on the beats of his heart against her ear to steady herself as she took in his admission. "I remember how obsessed you were with Marines when we were kids and then how much that recruiter affected you. I thought you were going to sign on the dotted line back then."

"You looked mad that day." Jack shook his head and grinned.

"Well, yeah. I didn't want to lose you." Rachael's smile held sadness in the corners as she pressed her hands flat against his chest.

"What do you think now?"

"I would be proud ... but so scared. I want you, not a flag." She looked up at him. Her tear-streaked face pled with him to wait. "Maybe there won't be a war."

"Maybe." He pulled her back against his chest. He'd seen his answer in her face. Not yet.

Autumn's chill finally beat summer into submission. Sadness rose to pride, pride to anger, anger to determination. Winter's ice melted into spring's showers as the country continued to pick up the pieces the terrorists had left in their wake. Wounds had begun to heal, but it would be a process that would take far longer than anyone could anticipate.

* * *

Jack's eighteenth birthday brought a house full of chatter and joy. He and Ben talked over last fall's softball season and speculated about the upcoming one. Rachael helped Becky with Jack's favorite dinner—ranch burgers with loaded steak fries and baked beans. After they handed off the burger patties to the men to cook on the grill, the ladies put finishing touches on an extra chocolatey cake.

"You're so good for him." Becky stopped mid-frosting to smile at her best friend's carbon copy.

As Rachael's cheeks flushed bright enough to match her hair, Becky laughed. "I remember when you two were toddlers. You had just reached the stage where toys meant play time but neither one of you had started talking a whole lot. We were right out there on that deck when Jack snatched this tiny baby doll right out of your hands, tossed it as far as his chubby little arm could and giggled like he'd discovered the best game ever. I thought for sure we were about to see some waterworks from you.

"Instead, you pushed yourself up to standing, put a fist on either hip and stared him down. His little lip started to quiver, and you pointed to where your dolly lay out in the grass. He toddled right on out to retrieve it.

"The next day, at y'all's house, Jack made a beeline for that doll. He picked her up, as gentle as you please, and carried her to you with the biggest smile on his little dimpled face. Y'all played with that doll for half the morning—he rocked her, fed her, pushed her in the stroller. Then, you put her in her bed, and Jack brought out his ball. He threw it and clapped when you padded after it and threw it right back. That's how you spent the rest of your morning. Even back then, you two learned to communicate and listen and share. You showed him that."

Becky smoothed back Rachael's hair after she added a candle to Jack's cake.

"The question is, what has he taught you? Is he as good for you as you are for him? That's a question you—and only you—can answer. And it's a question you have to answer honestly."

Rachael looked up from beneath lowered lashes with a thoughtful smile. "You sound just like Mama."

"That's quite a compliment; she was the wisest woman I've ever known. She'd be so proud of you now."

Becky cupped Rachael's cheek with her hand and kissed her forehead as the back door opened. Ben and Jack reentered the kitchen with a tray full of steaming burgers and an ongoing argument about the Braves' season potential.

Conversation flowed around the dinner table. They discussed the value of fried versus baked fries while they gobbled up Jack's less healthy preference.

"How're you feeling about Saturday?" Ben asked Jack.

"Good. If I'm not ready by now for these tests, I'll never be. I'll take all of them at once. There's no sense draggin' it out."

"You're going to do great; I just know it." Rachael squeezed his hand as their gaze locked for a moment.

Ben noticed the depth of their exchange and cleared his throat. He had seen a big change in Jack, but he felt he still had a ways to go. Not to mention, they were still just kids. He could hear Carolina, as clearly as if she were still living, "We were just babies when we meant forever." They may have drifted apart for a while when he had to chase the next big trip, but she had waited for him. They had lasted until death parted them.

"Have you decided on your next step?"

"Subtle, dad." Rachael tossed her father an eye-roll.

"What? I'm interested in this fine young man's future."

"Well, sir, I'm pretty excited about a career in sanitation. Either that or pooper-scooper. You know, someone's gotta pick up after the ponies in parades."

"Very funny, smart aleck." It was Ben's turn to roll his eyes. He did love both of these kids. He prayed for wisdom for them. And, there was one thing he pleaded with God for in the man his daughter may marry. Belief. He wanted Jack to know God, like his daughter did.

"Fine, if you want me to be serious ... I'm planning to apply to Georgia Tech. If they'll let me in without a high school diploma, that is. I'm considering being a construction manager, but I need a civil engineering degree. There's something about watching a house come together, piece by piece, that's exciting." Jack smoothed out his crumpled napkin on the table as he added, "But, longer than that, I've wanted to be a Marine."

Ben recalled Jack mentioning that during their first session at the mission. Uneasiness draped Rachael's shoulders as she examined the hands twisting in her lap, and Becky cleared her throat. Ben noticed their reactions and lessened the tension around the table by telling Jack he'd give Tech's assistant baseball coach a call for him. Ever the peacemaker, Ben thought a call to his old roommate could open that door wider and make the Marine option less appealing.

After supper and cake, Jack's mom left him speechless with a gift. She handed him a plain white envelope. He opened it and found a bank statement. His eyes widened at the total. In those digits he saw all the new clothes his mom never bought, the salon trips she never took, the fast food they never picked up and the movies they didn't see. Tears threatened to overflow.

"I started saving as soon as I found out I was pregnant. I know it won't pay everything, but it'll be a start for college. Maybe you won't have to work quite so hard. I want you to get good grades without stretching yourself too thin."

"Thank you, Mama. I love you. I'm so sorry; I ..."

"Now's not the time for sorries, sweetie. I love you, and I'm so proud of you. Happy birthday!" Mother and son embraced, spreading a healing balm on deep wounds.

After more chatter about Ben's recollections of his alma mater and Jack's shots at his age, Rachael winked at Jack as she stood. "I've got something for you, too." Holding out her hand to his, she asked, "Will you walk out back with me?"

Jack eagerly followed her to the edge of the deck where Rachael leaned back against the rail.

"I don't have anything to give to you, but I do have something to ask you." Jack smiled at her odd delivery. "Would you escort me to our senior prom?"

His grin spread like jam across fresh-baked bread as he responded with, "M'lady, it would be my lifelong honor so-with to do … that … thing which you asketh me … -eth."

With his goofy reply, Jack received the only gift he desired—Rachael's musical laughter. He took her in his arms and held her close to his heart. It was full of love for her and thankfulness for a future bright with her at its center.

***

That Saturday morning, Jack woke up early and drove an hour to the testing center. He was nervous but knew he'd prepared all he could. Even if he scored in the highest tier, he may still not be accepted into the college program he wanted. Mr. Dickson had told him he'd love to promote him on his crew, even without a degree. At least he had a plan B in place. The thought of enlisting hung in the back of his mind, too, but he had tucked it away as a distant plan C since Rachael wasn't fond of the idea.

Eight hours, four pencils and two water bottles later, Jack sank onto a bench outside the center and rested his face in his hands. He'd done his best. He just hoped it would be enough.

A month later Jack held the results in his hands. His hard work had paid off. He scored almost as high as he could. If this didn't get him in, nothing would. He reached for the phone to call Rachael but decided he'd rather see the sparkle in her eyes over dinner that night. They'd be dressed up for their senior prom. It would be the perfect time to share his news.

He grabbed his keys to head to Willard's Florist for the corsage he'd ordered to match Rachael's red dress. She'd chosen his favorite color, and he couldn't wait to see her in it.

Though, she could show up in a muumuu, and he wouldn't care. He loved her—the inside her—not the clothes she wore or the way she looked. It seemed odd to think like that; he wasn't sure many eighteen-year-old boys felt that way about their prom dates.

He climbed into the old truck. It might have been black at some point; now it was more of a rust-on-gray shade. Before Jack cranked it up, he checked the glove compartment. He really should keep the little box in the house, not in an ancient vehicle without working locks. The ring wasn't much, but he couldn't wait to see it on Rachael's finger. He'd worked out a deal with the DJ to play their song midway through the night. He'd lead her out to the quad and propose to her. It should be a clear night, too. The stars would be out in force. He smiled. She'd like that.

Jack twisted the key in the ignition of the old PT-50. It took a few seconds, but the dinosaur of an engine eventually roared to life. First on his list of big purchases was a reliable vehicle for his mom. This one had left her stranded more than once. He thought again, as he leaned over to roll down the passenger window, about the account she'd kept for him all these years. He shook his head. She had to be the most selfless person. He tried to recall a time she'd done anything for herself. Massage? Haircut? Nails? Weekend getaway? As far as he could remember, his mom had always been there. Work. Home. Providing for him. Preparing his food and clothes and home. Everything she did was for him. He'd make sure she was taken care of.

He may have to leave Bellum to do that. Much of the town's population still blamed Jack for anything out of the ordinary—from an unrest amongst local teens to temporarily missing car keys to less-than-ideal weather. Blaming the local drunk kid came easy. It didn't matter much to them that he'd gone through rehab and come out sober. He was their chosen scapegoat, and the guilt he couldn't relinquish made him accept their blame as his necessary burden.

Jack squinted ahead as the sun flashed off the glistening blacktop. He'd worn a hoodie that morning when he headed to the gym. No need for that anymore; summer came early in the South. He was contemplating how much he didn't want to work on blazing roofs again this summer when he turned onto Hyram Cutter Road.

Like many streets across the town, this one was named after the patriarch who owned the most land along its way. Jack crept along the street. Hyram and his wife, Margaret, had raised two things—cotton and kids. The cotton brought in a lot of money, and the kids brought more and more kids. Eight of their ten children lived on the same street. They even had great-grandkids staking out spots for their own houses these days. To the younger Cutters, the road was as much their property as their living rooms. Jack knew to look out for runaway toddlers, ball-chasing kids and abandoned scooters and toys all along the mile-long stretch. He wished there were another way to town.

"Shit."

Hyram stood at the end of his driveway, arms crossed. His glare made it clear he'd seen it was Jack driving the Plymouth instead of his mom. Hyram Cutter had saddled Jack with every negative aspect of his sister's life. Ever since Jack had robbed Ruby Appleby in his final days of rebellion before entering the mission, Hyram sought out reasons to send the boy packing. Mid-way through Jack's time in rehab, Mrs. Appleby had taken a tumble down her front steps. That was the end of one hip and the beginning of the end of her good health. Her days were numbered from that point, and no one but Hyram was surprised when the pneumonia took her that

November. Hyram had failed his older sister, but he couldn't bear guilt's load. So, he intertwined her death with Jack's stealing in his mind and wanted retribution. He had played judge and jury and was looking for an opportunity to become executioner.

Not today, of all days, Jack thought. Hyram stepped to the middle of the road and waited for the truck to stop before he swaggered to the driver's window. He was every inch of six feet and then some, and God must have used a barrel to shape his upper body and tree trunks as molds for his limbs. The man made an imposing figure.

"Good mornin', Mr. Cutter." Jack tried the polite route.

"Boy, what the hell d'you think you're doin'?"

Jack took a deep breath and gazed across the Cutter property. Children ran all over—too many to count in a glance. They were immersed in a massive game of tag. Houses and trailers clustered together in family plots with baby cotton plants filling the space between.

"Well, sir, I thought I'd drive into town."

"I don't want to see you anywhere near my land."

"How do you propose I get into town then, sir? This is the only route."

He resisted the urge to remind the man that his name on the road sign didn't mean he owned the black top. The breeze picked up, and Jack lowered his head to keep from throwing up. Hyram Cutter may have been richer than God, but he didn't use a cent of that money on soap or shampoo. A thick yellow film perpetually coated the hair that might have been white.

"You can take the county road."

Jack looked up, shocked at the old man's ballsy declaration. "You mean Route 17? You're jokin', right? It would take me at least forty minutes to follow that all the way around and into Bellum."

"I'm dead serious, boy. Now, you put this heap in reverse and get off my land."

"Mr. Cutter, sir," Jack kept his voice steady, but his tone grew deeper, ominous. "I have to get right around that corner up there to Willard's to pick up my girlfriend's corsage for tonight, and there's no way I'm going around Sister Mary's barn to do it. I'm sorry you hate me, sir, but I'm not the punk I was even a year ago. Now, I hope you have a good weekend; and I'll see you tomorrow in church."

Hyram's face had reddened with each word Jack had calmly but firmly spoken. If he didn't know it was physically impossible, Jack would've sworn the man had steam seeping out of his ears. The man's cloudy blue eyes took on a wild glint, like a predator eyeing prey that's about to make a break for it. And then, it happened.

"You little ..."

The man attacked, thrusting his beefy arm straight for Jack's neck. Surprise and fear took over, and Jack ducked and tapped the gas to clear the punch in motion and knock away the man's grasp. The truck's movement was just enough to send Hyram teetering, off-balance. It was also enough for Jack to hear a thud and feel the jerk of the wheel as he rolled over something.

Children came running and screaming, fear distorting their faces. They had been playing hide and seek. Two-year-old Abbie Mae Cutter, one of the youngest great-grands, had found a perfect spot to hide. No one would look for her there. She was the right size to crawl under the bumper of the funny-looking truck. She held in a giggle with her pudgy little hands as she waited for her cousins to find her. Her Papaw's growl startled her, though, and Abbie Mae hopped up to run when the truck jerked forward, knocking her down. Right in front of the rotating wheel.

Jack hit the brakes and put the truck in park, expecting to find a deflated basketball or, worse, a scooter that had damaged the truck's antique undercarriage. He swung the door open and jumped out to be only a step behind the man whose world was about to implode.

Both men turned the corner at the same moment to discover white-blond curls scattered out behind the front passenger wheel. Jack froze at the image that would forever invade his nightmares.

Hyram uttered a stifled cry—animalistic in its pain—as he ran to the broken child beneath the vehicle. He dragged her out as easily as he would a rag doll. There was no worry about causing further damage by moving her. Abbigail Margaret Cutter would never move again.

Guilt demands a scapegoat. So, on this day of a second accident in the sleepy burgh, it was no wonder Jack became the target of everyone's blame. The fact that he was behind the wheel this time didn't help one bit. The nail in his coffin was who the little girl's grandfather was. Jack willingly picked up the weight of guilt for the tiny life he had taken.

VI

A Ticket to Anywhere

April 20 to May 25, 2002

Out of six sisters, Ruby had been Hyram's favorite. And, out of his ten children, twenty-two grandchildren and eighteen great-grandbabies, Abbie Mae was the apple of his eye. In the wounded man's estimation, Jack Calhoun had taken both from him.

An injured animal retreats and hides away until healing or death relieves it. The same creature, faced with watching its young injured, attacks with full force and without hesitation or mercy. Hyram Cutter did just that.

Someone called Sheriff Pounds. Everyone was crying. No one looked at the boy who stood in the middle of the road, staggering under the burden of knowing he pushed the pedal that propelled the machine that crushed out the life of a two-year-old girl.

By the time sirens reached Jack's ears, the chaos around him had begun to pull him from the fog that engulfed him the moment he saw blond ringlets draped over a tiny fist. An ambulance raced past the sheriff's car and stopped short of the back of the truck. EMTs needlessly rushed around their ER on wheels. They set up a stretcher and unsheathed equipment. Hyram clung to the child's languid body. John and Jim, the first responders, tried to take Abbie Mae from her great-grandfather. He came alive and knocked John into the bed of the Plymouth with one mighty sweep of his arm. Jim took five quick steps back and looked around for Sheriff Pounds who had walked up in time to see the assault.

"You all right there, John?" the sheriff asked the groaning man. A quick glance told him the man would live to face another beating, so he didn't break stride as he closed the gap between his car and Hyram's side. The two had grown up together, won state championships together, served in the war together and raised families together. They'd lost together as well, but this one ... this one was different, harder, deeper. This was a lamb snatched from the fold.

Hank Pounds knelt beside his friend on the blacktop road. He laid a hand on Hyram's shoulder. Silence spread out from them—neither with a dry eye—and covered the mayhem surrounding the scene. No one heard what Hank whispered, but they all saw the moment reality hit Hyram. Emotion erupted from his reservoir of rage. The sheriff nodded back for Jim who slipped in to carry the lifeless child away. As the man lifted the toddler, Jack saw her face and would always wish he hadn't.

What happened next played out in fast-forward and slow motion at the same time. Sheriff Pounds asked Hyram what happened. It took a moment for the grief-stricken man's mind to rewind to right before he had clutched his favorite grandchild to his chest for the last time. When he remembered how they arrived at this nightmare, his mind hit stop. His rage reared its head again, and the papa bear attacked.

"Him!" He launched the word like a guided missile, locked onto Jack's crumbling heart.

Before Sheriff Pounds could react, Hyram lunged at Jack, lifting him off the ground and over his head with his bull-like strength. He swung him against the truck's windshield as easily as he would have a hay bale. Before Jack's head cracked the windshield and the world went dark, he saw Hyram Cutter's beet-red face and knew he'd never find forgiveness for that day.

* * *

The next moments of awareness for Jack included cool air drifting across his cheek, muffled voices, the scents of some sickeningly sweet flower and vanilla, an unbelievable heaviness on his chest and the worst throbbing headache he'd ever experienced. He tried to open his eyes, but the world around him was spinning and fuzzy. He squeezed them shut again, thinking he just needed to try again. The spinning grew worse with his second attempt, so he closed them again to keep the nausea at bay.

Voices around him grew clearer. A deep voice droned on his left. He didn't recognize it, but whoever possessed it had a lot to say. There had been another voice—softer, familiar. Where was it? The deep voice paused, and the softer one reached his ear. *Mom.* His mom was here with him. He wanted to call out to her, reach for her. He was pinned down, helpless to raise his own arm. *What happened?* And then his mom stopped talking; another voice rose right above his right ear. *Rachael. Rach, what happened? Where am I? Why can't I see? Why can't I speak. Don't leave me. Please.*

***

Jack later learned that he remained unconscious after the EMTs brought him in to the Bellum ER. After a quick exam, doctors requested an airlift to Atlanta to better evaluate the damage. While he should have been dancing with Rachael and proposing to her, doctors ran tests and speculated on how serious the injury to his brain had been.

Though he drifted in and out as his brain healed, Jack's first fully conscious recollection after the trauma was of an unusually bright room. He was propped up in a hospital bed. Across the room stood a dresser with a vase full of roses on top. His hand was enclosed in something soft and warm. Looking down, Jack saw Rachael's head lying against his leg, her hand on his and her eyes closed. She was the most beautiful girl on earth. He could watch her sleep for hours. Her bright red hair fanned out above her head and shone in the sunbeam that caressed it. Her lips pursed, and he could almost taste her kiss. She was his world, and he longed for nothing more than to hold her.

His head still hurt, but it was nothing like before. *What happened? Why am I in here? Where is here?* In one fell swoop, the memories crashed around him. The trip to town. Hyram Cutter. That horrible thud and then ... little Abbie Mae's lifeless face.

Oh, dear God, no, he groaned out his prayer. It wasn't just a nightmare. It happened. But, where was he?

Rachael stirred; her eyes fluttered open. When she saw him looking back at her through his anguish, her brows came together, and she sat upright. "Oh, Jack! You're really awake. All the way awake." She lowered the rail beside him and sat gently by his side. Her hands on his comforted him, steadied him, grounded him.

"It was an accident. I had no idea she was in the road. I don't know where …. She was so little."

"I know. I'm so sorry. I can't imagine how awful that must have been. Sheriff Pounds told my dad exactly what happened. The other kids said they were playing hide and seek. She must have been hiding."

"How did I get here, though? I don't remember anything after her face. Oh, Rach … her face … "

Rachael laid her head against his shoulder. He wanted to pull her close and breathe her in, but he couldn't move his head without searing pain. "That awful Mr. Cutter. He threw you into your own windshield, Jack. He picked you up and tossed you like … like a bag of potatoes or something." She looked into Jack's hazel eyes, golden flecks glistening in them beneath the sunlight streaming through the room's window. "I was so scared, Jack. Scared I'd lost you forever. You looked dead when I saw you in the hospital back home before they rushed you out to the helicopter. They didn't have to do surgery here like they thought they would."

None of this seemed real. Not one bit. Jack hoped he'd wake up from this nightmare at any moment. He had to wake up. But he didn't, because this was his new reality. He had killed a child. Her empty face would haunt him every moment of his life, and that afternoon would remain on instant replay in his mind.

Despite his potentially fatal injuries, Jack recovered. In the Atlanta hospital, he was surrounded by people who sympathized with him and saw him for who he was instead of what he had done. When Nurse Mary wheeled him out to his mom's rental car and leaned down to lock the wheels, her deep brown eyes pleaded with him. "You take care of yerself, Jack.

Don't you let any big bully keep you burdened with something that weren't your fault. You always got friends here, baby."

He stood up into her bear hug and leaned on her support and comfort. Those were two things he thought he may not find in great supply where he was going.

He was right.

***

Back in Bellum Jack was ignored at best. Hyram Cutter's rage had infiltrated the town the man held in his wallet.

Rachael's graduation was about a week after Jack's return. What should have been a joyous event, though, put the town's reaction to Jack on display in one packed arena. He did his best to pretend the entire crowd wasn't pointing at him and whispering about him all night. Rachael looked back to smile at him, but his forced return didn't fool her. She glanced around and frowned at what she witnessed. Following the ceremony, she pulled Jack to her side for a quick photo. After the fifth person pretended not to hear their request to snap a picture, Jack kissed Rachael on the cheek.

"Enjoy this night with all your friends. I am so proud of you." He continued with a finger on her parted lips. "No. Enjoy it. Please. I'm taking my leprosy with me."

Leaving a quick peck on Rachael's lips, Jack walked straight out the back of the sweltering gymnasium into the sauna of another summer-come-early.

***

Time inched past as Jack continued to heal. He went through legal proceedings to be declared not guilty, though he couldn't accept that verdict. The nightmares had returned, and Becky watched her son withdraw and worried. One month after the fateful day, Jack met the incident that finally pushed him over the edge and changed his future destination.

That Saturday afternoon, he ventured to Taylor's to pick up groceries for his mom. Snip-its of whispers followed him.

"... drinking again ..."

"... murderer ..."

"... drugs this time."

"Stoned out of his mind ..."

"... sped up to hit that precious little angel."

"... why the Sheriff hasn't locked him away yet."

By the time Jack reached the checkout, he'd heard it all. And then he looked up into the unforgiving eyes of one of the Cutters' granddaughters. His tongue grew cotton, and panic sprouted in his chest.

"For my mom ..." he mumbled.

Clara didn't care who the items went to because the drunk who killed her baby cousin held them now. She scanned each item and continued glaring a red-hot hole through Jack as she slammed the milk onto the bag carousel, cracking the plastic and sending up a white, frothy geyser. She tossed the eggs on top, so yolks mixed with the milk. Flour dusted it all; but, before she lifted the sugar bag, the manager rushed over.

"I think it's time for you to leave now."

Jack had kept his head down through the process, trying to decide what to do. He risked a glance up to thank the man when he realized it wasn't the girl with her grandfather's rage bubbling within her who was being ordered to leave. He opened his mouth, shocked. How could everyone in this town treat him this way? All around him, shoppers had stopped to watch the spectacle proceed in front of them so they could relay their warped versions to anyone they met in the coming week. Jack looked around at the eyes that couldn't seem to return his gaze for more than a half-second. Among them he recognized two deacons from Bellum Baptist, his elementary Sunday school teacher, the Rotary Club president and two well-known do-gooders in the American Legion Auxiliary. Backing away, Jack pulled a twenty out of his wallet, tossed it in the still-dripping paste and addressed the jury around him as he backed toward the door.

"One of you righteous ladies will need to get these items to my mom or find someone else to bake cakes for your missions bake sale."

Jack spun around and disappeared into the brightness beyond the sliding doors. He got in the rental car the insurance company had provided them and headed east. Clemson was just under an hour away. He could make it before his friend Misty closed shop. Jack kept his speed under the limit, but he couldn't slow his raging heart. He'd heard the Bible read and explained. Enough Sunday school teachers had outlined how to be a Christian from start to finish. What he saw in Bellum didn't add up. When he thought about Ben and Rachael and his mom and compared them to the people who'd done nothing but cast darts of hate and spears of accusation his way, he couldn't make the pieces fit.

To hell with the whole damn town. If I'm heading to hell, I'll see them there.

When Jack pulled into a space near the entrance to the package store, he raised shaking hands from the steering wheel and ran them through his hair. *How am I back to this point?* He quickly buried his memories of that first week without alcohol and took a deep breath. He emerged from the car and strode into the building that held his salvation from emotions and memories.

"Been an awful long while," said the bleach-blond cougar behind the counter when he slid the whiskey bottle in front of her. "I sure have missed your handsome face, baby."

Jack plastered on the smile of another person as he winked at his supplier. "Well, Misty, you know how it is. A man's gotta' drift around a bit. But, I had to come back here for that sexy smile of yours."

"You come on back any time, sugar. One of these days you're gonna take me up on my offer, too. You know you will." Misty called after him.

He waved back even as he shuddered under the dirty veil of the addict he had been. Tossing the brown bag on the seat next to him, Jack didn't think as he headed toward a park hidden off the road where he used to go to be undisturbed with his bottles. He pulled in to the familiar spot and eyed the pile of broken glass next to the warped picnic table. *Did I really put away that many here?*

Jack dropped the brown bag and ripped off the plastic on his way to perch atop the table. He unscrewed the cap, tossing it in the woods beyond him. The rim was nearly to his lips when the smell of the whiskey wakened his memories, bringing everything back to him in a rush like a rogue wave crashing into an unsuspecting wader. Lost nights, the foggy haze of two years of his life, an airborne muscle car spinning like a top, the rusty smell of blood, the explosion of anger within him, the pleading for death's refuge on that second day at the mission ... Rachael's angelic face looking up until those hypnotic blue eyes begged him to stop. The coolness of the bottle rested against his bottom lip as the tears spilled.

Rage overflowed like lava down the side of a mountain. Jack spun off the table and smashed the bottle onto the closest tree. Brown liquid showered him in its sweet-smelling seduction. He screamed the rest of his anger at the waning day around him. "Damn it all!" With a kick from his hiking boots that sent dirt and glass flying, Jack collided with the damp earth in that abandoned corner of nowhere and begged whatever higher power oversaw this world of horror to end his misery and spare the people he loved from any more of the pain he seemed to spread like an incurable disease.

Once every ounce of emotion had escaped the prison of his soul, Jack walked back to the car. He felt hollow. He knew what he had to do. No more would he sit by and watch the people he loved get hurt by whatever curse had claimed him as its host. The final tendrils of the sun's red hair slunk before him as he headed west. His mom would be at work until 10, so he'd have enough time. He hated that she had to work as a waitress on the weekends. That's another thing he would find a way to change. It was time for him to fix the mess around him.

* * *

"Can I meet you at the church in an hour? I need a ride to the bus station." Jack listened to the voice he had called as soon as he got to his house. "No. And, please ... please don't tell Rach."

It took him less than two minutes to pack his red duffle—change of clothes, toiletries, the ring his mom had rescued from their truck and three pictures. In one picture he and his mom sat on the back of their truck. His arm was around her. He remembered that day. It was the first day off his mom had had in a very long time, and he'd made big plans for them. They went fishing, had a picnic, raced his remote cars and drove to the next town for ice cream they couldn't really afford. Looking at her smiling face in the photo, he finally saw how tired she must have been. She had closed down the diner the night before and had to be in early at the factory the next day. That was the same day she ended up helping him with a science fair project he'd forgotten about. He wondered if she slept at all that night.

Jack had the photo with his mom after graduation from the mission—the one Rachael had taken. The third picture was of Rachael and him. Shannon—from his mission group— had snapped it one day during a reunion picnic with other former residents. Her eye for photography had grown, and the image was stunning. The sinking sun caressed their faces and shone on the love that passed between the two kids oblivious to everyone but each other. The joke they'd just shared hung in perpetuity with that photo. He would always remember that day and that moment, but not for the joke he couldn't quite recall or because of the photo. What Jack could never forget was that was the exact moment he knew he wanted to spend the rest of his life with the woman sitting beside him. Hers was the face he wanted to wake up to every morning for the rest of his life. Her lips were the last thing he wanted to taste before dreams carried him away each night. He saw all the future he could ever desire in her eyes.

And, he was running from her.

Jack tucked the photos inside the bag before zipping it closed. He sat down at his desk before he lost his nerve. Ten minutes later he folded the second letter and tucked it and some cash into an envelope he'd already labeled. He scooped up both letters, slung his duffle over his shoulder and speed-walked down the hall to the entrance. Before he could turn the handle, he paused to survey the house his mom had sacrificed so much to make his home. A single tear coursed unchecked down his cheek as he walked through the front door to a future far different than the one he'd seen in Rachael's eyes.

He took the long route to town. He refused to drive on that cursed road ever again. The only part of Jack's plan out of his control was whether Ben would understand and follow his wishes or not. He couldn't say goodbye to Rachael in person. He just couldn't. And, he had to leave. There was no other option for him. Besides, he wasn't good for her. She deserved more than an unstable recovering alcoholic who woke up screaming from nightly visits of dead kids and couldn't seem to do anything but hurt everyone around him.

Ben was leaning against his SUV under one of the streetlights in the church parking lot when Jack pulled in. Jack didn't realize he had been holding his breath until he saw Ben was alone and exhaled as he parked. He grabbed his bag and locked up the rental before tossing the keys to the preacher.

"Will you make sure my mom gets the car back?"

"I will." Ben watched the determined young man walk around to the passenger side. He leaned his head against the arm he'd rested on the vehicle before opening his own door. "Jack, are you positive about this? Running may not be the answer you're looking for."

"It's the only answer left for me. I can't stay in this town. It's not fair to my mom." He looked down before adding, "And, I'm not strong enough to handle the hate everyone here has for me. I had the bottle to my lips tonight, Ben. It was far too easy to go back there."

Ben saw the pleading look in Jack's eyes—eyes older than they should have been, with too much pain and heartache buried within. "But, what about Rach? Are you really leaving her without so much as a goodbye? She deserves way more than that."

"I know she does. That's why I'm leaving." Jack handed Ben the envelopes. "Please give these to them. There's a little money in the one for my mom. As soon as I get some work, I'll send money back for her as often as I can. Can I send it to the church, care of you? I don't want either of them knowing where I am. It'll be easier. Clean break. Fresh start for them."

"For them or you?"

"Both, I guess."

"If you had any desire to be the more Rachael deserves, you wouldn't run."

Ben's words stung, but Jack turned from their hard truth to the window. With his silent response Ben cranked up the car and headed out for the next town and the bus station that offered Jack his escape. After a few miles of tense stillness, Jack asked, "Will you give them the letters?"

An inner battle waged among Ben's father, preacher and mentor roles. Finally, he responded. "I will; but, Jack, it would be better coming from you than me."

"I can't. I may not leave, Ben. And, I cannot stay in Bellum another day. I've got to get somewhere I can start fresh and try to figure out who the hell I even am. I can't do that where everyone points me out as a murderer."

"Sheriff Pounds has made it very public that you are cleared of any charges. Hyram Cutter doesn't own everyone in this town. This will die down, Jack; I'm telling you. What happened today at the store—yes, I heard about it; Fred, the manager, came and talked to me, said he felt awful about how he handled everything—that's not going to happen again. Not all the Cutter family feel the way their Papaw does. I've been counseling some of them."

"This whole damn town needs counseling!" Jack's fist shook the vehicle as he side-punched the door. For a moment, the incessant rattle in the back of the aging SUV ceased. Jack's voice softened. "I see that little girl's face every single night. My mom can't sleep because I wake her up with my screams. And, I can't go anywhere because everyone's made it clear they believe all the gossip that I was drunk or high or whatever the latest scandal those old ladies have cooked up is."

"Jack, not everyone believes those lies. Honestly, I don't think the ladies 'cooking them up,' as you say, believe them. People are scared and hurting and looking for someone to blame."

"Well, they got one. I'm taking the curse away from them. And, so you know, most of the folks who're spreading the stories and giving me death glares sit in your pews every week. Aren't you Christians supposed to understand forgiveness?" He challenged the preacher with his final jab.

"Yes." Jack immediately regretted his words when he saw the sorrow wash over Ben's face. The preacher hand-picked words for his answer. "Christians understand forgiveness more than anyone because they've been forgiven the most. And, with that gift, come both the responsibility and the desire to forgive others. The thing you need to understand is, not everyone who calls themselves Christ's truly are. It's been one of the hardest things for me to handle in this community. Many families go to church as part of centuries' worth of traditions, passed down but missing purpose. They hear the truth week after week, but they don't understand it. They don't believe God's word or Jesus' message of forgiveness. Do you believe it, Jack?"

A street light brushed Jack's face as he contemplated his answer. "When I look at you and Rach and my mom, I want to believe. Then I see the rest of your congregation, and I'd prefer hell."

Ben's shoulders sagged as the heaviness of Jack's words settled there. He prayed for Jack to see past the fakes to the Gospel's truth. He prayed for belief in each member of his church as he wondered what it would be like each Sunday to look out from the pulpit at people he knew, beyond the shadow of a doubt, were Christians. Their community would be completely different, he decided. As Ben pondered the beauty of such a reality, he pulled into the bus station. Before he could say any more, though, Jack interrupted his thoughts.

"Thank you, Ben—for everything. You've done so much for me, helping me get my life back on track. Really, you're why I've got the possibility of a future. Thank you. Please take care of Rach and my mom. I'm sorry I have to leave, but I don't see another way … for me."

"What will you do? Do you have money? Do you have a plan?"

"I'm fine. I've got money and a plan—find work so mom doesn't have to work two jobs any longer. Try to forget."

Jack got out of the vehicle to face his next step. Ben called after him, "You can't outrun your past and your pain and guilt. They will follow you. Stay and deal with them … head-on." Jack looked away until Ben gave a parting word. "We'll miss you."

The weighted teen turned with a sorrow in his half-smile. "I'm glad *you* will, Ben." With that, Jack strode into the tiny station to purchase a ticket to anywhere but Bellum, Georgia.

VII

Start to Look Up

May 25-27, 2002

Ben kept his word. He drove to the diner and waited for Becky to untie her apron and head outside. He handed her the letter from her son. She clutched it to her heart. Mothers have a knack for knowing things about their children without being told. Becky took a deep breath before opening the envelope. She noticed the cash but removed the loose-leaf paper.

Jack's firm writing bled through the page, and Ben studied the slashes, loops and scratches as he waited for Becky to finish.

Mama,

I don't have the right words to thank you for the sacrifices you've made for me. You made me a home. You loved me. You taught me. You forgave me. I want to be a son you can be proud of and I'm working on that. I know you understand I have to leave. I need to escape the nightmares and the accusations. I hope my leaving brings you peace in Bellum.

I love you and I'm so sorry for all the pain I've caused you.

Love,

Jack

P.S. Please use this money to treat yourself to something special—something you've never splurged on before. That would make me so happy. I'll send more money to you as soon as I can through Ben. Please quit that diner job. I love you!

Becky would cry later. Ben had still only seen her cry twice, despite all the tragedy he had watched her walk through—the day they said goodbye to Carolina and That Night in the hospital.

"His mind was made up. Nothing I could have said would've changed it." Ben's roundabout apology brought a semi-smile to Becky's mouth.

"I know that, Ben. I can't say I'm surprised. This has been coming. I saw the shift in him and knew he'd reach this point sooner than later." Becky's shoulders sagged under the weight of her acceptance. "Jack's got that piece of his father in him, but I believe he'll figure it out—his purpose."

"True purpose only comes through knowing true peace." Ben's words lingered on the air between them.

"Carolina wouldn't want you to give up on Jack. Please don't give up on him, Ben." Becky's eyes pled with her pastor and friend.

"I won't. I promise you that. I pray for him every day, and that won't ever stop." Ben's sincerity clung to each word. "I've still got to deliver this letter, though, to Rachael. That's a conversation I wish I didn't have to have. I don't want to be the one to hand my little girl yet another heartbreak. She may not come out from under this one."

Ben had known about the ring. Rachael hadn't. One night soon before the latest tragedy that altered their reality, she sat in his lap as he read in his recliner. He smiled as she leaned back, her head on his shoulder. No matter how old she got, she'd always be his baby girl.

"Daddy?"

"Mm-hmm?"

"I have something very important to tell you." Ben put his book down and gave her his undivided attention. "I'm in love with Jack. He's the man I know God wants me to spend the rest of my life with. He's the reason I've read two more of Mama's letters—first love and when you know you've met 'the one.' Her words confirmed my thoughts. And, Daddy, I want you to be happy with me, too."

Ben's heart sank at her declaration. He wanted more for his girl. He wanted a man who shared her faith. He knew with certainty that Carolina would have known exactly what to say here. He did not.

"I know what you're thinking, Daddy; but I believe God's going to save him. I can't explain it; but, today, when we were laughing about something at the reunion picnic, I was looking into his eyes and ... I just knew."

Ben sighed at the memory of his daughter's words because he couldn't argue with her then and didn't know how to comfort her through this. God knows he understood exactly how Rachael felt. He had felt the same way about her mother years ago.

Becky was also thinking about Carolina. She said, "Rachael's got her mother's uncanny ability to read people. And her incredible strength. She knows what's best for her.

If that is Jack, no amount of childishness on his part will keep them separated. And, if it's not him, she will let him go with a greater grace and peace than you or I could ever muster."

"You do know my Rachael." Ben chuckled at Becky's summary of his daughter. "I still believe God's got great plans for Jack. I know he'll write me, and I'll do all I can to reach him."

Becky nodded. "I know you will. I also know his stubbornness can't outrun God. There's nothing I can do but pray and be here when he finds his way."

Ben drove Becky to her car at the church—to heck with what the gossiping old biddies may have to say about the appearance of it. He already had an earful planned for them. That week's sermon on Psalm 23 would go back in the drawer. It was time for pew sitters to finally hear a message of true forgiveness.

As he pulled in his driveway, Ben breathed a prayer for strength and glanced at the letter on the passenger seat. He saw his beautiful girl walking around the kitchen. It seemed he had blinked, and she had grown into an incredible young woman. She could cook pretty much anything—a gift from her mom. He smiled as he watched her spin around. She was always singing and dancing, especially when she cooked.

Rachael had told him once that she felt closest to her mom in the kitchen. To be honest, she looked exactly like her. Carolina would do the same thing, right down to the spin with the long red streak of hair sweeping around behind her. If only Carolina could see their baby girl. She'd know how to handle this situation. Ben breathed deeply. No need to put this off any longer.

"Supper's almost ready—finally. You made me hold it so long, I almost ate without you." Rachael smiled at her father as he entered.

"It smells amazing, as always." Ben gave her a hug and a kiss on her forehead before memorizing the blissful expression she wore. He feared he wouldn't see it again for a long time.

"What's wrong, Dad? Did something happen?"

Rachael had always been perceptive. Even as a toddler, she could tell when her father was upset. She'd put her hand on his chest, like she did then, to feel his heartbeat. This time, he placed Jack's letter against her hand. Recognition of the handwriting caused her to step back. "No." She shook her head hard, trying to toss away the sinking feeling coursing through her. "No." She took the letter, though, and sank onto the kitchen floor to open it. Her face lost all color, and she looked like the scared little girl who was once convinced an evil genie lived in her closet. She slowly unfolded the paper on her lap.

Rach,

You mean more to me than anything in this world. That's why I had to write you goodbye instead of telling you. Even now, thinking about your face as you read this is breaking my heart. I have to find another future. One far away from Bellum and all the people I keep hurting.

I'm no good for you. I'm broken. Not sure I can be fixed. You deserve much better. I never want to be the reason you hurt again, so please don't cry for me leaving. Go to college. You're going to be the best fitness instructor or nutritionist this world's ever seen. Go on with your life, Rachael. As much as it's killing me to write it, find a man worthy of all you are.

Goodbye, Rachael.

She didn't hold in her pain. Ben sat down and slid his arm around her shoulders. She looked up at him with her tear-streaked face. "Why? Why would he leave me?"

"This town turned on him, Rach. He's hurting bad. I don't think he could stand the thought of telling you he had to leave."

"I would have gone with him! I love him so much, Daddy!"

"He knows, baby girl, and he loves you, too. That's why he believed he had to leave you. He wants more for you—happiness and contentment, things he wasn't sure he could give you."

"But, he could. He did. Oh, Daddy!" Rachael buried her head in her father's shirt and wept until her tears dried. Emotionally exhausted, she fell asleep. Ben lifted his daughter and carried her to bed, covering her with the blanket that had been her favorite since she was five. He sighed again before kissing her forehead and wishing her tears' cause was still as simple as nonexistent fictional villains.

Ben returned downstairs to pray through a new sermon. He thought back over his years in this church. He had seen the signs. Some of the church's members showed no evidence of having a heart changed by God.

Why didn't I dig deeper in my sermons to clarify the vast difference between tradition and faith? Have I failed as a pastor? Maybe I'm not called to be a preacher after all.

Ben had always felt more at peace in the mission than in the pulpit looking out at bored and sanctimonious faces. Tomorrow would be his final sermon.

* * *

The choir hit the high note during their special music, and then the organist played one more verse of "I'll Fly Away" as choir members dispersed to sit with family members and friends. Rachael rested her head on Becky's shoulder as the women bore their sorrows together. Ben smiled gently down at them as he took his place behind the podium. For a moment he stood, head bowed and eyes closed, gathering his thoughts and praying again that God make it clear if what he was about to do was the right thing. The face he lifted to the congregation was one of resolve and peace. He launched into a litany of chapters and verses from the Bible.

"Psalm chapter 32, verse 1, 'Blessed is he whose transgression is forgiven, whose sin is covered.' Psalm chapter 130, verse 4, 'But there is forgiveness with You, That You may be feared.' Mark chapter 11, verses 25 through 26, 'And whenever you stand praying, if you have anything against anyone, forgive him, that your Father in heaven may also forgive you your trespasses. But if you do not forgive, neither will your Father in heaven forgive your trespasses.' Luke chapter 23, verse 34, 'Then Jesus said, "Father, forgive them, for they do not know what they do.'

"One of Bellum's sons left because you couldn't forgive. You couldn't see past your own blind anger to accept the truth and love a terrified, hurting boy who has to stare at the lifeless face of a two-year-old girl every time he closes his eyes. You didn't forgive or love him because you don't know this Jesus who came to forgive and to teach you to forgive. You don't understand his teaching and you sure as hell—quite literally—don't know him as your Lord and Savior.

"The masks have slipped since the tragedy in this town on April 20. You've shown your hearts, and I have wept over your hatred and your lack of understanding of this great Book, the message within it and the great God who gave it to us. Christ forgave the very men who tortured and killed him. Christ ate with and visited with and forgave men who stole money from others, women who slept around and friends who left him in his hour of greatest earthly need. Christ forgave us, not on our best day with our perfect masks firmly in place or when we're being 'good.' Romans tells us he forgave us when we were still his enemies.

"You claim the name 'Christian,' but you refused to forgive a boy who wasn't even your enemy. Far from it. He was your neighbor, your son, your brother. He was a scared kid who'd already been through more than any person ought to in a lifetime. He's a kid who made some bad choices in the past but got help. He was a kid who was working hard to prepare a bright and beautiful future for his family … and the family he wanted to make.

"He was a kid who found himself in a horrifying accident where he took the life of a child and has woken up screaming every night since. He was a kid who you condemned, spread lies about, hated, refused to forgive. Because many of you are the ones responsible for spreading destructive lies about him, I'm here to tell you the truth about Jack Calhoun.

"Jack said yes one night to a drink. That first sip led him to many more. His body lied to him, told him he had to have it. He believed it because he was a scared fifteen-year-old kid who almost died on a dirt road. He lost four of his classmates That Night. He had some of you blame him for those deaths, too.

"You know the story from there of how he got kicked out of school and how he stole to keep up with his addiction. That unquenchable desire nearly killed him again. But, he came to me for help. That seventeen-year-old kid did the hard work of battling a beast called Alcoholism. I watched him fight. He had the determination of a warrior and the commitment to a cause of a knight.

"He graduated from the program at the mission and got a job—a hard one—that he never complained about and did to the best of his ability. He tucked away money from his paychecks and began to pay back the people he'd stolen from.

"I see some of you haven't heard this part yet. Well, that's right; you wouldn't. See, Jack didn't want people to know he was paying them back, plus some. So, if Jack stole from you, think back. Did you ever have a cashier at Taylor's tell you your groceries had already been paid for? Ever go to pay your water or electric, only to find it already done? That was Jack.

"Everyone's been quick to blame ridiculousness on him— missing laundry, misplaced keys, late mail, falls from porches. But, no one wanted to look at all the facts and award praise to him for paying restitution with interest. Mrs. Appleby got most of his attention. Jack paid her water bill every month until her death, raked or mowed her lawn and replaced blown lightbulbs outside her house. After she died, he paid for new daisies on her grave every Thursday. She had told him once when he was a child that those were her favorites.

"Let me tell you another part of his truth. On April 20, Jack was on his way to pick up a corsage for his prom date— my Rachael. While creeping along the playground that's one of our primary roads, Hyram Cutter stepped in front of his truck and made him stop. Mr. Cutter proceeded to tell him he wasn't allowed to use this main road—the only road that connects Jack's house to Main Street. He told him he had to use the county road that loops all the way around Bellum. When Jack confronted Mr. Cutter with the ridiculousness of his demand and told him he was going on to town to reach Willard's before they closed, Mr. Cutter lunged at the kid's face. Jack's got great reflexes, though; many of you remember what a quick cornerback he was. He pumped the gas just enough to get away from Mr. Cutter's reach. What neither of them knew was little Abbie Mae thought underneath Jack's truck made the perfect hiding spot.

"And then, right after Jack looked into that child's tiny lifeless face, Mr. Cutter hurled him into his own windshield, put him in the hospital and left doctors unsure he'd even wake up. Now Jack's mama's got hospital bills she's unsure how she'll pay. And, as of last night, her son is gone. He got on a bus going anywhere that's not here. I've got a broken-hearted little girl, too. She'd given him her love, but your hatred made him believe he wasn't good enough for her and would only hurt her more by staying.

"I know some of you deacons are ready to throw me out of here—especially you, Mr. Cutter—but there's no need. This is my final Sunday. I can't continue preaching to a church full of people who think their heaven ticket's punched and they're above reproach. First Corinthians 13 tells us all about love; well, I'm gonna replace the word *love* with *forgiveness*. 'Though I speak with the tongues of men and of angels, but have not forgiveness, I have become sounding brass or a clanging cymbal. And though I have the gift of prophecy, and understand all mysteries and all knowledge, and though I have all faith, so that I could remove mountains, but have not forgiveness, I am nothing. And though I bestow all my goods to feed the poor, and though I give my body to be burned, but have not forgiveness, it profits me nothing.'

"You're sounding brass and clanging cymbals. Your lack of forgiveness sent a scared, lost kid—a kid who was just starting to ask good questions and seek for purpose—sent him running blindly away from God and the peace, purpose and forgiveness that can only be found in Him. Each one of you needs Jesus and his forgiveness. Get on your knees and repent of your unforgiveness and finally become what you've falsely called yourselves—Christians."

Ben walked off the stage, held his hands out to Becky and Rachael and led them down the aisle and out of Bellum Baptist Church. He never returned.

After they left, two-thirds of the congregation flooded down the aisle to get on their knees and pray at the altar. A couple of deacons ran to recruit help from their sister churches. The Presbyterian and Methodist ministers and a few elders came to pray with the people lining the front of the Baptist church. No one left until long after the buffet across town had closed.

Among the other third stood Hyram Cutter. His red face left no doubt about his reaction to Ben's parting message. Cutter's money had restored the steeple and its bell that sounded at noon. His money had raised the gymnasium in the back. His money paid most of the pastor's salary. But, Hyram Cutter found one thing his money couldn't buy him—passage on a golden chariot through the pearly gates above. His rage finally shredded his enormous heart as he stormed down the front steps of the church that day. Those surrounding him when it happened said it was a horrible sight to behold. His face twisted into a pained grimace. He grasped at his chest and pawed at the air, screaming, "No! Don't take me ... I paid for this church. Don't ..." Sheer terror etched his face.

* * *

While half of Bellum was finding Jesus, Jack wandered the streets of Columbia, South Carolina, in search of a job. He'd gone as far as he could afford and arrived early that morning, wide awake from his nap on the bus. He sat in the station until the sun rose and he could scope out businesses in the area.

He walked past a closed mom-and-pop hardware store but doubled back on a hunch. Jack peered in the window. Behind the counter was a board with some jobs tacked on it. He'd come back in the morning for a closer look. Jack wandered aimlessly most of the day. It seemed this part of town didn't see much Sunday afternoon traffic. He found a shady spot in a grove of trees on a vacant lot and sat down. At noon, chimes sounded from a nearby steeple. The tinkling sound turned to hymns familiar enough to Jack that he heard over the melody their words—in Rachael's voice.

Jack nodded off to sleep, Rachael's face in his mind and voice in his heart. He woke to find the trees' shadows had shifted and felt the innate need to acquire food and shelter before darkness descended. He walked back toward the hardware store by a different route until he found himself rooted to the spot in front of a liquor store.

Full bottles beckoned to him. The mind-numbing liquid seduced him with its siren call, replacing the earlier music with a tune promising relief and release. Jack longed for the oblivion of his mind under its sweet influence. No more pain, guilt, fear, dreams. Nothing.

The memory of its taste filled his mouth, coating his tongue and throat with the warmth that could spread through his chest to his extremities—one by one—and finally to his mind. He could so easily smash this window, grab enough to drown himself and be long gone before police could respond. Then he could drink until all memory had been drowned. Until this miserable life drifted away.

An ambulance's call wailed from a distance, breaking Jack's trance. Fear of the thoughts he'd just entertained clenched his heart and squeezed tighter as he thought of his mom and the promises he had made her. He could not give in. For his mom, he would fight and keep going. Jack shook his head and walked along the sidewalk until he reached an open gas station on the corner down from the store he'd found earlier.

He dug in his pockets for loose change. Fifty-six cents. Add that to the bills in his wallet, and Jack had a grand total of $8.56. Perhaps he should've brought more money, but he wanted to leave as much as he could for his mom. Looks like he'd have to sleep outside tonight. Maybe he didn't have as much of a plan as he had led Ben to believe. He entered the service station and bought a loaf of bread, some peanut butter and a can of beans. It wasn't until he sat down at a picnic table in a nearby park to eat his supper that he realized he had no can opener or spoon. Thankfully, the beans had a pull-top lid that he removed and bent to use as a makeshift utensil. After his meager supper of cold beans with two pieces of white bread, Jack rinsed the lid and can before putting them in his grocery bag and taking a long drink from the water fountain.

Night would fall soon. He looked around for somewhere to rest and remembered the church steeple. It was only a few streets over. He locked in some landmarks, so he'd know where to go in the morning before looking skyward. He kept his eyes on the cross as he walked down four blocks and over another two. Dusk had fallen by the time he reached his destination, and he cursed himself for not packing a flashlight.

The church was an old stone building—Episcopal, according to a metal sign. Jack tried the front door, but it was locked. He headed around the side and through a gate into a walking garden. He tried both side doors—locked. The path curved around the back building. He found no more doors but stumbled upon a wooden frame, likely used as a Christmas nativity manger. It was pushed against the outside of the building. He set down his duffle and put all his weight into inching the shelter away from the building. He tossed his bag in, headed back to the closest tree to relieve himself and shot a quick prayer heavenward that God wouldn't strike him with poison ivy in the wrong places for peeing in a church garden. He squeezed inside the shelter and did his best to push it closed again. He didn't want to draw attention to himself … or attract wildlife. He wasn't eager to share his den.

Jack couldn't stretch out since the lean-to wasn't long enough, but that suited him fine. He hadn't thought to pack a blanket or even a jacket. The May night temperatures dipped and left him curling up into himself to generate as much heat as possible. Even with the hard, cold ground and lumpy duffle as a makeshift pillow, Jack didn't take long to fall asleep.

In the early morning hours, though, his mind played a loop of both accidents in his past with filler moments of a dark corridor with doors flying open on either side as he ran to find an exit. One sprang open right in front of him, releasing flame licking its way toward him. He turned and tripped over a skull into a mound of bones. The flames neared, but he couldn't rise to escape. He kept slipping on the bones. He looked back at the fire. When he turned forward once more, he faced Steven's car flying toward him. He ducked and met Abbie Mae's face, holes like a skull's sockets where her lifeless eyes had been. Finally, Jack woke from the grip of the tormenting nightmare. He knew he'd been screaming and hoped he hadn't alarmed anyone. He hadn't looked for nearby houses during his haste to find shelter.

He dropped his head into his hands as he willed his heart to slow down and his breathing to steady. He recalled the way the liquor sang to him earlier that afternoon. Jack focused on his mom until he tempered the restless urge to break his sobriety. She was why he was here. To find a job. To make money to send home to her.

Jack sat up and edged toward the crack by the church wall. He peered out and saw that light was just touching the sky. He heard the occasional big truck rumble past somewhere in the foreign city around him. Soon, more traffic joined them, and he decided it was time for him to sneak out of his unconventional hotel room before the whole city awoke. He hoped this would be the only night he'd sleep on the ground. Today he'd find a job, and everything would start to look up.

Act II
Intention

VIII

Something Good Might Finally Happen

May 27 through Memorial Day 2002

Jack returned to his park for a breakfast of peanut butter, bread and water. He filled his bean can with water from the fountain and found an alley where he could brush his teeth, wash his face and change his shirt without attracting unwanted attention. Once he was somewhat presentable, he reloaded his bag and set off for the hardware store. No shops had opened yet, and he worried that he'd stumbled into a ghost section of town. Looking down the road he'd come across, he half expected a tumbleweed to blow past as he searched the line of unimpressive storefronts and rusty signs for his destination. The hanging sign above the dingy red door may have once been white. Its red border still popped, though. Something about its otherwise yellowed appearance beckoned to him and whispered a promise of opportunity. With his intention set, Jack strode down the street.

Hardy's had been a fixture in the Miller family since the late 1800s. The story behind the store's name had vanished, and there was no trace of a Hardy Miller or a great-grandmother Hardy in their genealogy. Pat Miller would likely be its last operator. At age eighty-two, he was still as active as when he was sixty. He kept the doors open to piss off his children more than anything else. His son, Pat Jr., ran a construction company and frequently reminded his dad that the big home improvement chains out-priced him every time. Senior would come back with some rendition of, "Some folks would rather buy from a Pat they know than a cashier they don't who doesn't have a clue the difference between a 3/4" particleboard and 3/4" MDF."

Each morning, Senior left his house by the Episcopal church and walked up several blocks to the American Legion for coffee with the boys before continuing two more blocks to unlock his store. He rarely had customers, but he could count on the boys to head down mid-morning for another cup of joe and some more bull shooting. They'd talk about the war and swap tall tales about anything from close calls to the fish that got away to the women who didn't. He'd lock up around one and walk home for lunch with his wife. Pat and Mabel had been married for sixty years in December. Their kids put on a big blow-out for them at the Legion hall. They danced like they did the day they were married. She'd been a wartime bride who answered the call of Rosie the Riveter and welcomed her man home with open arms once the war finally died. She worked beside him in the store until she decided it was time to take up bridge and pinochle and finish the quilts she'd started as a much younger woman. Senior didn't mind.

He loved his wife; but, after six decades, a little distance could do a couple a world of good.

As the sun glistened off benches and window panes, Senior whistled his way up Fifth Avenue, jingling his keys in time to the tune. He had never closed on Memorial Day, and he didn't intend to start this year. For him and the guys at the Hall, this was just another day to remember—something they did best in their regular routines.

He narrowed his eyes at the tall kid with the red duffle bag loitering in front of his store. He didn't have much use for lazy kids. They were everywhere these days, but he wouldn't allow them around his store. No sir! He'd call the police station; have an officer sent right over. That'd solve it, right fast and in a hurry. As Senior got closer, the boy's face caught his eye and made him forget a note or two. He was young, but—those eyes. They had seen things—none of which seemed to have been sleep. He'd only seen bags like that back in the trenches. If anyone wondered what hell could be like, the trenches were it. He could paint them a picture. But he wouldn't. Those weren't things he cared to recall aloud.

"You lookin' for somethin', boy?" Senior asked as he turned the key in his lock.

"Well, yes, sir. I think I'm looking for you." Jack paused until the man shot him a skeptical and appraising look. "I'm ... new in town and looking for a job. I've got experience in construction and thought you may have some listings up on your board in here."

"Might be. Not sure, though. Most of these folks only hire professional workers, you know." Senior eyed Jack warily. The jagged scar snaking down the boy's neck grabbed his attention momentarily. Back to the face, Senior wondered again how old this kid could be. Of course, he could get him on his son's crew—Junior was always looking for workers—but he wasn't laying all his cards out at once. A person couldn't be too careful these days. Why, just last week, some young punks whacked old Marshall Smith on the head with a baseball bat before he could lock up his gas station over on Twenty-eighth Avenue.

"What's in that bag?" Senior narrowed his eyes at Jack before he finished opening the store. He could fit a small bat in there, definitely a gun. If he was thinking he was going to rob Pat Miller Sr.; well, he had another thing coming all together. The store owner's eyebrows arched in challenge to the young man before him.

"It's my clothes and such, sir. I just got in town and haven't found a place to stay yet. Don't have anywhere to leave it."

Senior raised his right eyebrow slightly higher until it nearly joined his wispy gray hair. He appraised Jack a moment longer before he pursed his lips, shrugged and turned back to open the door. "Well, leave it right here, just inside the door."

"Yessir."

"You can take a look over there at the board. May be some jobs up there. I haven't paid much mind. They could be old, too. Just don't knock nothin' off that counter there. I've got behind on my shelvin', and stuff ends up there."

Senior busied himself with dumping out used grounds from his long-stained coffee pot. Jack took his time examining each posting. He saw a request for a dog walker next to a business card for a dog walker. There was a call for a hair stylist at Mamie's Hair Style-abration. On scraps of paper, he found handwritten needs for odd jobs around people's houses. One of them read:

WANTED: Strong young man to pull weeds, rake leaves, tidy the yard, wash outside windows and powerwash siding. $10 a day for a good worker.

Jack pictured the little old blue hairs who loved to sit around gossiping about him back in Bellum. He shook his head. This old biddy could keep her social security check. Though, $10 was $10 more than he had; so, there was that. He'd keep her in mind.

In the bottom right corner of the board, Jack discovered an ad for Miller's Construction Co. It didn't list any job openings, just the company name and a number for a man named Pat Miller Jr. In the center was a logo of a bright yellow duck drawn to look like a hard hat. Jack examined the ad further and didn't hear the door open. He asked the store owner, "Do you know if this Miller's Construction's hiring?"

"Depends on who's askin'." The booming voice drew Jack's head around. He looked up at a big-barreled man with a ruddy complexion and a Miller's Construction cap covering his bald head.

Jack recovered to extend his hand. "Are you Mr. Miller?"

"I'm Pat Miller Jr.; call me Junior, though. Hold the *Mr.* for my pop over there." Junior nodded his head back to the old man who was still puttering with the coffee pot.

"Us old coots appreciate the respect." Senior waved a dismissive hand back toward his son.

"Let me guess, you came in here lookin' for a job, and Pop didn't bother to mention his son's always lookin' for able-bodied young fellows such as yourself?" His laugh reminded Jack of waves crashing along the beach on a mild summer day. He'd gone there once with his parents when he was a small boy. It was the only memory he held of his father. "What's your name and how old are you, Kid?"

"I'm Jack Calhoun, sir. I'm eighteen. Last summer I started work on a construction crew in Bellum, Georgia, … until recently. I just came into town here and hoped to find something similar. My old boss said I was fast, but thorough. Plus, I gave his seasoned vets a run for their money when it came to roofing."

Junior chuckled at the boy's pitch. "With an advertisement like that, what more do I need to know? How 'bout you come on down to the office and fill out some paperwork? Can you start tomorrow?"

"Yessir. I can start today if you'd like."

More chuckles. "Tomorrow'll be just fine. My crews are off today for Memorial Day, but my son and secretary and I will be in … catching up on paperwork. Come to my office downtown and get the papers in order later today so you can start right off in the morning. I'll jot down directions for you."

"Can I walk there?"

"Downtown? If you want to get there after I've left for the day. Do you have a car, motorcycle, somethin'?"

"No sir. I just got into town on the bus and haven't lined up transportation yet."

"Tell you what, Jack." The man helped himself to a cup of his dad's coffee as he talked. "I like you; so, I'm gonna swing back by here and pick you up after I visit some of our sites to make sure everything's ready for crews tomorrow."

"Thank you, sir. What time should I meet you here?"

"I'll be back around one." Junior threw the response over his shoulder on his way out the door. "Later, Pop!"

A barely discernible grunt answered him. "Rich as he gets, he still comes by here for his mornin' cup. 'Spose those fancy coffee joints don't know how to make it right anyway. Well, you got your job. You gonna find you a place to drop off that duffle of yours?"

"Actually, sir, I wondered if you'd like a hand with this shelving that needs doing." Jack eyed the piles on the counter next to him. He didn't dare lean too close for fear he'd bump something and send it all tumbling.

Senior's eyebrows shot up again. "Well, boy, I sure as heck didn't say *I* was hirin'!"

Jack quickly responded, "No sir! I just figured since you helped me find a job—and I have a little time to kill—I could lend you a hand. If you'd like, of course."

Wild and bushy eyebrows continued a frantic dance on his forehead as Senior considered the proposal. Finally, they came to rest, and he voiced his decision. "Well, I reckon you can't do any worse than that lazy grandson of mine I had over spring break. Boy didn't know a Phillips head from a flat head and only wanted to play on his doggone video games. All the shelves are laid out how I like 'em; just put this new stuff up where it goes. If you got questions, ask. But don't get crazy with the askin'." He tossed out the final command with an edge of warning to it.

"Yessir."

Senior flipped his Open sign around and busied himself with dusting the window display. Jack was fairly certain the ladder with the tools, ropes and cords hanging from it hadn't been changed at all in the past decade or two. He grinned when he realized Senior had probably never considered he may need to update the display from time to time. By mid-morning the counter was cleared, and the shelves were straightened. Jack had even dusted some of the shelves that hadn't been touched in several years by customers or owner. There'd been no traffic. He was just wondering why the old man kept the place open and why stools and chairs cluttered the front of the store, when a chorus of greetings, cursings and pronouncements of the weather rushed through the open door. Senior's friends from the Legion hall had arrived for their daily bull session.

"Galldurnit, Pat, when you gonna start a fresh pot right 'fore we get here? We've been comin' down here at the same time every day for two decades now!" A stooped, white-haired man raised his cane to the store owner's reddening face.

"Heck, you hate it so much here, Gene, you can stop shufflin' down. Ain't nothin' wrong with what's left in the pot. Waste not; want not." Senior wore the quintessential get-off-my-lawn look of a grumpy old guy. Gene snarled at the store owner as he crossly helped himself to a cup of the hours-old coffee. Jack chuckled to himself as he deduced this conversation replayed verbatim every morning. The group of men fell into an easy give and take of ribbing and banter that explained why Hardy's was still open, despite the cobwebs.

"Humph, Pat. You finally do some work around here? Where's that galldurn pile of junk you thought you'd sell one day?" Gene and Senior apparently only spoke in condescending tones. Jack figured there might be a story behind their "friendship."

"Junior hired a new worker this morning, but he doesn't need him till this afternoon." Senior's nod in Jack's direction alerted the group to his presence. "I figured I'd put him on to work. Kids these days don't need any encouragement to be lazy."

After a confusing round of acknowledgements and welcomes, Jack had been introduced and inducted into the unofficial Hardy's Crap 'n' Coffee Club.

"How on earth'd you end up at this dump?" asked Murphy—whether that was a first or last name, Jack never found out. The candid questioner wore a Mr. Rogers sweater. As bald as the top of his head was, he had more hair on each side than most men have on their whole heads. Fluffy cotton ball-like hair tufts stuck out on either side of his thin head. Leaning on his cane, Murphy peered over a pair of spectacles that Jack thought might be as old as the man. "This ain't exactly on the scenic route of Columbia, you know."

"Well, I was just passing by looking for Hiring signs and thought there might be some listings in here. I've got construction experience." Jack shifted his weight under the scrutinizing gazes of the men around him.

"Passin' by from where, exactly?" It would come as no surprise to Jack to learn that Murphy had been a detective.

"I came into town on the bus just down the way. I'm from Georgia." Jack felt the little hardware store heat up. He tried to recall the chill that spread from his toes, up his spine, down his arms and into his lungs when he had tried to sleep in his makeshift shelter the night before. The thought only made him more flustered and less in control of the sweat beginning a slow trickle down his back.

Murphy gave him a hard look over his glasses that clearly said he didn't believe Jack was giving them the straight facts. Elmer, the youngest member of the group at age sixty-five, ran his fingers up and down the insides of his black and red suspenders as he rocked back on his feet. "You must've come in with my boy, then. Junior drove the bus in from Georgia. Got home early Sunday mornin', he said. Claimed he hadn't had enough sleep to take himself to church. If you ask me, I think he takes those late ones on purpose."

"Galldurnit, Elmer, what's it matter if that boy sits in them hard pews every week or not?" Gene interjected. "You need to worry 'bout somethin' else, like how he's gonna keep that little blonde of his happy. She seems to like an awful lot of flashy gems for a bus driver's salary."

"Why, you old gossip! You know, well as I, Junior makes a might better livin' than your good-fer-nuthin' with all them kids."

Their voices and blood pressures rose as they hurled more insults about each other's offspring. Once Gene started splashing coffee with his gesticulations and Elmer's face deepened redder than a homegrown Big Boy, Murphy stuck his cane between them and called for a ceasefire. The men spit out a forced peace treaty, and another member of their dysfunctional unit pulled out a checkerboard from somewhere. "Who wants to lose some money today?"

In the midst of the kerfuffle, Senior caught Jack's eyes. The boy knew he'd figured out he was withholding some pieces to his new-to-town story … like where he spent his time the day before and where he stayed overnight. As checkers tapped into their places, Jack sighed his relief. Hopefully he'd dodged any further interrogation. He wasn't sure how the law read on sneaking into the side yard of a church to sleep in a manger during its off-season.

After more chatter and tales, a couple more close calls for blows and a whole lot of dimes exchanging liver-spotted hands over the checkerboard, all the men answered some call—inaudible to Jack—that roused them up and out the door right before 1 p.m. He rose with them and quickly grabbed his bag. Perhaps he'd have time for some more of his peanut butter and bread before Junior picked him up. He'd hoped no one had heard his stomach growling most of the morning.

"Y'all head on. I'm gonna wait a bit on Junior. Forgot to tell him somethin' this morning." Senior flipped his sign as he swung the door behind his friends. He met Jack's nervous grin.

"I was gonna wait on that bench out there for your son. Need me to tidy up anything else while we wait?"

"Nothin' in dire need right now. How 'bout you sit a spell? Where'd you stay last night and the night before?" Senior's steely gaze held Jack's.

"Well, it really was quite late … or early, is better to say … on Sunday mornin'. I'd dozed off on the bus, so I walked around a bit. This part of town is nice … in some parts."

"And last night?" Like a bulldog, Senior had bit down and wasn't letting go of his question until he found a partnering answer.

"Oh, you know … I just found a place. I was pretty tired after walking around all day looking in windows and checking for signs. When I saw your store, though, I thought it was my best shot, so that's why I came back this morning early to be here when you opened." Jack's laugh revealed his nerves. "Course I forgot it was a holiday. Lucky for me you opened anyway, right?"

"Boy, you may be quick as a jackrabbit, but I'm slyer than a fox. Now, answer me. Where'd you sleep last night?"

Jack flushed as he knew he'd been beat. He thought of how he'd considered stealing and drinking himself to death. "I don't want to get in trouble. I didn't damage anything. It's just … I didn't have any money." Jack's words tumbled over one another as he tried to explain and apologize and satisfy the man's stern expression. "The Episcopal church a few blocks over. They have this thing against the side—a manger, I think—I pulled it out just far enough to slip inside and pushed it back for overnight. I put it all the way back when I woke up this morning. I mean, I did pee on the tree there a couple times; I'm not going to jail for that, am I?"

His heart nearly leapt out of his throat where it had risen during his confession. The old man switched from a judge's scowl to a full-on belly laugh in less than a second. He rocked back onto a stool as he slapped his thin, wrinkled hand on his knee. "Last time I read the lawbooks, it wasn't against 'em to relieve yourself by a 'piscopal church tree when you've got nowhere else to go. Now, if you'd taken to fertilizin' their flower beds, they may have some legal standin' against you." Senior wiped the tears from his eyes as he sobered up to continue his questioning.

"Now, I have to ask—and you need to give me the truth— are you runnin' from the law?" He fixed his truth serum eyes back on the young man in front of him.

"No sir. I'm runnin' but not from the law." Jack's honesty shone through the words he used. When he saw the man's sincere concern, he continued. "I made some bad choices with alcohol, but I sobered up. Got the job with the construction company right after graduation from the mission there, studied up and aced my GED tests a couple months back. I'd hoped they might let me in to Georgia Tech. I wanted to work on a civil engineering degree."

Jack's words stopped coming. He broke eye contact and looked down at the hands clutching the fraying strap of his duffle. Senior prodded him to continue. "Sounds to me like you were doin' just fine. What'd you think you had to run from?"

Seconds passed like a turtle convoy, and Jack worked his jaw muscles to get the next words ready. "There was an accident. Not on the job site," he added quickly with a pleading glance in Senior's direction. After he lowered his head again, Jack continued. "It was in my truck. There was a girl ... so little. She was playing hide and seek. No one saw her. I didn't see ..."

Senior didn't need to see the tears. They dripped from each word as Jack pushed through. "There'd been another accident, the first night I drank. I wasn't involved, but I almost died." Jack tugged on his shirt collar to reveal more of the scar from That Night. "A bunch of people blamed me for it, though. So, the whole town blamed me for the girl, too. Most of them thought I was still a drunk anyway. Bellum's a small place; nowhere to hide from people's rage ... or my guilt. Accident or not, I killed that little girl. Her face ... I see her face every night."

Jack sat up, brushed away his emotions and cleared his throat. "Anyway, I'm running away for a real future—for me and the people who do still love me. That town will never forgive me ... or let me forget. I want a job so I can send money back for my mama; it's just her and me. I don't want her to have to keep working so hard. She's put up with so much."

Senior targeted Jack with his fixed stare again for a moment before saying, "Forgive and forget happens in your own mind when you're ready to accept 'em. You sure you're not runnin' away from the very future you claim you want?"

Junior chose that moment to open the shop's door. "Hey, Pop! What're you still doin' here? Mom'll let you have it if her roast gets cold on your plate. You ready, kid?"

"Sure!" Jack hopped up and slung his bag over his shoulder before returning the stool to behind the newly cleaned counter.

"Well, ain't that somethin'! You've still got a register there, Pop! Did your buddies finally earn their keep?"

"Nah! The boy here is fairly handy. He cleaned it up for me in exchange for room and board for a bit. You know, till he gets settled in."

Jack's head shot up, and their eyes locked again. This time it was the older man who broke the gaze first.

"Now, hurry up! You're droppin' me off at the house since I had to sit round here waitin' on you."

Jack's shock lingered as he processed this change in his situation. He wasn't sure what future he really wanted, but he did know the next step he took could get him closer. As implausible as it seemed, something good might finally happen, and Jack chose to accept it.

IX

Far from Home

May 27-28, 2002

"Pop doesn't impress easy." Junior shot Jack a sideways glance as he maneuvered his white F-350 through downtown Columbia's holiday traffic.

"Your dad's a real nice man." Since they dropped Senior off at his house next door to Jack's makeshift hotel, Jack had spent the twenty-minute drive trying to figure out why the man—a perfect stranger—would offer up his home to him. He thought about Rachael. She was a favorite with all the older men at their church. One afternoon after work, she'd brought some peanuts to Jack's job site. They leaned against a stack of 2x4s and tossed the shells into the woods. He asked her then why she always went out of her way to speak to that particular crowd. She told him she had a soft spot for grumpy old guys.

"Besides, they're not really grumpy. When you take the time to pick your way through their tough shells, they're big ol' softies on the inside ... like boiled peanuts!"

He shook his head at her cheesy comment and retorted with his own. "They're certainly salty." He could still remember the way her lips tasted that day—spicy and tangy.

Darkness covered the cab as they jolted over a bump into a parking garage. Junior saluted the attendant, a gentleman who looked like an ideal candidate for the Hardy's Crap 'n' Coffee Club. They wound around until they reached the top floor. Junior pulled into an extra wide spot. The sign in front of the windshield read:

Pat Miller Jr. CEO
Miller's Construction Co.

Perks of the job, Jack thought as he climbed down from the truck and jogged to catch up with Junior. The big man walked fast, talked loud and stood tall. He led Jack across a windowed bridge overlooking the street beneath. The door to the connected building opened into the construction company's office.

"Jack, this is Elaine Bell. We call her Aunt E. She's been with me from the start of this company, and I couldn't live without her. Keeps me straight." Junior leaned over to give his secretary a kiss on her time-creased cheek. With her recently-curled white hair, carefully-done makeup and smart little suit, Aunt E. looked like everyone's southern grandmother. She was just missing a bowl of corn to shuck and a freshly-baked apple pie cooling on her desk.

"Nice to meet you, ma'am. I'm Jack." He reached out to shake her hand. She dismissed his hand and said, "None of that here, sweetie! Little Pat brings you in, you're family; and I hug my family. Now, get over here!"

Jack smiled and approached for his welcome-to-the-family hug. She got up on her tiptoes and wrapped her soft arms around his neck. As an added bonus, she gave him a kiss on the cheek and asked her boss, "What's such a young boy doing comin' to work for us?"

"Well, he's not all that young and he's got experience. He just moved here from Georgia and stopped by Pop's store this morning searchin' for a job."

"Mercy! Are you away from your family?" The look she cast his way was sweet and warm enough to conjure that missing pie out of thin air.

"Before you adopt him as one of your strays, Aunt E., Pop and Mama have taken him in for a bit until he gets settled. Though, I'm not sure if Pop's told Mama yet."

"Oh, well then! Let me get Mabel on the phone right now and let her know just how skinny this sweet young'un is. She'll need to get some fat on those bones of yours."

Junior's booming laugh reverberated in the small office. "Go right ahead ... *after* you pull out the paperwork for him."

"Of course, dear." Aunt E. reached up to tap "Little" Pat's arm as she turned to the file cabinet beside her desk.

Jack had observed their exchange with an amused expression. When he received the paperwork, he picked a pen from a bright yellow duck pencil holder and sat down on the guest side of the secretary's desk to fit his story into the empty blanks.

"Bring those in to me when you finish 'em," Junior requested as he passed Aunt E.'s desk and entered his own office.

The Miller's Construction headquarters wasn't huge, but it was in a prime spot—the corner top floor of one of the city's tallest buildings. Jack later learned that Junior's crews had built it and a number of other buildings nearby. A window provided a picturesque view of the city's skyline and historic Arsenal Hill. This view spanned the entire left side of the main office. To Jack's right, a hallway led to more offices, meeting rooms, bathrooms and a kitchenette. All their outer walls were glass as well, which meant Junior had a surrounding view in his office. Jack considered how he'd never spent much time in a bustling city before. The beach vacation was the only trip he'd ever taken. Other than short treks to slightly larger towns around Bellum—most for football games—and the occasional field trip to Atlanta, his travel experience had been limited. With a final entry on the paper before him, Jack stood to join Junior in his office. On his way, Jack took in his surroundings.

Dark hardwood floors and accents on the walls contrasted with strategically placed natural design touches—magnolia branches, bright green plants and a driftwood shelf. The combination made the area feel like anything but an office, especially a construction one. Black and white photos of buildings and houses dotted the walls throughout, showcasing some of the company's favorite projects. Bright yellow duck décor added splashes of whimsy that somehow fit the company perfectly. Jack decided if he'd been a potential client, he'd choose Miller's based on the happy feeling the ducks gave him. Though, a duck did seem an odd mascot for a construction firm.

Junior waved Jack in when he rapped on the door. He gestured to the plush wingback chair in front of him and said, "Jack, meet my son and our COO, Pat Miller III."

A young man in a yellow Miller's cap stood and turned to greet Jack. "Call me Ducky!" he said after his father's formal introduction. He stood a great deal shorter than his giant dad and looked at Jack with kind eyes that turned slightly upward.

Jack returned the offered handshake while fighting a wide-mouthed look of shock. The COO who stood before him was a guy who just happened to have Down Syndrome. Ducky laughed at Jack's poorly veiled wonder.

"It's okay. I surprise everyone when they meet me and find out what I do. But, that means I get to share my secret." Ducky leaned in and lowered his voice before speaking through the widest smile Jack had ever seen. "My *dis*abilities are really my super special abilities. God just filled me full of extra goodness before he sent me down."

"Ducky here is the reason this company's as successful as it is today." Junior beamed with pride. "He was only six when he picked up a business card I'd just had printed and told me, 'Dad, you need a duck on these—a bright yellow duck.' I laughed it off as a kid's cute idea. He'd adored ducks ever since he was a toddler and we took him to the lake where he first saw those fuzzy little ducklings."

"They're just so cute!" Ducky's declaration launched a new round of laughs.

"I didn't think much more about it until a couple weeks later when he was ridin' around with me. After about the tenth stop, he just sat in his seat and sighed real big. I asked him what was wrong. He said, 'You didn't listen to me.' I'm racking my brain now, right, wonderin' what I missed. I asked him when, and he said, 'On the day you got those awful cards.' It hit me—the duck idea! I said, 'Well, buddy, you know, I did hear you; but I'm not sure how a duck would fit our company. We make buildings.' He looked at me and said, 'You wear them on your head when you *make* the buildings, silly.' With that, he tapped the yellow plastic hat he wore whenever he joined me at work."

"Took him long enough!" Ducky playfully punched his dad's arm as they chuckled.

"That's when his idea of a duck as a hard hat became reality. I found an artist who designed our logo, and we got new cards made up right away. That was the beginning of somethin' really special with this company."

"Yep! That's one lucky ducky!" Jack could tell this was a joke the young man made often, but he also knew it was one that never lost its ability to spread smiles.

"In all seriousness, when Ducky came on to help more with the marketing and promotion of the company was when we really skyrocketed. That's been almost five years now—the best five years for us." Junior's eyes misted as his son gave him a side hug. "I cut the ribbon on our first office trailer on my thirtieth birthday, and we'll celebrate 30 years in September."

"We're planning a huge celebration for September 23. Thirty—and sixty—are big deals!" Ducky gave his dad a wink before walking with Jack into the main office. "Welcome to our crew."

"Thanks, man! I really appreciate the opportunity, and I'm excited about working with you guys."

"Well, you're family now!" Ducky embraced Jack and patted his back. Aunt E. popped up from behind her desk and chirped, "Oh good! You met my Ducky Day!"

"Of course, Aunt E." Ducky smiled at the secretary who had done a quick and satisfactory assessment of Jack's reaction to her favorite boy. She'd been a close family friend for far longer than Ducky had been part of it, and she was his fiercest protector. If anyone gave the slightest indication that they viewed him differently … well, she wasn't quite as sugary to them. Jack earned another hug.

"Jack, I gotta get you back to my folks' house. Mama'd never let me hear the end of it if you're late for dinner." Junior clapped Jack on the back before gathering some folders and leaving a few notes on Aunt E.'s desk.

"Just wait! Mawmaw and Aunt E. are the two best cooks in the South." Ducky shone with pride. "See you tomorrow, Jack. You'll be going out with me to a new project I can't wait to start."

"Sounds great. I better rest up; you'll probably want to work the new guy pretty hard, huh?"

"You bet!"

Jack's smile lingered all the way to the parking garage. He realized this family he'd stumbled upon exuded true joy. It warmed him from the outside, filled him with light and made him want to do cartwheels down a grassy slope. The very center of his heart, though, remained hollow, and he had nothing with which to fill that empty ache.

Junior's words pulled Jack's thoughts back into the truck's cab. "Either Ducky or I will pick you up and drop you off at Pop's. Plan for Ducky tomorrow. Y'all will need to get to the site early since it's a new project. He'll get you around 5:30. You up for that?"

"Absolutely, sir; I'm used to construction hours by now. Not sure I could sleep in, even if I got to try!" Jack didn't share that he didn't sleep much on the front end or in the middle either. The truth was—with the exception of his time in the hospital, thanks to Hyram Cutter—Jack hadn't slept more than a couple hours at a time since the accident.

Junior eyed the bags under the boy's eyes and guessed pretty close to the truth. "I don't know your whole story— and I don't have to—" he added with a pointed glance in Jack's direction that left room for Jack to make that choice at a later time. "But, I sure as anything know pain when I see it. I also know what it looks like when a person's seeking for peace. I saw that enough in the mirror after I lost my Mary Anne when our Ducky was still young." Junior cleared the emotion from his throat. "Anyway, it's obvious you're carrying pain—it would take a pretty dense person to miss that. Peace isn't an easy commodity for many people, especially anyone with tragedies in their past."

It was Jack's turn to hide the feelings churning inside as Junior's words hit home.

"Just know that we're all here for you. I'm a big believer in God's perfect timing. You didn't stumble into my dad's hole of a hardware store on accident. If it's family you're huntin', you've found a good one." As he swung into his parents' driveway, Junior leaned toward his passenger with one final thought. "If it's peace you're needin', though ... well, there's only One who's got that; and His line's open all the time, from any place."

Jack considered how this mountain of a man beside him had summed up every sermon he'd ever half listened to in the simplest of ways. He examined the man's face and discovered only truth and sincerity etched in every line. He gave him a smile and a nod. "Thank you. Truly. I can't tell you how much it means that you'd take a shot on me. Your whole family is just ... incredible."

"We Millers are certainly somethin'—incredible may not be quite right, though." Through his laughter, Jack eyed green shutters beneath the porch of a brick house, neatly lined with holly bushes, all illuminated by the truck's headlights. The front door swung open, and Jack got his first view of Mabel Miller. Her apron bore the marks of the home-cooked meal waiting inside. With her slightly disheveled look, her wiry gray hair that never did quite set right when she visited the beauty parlor and her thick-rimmed glasses that perpetually slid down her nose, Mabel appeared to be a doughy, lovable lamb of a woman.

She had perfected not needing to take a breath while speed-talking. "It's about time! I wanted to start the gravy five minutes ago, but I didn't want to have to leave it when y'all arrived. Hello, Pat dear." She pulled her son down from his towering position above her to plant a kiss on his cheek. "I just knew you'd be along any moment. Didn't want the gravy to burn on me. Mashed potatoes are just a lump of white mush without the gravy, you know. Well, you must be our Jack. Elaine was right as rain; you're skinny as a beanpole." She clucked—still without a breath—as she shook her head and narrowed her eyes to examine him from head to toe. "We'll get you fattened up in no time, honey. Now, you come right on in. Is that all the luggage you've got? Oh my! We'll have to see about getting you some more clothes, I'd imagine. Well, first things first. I'll show you to your room. You can wash up while I get that gravy going. Should've started it five whole minutes ago …. You go on home now, Pat dear. Kiss my Ducky for me and you tell him to get here early for breakfast." She flipped a dismissive wave in her son's direction as she walked toward the front door. Jack shot Junior a grin and wave as he heard him chuckling. Mrs. Miller greeted a white Maltese who'd cautiously planted one paw on the sidewalk and held another daintily raised in midair. "Now, Missy! You get your furry little bottom back in that house. Yes, ma'am! No need to get those little paws dusty. Let's go get that gravy on, Missy Mee. Now, you just go on down this hall, honey. Second door on your right is your room. First door's the bathroom. You've got towels out for you. Make yourself right at home. Come on,

Missy. Back to this kitchen. Those potatoes better not be lumpy …"

Jack took a deep breath for his hostess. The house contained a distinct smell—one Jack had never before experienced. It was a mixture of countless meals and memories, love, laughter and tears, hopes and dreams come true and lost along the way. It was warmth and comfort. A soft place to land. A home raised on memories.

Missy took to Jack right away. To say she was smitten would be an understatement. She sat in her high chair for supper. At first, the pup let her plate of pork, potatoes, gravy and peas grow cold while she stared, mesmerized, at the young man next to her. Mrs. Miller frequently interrupted her stream of chatter to urge Missy to eat her dinner. Finally, Jack grew concerned for the little fluffy dog with her charcoal eyes pinned to him. He set his fork down and shifted her plate closer to her. "Here you go, Missy girl. Your food's gettin' cold there." Missy blinked for the first time since she laid eyes on him. Her tongue flicked out as if testing the safety of the air. She gave his hand a timid lick, looked up at him and then dove in to her supper, though she continued to cast side glances in his direction. When he patted her head gently after she licked up the remnants, she took that as an invitation and hopped in his lap.

"Land's sakes! She's just taken right to you. I tell you, that Missy Mee isn't an easy one to win over. I've still got friends who come over for pinochle who she shows her teeth to—just shows, doesn't growl, mind you—she'd never growl. She's too sweet to do somethin' like that, but she lets it be known when she isn't fond of someone. Betty Sue and Mamie fret over how she shows them her teeth. I tell them not to take it personal, but they do, you know …" Mabel's voice floated with her as she went into the kitchen to dish up four bowls of peach cobbler with ice cream. "… minute more in here. I have to heat up Missy's ice cream before I put it on the cobbler. Missy doesn't like cold foods. She likes her water tepid, too. Prissy little thing, I tell you …"

Jack raised an eyebrow in Senior's direction, wondering how on earth the man had put up with his wife's ceaseless chatter for so long. "You get used to it 'fore long. Once you figure out she doesn't require a response too often, you'll relax and tune it out. I don't even hear her anymore."

His host's candid admission made Jack snicker and wonder what happened when Mrs. Miller did expect an answer. He felt an ache again as Rachael's face flashed into his mind's eye. The sunset glowing on her cheeks and those perfect pink lips. He had wanted to grow old with her. He had wanted to dance to sixty years together with her. *I've got to get these emotions under control*, Jack thought. *I said goodbye so she could say hello to the life she deserves. I've gotta remember that.*

Remembering his reason drew his brain back, like a magnet to a steel door, to Abbie Mae's empty face, to Mr. Cutter's face purple with rage, to Bellum residents' looks of distrust and judgement.

Those images flowed freely through his brain as he sank in to the worn mattress a while later. He felt the weight of the history and memories in the patchwork quilt pulled to his chin. As his eyes shuttered closed, faces blended and blurred together like a kaleidoscope. His brain twisted the images round and round, back and forth until the center came into focus. Rachael. She was crying. Before he could reach her and ask why she was hurting, she turned and walked away. The kaleidoscope clicked around and around and back again. She drifted farther and farther away, smaller and smaller until she was a color speck lost amidst an indiscernible pattern.

A sound reached him, a scratching. Soft at first. Then more insistent. Next, a whimpering joined the chorus. No ... the dead were trying to get out of their graves. He could hear them. They were calling to him, tormenting him. It was his fault. Their faces combined with the sounds—Steven with his jet-black hair so long ... hanging in his face ... blood and gray matter dripping down. Leslee dragged her top half toward him ... the sports car had left her eternally torn asunder. Bobby Lee. Susan. Abbie Mae. Too many dead faces. He'd killed them. Killed them all.

And then he was awake.

The top light shone down on him as he sat straight as a board, sweat—and tears—streaming down in a unified waterfall along his face and neck. Senior and Mabel stood on either side of his bed, fear and concern coating their faces. Missy bounded into his lap. She licked his cheek, the scar on his neck, his other cheek and then she turned around a few times in his lap before lying down so she could look up into his face.

"We thought somebody was murderin' you in here. You okay?" Senior's voice filled the recent silence first.

"I'm ... I'm so sorry. It's just my dreams, they don't let me sleep. I didn't even think. It won't happen again. I'll find somewhere else to stay. Don't want to scare you like that again."

"Nonsense. This is your home now. Long as you need it," Senior replied.

Mrs. Miller crossed over to kiss Jack on the forehead, and it struck him as she shuffled back to her room that he'd found a way to render her speechless.

"These dreams of yours—terrors, more like—they'll drift away one day. Took mine a long time, after the war. Every now and then another one'll pop up, but they've mostly left.

So will yours. You'll see." He patted Jack's leg on his way out. "Now, you keep Missy in here and don't close that door all the way shut, y'hear? She near scratched through the doorframe tryin' to get at you. That little girl loves you somethin' crazy."

Senior shook his head at the sight of the tiny dog curled up in the lap of the sweaty, terrified boy far from home.

X

A Growing Sense of Restlessness

May 28-31, 2002

Despite the interruption of the night before, Jack woke more rested than he could remember feeling. Missy lay curled against his chest, and his hand rested in her warm fur. Jack had never had a dog, so this was a new experience—one he rather enjoyed. He smiled as he stroked the dog's silky fur and scratched her ears. When he leaned up on one elbow, Missy pressed back against him as she stretched all four legs out straight and yawned, her bubblegum-pink tongue curling out of her mouth. She hopped up, shook herself and then proceeded to wash Jack's face. Once satisfied she'd given him a thorough cleansing, Missy hopped to the floor, bounded midway to the door, then glanced back over her shoulder at her new friend. He chuckled and followed her lead. She had him wrapped around her tiny, snowy paws.

The enticing aromas of bacon and butter and hand-squashed biscuits drifted down the hall toward Jack as he responded like a stray dog sniffing out a sausage cart. Missy hopped in her seat, front paws propped on the tray of her high chair, tail wagging expectantly.

Mrs. Miller set Missy's plate down. This time the pup didn't wait before she began daintily chowing down. "Good morning, dears! Now, you just sit right down there. I'm filling you up a plate now. You want bacon or sausage? Of course, you'll want some of each. So skinny. Heaven help us! Sweet boy … just a shame …" She returned a moment later, still talking, with a heaping plate for Jack.

"I'm not sure I can eat all this, Mrs. Miller. This is a lot of food." Jack warily eyed the mound in front of him. And, he didn't consider himself skinny. In fact, he was proud of the muscle tone his shirt covered, thanks to construction work and the running habit he'd started back at the mission.

"Nonsense, sweetie! You need some fat on those bones. Eat away! And, you call me Mawmaw Mabel; no need for formality around here. Now, I'm fixin' you a good workin' man's lunch to take, so you just finish that up and I'll have it all ready before you walk out the door. Got some of Senior's old work clothes laid out for you in the bathroom. I wasn't sure what you'd managed to fit in that little ol' bag of yours. Leave any clothes needin' washin' in the bin in there. I'll be doin' laundry this morning. And, you be thinkin' what snacks and foods you'd like. I'll be makin' my list tonight to go tomorrow right after bridge with my ladies. Oh, don't you show your teeth, Missy Mee! Betty Sue and Mamie won't be here. I tell you, sweet as a flower, but those teeth …"

Jack and Missy found themselves alone with their taste buds and another meal of delicious home-cooked foods. The biscuits flaked apart in layers. The tanginess of the buttermilk floated on Jack's tongue with the lightness of its consistency. He wondered where Senior was and why Mawmaw Mabel hadn't mentioned the night's upheaval. His thoughts kept him from realizing he ate his plateful plus some, despite his earlier objections. This kind of food didn't take no for an answer, much like the Mawmaw who made it. He was wiping up the last of the buttery grits with his third biscuit when he heard the door open.

"... knew he'd be soon." The back half of a sentence drifted from the kitchen before Mawmaw Mabel appeared with more chatter. "There's my Ducky! You come over and give me a kiss; I'm dishin' up your breakfast now, my sweetie." She handed him a biscuit and reached up for a hug.

"Thank you, Mawmaw. I'm starvin'!" Ducky planted a kiss on his grandmother's forehead. "Hey there, Jack! Ready to work?"

"You know it! I'm gonna get dressed now." Jack carried his plate to the kitchen as he drained the last of his orange juice.

He reemerged from the bathroom as Ducky's plate clattered into the sink. "Wait till you see what we're workin' on today, Jack!" Ducky's grin shone around another of his Mawmaw's "angel biscuits." He had dubbed them that since, in his words, "they float on angels' wings" and "come from Mawmaw who's pretty angelic herself. "Dad gives me the best projects to oversee. We do a few charity ones each year. Last week we finished clearing and land prep for a huge build. Four houses!"

Ducky raised his eyebrows at Jack and held up his fingers to emphasize the scope of the job they would be working on.

They got into his truck, one smaller than his dad's but that also sported the Miller's duck logo on each door. "Our church, Sovereign Grace Presbyterian, got a whole bunch of money from this sweet older couple who wanted them to use it to help hurting families. That's where we come in!"

The pride in his father's company and their help within the community enveloped Ducky's face in a heavenly glow of his own. "Our company donates the labor, and local businesses partner with us to provide all the materials. It gets everyone to work together. We're going to build these four houses so families who've lost their homes can have one again."

When Ducky spoke of this massive project, it all seemed so simple. Jack thought how many more families could benefit and find a little help through their storms if every community pooled its resources in this way. He certainly never witnessed a spirit like that in Bellum.

"Wanna know the best part?" Ducky leaned toward Jack as they pulled up to a large tract of cleared land. "After the houses are built, we get to put up a playset and playhouse for all the kids who're gonna live there!"

Jack had to admit, Ducky's joy and excitement were contagious; and he found himself eager to get started. "We're breaking ground today on the foundations, and our first family will be here to help!"

"Hey there, Ducky!" A young blonde with a Miss America smile walked over to them. She wore a pantsuit and carried a reporter's notebook and pen in one hand with a camera bag slung over her right shoulder.

"How's my favorite reporter?"

"It's groundbreaking day. How do you think I'm doing?" Daisy gave Ducky a hug before she turned to Jack and extended a hand. "You must be the new guy. Jack, is it?"

"News sure travels fast around here." Jack couldn't get over how he'd come to a much larger city, but everyone he met knew his name.

"Well, Ducky and I chat all the time, so he keeps me up to date on all the goings-on with the Millers."

"Daisy's the best reporter. She used her stories to make this happen. Her words are pretty convincing." It seemed Ducky's pride in others extended to the local media. He fake-whispered to Jack, "I think she puts a spell on them before they toss out the papers."

She swatted his arm with her notebook. "Stop giving away all my secrets! Now, let's go check out the site for the ceremony."

Jack's jaw dropped when Daisy grabbed Ducky's hand and pulled him close while they walked. He followed them and shook his grinning face when he realized Daisy was more than a media contact to Ducky.

"What time will the Tuckers be here?" Daisy asked Ducky as she straightened his shirt collar.

"A little before eight; mornings are better for Tara," Ducky responded. He spread out some design plans on the hood of Daisy's aqua Saturn so they could all look over them. Jack immediately realized this house was special.

"Wheelchair access?" he queried.

"Throughout." Ducky nodded as he pointed out specific parts of the plans. "All door frames and bathrooms are bigger than in most houses. They'll have huge open showers and built-in lifts in certain areas. It's all for Tara."

Daisy explained, "A few years ago, a drunk driver crossed the median of a local highway and plowed into the side of Dante and Mary's minivan. Tara was on the side that caught the brunt of it. She was only eight and stayed in a coma for almost three months. Doctors didn't think she'd live. She's got severe brain damage but hasn't lost her joy."

"She loves our ducks!" Ducky added, pointing to his truck's logo.

"Anything bright really makes her smile," Daisy added.

Jack looked back at the plans. This little girl and her family had done nothing to deserve this. He thought about the times he'd driven drunk. He could have very easily caused a tragedy like that for another innocent family. But, he'd done enough as it was. He clenched his jaw and willed the moisture in his eyes to evaporate.

Junior's crew cab pulled up then. He had brought the preacher and some of the elders from Sovereign Grace. As if on cue, trucks and SUVs began rolling in. The workers had arrived ready to get started. After a full round of introductions Jack was positive he'd never remember, they laid down a makeshift sidewalk and stage over the bumpy ground to make maneuvering Tara's wheelchair easier.

The crew finished its setup and discussed plans for their work following the ceremony, until a white wheelchair van pulled up. Dante Tucker's smile lit up the windshield when he spied the makeshift parking sign Daisy had made.

Parking
for the
Tucker Family
ONLY!

He emerged and lifted two massive arms in a victory pump over his head. Jack wasn't surprised to learn he'd played linebacker in college.

Everyone stood at a respectful distance as Mary lowered the wheelchair ramp. A mini-sized Dante bounded down first. Little David looked like someone had cloned and shrunk his father. Jack chuckled at the mischievous glint in the boy's hazel eyes. He was full-steam ahead and ready to take center stage. Alyssa took her father's hand as she carefully stepped down onto the dirt lot. She looked far older than her thirteen years, despite the braces she tried to hide. With a head of curly hair and a kind, shy smile, she was already a beauty. When Mary turned, Jack discovered Alyssa was an even more exact copy of her mom than David was of their dad. They could almost pass as twins.

Jack found himself staring at Mary's eyes. They told a story of exhaustion and worry and sadness. For a moment, a vision of his mom took the place of this other mother. He had put a similar worn and burdened look on her. Jack longed to hear his mom's voice.

Mary disappeared into the van for a moment before returning behind an extra-small wheelchair. Tara's shaky features lit up when she saw the crowd waiting for her; and she slowly raised a fist, without the strength of her father's earlier motion but with all the same passion. Tara's smile warmed the morning better than the sun that lit up her brown hair. Tight curls on either side of her face bounced with the motion of her chair. The rest of her hair lay on one shoulder in a loose braid. She wore a pretty yellow dress with a skirt that spread out around her lap like the most regal of gowns on the fanciest of princesses. Although her eyes bounced around continuously, never focusing long on one spot, Tara drank in every movement, sound and sight she could.

The family progressed to the stage area the crew had set up earlier. Daisy and Ducky hugged them all and set everyone in the right places. Local politicians and citizens had arrived as well, swelling the crowd to more than three times its original size. Jack stayed behind the audience with other crew members. Every time he looked at Tara, he thought of a different occasion he'd driven while intoxicated.

Once he'd taken out poor Widow Jenkins' mailbox. That was early in his drinking days when he was still only getting drunk on the weekends. He'd been half asleep as his mom drove them to church the next morning. When they passed the downed and crumpled mailbox, memories from the night before drifted back and he couldn't stop laughing. His mom didn't understand why he wouldn't tell her what was so funny.

It didn't seem so funny anymore.

The pastor, the mayor, Junior and Ducky each spoke briefly before Dante took the shovel and turned to the crowd. "I didn't plan to say anything to you folks today, but maybe Jesus had another idea. I'm gonna be honest with y'all. To say the past few years have been hard is an understatement. We almost lost …" Dante's voice cracked as he narrowed his eyes to squeeze back the tears fighting to escape. "… almost lost our Tara. I've battled. I thought anger and rage would consume me, but God beat those for me. There was somethin' else, though. Somethin' you may not think of. It kinda snuck up on me, but that didn't make it any less real—or destructive. Guilt.

"Ever since the night that guy—that kid, really—made his decision and got behind the wheel, I've blamed myself more than him. What if I'd swerved the other way? I should have. Driving 101—don't swerve into another lane if you can help it. If I'd turned into the median instead, I could have taken the hit. Me. Not my Tara. Back it up more, why was I even in that lane? I didn't need to be on that side. I wasn't passin' anybody. So … the questions. They fly at me. At night, when I try to sleep, I hear an endless loop of questions playin' in my head. When I do fall asleep, I see that car barreling toward us; and then it's like I'm lifting her up and offering her out to that car to take. So, guilt; it's real, powerful. But it isn't the most powerful force. The past few weeks, the pastor here's been meetin' with me, walkin' me through what the Bible says, talkin' me through my thoughts, prayin' with me. Let me tell y'all, God is so much bigger than this guilt—no matter how heavy or dark it is.

"Today, we're breakin' ground on a bright future for so many families, and I'm diggin' up that guilt and tossin' it aside to claim somethin' that the pastor showed me just yesterday. Nothin' can be done about the past. It was. But it doesn't have to be our present or future. We get to move on. We get to make wiser choices based on what that past taught us. We get to serve and bless others using that past. So, let's use it today for this building project. Let's do this!"

With that, Dante walked off the plywood to the dirt. He showed no exertion as he stomped the shovel into the soil and came up with a heaping mound. He paused to smile beside his family as at least a dozen camera shutters clicked. Then he tossed away most of the earth before resting the shovel on Tara's lap. Her eyes lit up as she offered her biggest smile yet for the cameras.

Ducky made sure that was only her second biggest of the day, though. He pulled out a yellow hard hat with a duck on the front and put it on her head. "Now you're one of the Miller crew!" He said as he bent down to give her a big hug before they posed for a few more photos.

Jack found himself wanting to talk to Dante about guilt, but he shook it off. *This man's got no reason to feel guilt. No right. He didn't drive drunk. He didn't plow into another car. He didn't pressure a drunk teen into drag racing. He didn't terrorize a town full of old people. He didn't steal. He didn't end a child's life.*

The rest of the day, Jack steered away from the crowd and channeled all the energy of the rage pulsating inside him to attack the foundation work. He had worked most of his frustration out by the end of the work day and pulled himself into Ducky's truck with the last of his strength. He sent a silent thanks out to Mawmaw Mabel for the "workin' man's" lunch she'd sent with him. Even with a roast beef sandwich too big for his mouth and a tightly-packed container of potato salad, two still melt-in-your-mouth biscuits and homemade brownies, Jack felt a twinge in his stomach. He decided he worked harder than he'd realized.

"How'd it go on the site today?" Ducky asked when Jack buckled himself in for the ride. The COO had spent his afternoon in town, marketing and giving a few more news interviews.

"Not bad. We got a really good start on digging out for the foundation. Should be ready to start another one end of the week."

"Thanks for all your hard work today, Jack. Bob called me earlier. He said you were pushing the pace." Ducky shared a smile of appreciation with his passenger before backing away from the site.

They drove a few miles in silence before Jack spoke. "Daisy's really nice. How long have you two been together?"

Ducky blushed his response. "A few months. We've known each other since back in school. I've liked her as long as I've known her, but well ... no one's more shocked than me. She chose me! We've got lots in common. Space stories, comic books, 80s hair bands and helping people. We've always got somethin' to talk about."

In the quiet, Jack thought about how he and Rachael could have talked for hours or just sat in comfortable silence together for a week. Either worked because, even in stillness, they communicated. Jack began to view much of his past in a new light as he considered how Rachael had always known he could be more than what he allowed himself to be. It was her cheering him on that pushed him to prepare for the GED tests. If she hadn't asked "Why not?" he'd have never considered applying to Tech. She was the only one who knew how much he loved the idea of building things. To be honest, she understood that drive inside him more than he did.

"Do you have a girlfriend?" Ducky's question brought Jack back to the present.

"I did." He nodded and offered a half-grin. Jack looked out his window, and Ducky didn't ask more.

They rode the rest of the way mostly in silence with an occasional discussion of the Tucker home project. Ducky explained how their crew would stay intimately involved with the project through to framing. Sub-contractors would take it from there, but he and Bob would still oversee all the details. He hoped all four houses would be framed out by the end of the summer. They had other construction companies who were donating some labor, so they'd be able to throw the houses up in no time. "Like a modern-day barn-raising," he joked. "Back then they only had their neighbors, so they got things done for each other. That's how it should still be, I think."

Jack offered his most words of the day then as he spoke through his thoughts. "I'm thankful to be a small part of all this. The way your whole family cares for others and gives so much—like with taking me in—I can't say I understand it all, but I sure do admire it." Jack wasn't certain what he was trying to say, but he knew the warmth he felt in his chest had to do with all the kindness and peace he'd stumbled into. He found it hard to believe only two nights ago he was sleeping outside, fighting his inner demons in the darkness … alone. Today he took part in something far bigger than himself. Even his pain and guilt seemed inconsequential when he considered all the needs in the world around him.

Junior had shared his secret of peace with Jack the day before, and Jack was starting to believe he might be right. The Millers, Ben, Dante Tucker, Rachael—they all had two things in common—peace and Jesus.

As the week progressed, Jack continued to impress Bob with his work ethic and drive to complete a task quickly and carefully. By Friday, Jack was sore and exhausted but pleased with his labor. He eagerly cashed his check and put most of the money into an envelope with a letter he'd written the night before.

Dear Ben,

Thanks for looking out for my mom and for keeping my location a secret. It really is best for everyone. (I know you agree when it comes to Rach.) I may call mom soon but would like to have some sort of plan in place when I do. Please give her this money. This is the first of a lot more, I hope. Don't worry, I have a legal job and all. I'm working with a family construction company. The family's taken me in, and I'm staying with them now. You'd love these people, even if they are Presbyterians. Ha! We're building a house for a family whose little girl's in a wheelchair.

Anyway, I'm safe and well, so no need to worry—or consider telling Mom where I am. Just give her the money and tell her I'm doing great. I miss her and love her, but I want to make her proud and do all I can to make the rest of her life easier since I've only ever done the opposite.

Take care of Rachael, please.

Jack

As Jack sealed and addressed the envelope, something within him stirred. A growing sense of restlessness expanded, pressing him to make a move; but, toward what destination, he couldn't tell.

XI

The Darkness Inside You

June through July 2002

Every night since his first with the Millers, Jack would leave his door cracked and wake with Missy snuggled next to him. He usually remembered his nightmares and figured she must have come in when he grew restless. Senior and Mawmaw Mabel didn't mention his screaming waking them up again. He sure hoped he wasn't. He thought he was sleeping until morning once Missy joined him. The previous night, she had joined him as soon as he fell into bed. The Sunday morning light flooded through his window by the time he finally opened his eyes. Missy's head perked up as she turned toward the door. A gentle tapping came again. Jack shook his head to clear any lingering strands of sleep before calling, "Come in."

Mawmaw Mabel's gray perm appeared around the door. "I'm so sorry to wake you up, sweetie. You were sleeping so soundly, but I want you to get a good breakfast in you before we head out to church. I hope you'll come with us; course we won't make you. You just come on out, and I've got breakfast all ready for you. I put some cheese in your eggs this mornin', too. I'm just gonna give the bacon a final flip and then …" With that, she was off down the hall, talking as she went. Missy gave Jack his morning kisses before she hopped down and bounded off for her own breakfast.

Church. Jack wasn't anxious to go to some church he didn't have an obligation to attend, but Ducky had said they'd all meet at his grandparents' for lunch. Sundays were a big family day for the Millers. Jack figured he ought to go, considering all they had done for him. They wouldn't even let him pay room and board, though he'd tried with his first paycheck. He also knew his mom and Ben would want him to go. As Jack stretched his way out of bed, it hit him.

I slept all night. No nightmares.

He floated to the kitchen on the lightness of that realization. He watched Mawmaw Mabel dish up everyone's plates and then offered to carry his and Senior's to the table. On the way he passed a framed photo of a much younger Junior and Ducky next to a pretty woman with a kind smile.

Mawmaw Mabel saw Jack examining the family photo, and a cloud crossed her face as she spoke. "Mary Anne passed away when Ducky was only ten. Multiple sclerosis. She was the sweetest girl. Nearly broke Little Pat's heart. And, of course, Ducky … poor lamb." She didn't say much through the rest of breakfast, but she gave Jack's arm a pat and kissed his cheek after he cleared the table for her.

Despite his dread, Jack enjoyed the service and felt as much at home there as he had at the Millers' house. Aunt E.

made sure he met all her friends. Soon Jack found himself surrounded by a cloister of grandmothers, each one fussing over him in her own way. He had offers for pies, home-baked bread, dearly departed husbands' clothes and granddaughters' phone numbers. Never before had Bellum's black lamb felt loved by so many people.

"I think Aunt E.'s circle ladies have got you enough dates for a month of Sundays." Junior's smile carried his greeting to Jack after the service.

"Some of them're already picking out china patterns, I'm afraid," he shot back as they walked toward the row of vehicles belonging to members of the Miller clan.

"You'll find they're relatively harmless and eventually stop fussing over you once they think you're properly settled in." Jack chuckled at Junior's assurance as he slid into the back of the elder Miller's station wagon.

Back at his hosts' home, Jack found himself surrounded by more Millers than he could count. Senior and Mabel had five children, and four of them lived within Sunday driving distance. Junior was the oldest and the only son. His three sisters fussed over him and Ducky nearly as much as his mom did. Jack did his best to tuck himself away in a corner to observe and laugh. Of course, before they'd even filled their plates with Mawmaw's Hearty Chicken and Dumplin's—as her recipe was listed in the church cookbook—he'd attracted almost as much clucking as he had back at the church.

The only one who didn't seem overbearing was Gabrielle, the Millers' youngest child and mother to the "lazy" grandson Senior had referenced when Jack met him. She stood behind him in the line that wove through the cozy house. He thought she should be wearing bell bottoms and sporting flowers in her long brown hair. She had a free spirit lingering around her. He felt her nudge him with her plate and turned his ear toward her so he could hear over the din surrounding them. "You're in luck, you know. No one else entered a dumplin' recipe for the church cookbook once Mama put hers in. Hers are like …"

"'… pillows of air wrapped in a sea of silk with a taste of heaven.'" Gabrielle and Eleanor, the oldest daughter, laughed as they ended in unison. Gabrielle explained, "Those were the words our brother came up with when he wasn't quite as big as he is now."

"Watch it back there!" Junior tossed a warning at his sisters. "You may get up here and not find any left for you."

Ripples of laughter floated through the house and out into the backyard where kids ran around and husbands had already joined Senior at a giant picnic table. Jack wondered where they had found one massive enough to accommodate this crew.

Gabrielle continued, "Mama's quite famous for this recipe, and we're all pretty fond of Sundays."

Jack could see why.

They followed lunch with a dessert of her homemade apple crumble—Ducky's favorite. Mawmaw Mabel had a dessert rotation to make sure everyone got a turn for their choice. With so many family members, Jack guessed they may have to wait a few months for their turn to roll around again.

He and Ducky sat on the back porch swing, their bellies full and their hearts light. Senior kept a steady rhythm in the rocking chair beside them as he whittled a block of wood. Jack eyed his progress intently for about five minutes until he exclaimed, "I know what that's gonna be!"

The older gentleman paused mid-stroke across the still-rectangular figure and raised bushy eyebrows toward him. "You think so, huh?"

"I sure do," Jack responded confidently. He received an amused expression in response.

"How 'bout you, Ducky? You got it figured out?"

The swing stopped as Ducky leaned toward his grandfather for a closer look. He squinted his eyes and observed the process for a couple more minutes. "I think I do now."

"Gabrielle, bring these boys each a slip of paper and somethin' to write with." When she headed inside, Senior gave them instructions. "Y'all write down what you think I'm pullin' outta this wood and your name. Fold it up. We'll get Gabrielle to hold on to 'em for you. I'll have it finished next Sunday."

The following week, Senior handed Jack a wooden duck. "How'd you know?" Ducky asked him.

"I'm not sure. I just saw it ... in the wood. It was almost like the tail was trying to waggle its way out." Jack blushed. "I guess that sounds crazy."

"Only if you're callin' me crazy. I saw the same thing you did ... a second before you spoke up," Senior said. "That's yours to keep since Ducky here thought it was a cat."

They laughed, but Jack held the duck out to his friend. "You should really keep it, though. It's only fitting."

"No, thanks. I only like them if they're yellow." Ducky flashed his earth-brightening smile. "Say, Pop, can we show Jack your shop?"

"Reckon we should." Senior's eyebrows continued to contemplate Jack's recently tapped skill.

The trio walked around to the side of the house where Jack had never been. He was shocked to find another full lot with a large metal building. As soon as they stepped inside, they took a collective breath. A mixture of smells—cedars, pines, oaks—greeted them. It was the smell of nature, domesticated.

Jack felt the potential all around him. He'd never stepped foot in a woodshop before, but he instantly saw each piece of wood for what it could become. A table and chairs to host family dinners. A picture frame to hold a memory. A bench for two lovers to carve a heart and their initials on—like he and Rachael had done back in Bellum's park.

Jack surveyed the shop. Everywhere he looked, he spied another tool. Some took up a great deal of space, like the lathe to their right. Others were smaller hand tools. The entire back wall was covered with those. There were dozens of the same tool in some cases, but Jack picked out subtle differences amongst them. He must have looked like a kid in a candy store to the other two. When he realized his jaw was hanging open, he closed his mouth and swallowed.

Senior explained, "Mabel'd always buy me tools. Other folks started; now I've got all this. Junior learned to use it all, but he hasn't done much since the company took off. Ducky here's pretty good with some of it. Even made me that stool there."

His grandson blushed as Senior nodded at a beautiful stool standing just the right height for the work bench. Jack admired the wood grain of the maple. "It's unfinished, but I didn't want to cover it up. Even with stain," Ducky explained.

"It's perfect like this." Jack ran his hand around the top and then bent to examine the detailed work around the legs. He lost himself in the feel, the smell, the craftsmanship around him. Senior understood the shimmer in the boy's eyes and began teaching him that evening. He put names to the tools Jack instinctively knew how to use. He walked him through a few types of wood and their best uses. He showed Jack all the pieces he had scattered throughout the shop, the yard and the house.

That began a daily education they both looked forward to. Jack took to woodworking like nothing Senior had ever seen. His typically grumpy expression even broke into a full smile a few times while his eyes held a light they hadn't for many years. For his part, Jack felt purposeful when he was whittling or sanding or shaping a piece of wood. Building houses was one thing—a thing he was only part of. This, though, was tangible, fulfilling. He built planters for Mawmaw Mabel's herbs, stools for the bar in Junior and Ducky's den and a raised dog dish holder that bore a higher quality of craftsmanship than any Senior had ever seen. He joked and said he must be a heckuva teacher and had missed his calling. The pair spent most of their time together in the shop in silence, but they had a few conversations that helped Jack sift through some of his deepest thoughts about his future.

"What branch were you in?" Jack asked one evening.

Senior answered simply. "Marines."

Jack stopped sanding the board in his lap and looked up. "Did you like being a Marine?"

"I did. Back then, joining was a given. I wanted to choose the branch for me. They were the few, the proud, and I've never cared to be second rate in anythin'."

After a silent moment, Jack leaned forward to study the grains on the wood in his hands. "The Marine Corps is the only branch I've ever thought of joining. Up till now I've told everyone it's because of my favorite movie. You know, the one with John Wayne."

Senior's eyebrows twitched his approval of the boy's preference.

"Well, that's only part of the reason," Jack continued. "Seems silly now, but when I was a little kid I used to pretend my dad was a Marine. He had gone off on a special mission ...

far away. He saved a whole village, but the enemy had captured him. In my mind, I was waiting on my daddy to return. As time went on and I gained a few years, my story switched. Maybe the enemy had killed him."

Jack vigorously sanded a stubborn spot. "Once I accepted the truth—that my old man had just run off—I ditched the story but always kept a soft spot for the Marines. They embodied 'hero' to me, I guess. A recruiter came to my school when we took the ASVAB, said I had impressive scores and told me all the opportunities I could have. He could see I liked the sound of seeing the world, I suppose. I would have joined up then if I'd been old enough. Anyway, when I watched the Towers fall, I wanted to enlist; but ..." Jack pictured Rachael's pleading eyes. "I guess I wasn't ready. It's been on my mind a lot lately, though. It looks like we're really headin' to war, and I want to defend freedom."

Suddenly Jack realized he had no reason not to join, and he turned to Senior. "I don't have a diploma, just my GED. Would that matter?"

"Shouldn't. You may need a waiver, but those aren't as hard to come by as you might think." Senior evaluated the young man before him, and his gaze grew guarded. "Now, the military isn't for everyone, and it isn't an easy option. It's not a decision to make lightly, 'specially with another sandstorm brewin'."

"Yessir." Jack lowered his head as he nodded. He knew he couldn't even imagine what war was really like.

"The military means more than donnin' a uniform and bein' a hero." Jack nodded as he attended Senior's words. "Takin' a life changes a person, rips the soul. Those actions stick with you. Some fellas can't live with it. No matter the foe, we're all human bein's, no matter how much the drill instructors and officers set out to dehumanize 'em." Senior's expression held bitter truth.

Silence wove around the two as they each returned to the work in their hands. Jack pieced together his thoughts as he spoke. "I have thought about how it would be to intentionally end a life. I know I can't fully imagine it, of course; but I can't stop thinking about those villagers I created in my stories as a kid. They were old people, women and children whose freedom and lives had been taken. Like Saddam Hussein's victims. Like all those people in the Towers. They all deserve a hero; and, if killing is the only way to give them that, then I'm willing. I already see skeletons in my dreams. At least I won't know the names of the new ones."

He turned to Senior and asked, "Do you regret your choice?"

"I regret the need for it." The old warrior's shoulders sagged. "I don't regret my choice to answer that need. I still ache from the actions I had to take, but talkin' with the guys at the store eases the pain. Reminds me I'm not alone."

A man of few words, Senior occasionally caught Jack off guard with a lengthy observation that dove deeper than the boy could always follow. Jack understood him this time, though. He sat for a few minutes as he reflected on what future he should be running toward.

* * *

One afternoon, the carpenters had been working with some pine Junior had recently chopped down and discovered unique markings in the wood as they planed it out. Senior explained how the tree had developed a knot at some point in its long life.

"This here tree faced some kinda rough patch. Coulda been a whack from a kid's new hatchet or some sorta disease."

Senior paused before he mused, "When hard times hit it, a tree toughens up. It takes that outside abuse, covers it over and keeps on growin'. It doesn't run from the rough stuff; it embraces it as part of itself."

As they stepped back to examine the oddly marked pieces of wood, Senior let out a loud "humph."

"It's in the natural imperfections that the wood shows its truest beauty. A skilled woodworker seeks to highlight 'em and create somethin' special." With that declaration, Senior walked away from Jack, whose mouth was catching gnats. Before he closed the door behind himself, Senior tossed back over his shoulder, "Let's see what kinda craftsman you are."

Jack pondered the man's message. He'd faced some tough times, like this tree. The question he mulled over as he inspected the wood before him was if he were trying to cover up or embrace his own hardships. Could he turn the giant knot of his past into a stunning pattern?

He recalled Dante Tucker's words about finding peace. Jack was surrounded by peace-filled people here—such a switch from his birthplace. But, just because he was surrounded by it, didn't mean he had it. Maybe this tree had made peace with its rough hits in life, but he wasn't sure he could. Perhaps he had more growing to do in order to embrace his own past and find peace. As easy as life was here with the Millers, maybe it was too easy for him to grow as he should.

A few weeks later, Jack presented Senior with a chest for his store's paperwork that left the old man speechless. He had taken each piece of wood and found its most unique knots and patterns. He arranged each panel in such a way that the entire outside of the chest told a story of growth and continued life around death—a break in the typical pattern that exemplified change and adaptation to it.

***

Whenever Jack worked on a piece, he spent the time deep in thought. He considered his future and ran over the options he thought he had to choose from. He had already contacted the University of South Carolina for registration information and details on their civil engineering program. Since he'd begun carpentry, though, Jack wondered if he could turn that into a career. He looked into woodworking schools, just in case.

In the back of his mind, always, was the call to the Corps. The call to fight for freedom for people who couldn't. Perhaps the Marine Corps could grow him in the ways he needed to embrace the knots of his past and find his purpose.

Jack took up reading military history and military fiction books in the evenings. Missy enjoyed snoozing in Jack's lap as he read. She wasn't a huge fan of all the time he'd been spending in the shop. Mawmaw Mabel barely let her paws touch the grass to do her business, let alone allow her to run around outside unhindered.

The routine Jack had drifted into with the Miller family was easy and comfortable. Their house already felt like home to him. *Home* was exactly what Jack's worn heart desired, so he embraced the scents of the decades of memories, the scratchy towels, the southern-seasoned meals, the endless chatter of Mawmaw Mabel and the quiet sullenness of Senior. They meshed … like they'd always been together.

He'd accepted Sundays at Sovereign Grace as routine and discovered messages and verses he remembered from Sunday school or Ben's sermons. He noticed other similarities. He never understood how Rachael and her father could be so forgiving, so open-armed, so kind. It didn't make sense. He felt the same way when he arrived in Columbia and experienced it again with the members of the Miller family. When he entered Sovereign Grace, he found himself surrounded with more examples.

The more he reflected on his observations, the more restless Jack felt. He knew he needed to move on—but, to where? From the time he recognized his desire for peace and accepted his need to embrace the past and grow around it—like the tree with its unusual patterns—he understood. This was just a stop on his journey. He wasn't sure what the next leg of the journey was or how long his layover would be.

He rarely had nightmares anymore, but during the day he still had moments. One of the Millers' great-grandbabies reminded him far too much of Abbie Mae; so much that the first time he saw her, he had to shut himself in his room until he calmed the panic rising within him. He pulled out the family's photo albums tucked away in his closet in order to logically explain he was not seeing a ghost.

Jack couldn't embrace forgiveness for his past mistakes or find freedom from the guilt to which he clung. As far as he was concerned, he could never be forgiven. While forgiveness may come to good people, he wasn't one of them. Sometimes the thoughts and grief and guilt converged to attack. He was fighting—fighting to stay on an even keel and keep going. In those moments, he'd let his mind linger on the release alcohol used to bring him but then reminded himself of the chains it carried and the promise he'd made his mom.

The more Jack pondered his past and wrestled with his future, the more he thought the military held a place for him. His life already felt like a war; he may as well enter a real battlefield and fight a visible enemy that he might be able to defeat. He had nearly made his mind up about it, but he had another problem. He'd grown to love the Millers, their friends and this place.

***

Each Saturday Jack and Ducky worked on playhouses for the big home complex. They had decided it would be fitting to build four instead of one and fashion each after the big houses. On Sunday evenings after their big dinner, they would sit on the porch, watch the news and whittle. Ducky could always tell when Jack drifted into deep thinking. On one of these occasions, he asked some questions to find out just what weighed on his friend's mind.

"Do you miss your home, Jack?"

"Yeah, sometimes." Jack slowly withdrew from the war waging in his mind to focus on Ducky's question. "I do miss my mom."

"What about the girlfriend you mentioned?"

"All the time, but I try not to think about her. She deserves so much better than a guy like me." He frowned as he concentrated on adding the detail of some whiskers to the cat he was whittling for Ducky's youngest niece, Sophia—the one he'd once thought was a ghost come to haunt him.

Ducky stopped whittling and asked, "Did she say that?"

"Well, no; but I could see it." Jack paused as he reflected on the unexpected question before adding, "Even if she couldn't."

"Maybe you shouldn't be here. Maybe you've got something more important you need to do."

It was Jack's turn to stop and look up. "Maybe you're right, Ducky."

The picture in the top corner of the news broadcast framed a man with an aura of evil about him. Saddam Hussein's face and name spread fear to most, but Jack's anger grew each time he saw him and thought about the innocent people he'd tormented. This monster didn't seem to feel one lick of guilt for all the pain he'd caused. Maybe it was time someone made him.

"We're going to end up at war, aren't we?" Jack's words were more statement than question.

"Pop and Dad think so." Ducky sighed. He looked from Jack to the TV and back. All that thinking he'd observed made sense. "Is that what you think you need to do?"

"Yeah." Jack could feel Ducky's concern already.

"I don't know about that, Jack. I don't think that's what you've got to do at all." Ducky shook his head. "I was thinking more about your mom and ... and the past you left back in your home."

"Ever since 9-11, I've been thinking this. I knew Rach wasn't much for the idea, or I'd have joined up then." Jack set the wooden cat aside with his tools before adding, "I can still send money to my mom; plus, I'll finally do something she can maybe be proud of."

Ducky stared at the screen for a moment before he pointed to it. "Jack, if you run across the world to that darkness, you'll just be adding to the darkness inside you. I think you know that, too. Deep down ..." He reached out and placed his hand over Jack's heart. "In here."

XII

Pride in Something

August 2002

Ducky's words didn't deter Jack from claiming his future that night. As soon as he returned from work the next day, Jack found Senior in his shop. "Any chance you could drive me to the recruiter's station?"

Senior set down the chisel in his hand and studied the young man before him. "You sure?"

"I've thought about this every day for a couple months now, and it's been in the back of my mind since September. All I know is, I feel a tug every time I watch the news. If my country's going to war, I'm going to fight."

Senior held Jack's gaze as he weighed his sincerity and commitment. "Let's go."

The older man led Jack through the house and past a flummoxed Mawmaw Mabel in her flour-covered apron. "Be back for supper," Senior mumbled as they exited the front door. The drive began silently. Cleared land rose up to wooded lots, and Jack's thoughts wove amongst the pines that drifted past, like some wild mystical stallion running free through a forest of endless possibilities.

That's how Jack viewed his future since he'd planted the Corps firmly in its center. He knew their values—honor, courage, commitment. Those were three mighty words. They were also three words no one had used for him. If he could take a step toward an opportunity where he knew he could help, could right wrongs, could fight battles for those who couldn't, then maybe—just maybe—he'd take on pieces of those values. If his mom could see any of those things in him when this was all said and done, then that would be even better. He knew she loved him and would use the word "proud," but that's one of those things moms are supposed to say. He wanted to make up for all the crap he'd rained down on her the past several years, maybe even make up for some of the hurt his dad had left behind and start his apology for taking a similar step out the door. She deserved better than the mess this life had handed her.

As he thought through his reasons for joining, Jack's resolve grew. This was the answer, his next step. He knew becoming a Marine was more than an escape. It would metamorphose him even as he became part of something beyond himself. The man sitting next to him was proof of that.

Jack broke the silence. "I know the training won't be easy. Any advice?"

Senior raised an eyebrow and snorted. "Well, I'm not sure nowadays. Back when real men went through, we sweated bread and bled water to provide our own sustenance in the field. Nowadays I think waiters bring in fancy dinners on silver platters for you and blow on it so you don't burn your tongues."

Jack howled until his sides ached, especially when Senior joined in with a chortle as rusty as a forgotten gate. As they wiped the moisture of mirth away, Senior gave Jack his first round of advice.

"You'll loathe your drill instructors, but DIs will mold you into a lean, mean warfighting machine. They'll squeeze out every drop of arrogance and selfishness you got. Once they've broken you completely, you'll view yourself as they do—the lowest form of scum on earth ... barely on par with plant life."

Jack shifted in his seat as Senior continued. "Once you're broke, they'll build you back. Piece by piece. Until you're efficient, effective. Remember, not a single thing they do is about you. It's about making you one with your fellow recruits."

His gray eyes donned a silver shimmer that glowed in the sunlight. Jack watched the lines and years slough away from his face. It was as if he were observing some magical transformation to Marine in the man before him.

"'The few, the proud ...,' huh?" Jack whispered.

"Semper Fi," came the throaty response as the Marine pulled into the lot of the recruiting office and parked beneath the Eagle, Globe and Anchor.

Jack sat for a moment, breathing deeply, sifting through what he'd just heard. He would be part of something so much bigger than himself, he could barely fathom it. He hit rewind on his life and realized he had never truly belonged. Not in Bellum where he was the drunk's kid until he became the drunk kid. And not here in Columbia. As kind and welcoming as everyone had been, he wasn't part of this family. He didn't have Miller blood running through his veins nor had he been "washed in the blood of the Lamb," as the choir sang on Sunday.

He also hadn't defined his purpose. He had bounced from a kid who cared only about football and girls to an alcoholic to a builder of houses and of a foundation for his future until it slipped out from under him. He was still scraping up the pieces to rebuild, but where his purpose rested, he couldn't say.

That bit Senior had said about being broken down and rebuilt—piece by piece? That's exactly what he needed—to be remade. Recreated. It was time to find his place in this world and be more than he could ever push himself to become on his own. Jack flashed a confident grin to his driver. He was ready.

For the next hour and a half, Senior and Jack went through questions and paperwork with the recruiter. Jack answered honestly about his GED and his scar. He breathed a thanks to the heavens when he could answer in the negative for arrests.

When they left, the sun waned in the western sky. Jack's head spun with all the information he'd consumed. He ran over the list of documents he'd have to get or fill out. He understood why adults complained they'd drown in paperwork one day. As he rubbed his aching wrist, Jack realized he was an adult. He was eighteen after all. Soon he'd be a United States Marine. Jack straightened against his seat as street lamps signaled close proximity to their destination.

Mawmaw Mabel had a heaping, steaming plate of food ready and waiting for each of them. As the front door opened, she was already mid-conversation. "... dark as midnight out here. And—heaven declare!—I believe my sweet boy's lost any little weight I've managed to put on him. Workin' all day so hard with supper so late. Knew I should've packed extra food for some afternoon snacks. I've got plates all ready for the two of you. Oh, Missy Mee! Don't fuss ... come on along. I'll just heat them ...."

Cream of mushroom chicken breasts with butter-laden baked potatoes, fresh green beans and homemade cornbread threatened to overflow their plates. After hand-churned ice cream served over angel food cake with some of the season's last peaches crowning the top, Jack was almost ready to change his mind about joining the Corps and stay put at Mawmaw Mabel's dinner table. Senior and Jack lumbered to the den, each with a hand on his full stomach.

Senior sank into his recliner and looked toward the empty fireplace. Jack lowered himself to the floor and leaned back against the ottoman. The steps he'd taken earlier that evening soaked in to the shag carpets and paneled walls around them. Even Missy felt a change brewing. She lay on his lap, looking intently into his face, as if waiting for more ... or less. Senior nodded his head with his rocking until he stopped mid-motion and turned toward Jack. "You know she's gonna fret and worry like crazy, right?"

He didn't need to nod back toward the kitchen. Jack had already considered that and wondered if he really had to tell Mawmaw Mabel. The letter thing seemed to work before.

Senior had turned back to nodding at the fireplace. "There's Junior, course. And Ducky." Jack wasn't overly fond of these reminders of the goodbyes he'd have to make. He ran his hand along Missy's back and wished he could move on without leaving anyone behind. This may be harder than he thought. He could have never imagined a couple months ago how much this foreign city would become a home like he'd never known.

* * *

The next few weeks swirled past in a whirlwind of activities. Gathering all the information and documents required for Jack's application. Enjoying "just one more special meal." Visiting more places he "just had to see before he left Columbia." Ramping up for the framing and roofing of the Tuckers' house and completing one final woodworking project. Not long after he arrived at the Millers', he had overheard Mawmaw Mabel mention how nice two pretty rockers would look on their front porch. As soon as his hands lost any clumsiness with the tools he'd need, Jack began work on two rockers. He ordered some special maple from Pennsylvania through Junior. He forced himself to slow down on this build. It was hard to explain, but—though he could fly through project after project—he wanted to really feel this one. As he sanded and planed, he memorized each grain, each darkening, each pattern in the wood beneath his hands. Working with such details forced Jack to focus, even as the smell of the wood cleared his thoughts and set them free.

Pat and Mabel Miller had opened their home and their hearts to him. They'd become the grandparents he'd never known and a family he'd unknowingly longed for. They had continued to refuse his offer to pay for his room and board. But this, this was one thing he could give them. It would be his thank you and farewell. It would be something they could remember him by, but it would also be something he would remember them by. Wherever he ended up, he could close his eyes and picture them sitting there, side by side, rocking together through the rest of their lives. They were the essence of what he'd subconsciously desired for Rachael and him to become.

In those last few weeks, Jack tucked away more mental snapshots he'd carry away with him. Missy's adoring gaze lifted up to him. Ducky and Daisy holding hands and laughing together as the sun set after another beautiful Sunday at the Millers'. The entire Miller clan tucked into the picnic table, a feast spread among them. The shimmer of sawdust in a sunbeam near the window of the woodshop.

***

"I love that view," Jack admitted to Ducky one day at quitting time. They had been framing the Tuckers' house and had just hammered the final nails. They stood back, admiring the sight of the house's bones, tall against the landscape beyond. One more picture to file away in his memory scrapbook.

"Me too."

Jack would miss watching those houses reach completion. He would love to see the look on little Tara's face when they wheeled her into her new home for the first time. He could imagine it, though. That image brought a smile to his face. He was part of something here—it may have been a mostly inconsequential one, but it was a part nonetheless—of something life-changing and lasting.

For the first time in his life, Jack felt pride in something he'd done. He thought of the future he'd signed up for and decided this wouldn't be his last experience with that feeling.

XIII

One Final Sentence

August to September 1, 2002

Time alternated between slow motion and fast-forward as boxes earned checkmarks, forms received approval signatures and Jack's adopted family accepted his goodbyes. He'd passed all physical and psychological tests at Fort Jackson and taken his Oath of Enlistment into the military. Jack's road to Marine felt like the German autobahn. It seemed no speed limit had been placed on his process as it took only a few weeks from signing up to shipping out.

The recruiter made use of every day of it, though, and had Jack and his other poolees meet up for running, pull-ups and push-ups a few times a week as they waited to report to Marine Corps Recruit Depot, Parris Island. Jack was thankful he'd continued running throughout his time in Columbia, especially with all the heaping plates Mawmaw Mabel fixed him. Of course, there was also something freeing about running, full out, with no reason to stop, no set destination in mind.

His speed caught the recruiter's eye. He told Jack if he kept that up at Boot Camp and put as much effort into everything else the DIs required of him, he could graduate a Private First Class rather than a Private. The seasoned Marine turned out to be an able story-teller and easily held their attentions as he shared tales from both USMC history and legend as well as a few of his personal stories.

Jack heard many more tales from the Hardy's Crap 'n' Coffee Club members. Each found a way to express the commitment to the cause without skimming over the cost.

"War's comin', sure as I'm sittin' here," Murphy mused. He wasn't one to skirt around a delicate topic. "It'll change you. No doubt 'bout that either. You just have to find a focus and a forgiveness you can cling to when the ghosts rise up."

"And, we'll still be here when you get back." Senior couldn't hide the emotion moistening his words.

Gene gave a loud snort. "No doubt still drinkin' this galldurn tar."

"I'll tell you where you can keep your cuppa tar there …" Senior's eyebrows shot up a warning as he ended mid-threat. Jack chuckled as he crowned another piece in his checker game against Murphy. He knew he'd need these men one day. As much as he could tell himself this type of death would be different, he knew easy didn't exist in a war zone.

* * *

Jack continued to correspond weekly with his former pastor. After a couple months of uncertainty, Ben had moved to Savannah, Georgia, where he took a job as director of a Christian rehab. Jack wondered every day if Rachael were there too, where she had decided to go to college and if she'd moved on from him yet. These were questions he'd never ask—whether out of commitment to his choice, concern Ben wouldn't tell him or terror of the answers, he wasn't sure.

Each Friday, Jack mailed a money order made out to his mama with an update on his week. Ben read and responded to each note. They wrote about books, the mission, their jobs, his mom and his enlistment. Jack asked Ben not to tell his mom that he'd joined—not until after Boot Camp. He couldn't shake a nagging voice that he may not be able to hack it. It would be bad enough to disappoint the Millers and Ben. He didn't want to add his mama's face to the mix. Ben kept his word to Jack and forwarded on the money to Becky, along with an assurance that her son was slowly discovering his place in the world.

After his final Friday on the job site, Jack found a letter waiting for him beside a plate of fresh-baked chocolate chip cookies. He tore into both eagerly while Missy curled up in his lap, her nose sniffing at both the letter and the treats. He could almost hear Ben's voice as he read the message.

Dear Jack,

I hope the post office doesn't disappoint me; this should reach you right before you ship out to Boot Camp. I know it'll be a while before you get to write again.

You will be in my prayers—not just that you won't pass out on one of those "marches," but also that you'll find some peace. I know you've been seeking for the right path to take. If this doesn't turn out to be it, though, don't get discouraged.

I can see your eyes rolling as you read this, but God's got a plan for you, for your life. You'll know what it is as soon as you find it.

Wishing you all the best,

Ben

Jack smiled and tucked the note away with all the others in a special pocket inside his duffle. The weekend ahead wouldn't be an easy one. Mawmaw Mabel had instructed the entire Miller clan and half the church to come eat all Jack's favorite dishes and send him off in true southern style. All these goodbyes made Jack wish for another escape on a midnight bus.

"Now that we're alone, I've got something to show you," Ducky whispered as he glanced around the recently cleared backyard. It was the first Sunday of September and Jack's final Miller family get-together. He had to catch a later bus to Parris Island. Jack could tell his friend had something exciting to share by the color that had risen in his cheeks. Ducky leaned to one side and pulled something out of his pocket. It was a ring box. "I'm going to ask Daisy to marry me. What do you think of it?"

He held out a princess cut diamond ring. Sunlight caught its edges and cast shimmers onto the thin gold band that looked custom-made for Daisy's slender fingers. "Man, Ducky, that's awesome! I'm sure she'll love it. When are you gonna pop the question?"

"At the Miller's thirtieth anniversary celebration." His smile rivaled the gem's sparkle. "Do you think she'll say yes?"

"Absolutely, man. No doubts there. You gonna get down on one knee?" Jack grinned back.

"You know it!" Ducky grew serious as he returned the box to its hiding spot. "I'd really hoped you'd be there."

"Me too." Jack sank back against the swing's wooden slats. "You know, I never could have imagined how many friends—family, really—I would have met in my few months here. You guys have made a world of difference in my life. I hate to leave y'all; but, in one way, you're the ones giving me the strength and courage to go. Back in Bellum I was judged as the kid who wrecked lives, whose own life would never amount to anything. Y'all treated me like I could be more."

"Aw, Jack. You're one of the best workers I've ever seen." He put a hand on Jack's arm as he continued, "And one of the best friends."

"Thanks, man. Right back at ya'!" The emotion rose in Jack and threatened to overflow. He sprang up and said, "I could use some help packing. I've got to leave soon."

"You got it!"

Jack didn't have much to pack. A few more articles of clothing and one more picture totaled all he'd added in the last few months, though most of his clothes would stay here. He wouldn't have a need for them where he was going. The new picture was of him and the entire Miller clan. They'd stacked up on that crazy table in the backyard in a big jumble of mass confusion. No one was looking in the same direction or making the same kind of face. Some were laughing; some striking a pose; some making faces. In the center of it all sat Mawmaw Mabel—prim, proper and proud—and Senior right beside her. The patriarch observed them all with crossed arms, puckered lips and sky-high eyebrows. Jack smiled down from atop the table at Ducky with Daisy's head on his shoulder.

He recalled his thoughts when the Millers' neighbor snapped this shot: *In another life, I could have had a family like this. Old and ornery like Senior, with Rachael—the ultimate hostess—by my side. Kids and grandkids around us. Maybe I shouldn't have left. Maybe it could have ...*

Nope. He wasn't going down that rabbit trail. No regrets over past decisions. This day was about embracing and mentally preparing himself for the big decision he'd made. Rachael was his past—such a beautiful past—but his focus had to be on where he belonged and what purpose lay ahead.

The photo joined the other three. He tucked them in the side of the bag, nestled against the little box he'd kept hidden away—out of sight, not out of mind. He zipped and shouldered his bag and clapped Ducky on the back as they walked out of his room and down the hall to face the final goodbye process.

"Now, don't you tell me no again. You know they won't have good food there, Pat. I had almost started to see some insulation around that boy's skinny bones. Oh, Jack! I've got you a bag all packed with food. You need to take it and ignore Mr. Pat here. I want to make sure you have some good food while you're there. I'll send you a care package with all your favorites every week: biscuits, pies, cookies—now, was it the peanut butter or the snickerdoodles you liked better? Never mind, dear. I'll send both. You can share with all your new friends."

"Mawmaw Mabel, they won't let us get care packages like that. It's against the rules. They'd just throw them away, I'm afraid. You can write me letters once I'm able to send you my address, but you can't send any food."

"Told ya." Senior's stoic face spoke volumes. His wife narrowed her eyes at him before turning back to Jack and patting his arm. "I'm just so worried about you not gettin' enough to eat there. And, I don't think they use salt ... or butter." She breathed this last statement with a tone of sheer horror. "Or make desserts." At this realization, the little woman shook her head and dabbed at the tears trickling out of the corners of her eyes. She pulled him down for a bear hug and a kiss on each cheek.

"I'll write you," Jack promised as he gently pressed his own kiss to her worry-lined forehead. "And, I'll be just fine."

His words, meant to be reassuring, opened the floodgates on her emotions. She shoved an over-stuffed paper bag in his hand and headed to retrieve a box of tissues from the coffee table. Jack bent down for a bath of Missy kisses. She knew something was about to toss her little world upside down, and she wasn't happy about it. She leapt up in his arms, continuing her thorough licking of his face and neck. "I'm gonna miss you, Missy Mee." Jack buried his face in her soft, white fur as he whispered so only she could hear, "Thank you for chasing away my nightmares."

Ducky gave him one final hug. "See you soon, Jack."

Junior heaved himself up from the low living room sofa and wrapped Jack in an engulfing hug. "You stay strong, Kid. Do us proud." Jack smiled and nodded, a tightness in his throat halted any response.

Senior waited by the front door. He opened it as Jack approached and followed him through it.

The car ride to the bus station fluctuated between a silence charged with Jack's anticipation of all that lay in store for him in the coming weeks and unusually long chunks of conversation from Senior.

"Remember, it's not about you. Once you reach your destination, you won't use the pronouns *I* and *you*. You'll learn to rely on and answer to the men around you. They'll be your brothers. That's something that's harder for some than others to make peace with. The day you do, though, you've made it."

Jack stared straight ahead as he processed the information he'd just been given. What Senior told him sounded simultaneously simple and impossible. He'd read and heard time and again about the importance of trusting the men around you. The thing was he wasn't sure he'd ever really trusted anyone. His mom, of course; but that was different.

They passed a sign for the bus station, and Jack shifted in his seat. He was supposed to trust his life to total strangers. Quite honestly, he wasn't sure he could. He trusted himself to overcome the mental and psychological pressures he would face from day one—specifically at zero dark thirty when the yelling began. But to trust another person that completely? Most of the people in his past had let him down, left him when the going got tough—like all his friends and the guys on the football team after Steven's death. They'd vanished then, never to be seen again. Who was to say these guys wouldn't do the same thing if he needed them? Doubt bred worry, and worry grew until it exploded from Jack in the form of a single word.

"How?"

The abrupt question drew Senior's eyes to evaluate his passenger's face. After a moment's consideration he answered. "Everybody breaks in Boot Camp. Your trigger could be trust—or the lack of it. You push on through whatever it is, you'll find the one thing that defines you, makes you a Marine."

After a heavy silence, Senior added, "This ain't gonna be easy, you know."

Jack nodded.

"You'll make it, though. Remember, you're part of the latticework of these United States of America. Each piece gets sanded, shaped and stained to be the part it needs to be to make a finished product the craftsman can be proud of. The sandin' and shapin' ain't much fun. After, though, you can see how you fit with all the other bits. Guys like me and the boys at the hall and the kids who'll become your band of brothers—we're what keeps this country together. We're who the world sees when they look up to this country—beacons of light and hope for the hopeless, a warning warrior eye on the world's evils. Remember that big picture and forget about any of this bein' about you."

They pulled in to the station then. Senior left the car running as he got out to walk around to Jack. In his hands was a small brown leather Bible. "Mabel and me want you to have this. I don't reckon it's a gift you really want right now, but there may just come a day when it leads you to the greatest gift of all. For now, fine-tune your focus and keep your eyes on the prize."

"The prize?"

"Eagle, Globe and Anchor." He held up his Marine Corps ring for the boy to see. The old Marine's eyes twinkled. Jack smiled at the emblem he would come to know intimately over the next few months. Jack locked eyes with Senior and said, "Thank you. For everything."

"God bless you." Senior's eyebrows waggled as he puckered his lips to push his emotions back inside himself. His verbosity through the evening had shocked Jack so much, the recruit hopeful's tears were kept at bay until one final sentence. "Love you, Son."

With a firm grip on each arm, Senior left a rough kiss on the boy's forehead before turning back to the idling station wagon ahead of any response Jack could have summoned.

XIV

These Guys Could Move Iwo Jima

September 2 through December 4, 2002

As Jack waited for the bus that would carry him to whatever lay ahead, he pondered Senior's pronouncement of God's blessing on him and looked down at the gift in his hands. He wasn't convinced God had many blessings to sprinkle on him, but he'd take whatever good will he could get for this journey. As confident as he was in his abilities, he was equally worried that he would—yet again—disappoint the people around him. Knowing he had a posse of people believing in him and cheering him on was more terrifying than facing down a town of rage and judgement. This was his chance, though. His opportunity to do something bigger than himself, better than his past, brighter for those he loved. He took a deep breath and pictured his mom with a smile on her face—one without the strain of worry masking it—and Rach … *No.* He shook her from his mind.

Jack eyed the other passengers and picked out fellow recruits. Several he knew from time spent exercising together with their recruiter. They nodded the matter-of-fact head bobs of young men bound for the same uncertain fate. When the time came to board, he took a moment to thaw out from the freezer of the room he'd just exited. He listened to the rumble of the waiting ride and did his best not to look as terrified as he suddenly felt. Once he felt his blood flowing again, he boarded the bus and filed down the aisle to sit next to a guy who looked like he should play offensive line for the Gamecocks. He tipped his red face toward Jack before leaning against the window where he promptly fell asleep.

This bus ride began the psychological breaking down. Each mile that ticked past brought a dozen more questions or doubts into Jack's mind. With each star that appeared in the night sky, though, the young recruit's worries lessened and his determination grew. The bus rocked and swayed as Jack recalled Senior's latticework analogy. He smiled at how the man of so few words often dropped a truckload of truth and wisdom when least expected.

Midnight must have passed, Jack thought as he stared into the blackness around them. He pondered all he'd read about the Island, the training and the Corps. He knew their peace was about to be shattered and they would all be a whole lot closer very soon. They'd have no privacy, no relief, no down time. Every movement would be scrutinized, analyzed. Jack would have to stand stone-faced while enduring all manner of attacks. While that didn't seem so different from overlooking gossip and hateful comments, he knew he needed to heed Senior's advice. Focus. Eagle, Globe and Anchor.

***

Jack took a deep breath as the bus jolted to a stop with a squeal of brakes. He could smell the exhaust, choking with a hint of sweetness; he filled his lungs with it and braced himself for the welcome that would follow the opening of that door. The Drill Instructor greeted them with a tone that heralded the storm to come.

"On behalf of the Marine Corps Recruit Depot Commanding General, I'd like to welcome you to my Island."

And then the switch flipped.

"Now! Get off my bus! You will walk fast—not run—and stand on my yellow footprints. Now, scream, 'Aye, Sir!'"

"Aye, Aye, Sir!"

"Walk faster; walk faster. Get on my footprints now. Now scream, 'Aye, Sir!'"

"Aye, Aye, Sir!"

Each young man filed onto bright yellow footprints lining the concrete in perfect formation. They filled spots covered by countless young recruit hopefuls across the decades of training at Parris Island. The seriousness of tradition radiated through the soles of their shoes and up to their hearts.

The Drill Instructor continued to bark out his welcome. "You are now aboard Marine Corps Recruit Depot, Parris Island, South Carolina, and you have just taken the first step toward becoming a member of the world's finest fighting force—the United States Marine Corps. Starting now, you will exist as a team. You will live, eat, sleep and train as a team. The word *I* will no longer be part of your vocabulary. You will become the collective *you*—the Marines before you, behind you, beside you. You will learn to work together to achieve the unachievable, to reach the unreachable, to defeat the undefeatable. Only then will you earn the title United States Marine. Now, scream 'Aye, Sir!'"

"Aye, Aye, Sir!"

Jack welcomed a numbness around his senses as the yelling continued. He did his best to follow the orders, the explanations, the commands. Senior's advice was certainly accurate. This wasn't about him one damn bit.

He and his bus-mates found themselves facing silver double doors, each with its own gold emblem. Eagle, Globe and Anchor. Its sheen was both a siren call and an omen to Jack. His eyes fixed on one of the emblems. He memorized every line, indentation and ridge as though his life depended on it. This laser focus branded the DI's barked words into Jack's mind.

"Passing through these silver hatches signifies your transformation from civilian to United States Marine Corps recruit; therefore, you will pass through these hatches one time, and one time only. Do you understand? Now, scream, 'Aye, Sir!'"

"Aye, Aye, Sir!" Their response echoed back at them in perfect unison, like the bark of one mighty dog.

"You will walk—not run—up my stairs and into my building. Do you understand?"

"Yes, Sir!"

"You will walk quickly. You will not run. Do you understand?"

"Yes, Sir!"

"You will keep an arm's distance from all other people in my building. Do you understand?"

"Yes, Sir!"

"Two recruits grab the hatches. Now, scream 'Aye, sir!'"

"Aye, Aye, Sir!" Jack rushed up the stairs and grabbed hold of one handle. A shot of straight adrenaline coursed up his arm as he grasped the metal. That shock launched his transformation. He would soon be a Marine. No turning back. No giving in. No bowing down. No defeat. He would succeed. He would persevere. Eyes on the prize.

* * *

The first few weeks passed in a fuzzy blur of motion and movement and orders and rules and regulations. The razors and uniforms left them unsure which recruit they were in the glass doors they passed in formation. They fell into their platoons and began to discover each other's strengths and weaknesses. Jack filed into 3rd Recruit Training Battalion, India Company. Despite his exhaustion toward the end of Receiving Week, Jack sailed through his Initial Strength Test, catching the eye of the DIs by surpassing all requirements.

Jack met every physical fitness milestone, beating the minimum by a little each time. If he thought the DIs wouldn't notice his ease in running, he was wrong. They didn't miss a thing. That included Jack's polar opposite—his bunkmate—Recruit Nathaniel Dawson from Charleston. Dawson was a skinny kid with zero confidence, negative muscle mass and even less coordination and skill. He was always earning the platoon extra push-ups or pull-ups.

On Black Friday, they met the men who would motivate them for the rest of their journey. Staff Sergeant Henry Dubois barked at them with a Cajun accent that took careful attention and practice to understand. Sergeant Marcus Green earned the nickname "Heavy Hat" with his dark, beady eyes that never missed a lag in pace, a cheating rest or a mis-step. Rounding out the team was Sergeant Solomon Marshall. Jack decided early on this bulldog was one of the most brilliant men he'd ever met. What he wasn't sure of was whether or not he could one day think of him with anything besides malice.

Marshall rode the recruits mercilessly. His specialty was lurking in the shadows of whatever they were doing. He would drift and circle until he became part of their surroundings—unseen, unnoticed. Until they screwed up. Immediately, he'd be in their face, issuing an ever-revolving assortment of insults.

"Did your mother have any children who lived?"

"Were you born this incompetent, or did your granny drop you on your head when she first saw your ugly mug?"

"Why are you here? Marines are the best, the elite, the top. So, why are *you* here?"

Jack managed to mostly tune Marshall out on the unfortunate occasions he earned his attention and didn't bother to dwell on whatever words he flung his way, but it irked him to see the toll it took on some of his fellow recruits, including Dawson.

Marshall laid into Dawson every time he made a mistake, which happened often. "Maybe you should have joined the Army instead, Recruit! Perhaps you could keep up with the Doggies. Maybe you're not quite Devil Dog material, Recruit! Get down and give me 30 frickin' push-ups and keep that butt down."

At first Jack felt sorry for the kid, but he got pretty sick of all the extra physical activity he caused them. Marshall picked up on the rising frustration and started sending Jack back in the group once he completed a run to finish again alongside Dawson. "Calhoun!"

"Sir! Yes sir!"

"You will circle back and run with your bunkmate. You will speed up Recruit Dawson."

"Aye, Aye, Sir!"

Jack held his tongue, kept his head down—eyes on the prize—powering through until evening when he could disappear within the inner workings of his weapon.

The highlight of that initial week for Jack had been when they put his weapon in his hands. As a kid, he didn't have the same experiences with rifles that all his friends did. He didn't have a dad to teach him to shoot and take him hunting. When his friends first invited him to go along with them and their dads, he headed to the local library to check out videos on hunting and shooting and weapons. Jack taught himself the parts of a weapon; so, when he got to hold a borrowed rifle, he knew exactly where everything went and how to hold it. He knew how to load them, how to cock them and how to shoot them. He never told his friends how he knew what to do. He'd always shrug off their questions with a muttered tale about his dad giving him lessons.

Jack had taught himself to respect a weapon. He'd learned to be one with it. That familiarity—that skill—led him to the two things Senior had promised him—a breaking point and a defining moment—together.

One evening, Jack bent over his rifle, mentally reciting "The Marine Rifleman's Creed" they had memorized, as he examined each piece methodically.

This is my rifle.

There are many like it, but this one is mine.

My rifle is my best friend. It is my life.

I must master it as I must master my life.

My rifle, without me, is useless.

Without my rifle, I am useless.

I must fire my rifle true.

I must shoot straighter than my enemy

who is trying to kill me.

I must shoot him before he shoots me. I will ...

Cleaning the M16 became both a release and a relief for Jack. In those precious moments of square-away time, he could escape the yelling, the orders and the constant psychological onslaught of the DIs. He lost himself in the order and function of each part of his weapon as he meticulously cleaned, lubricated and oiled each one. In Jack's mind this weapon was the one thing under his command. He would disassemble and reassemble it over and over, timing himself and rewarding a new time with more practice.

Jack's aptitude with a weapon did not go unnoticed. He may have found himself self-conscious had he overheard the DIs' conversation about him one evening.

"Ever seen a recruit more intent on his weapon?" Green questioned Dubois mid-way through the first phase of training.

"Only a few times. Never this efficiently, this early on. You timed him yet?" Dubois asked Marshall.

"I have. Never seen times like these, especially at this stage." Marshall never took his eyes from the silent recruit. "If he shoots as well as he handles that weapon, he may not be able to handle his platoon's failures on the range. No doubt he can do alone. Can he do Marine?"

Dubois watched Marshall as he walked up and down the squad bay to more closely observe each recruit's activities. Some prepared their weapons or uniforms for the next day. Others tidied lockers. Others wrote letters. The DIs could look down the rows of metal bunks and tell which recruits would remain standing after their final run and which ones wouldn't even participate. They also had the ones pegged who were wild cards. Jack landed there. Marshall had summed it up. Jack was squared away—arguably far more squared away than most of the other recruits. How would that work, though, when they broke them down and forced them to rely on one another to succeed or fail as a team? How would Jack handle the pressure of failing at something he appeared to do better than the Senior Drill Instructor had ever seen anyone do?

"Hey, Calhoun, can you show me how you do that so quickly?"

Dawson's interruption came mid-process and mid-line of the Creed his bunkmate silently rehearsed. Jack didn't look up as he answered. "Nope."

The recruit wouldn't give up so easily. He awkwardly passed his rifle from hand to hand while looking at it like it was an unfathomable mystery. "The harder I try to assemble and disassemble this thing quickly, the slower I seem to go."

"Then quit trying."

By this point the DIs' ears had tuned in to the conversation happening mid-bay. Jack's clipped response reverberated, though he'd made it softly. Dawson stood, dazed and dumbfounded, his rifle dangling at his side.

After an eternal moment, Jack looked up from his process, sighed and said, "Look, Dawson, you're tryin' too hard. With everything. Lighten up; breathe. Let's see what you've got."

Jack stood up and motioned to the weapon a hopeful Dawson nearly dropped in his excitement. It took a few seconds of fumbling before Jack repeated, "Lighten up; breathe. One step at a time. Upper receiver first—one piece at a time. Call the part as you touch it."

From each receiver, down to the firing pin and back again, Dawson went through the entire process quicker than ever.

At the final click, he looked up and beamed at Jack. "I did it. I actually did it."

"Now, do it again. And clean that mess this time. Then do it again and again the exact same way. In a few days you won't be thinking about it anymore. Maybe then you'll have put some speed to it." Jack returned to his own weapon and blocked Dawson from his mind.

The DIs moved on about their duties but continued to contemplate what they'd witnessed. Marshall furrowed his brow and kept his thoughts to himself. How would this newfound leadership translate to the field in a few weeks? And, would it make him a true leader under the pressure he'd find there?

* * *

Jack took water survival and rappelling into stride. He survived the gas chamber … mainly because he sure as heck didn't want to repeat that. The one aspect of Boot Camp that nearly tripped Jack up—literally, a few times—was Drill. Green tortured the recruits for what felt like days on the sizzling Parade Deck. They would Drill over and over— marching with the precise footwork of a unified force. For Jack, this came as naturally as ballet to a pig. The entire first week, he kept confusing his right and left. The next couple of weeks, he either strode too long or too short, causing collisions at best and pile-ups more often.

"Recruit Calhoun!"

"Sir! Yes, Sir!"

"Do you know how to walk?"

"Yes, Sir!"

"Were you born with two left feet?"

"No, Sir!"

"As far as I can see, Recruit, you have no excuse for this shocking footwork. You will learn your left from your right, Recruit Calhoun."

"Aye, Aye, Sir!"

"You will learn to march like a Marine or you will get off my Parade Deck."

"Aye, Aye, Sir!"

Phase One's end fast-forwarded into Jack's vision. If he didn't get his act together on the parade deck, he could very well be headed out on a return bus. The thought of that flooded his mind with disappointed faces. After more push-ups than he could count on that Monday morning, Jack's heart sank when they were ushered back out to the steaming asphalt to stand at attention for so long Jack was thankful when Green ordered them to Drill.

"Attention!"

The recruits snapped up as one.

"Right, face!"

With one motion, the entire group faced right.

"Forward, march!"

"Aye, Aye, Sir!"

This time, Jack closed his eyes. He thought of the advice he'd given Dawson.

Lighten up. Breathe. One step at a time.

Slowly, surely, his heart matched the beat of the boots surrounding him. The timing and rhythm finally clicked into place.

He had subconsciously tensed his body for the mistakes he'd come to expect from himself. Instead, he heard the beat of his own feet on the deck. He felt it match with all the others. He had mastered his nemesis.

* * *

Jack found further opportunities to develop his leadership skills when he got sent back to run alongside Dawson. He tossed pointers on breathing and form to his fellow recruit as they ran. He also pushed him ... and managed to cover his shock when Dawson rose, bit by bit, to each challenge.

"Calhoun's setting the pace today." Marshall called out the one bit of news that caused a collective groan in their platoon. Jack had served as guide a few times already as the DIs made the rounds, seeking out potential leaders worthy of a First Class designation. "Recruit Dawson, front and center!"

Everyone exchanged furtive glances. Calhoun in the front? Every day and twice on Sundays. Dawson in the front ... with Calhoun? Their bulldog DI was smoking crack with this one.

Jack didn't look at his running companion as his knuckles paled around the platoon's guidon, their platoon number 3086 fluttering in the breeze at its top. Jack decided he'd lead them on a brisk—but easy for him—run. "Recruit Calhoun, full out. Do not hold back. Do you understand?"

At Jack's hesitation, Marshall barked, "Did I stutter, Recruit Calhoun?"

"No, sir!"

"Is something wrong with your ears? Did God make 'em that big so you can fly but not hear?"

"No, sir!"

Marshall got within inches of Jack's face and lowered his voice. "This is your chance, recruit. Lead, follow or get out of my way."

"Aye, Aye, Sir!"

Jack recalled a line one of their football coaches used to shout at them. "A chain's only as strong as its weakest link." That was Dawson. As the strongest link, it was Jack's task to bridge the gap between them and help this platoon become a stronger chain.

"Full out, Calhoun!" The DI bellowed his final order and stepped back to see what happened.

"Aye, Aye, Sir!"

Jack adjusted the guidon and took off. Dawson resigned himself to his fate and muttered, "This is it then." Jack pounded the concrete with his go-fasters and cranked it up a notch. A few yards in, he heard Dawson's breathing coming ragged already.

"Dawson, this is your choice. You gonna be a Marine one day or not? If you are, this is where you'll earn it. Now, breathe like I taught you." Jack's voice drifted calmly and steadily to the pale, freckle-faced kid next to him. With those words, Dawson straightened.

Jack nodded, eyes facing straight ahead, and yelled, "Let's do this, Dawson." He picked up the pace to a real "full out." Dawson felt like an IED had exploded in his lungs and decided his legs had fallen apart somewhere about three-quarters of the way through, but as they reached their destination, the recruit smiled for the first time ever following a run. And, Jack, finally winded, turned to his bunkmate and gasped, "Dawson, you may just make it after all." He planted the guidon and filed in for showers with his platoon.

Behind the dripping and winded recruits, the DIs huddled to discuss the run. Dubois slapped Marshall on the back and said, "He may just make it after all as well."

"Phase Two will tell."

"Phase Two always tells," Dubois agreed.

* * *

During Grass Week, Jack was in his element. All the hours spent becoming one with his rifle paid off. It was simply an extension of himself at this point. The four firing positions required a bit of practice—he'd never even fathomed the need to lay down to shoot before. Soon the field became as comfortable for him as Senior's woodshop had been. For whatever reason, the weapon—like the tools—felt as natural in Jack's hands as air. He eagerly anticipated the following week, when he would finally get to shoot his rifle.

He blew away the rest of his platoon, hitting his targets nearly every time at each range and from every position. When he had a target in his sights, his entire focus zeroed in; his breathing steadied; his body zoned in to the task at hand. The shooting instructors didn't yell or bark orders. They taught calmly. They reminded calmly. They spoke calmly ... and they listened.

Jack felt this could be a new normal he'd actually get used to. With the strong surety of his rifle in his hands, Jack relaxed for the first time since boarding the bus. He soaked up the instructors' advice and correction. Evenings in the squad bay became a time for him to assist his fellow recruits with their form and precision. It struck him after the day Dawson crossed his hurdle, these men all around him could be the very guys he had to rely on in a firefight. They sure as hell better have a frickin' unbreakable chain. By the end of the week, Jack's platoon had the cleanest weapons and the highest shooting scores, winning their DIs the honor of top Shooting Platoon. Jack was officially an expert rifleman. He held the guidon a little higher that Friday.

With the final physical fitness test coming up, Jack pushed himself harder with every run. He was still just over eighteen minutes for three miles. He could do better. He pushed harder, faster. On test day, he saw his reward at the finish line—17:56. That was the first time Jack smiled in Boot Camp.

Letters poured in throughout the weeks. Mawmaw Mabel, Ducky and Ben wrote him at least once a week each. Ben didn't answer Jack's one unasked but burning question—how was Rachael? Her face had replaced the nightmares he used to have. In some ways he preferred the terrors. Picturing her night after night and knowing he should never see her again left his heart feeling like it'd gone through a shredder. But, during the day, on the long runs and in each challenge, every exhausting or overwhelming moment became suddenly bearable when he pictured her smile. She carried him when he wasn't sure he could carry on.

It was her face that motivated him at that halfway point in the Crucible, the final major challenge of Boot Camp. Fifty-four hours with barely any sleep and very little food under simulated combat conditions are enough to drive anyone nuts. When he felt he could go no further—when the exhaustion had sunk deep within his being and Jack didn't know where he could find another reserve of energy to get him through the remainder of the assault courses and obstacles—it was then that he saw Rachael the clearest. His delirium drifted away. The searing pain in his legs and the itching from being covered in dirt and sweat disappeared when his focus shifted to her image. She was there—in the field in front of him, twirling and laughing. Her red hair fanned around her as she spun in the sunlight. Her lightness and musical mirth gave him much-needed spirit. It was time to finish this. He was so close. His men needed him.

In their simulation, one man was severely wounded. They had to extract him—no Marine left behind. He was heavy— so heavy. Their gear pressed down on their aching shoulders and backs. They'd forgotten the taste of food or the sweet release of sleep.

Ahead, the mirage of his love dissipated. In her place loomed the reality of hidden mines and other dangers. He turned to the men beside him, recognized their desire to give it all up and took charge.

Throughout the Crucible, they'd heard tales of Marine heroes who'd paved their way. They heard of these men's honor in battle, courage in the face of insurmountable odds and commitment to Corps and country. Jack soaked up every story, despite his exhaustion. Each one added fuel to the fire inside him to rise up to the challenge and call of United States Marine and gave him a desire to learn more about the history of the Corps and the warriors who'd made it great. It was their influence, coupled with Rachael's inspiration, that drove him to rally the men around him through the final phase of their grueling ordeal.

"Almost there; we can do this, guys. We're so close. The prize is in sight. For our Marine Corps!"

Their echo brought a moment of emotion, even to crusty Marshall. "For our Marine Corps!"

Jack gave them a game plan they snapped to by hoisting their wounded brother and communicating their way safely across the simulated minefield.

The final task faced them. A nine-mile hike, forty-five pounds of gear, one goal—completion. They buckled down and marched on. Mile by mile slowly passed beneath them until the Marine Corps Memorial stood resolute ahead. The Stars and Stripes rose with the kiss of the dawn's earliest rays, catching in the breeze and snapping to attention at their approach. Jack's throat tightened around the pride he felt at that sight. Just a few more yards. The breeze caressed his damp forehead as its chill cooled the heat of the last nine miles.

All exhaustion sloughed off onto the path as they caught this glorious sight. They arrived at the parade deck where they stood at attention—tall and proud.

First Sergeant Hank Townes spoke the most welcome words as the sun continued to rise. "You have earned the title of United States Marine, and that's something no one can ever take from you."

Jack's breath caught with the realization that he would defend that fluttering flag to his last breath, if necessary. He had made it through the hellish moments, the uncertainties, the self-doubt. He was no longer This Recruit; he was now—and for always—a United States Marine. His drenched shoulders and neck straightened as Marshall made his way down the line toward him, a tray in his arms. Jack knew on that tray rested the prize Senior had instructed him to keep his eye on this whole time.

"Calhoun, I'm proud as hell to be the first to congratulate you ... Marine ... and welcome you to our Corps." He pressed a shiny black Eagle, Globe and Anchor into Jack's left hand before shaking his right. "You better live up to this title!"

"Aye, Aye, Sir!"

Once every Marine received individual congratulations, they relaxed and meandered back to the mess hall for some much-needed chow. Graduation was right around the corner.

"I actually made it, Calhoun! I'm a frickin' Marine!" Jack smiled and returned his bunkmate's embrace. He was pretty sure there wasn't a dry eye in their platoon. And, that was okay. Fifty-four hours of pushing themselves in every possible way, but these guys could move Iwo Jima.

Act III
Implosion

XV

Prepare Like Hell to Go ...

December 6, 2002, through February 2003

Jack woke to darkness and snores on graduation morning. The recruits—now fresh Marines—around him slept on blissfully while he thought through his guest list for the big event. He wasn't sure who all was coming, but Mawmaw Mabel's last letter declared not even the Commandant could stop her from coming—or from bringing goodies. Every letter bemoaned the fact that she couldn't smuggle him contraband and speculated on how skinny he had surely gotten. If anything, Jack thought, he'd gotten thicker. His muscles felt bigger, heavier. He looked down at his arms. They hadn't been that round fourteen weeks ago.

Ben planned to be there as well. Jack had sent one other letter, but he wasn't sure it arrived in time or how it would be received. He'd had no response, so he'd just have to wait and see.

His fellow graduates finally joined him to make their last-minute uniform preparations. Most of them had met with family the day before, but Jack took advantage of that extra time by preparing his uniform for the ceremony, making sure his PFC insignia were on correctly. He even shined his shoes two extra times. As Platoon Guide, he got to wear his dress blues, a privilege reserved for an early promotion to Private First Class. He hadn't written to his adopted family about how well he'd done. Giving them the surprise would be much more fun than writing about it. He was excited and nervous, thankful they'd take the time to be here for him.

He looked again at the uniform. Sharp creases. Exact placements. Rules. Regulations. Jack understood this world. Everything was clear-cut; his way pre-determined. When he put on this uniform, he placed himself in someone else's hands and no longer felt the sense of impending implosion that had haunted him since That Night in Bellum.

Time spun forward, and Jack found himself staring at a sea of people in the stands in front of the parade deck. He stood at attention; his platoon's guidon firmly grasped. No way would he drop it that day. Subconsciously, he knew he was sweating in the heavy uniform, but he didn't give it a single thought. He was a United States Marine, and in those stands were a group of people who believed in him and wanted to celebrate with him. The ceremony passed in a blur, and his heart raced as he heard the words they'd all been listening for: "Senior Drill Instructors, dismiss your platoons!"

With one final, mighty "Aye, Aye, Sir!" each platoon broke up to find loved ones who flooded the parade deck. Jack spotted Senior first. He was decked out in his dress blues. Despite the many years since he'd donned it, the older man looked comfortable, like he'd never worn anything less. The first to reach him, though, was Mawmaw Mabel.

She threw her arms up and pulled him down for a big hug and a kiss on each cheek. "I'm just so proud of you. And, look how handsome you are! Not everyone's wearin' that fancy uniform. I'm so glad you are. It looks so much better than those dull green and khaki things. I've never liked those. You've definitely lost weight, but … don't you worry … I've got a car full of goodies for you. Been baking for the past two weeks. I told Mamie and Betty Sue I just knew they weren't feedin' you right. Was I right? They don't use salt or butter, do they?" As she'd done in her home, Mawmaw Mabel whispered this last bit of culinary blasphemy.

Jack's smile stretched from ear to ear as he realized just how much he'd missed the kind woman's fretting and chatter.

Senior strode up to pull his wife back a bit. "The boy just survived a grueling hell on earth, Mabel; don't talk him to death now."

Ducky and Daisy hugged Jack next. She eagerly showed off her new ring.

"Looks even better on your finger than it did in the box." Jack returned the blushing bride's glowing smile.

"You're too sweet. Ducky picked a perfect one, didn't he?" She raised her sparkling hand to her fiancé's cheek.

"He sure did." Jack agreed. "And the ring's nice, too."

"Hey now! My groomsman's not supposed to flirt with the bride!" Ducky punched Jack's arm as the new Marine's eyes widened.

"Groomsman?"

"Of course … if you can. It won't be until the spring of 2004, so I hope you're not on the beach in Hawaii. I can't picture our big day without you up there by me."

"Man, I'd be honored, and I'll do everything I can to be there." Jack smiled and hugged them each again. "Congrats, you two!"

"Ben!" Jack caught sight of his mentor. As they embraced, Jack's gaze locked with the love-filled golden eyes and forgiving smile of the woman who'd sacrificed her happiness and comfort for his own.

"You came." Jack moved around Ben to his mom's open arms.

"Did you really think I wouldn't?" Full teardrops clung to the corners of her eyes as she held him out for a proper examination. "My sweet Jack ... all grown up. I am so proud of you."

She cupped his cheek as she studied the face of a man where just yesterday had resided her boy's carefree impishness. Jack caught Becky by surprise as he swung her around in a wide circle before giving her a proper bear hug.

Once her laughter had subsided and his grip had loosened, Jack searched her expression as he asked, "Will you forgive me for leaving like I did?"

"Oh, Sweetie ... of course I forgive you. My heart ached for you because you have always been the sunshine in my life, but I understood. I knew why you needed to leave. You needed clarity Bellum's chaos didn't allow. I saw that." Becky placed a hand over her son's beating heart and held his gaze as she continued. "I'm so happy you sent me that letter. You made my year!"

"I love you, mama!" Jack pressed a kiss to her forehead.

His entourage had stood nearby during the reunion, so Jack made introductions around the circle before returning to Ben for a continuation of their greeting. Ben noticed the quick, searching look Jack sent over his shoulder. "She doesn't know I'm here … or that you're here, for that matter. I've kept your secret, like I promised."

Jack swallowed his disappointment and replaced it with the conviction that he made the correct choice for the woman he loved. "Thank you."

Mawmaw Mabel wrapped Becky up in a motherly hug. "I just love that sweet boy of yours, and I'm so proud he finally told you what he was up to. It's about time I get to meet his sweet mama. I told Missy Mee—that's my little pup—and I told her a hundred times how much I wished he'd call his mama. A boy needs his mama … whether he realizes it or not. Plus, I wanted to give you a great big ol' hug."

Becky laughed as the little lady finally paused to breathe. "Thank you so much for taking care of my Jack. He's been a little lost for far too long." The women looked over at him as he and Ducky pretended to box each other. Becky's smile held a hint of hope as she said, "Perhaps he's finding his way now, despite it all."

The entire group headed out for a celebratory meal. Their time together was full of non-stop chatter as they caught up on everything that had happened over the past few months—and longer for Becky. The group from Columbia filled her in on how her son arrived and fit right in with them. The Marines swapped stories, and everyone laughed at the tales of gas chamber tears, barely edible food—that caused much head-shaking from Mawmaw Mabel—and stories about hardcore drill instructors. When they discussed the contents of MREs, Mawmaw Mabel clutched her chest in horror. The meals may have been ready to be eaten, but the Marines who relied on them for sustenance weren't always ready for their tastes and textures.

"First MRE I pulled on the Crucible, I got the four fingers of death." Jack recalled his misfortune with a grimace.

Senior answered the unspoken questions of the civilians at the table. "Worst field meal you can get these days. 'Sposed to be hot dogs of some sort, but they look like severed fingers."

"Taste ten times worse," Jack added.

After appropriate reactions to the mental image, Senior asked, "Which DI had it out for you?"

Jack shot him a quizzical look but offered, "Sergeant Marshall rode my butt the entire training."

Senior said, "You know he pulled that out special for you, right?"

In response to Jack's clear confusion, Senior continued, "Ev'ry so often, there'll be a DI that chooses a guy to ride harder than the others. The kid he wants to push to his breaking point quickly, so he can improve faster and motivate the others. DI'll do everything from pairin' the kid with the weakest bunkmate to pushin' him beyond normal physical bounds to stayin' in his face even for minute flaws … and pullin' the nastiest MREs just for him."

"Congrats, Jack. You were Marshall's guy!" Ben chuckled as he lifted his glass of water in a celebratory salute.

Jack shook his head and grinned as moments over the last few months popped up in his memories with new meaning. "You think I lived up to desired expectations?"

"Who gave you your emblem?" Senior asked.

"Marshall."

"There's your answer."

As Jack's group rose to leave the restaurant, Private Dawson walked past with his family. As soon as Dawson introduced Jack to his parents, Mrs. Dawson, a plump little lady with red cheeks and evergreen eyes, grabbed his hands in hers and said, "Thank you. You helped my boy through, and I can never find a way to thank you for that. This uniform has been his dream since he was a tiny kid, and you helped him achieve it."

Jack considered the impact his leadership had made within his platoon. He flashed back to the night he wanted to chuck Dawson across the squad bay for interrupting him. It never occurred to Jack then that this kid had placed his life-long dream on a delicate balance in Jack's own hands. He hadn't considered the profound effect his words would make the morning of their full-out run either. He saw it standing in front of him—ramrod straight and Devil Dog proud.

Dawson's switch from dangling by a fingertip to a superhuman resolve to hoist himself up and over had replayed itself in the guys Jack took the last field simulation with during the Crucible. Maybe—just maybe—he could improve that skill over the years and eventually earn some more stripes and stars, even. This could be more than just a layover for him.

***

Becky and Jack spent some extra time one-on-one after they ate. He had grown up more than he realized since the spring that felt much more than a couple of seasons ago. He found himself in a new relationship of sorts with the woman who'd always cared for him. She was still his mom, but he was no longer her little boy. He was the man she'd raised.

"Thank you for all the money you've sent, Jack. It's made a big difference in my life." Becky smiled up at her son, as she wondered if he'd actually grown taller. "But, I don't want to keep taking your money. You need to start saving for your own future."

Jack took his mom's hands in his own. "Mama, sending you that money is the proudest thing I've ever done. There's no way I'm gonna stop now. Don't worry; I'm being wise with my money. I'm saving and investing most of it. Living on a military base, I don't need to spend a whole lot on basic necessities. Plus, I'm pretty sure they're not going to give me enough free time to get in any trouble."

Their jovial mood faded to serious. Becky said, "I do understand why you left Bellum. I really do, but I need you to ask yourself if you're running from a past you haven't dealt with. Too much bad happened to you too young. It's a lot to process for anyone, let alone a teenager. And, I know you've never really talked to me about anything—which is fine. You just need to have someone you confide in, someone who can guide your thoughts as you seek to make sense of it all."

"Ben has been incredible. He and Senior have a way of getting me to see things from a different perspective." He lowered his head as he considered his next statement. "When I set out, I was running; but I didn't feel like I had a choice. Once I decided to enlist, though, that running changed. For the first time, I'm running with a purpose."

"Just as long as you're not trying to run with the burden of your past strapped on. That'll eventually weigh you down, especially since this purpose you've chosen isn't exactly an easy one." Becky's eyes grew misty as she searched her son's face. "That storm that began brewing on 9-11 is ramping up, and it's had a lot of time to grow into a massive tempest. Have you thought through what war could mean for you—what pain it could add to the past you may not have fully left behind?"

Jack placed his hands on his mom's shoulders as he replied, "Guys like Senior and his buddies have been there. They've talked to me, answered my questions—even when I haven't known how to ask them. I'm as ready as I can be. This world's full of hate and evil. If I can take down any piece of that, then it's worth the cost to me."

"I'm so proud of you, my sweet boy." Becky placed her hands atop her son's. "But, as your mama, you know I worry. Just what will that cost be, especially if you're running forward under a weight you don't have to carry?"

His mom's words rushed through him, rippling the curtain of his heart and revealing the truth of what he sought to hide from everyone, including himself. He pulled her to his chest as he rested his chin on her head. "Don't you worry about me, Mama. I know this decision is the right one. Whatever lies ahead, I have to believe this path will help me at least make up for some of my past mistakes. I've got great people in my corner—you, them." He nodded over to the group of friends approaching to say their goodbyes. "I'm gonna be just fine."

Becky did her best to smile at him. The tightness in her chest squeezed her breath as she kissed his cheek. She did then what she'd done every day of Jack's life—she prayed for the child God had given her and lifted him and all his needs up to his Creator. It was the most she could do.

* * *

Jack enjoyed the normalcy of an evening with his family and friends, but he didn't regret passing up his ten-day leave. He was ready to get to the next stage of his training, settle in and get back into the field. He was a Marine and couldn't imagine himself doing anything but continuing his training. His trigger finger itched to shoot, and he didn't want to lose the momentum of his run times.

Once he arrived at Camp Geiger, Jack had a full week before Infantry Training Battalion—ITB—kicked off. Plenty of time for him to learn where everything was and who to talk to about further learning. The Crucible's simulated combat situations made him want to learn more about military tactics. He discovered he could take courses through MCI—the Marine Corps Institute. Perhaps missing out on his final years in high school made him crave knowledge. He made a list of some of the subjects he wanted to take and added a few he knew would help him get to the next rank more quickly. He'd never been anywhere near the top of the class, but Boot Camp showed him he liked the view there.

As training ramped up again, Jack thrust every ounce of energy into it. The few times he struggled with a new concept, he focused harder and practiced longer. In the classroom, Jack furiously scrawled notes. In his rack that night, he'd rewrite them and write a third time anything that wasn't sticking. He was one of the few who was okay with running everywhere. In the field, he observed his fellow Marines whenever possible. Through assessing his brothers, he recognized strengths and weaknesses in each. With his easy-going nature, it didn't take long for them to accept his observations—both positive and negative—with appreciation ... and a bit of awe. He earned the nickname Eagle Eye, both for his ability to advise everyone around him and for his expert rifle skills.

Jack settled easily into the Marine way of life—the schedule, the discipline, the clear expectations. He knew what was required of him and ... best of all ... he could deliver it most of the time. Above all of this was the constant reminder that he was part of something bigger than himself and that he could, in some small way, make a difference in the world. Tensions continued to rise in the Middle East, and Jack was ready to answer the call to promote peace. Deeper inside—on a level he didn't care to admit—Jack wanted to carry his pain with him to the desert and leave it there.

Nightmares reared their heads a few times, especially after particularly intense training days. One night he woke up screaming. Looking around, Jack saw his buddies in the squad bay surrounding him, on high alert. He apologized and shook his head to clear it. Some of the guys gave him wary looks as they returned to their racks.

"Maybe Harrington should sing you a lullaby before bed," Private Matchiss joked to dispel the darkness that had settled like a shroud around them.

Private First Class Trayvon Henry slept across from Jack and accepted he wouldn't be falling back to sleep any time soon after the jarring alarm. He joined the flushed and disheveled Marine on his rack instead of staying in his own to toss and turn. He leaned toward Jack and said, "You need to get those night terrors under control. You know that, right?"

"It's been a while since I've had one; I'm not really sure why I still have them sometimes. I am sorry I woke you up." He ignored the true cause of their wake-up call and shared about the night he lost four classmates. No one needed to hear about the tiny face that haunted him most. Jack nodded at the one guy who was giving him a run for his money on the shooting range. "Man, where'd you learn to shoot?"

Tray shook the somber realization that this was a fellow Marine who had already witnessed death in real life; something he knew lay in his future. He replaced that heavy thought with a grin and replied, "Corps taught me. I never shot a day in my life until Boot. The instructors say it's easier for someone who doesn't have to unlearn everything they already know just to relearn it different. I guess they're right."

"Seems like it. I didn't have much more experience than you." Jack replied. In those early morning hours after Jack's terrors, he and Tray sparked a friendship that centered mostly around shooting.

Jack stayed awake with his guilt most of the next week. He knew no one trusted a guy who could wake up screaming in the middle of enemy territory. This was the only time he'd ever woken up like that here. Typically, he'd simply thrash himself awake. Still not ideal for stealth sleeping in a combat zone.

More often, though, Jack's sleep carried him to a plain of pleasure where Rachael remained part of his life. She waited for him to finish training and come home to her. He'd reach her, drop to a knee and open the little velvet box like he'd wanted to do so very long ago—had it really been less than a year? Her warming smile, those captivating blue eyes under curling lashes, thick red hair and every precious freckle that decorated her cheeks and nose ... each detail of her face imprinted on his mind's eye. He would pull the vision of her up when he needed an extra boost in the field or when he found himself missing home. Without fail, Rachael would give him whatever it was he needed in that moment. She was his unfailing compass, always pointing him straight.

* * *

A few weeks in, Jack's platoon got to choose their specialty. Jack didn't think twice when he requested 0311. He was a born rifleman. The powers that be didn't disagree with him ... or Trayvon. Both of them poured themselves further into the specialized training. Jack ate, slept and breathed shooting. When his group got their first liberty, his friends primped and preened to head to the bars and taste some of the local flavor. Jack had found out where a local range was, and he and Tray had already reserved time to shoot.

Matchiss howled when he heard Jack's plans. "Who forgot to tell Eagle Eye he could potentially sleep with a woman tonight instead of his weapon—if he heads to a real dim-lit bar, that is? Don't you get enough of that crap every day?"

"Never," Jack replied with a grin as he headed out the door.

Harvey's Shooting Range became Jack's home away from base in Jacksonville. Every chance he got, Jack hung out on the range. It kept him away from the seduction of bars. He still found himself longing for whiskey—usually when he was exhausted or bored. He saw no need to tempt his resolve, so he became part of an inner circle of former military guys who met to exchange stories and give each other some friendly shooting competition. The eclectic shooting club willingly accepted Jack and Tray. For their part, the Marines brought some young blood to the group. They also solidified their friendship across from targets and turned it into a bond over whittling. Tray showed Jack the shop on base where he snagged end pieces of wood.

"It's not the highest quality, but it's good to whittle away at until something emerges." Tray studied the block he had just picked up. Jack saw his friend's wheels turning and wondered how long it would take him to see the horse rearing its impatience to be released from the wood. Jack stared intently. Yes, there were the legs. Here, definitely, was the mane and the tail. He could almost see the breeze lifting the strands of each in an imaginary wind. He hadn't realized how much he'd missed the feel and smell of wood and the satisfaction of pulling a lifelike creature from an inanimate block.

"Where'd you learn to whittle?" Jack finally asked his friend one unusually quiet Saturday afternoon.

Tray smiled, but the darkness in his eyes and the emotion in his voice told Jack his past lay darkened by loss. "My dad. He was amazing. He made this hummingbird once ... I'll have to show you a picture. That's the one possession I have that was too special to risk bringing here. I left it at my Grandma's. Anyway, this hummingbird, man, I swear it looks like it's flyin'. I still have no clue how he could put so much life into his pieces."

Jack didn't ask the question he wanted to, but he was sure his face did. Tray continued as he made a few adjustments to the piece in his hand and turned an alligator into a lizard. "My parents went to D.C. for their anniversary. I was eight, staying with my grandparents. Dad and mom never went anywhere together—just the two of them. They usually had me tagging along, but this was special—they were celebrating a decade of marriage. They took a wrong turn and got a flat tire. My dad got out to change it." Tray's voice cracked, and his knife stalled mid-slice. "Car drove by—kids trying to prove themselves for a gang spot. They unloaded their guns. My parents were dead before the car took the next corner."

Both Marines sat motionless, reflecting on the horror of a boy's realization that he's suddenly an orphan. "We were supposed to get ice cream together when they got home," Tray continued. "Amazing how quickly a mundane weekend can turn into a living nightmare."

He shook his head, as if to clear out the terror of that time. "But, you know, I've got the most precious Grandma on the planet. She loves others and she loves Jesus. There's not a thing on earth Grandma Ethel wouldn't do for another person. She's been good to me. She's the one who taught me all about God's forgiveness and how we can forgive, too. And, her sweet potato pie will make you believe heaven is an eternity of eatin' it."

They turned their attention back to the wood in their hands and crafted in silence until Tray spoke again. "Whenever we get time away on the weekends, I head over to a community center in my old neighborhood to join in some pickup basketball games with the guys there. You wanna join me sometime?" Tray grinned. "If you can ball, that is."

Jack shook his head. "Don't worry about me. I can hold my own."

"We'll see about that. Just try not to embarrass me too bad."

* * *

The Marine instructors picked up on Jack and Tray's dedication to the art of shooting. Jack was always too zoned in to notice, but he also attracted attention from some of the higher NCOs—non-commissioned officers—whenever he shot. On one of those occasions, Sergeant Major Dwight Strickland asked Master Gunnery Sergeant Trevor Browntree, "Have you had a discussion yet with Calhoun about his future?"

"Not yet. I've been thinkin' I should."

"Background like his, I'd hope you would. We need to keep him close and get him ready to slide in to Scout Sniper as soon as he's eligible." Strickland kept his focus on Jack during his entire round. "I want to see his daggone groupings after they finish."

"Copy."

Jack studied his targets as he always did after shooting, looking for ways to improve. Browntree approached him and jumped straight to the point. "Calhoun, that was some frickin' outstanding shooting. What are your goals in the Corps, Marine?"

"Thank you, Master Gunnery Sergeant. I just want to be the best Marine rifleman I can be to serve and defend my country."

"That's outstanding, Calhoun. But, have you thought about more?"

"Not sure I follow, Master Gunnery Sergeant."

"The Scout Sniper Course over at Lejeune. You thought about that?"

"I hadn't, but anything with shootin's got my full attention."

"Outstanding. Keep it in mind, Marine. We'll be keeping our eyes on you until you rank up."

"What happens next, though? After ITB, I mean." Jack tossed out the question he'd been chewing on since before they even began training.

Browntree crossed his hands behind his back as he evaluated the newly minted Marine in front of him. "You'll either hit the Fleet or advance your training. You may head to Lejeune for the designated marksman course."

He continued to consider Jack as he rocked back and forth in his boots. He saw a hint of fire in the boy's eyes that told him this Marine had something special in him.

"Do you think we're going to war, Master Gunnery Sergeant?" Jack could tell he nearly caught the seasoned Maverick off guard with that one. The response he received was one he'd never forget.

"Prepare like hell to go; pray to heaven we don't."

XVI

... Pray to Heaven We Don't

February 10, 2003, through December 2004

Jack and Tray took the twenty-minute hop over to Camp Lejeune following ITB graduation to continue their training as designated marksmen. Their training at Geiger, with added time at Harvey's range, had more than prepared them for the new rifle challenges. From there, they filed into the 3rd Battalion, 8th Marines, where training remained an ongoing part of life. Such was the life of a rifleman—physical training, field exercises, shooting, more PT; shower, rinse, repeat.

They did have more free time, though. Jack used his to hit the library. His first checkouts included books on his regiment's famous battles of the past—Okinawa, Tarawa and Guadalcanal. Understanding the history he was part of lit a fire under Jack to be the best for its future. He continued taking MCI courses and worked his way from Math for Marines up the list, learning everything he could get his hands on. His days bounced from chow to training to studying to shooting.

The United States launched its invasion of Iraq on Jack's nineteenth birthday. The cold, rainy day matched his emotions.

"Hey man! You wanna grab a burger or somethin' to celebrate?" Tray asked when he found his friend staring out a window at the dampness.

"A burger would be good to go."

Jack didn't say much as they scarfed down a few square burgers at the food court. Tray licked his fingers and wiped them on his napkin before asking the question that had been dancing on his lips since they'd sat down. "Spill it. What's got ya' lookin' like that gloomy cartoon donkey?"

Despite himself, Jack had to laugh. Tray did have a way of making him talk.

"It's just hard to think about celebrating when so many guys are on the ground right now, you know? I'm just ready to be there." He pulled pickles off his last burger and popped them all in his mouth before continuing. "I keep thinking about Dawson—guy from Boot. He's in the 3/2. He was the one I encouraged along and came to think of like a kid brother. He's got the skills, but he needs to keep his focus and confidence. And keep his head down."

Tray nodded and smiled. "He's a Marine. He will. Just like we will when the 8th gets its shot."

"Hoorah!" Jack responded as they stood with their trays.

"We've got liberty next weekend. You up for some ball?" Tray asked as they dumped their trash and headed back across base. Jack knew Tray's grandmother lived nearby because his friend came back many Sundays with tales of her cooking.

The usual glimmer returned to Jack's eyes. "Depends ... do I get some of that sweet potato pie you rave about?"

"That could be arranged." Tray grinned his response.

***

Weekend liberty arrived and found Jack going somewhere other than Harvey's for the first time since arriving in Jacksonville. He proved to Tray he could hold his own on the court.

"Good game, man!" Lewan Johnson had eyed Jack with suspicion when they ended up on a team together. By Jack's second basket, he started seeing him in a different light. The fifth time Jack spun around Eli Chalmers, the best defender Lewan had ever played with, he transformed into a fan.

"Back at ya'!" Jack responded with a handshake before he finished toweling off the sweat. "You go to school around here?"

"Yeah. Just down the street there. I graduate in a few weeks." Lewan chugged down some water. "Been thinkin' bout joinin' the Corps ever since Trayvon did. Why'd you join?"

"I wanted to do something bigger than I could in a regular job. I wanted to really make a difference. When I watched the Towers fall, I felt the call to defend my country. Took me a while, but I finally answered it."

Lewan looked down at the basketball he fingered. He tossed Jack's answer around as he carefully chose his next question. Without raising his eyes, he asked, "You scared?"

"To go to war?" Lewan met Jack's eyes and nodded. "Of course I'm scared, but that doesn't mean I'm not ready. Freedom's a helluva lot bigger than fear. The Corps trained me to use my rifle efficiently and effectively, so I'm ready to defend freedom. No one deserves to live under a tyrant's boot."

"Any regrets on signing with the Marines?"

"Not one." Jack shook his head as if trying to shake off something too inconceivable to consider. "They broke me down and reassembled me into something I never could have been on my own. I'm squared away now, focused and driven. I never would have used those words to describe me before."

"Any advice to get ready for Boot Camp then?" Lewan's smile lit his face, and Jack could tell the boy had just chosen his future.

"Run. A lot." Jack laughed. "Seriously, just being in great shape will help with the physical stuff. Keep yourself out of trouble. Also, stop thinking of yourself as an individual. They'll drill that out of you in Boot Camp, but start getting used to the idea now. The quicker you figure out a way to work with the guys around you, the better off you'll be. Those guys who go in with you and get screamed at alongside you and screw up and cause you all to run extra, those same guys are your brothers. They'll be the ones to have your back in a war zone. Make sure you've got theirs."

"Like you guys?" Lewan nodded over to Tray who was surrounded by a group of junior high boys. They were all trying to knock the ball out of the hand he held high above his six four frame.

"Exactly like us. We've trained together every day for a while now. I know he's one of the absolute best riflemen around. If something were to happen and I had to rely on him to have my back, I could trust him with my life."

"Not sure I can trust anybody that much."

"I wasn't either. It comes down to losing that individual mindset in Boot Camp. Once I did, I saw myself as one link in a chain. When we work together to strengthen our weaker links, that chain only gets stronger."

Tray burst out of the circle, tossing the ball over his shoulder. He joined Jack and Lewan.

"I made my decision," Lewan said. "I'm joining the Marines as soon as I graduate."

"Man, I've been working on this kid for over a year. You get five minutes with him, and he's signin' on the dotted line?"

"Everyone knows I'm the more charismatic speaker of the two of us," Jack laughed.

"Says the man who uttered a grand total of two dozen words on our last five liberties combined." Tray shook his head before adding, "And half of those were to his rifle."

"I don't need as many words as you to make a point."

"Yeah, yeah. Come on, man. There's a sweet potato pie with my name on it, and that's one date I won't keep waitin'."

"Only date you'll ever get." Jack rolled his eyes as he followed Tray out to his beat-up, apple red Ford Ranger.

* * *

Grandma Ethel met them at the front door of her tiny one-bedroom home. She clearly had a green thumb in addition to a magical whisking hand. Under each window on the front of her white house, planters overflowed with flowers in every color of the rainbow. Beneath them, her flower beds showcased more of the same talent. Jack recalled the glow on Rachael's face whenever she talked about her mom's green thumb. He remembered chasing her around her mom's vibrant garden when they were just kids. They were ten when he snuck his first kiss. Only the host of bright rose bushes saw his awkward peck on the sweet lips that matched their hue. Jack shook his head to return to reality and greet the little lady walking their way.

"There's my boy! You get up here right now and give your ol' grandma a hug and a kiss." Grandma Ethel's gray hair was pulled back into a tight bun. Her eyes twinkled, and all the lines on her face spoke of a lifetime full of laughter despite loss. The pockets of her green ivy apron overflowed with spatulas, dish rags and oven mitts, and the timer clipped to the top of one sounded its reminder right as Tray bent over to scoop her up in a bear hug.

"Is that for my pie, Grandma?" His nose was already aimed toward the open door.

"You know it is. Now, you take these and get it out of the oven while I welcome this sweet boy I've heard so much about." She pressed a pair of mitts into Tray's hands and pushed past him with arms open to Jack.

"I had no idea your grandson thought of me as sweet. It's nice to finally meet you, Mrs. Henry." Jack returned her hug, a smile stretching his face.

"Lord have mercy! You call me Grandma Ethel, same as every other child for miles around." She continued in a whisper, "I added the sweet part. My Tray's not one for flowery speech, but I've learned to find the pretty bits amidst all the weeds he spits out."

"He certainly is a talker, ma'am," Jack replied as she took his hand and led him through the house to a brightly lit kitchen.

Jack's eyes shifted to a giant bay window on his left. Hanging pots and planters covered the space in front of it. They held more herbs than Jack had ever seen in one place. He thought again of Rachael and how much she'd love to cook with those. The next thing he noticed was Tray holding one of two sweet potato pies up to his nose. He was breathing deeply with a look of pure bliss lighting up his face.

"You put that pie down right now, 'fore you snort out a booger on it, Marcus Trayvon. You boys go wash up. Supper's all ready and waitin' for you. We'll eat first and chat later."

"Smells amazing." Jack's nose was working about as hard as his friend's as she shooed them out of her kitchen with the slap of a damp dish towel.

They passed photos of Grandma Ethel and her husband Edwin. Tray had told Jack how they had lost him the year before to a heart attack. Jack noticed a family portrait that must have been taken soon before Tray's parents were shot. Grandma Ethel's house was full of reminders of the loved ones she'd lost, but her cheeks were rosier and her smile wider than a person who'd never known pain.

Jack worked up a lather around the bar of soap in his hand. He considered the suds as his mind wandered. What force could keep such visible joy flowing from people who'd experienced loss like Tray and his grandma had? He watched the bubbles pop as the water carried them and the grime they'd lifted off his hands down and away. As Jack gently patted his hands dry on the tiny guest towel, he envisioned Grandma Ethel carefully sewing it, adding a pinch of love with each stitch. He put the towel back in its spot and decided he could use a little of whatever it was Tray and his grandma had that made them content.

The dinner companions held hands around the wobbly metal table in the kitchen as Tray blessed the fried chicken, greens, mashed potatoes and cornbread and the hands that made it all. Conversation came easily as Grandma Ethel pulled details out of Jack about his past, including how he'd said goodbye to his mom and girlfriend. She scolded him for leaving his mama in silence for so long in a way that was so kind, he wished he could go back in time and do better.

Tray's eyes lit up as his grandma delivered heaping plates of dessert. Jack discovered in his first bite that his friend's praise for his grandma's signature dish hadn't done it justice. The filling set off a flavor bomb in his mouth as soon as he bit down and the crust melted away to a buttery silkiness that offset the bold spices in exactly the right way. Jack took seconds even though he was ready to roll out the door as it was. He knew he'd regret it if he didn't have another piece— even if PT would be hell on Monday.

The car ride back to base coasted silently except for the occasional boom of thunder from the storm around them. Tray broke in, "Thanks for coming with me to the center— and for talkin' to Lewan. I did all the hard work on him, but I suppose I can share the glory with you."

"Gee, thanks, man!" Jack grinned. "They're good kids."

Silence filled the space between the thunder's rumbles again before Tray nodded thoughtfully. "At the end of the day, these kids just want to belong to something. Be part of something. Know someone cares. Some look to gangs, but they know they're built on lies. Even more, they want to know that someone else turned out okay despite all the worry he couldn't power through his past to turn out into anything—good or bad."

"I suppose I fit that category pretty well." Jack watched a bolt of lightning rip the heavens apart. "By all accounts, I shouldn't be where I am."

"You ever gonna tell me the whole reason for those nightmares of yours?"

Jack gave a half chuckle at the way his friend saw through him before he gave a slow nod and turned to Tray. "Yeah. One day."

***

Whenever Jack sat still too long, he grew restless. So, when he wasn't on duty or training or shooting or whittling, he studied. Gunnery Sergeant Carl Brighton had kept a close eye on Jack since his arrival at Lejeune. One early summer afternoon he watched the young Marine carrying another bundle of course packets back to his squad bay. "Calhoun, what're you gonna do when MCI runs out of courses for you?"

"Well, Gunny, I reckon I'll work my way through all the books in our libraries." Jack smiled, though he realized he was half serious. Never in a million years would he have pictured himself as a book nerd.

"That's good to go, Calhoun. See you in the field. Better be ready to run in the mornin'. Your company's butts have been draggin'. Too much beer, I think."

"It's about time you give me a challenge, Gunny. I'm gettin' bored around here. No beer to sweat out of this Marine. Hoorah!"

"Careful what you ask for, Marine!"

Jack may have regretted his statements toward the end of the nine-mile hike—more like sprint—the next morning. His fellow Marines definitely did. He hadn't figured on Brighton letting everyone know that morning's run was brought to them courtesy of PFC Calhoun's boredom. That taught him when to keep the boasting to himself.

While Jack didn't care for the summer heat any more than he had when he had baked on roofs, he didn't complain. They had plenty of water whenever they went on hikes or into the field for training or shooting. Any time he thought about cursing the heat, he thought of Dawson and his other brothers in the desert across the world.

Time passed steadily until the seasons morphed again. Jack welcomed the cooler mornings and evenings and increased his distance on the personal night runs he took. A couple of those nights each week, he'd kick it in high gear and push himself to shave a millisecond off his time. Running cleared the haunting memories from his mind, allowing him one space of peace.

***

One Monday Brighton instructed Jack to stop by the First Sergeant's office. Though he couldn't think of a thing he'd done to warrant a reprimand, Jack felt his nerves pop as he approached Smith Hall. First Sergeant Mack Thornton called Jack into his office. What stood out about the man behind the desk was his face. It bore the trenches and battle lines of a born Marine.

Thornton's gruff voice filled the office, even with its high ceilings. "At ease, PFC Calhoun. I won't keep you long; no one wants to miss chow time. You are eligible for promotion to Lance Corporal, and I have signed the necessary paperwork for that to happen this fall."

Jack's chest swelled as he managed to utter a respectable, "Thank you, First Sergeant."

"Continue doing an outstanding job, Marine, and I'll see you back here in a few months. In the meantime, your Gunny's proposed you for the Scout Sniper Course. From what I've seen, you're more than qualified. Would that be something you're interested in pursuing?"

"Absolutely, First Sergeant! It would be an honor."

"Outstanding, Marine. And, it is an honor. You'll be representing your unit. We expect your best—all in."

"Yes, First Sergeant."

"Scout Sniper's got a high attrition rate, but we don't want one of ours to be a statistic." Thornton's gaze bore through Jack as though he could see his future. "From everything I've seen and heard, I believe you can do this. I'm not used to being proven wrong."

"Understood."

"We'll get you into SSC after the new year. Gunny Brighton will be in touch with you about that. He'll need you to fill out some paperwork once your promotion's finalized."

"That's outstanding, First Sergeant. Thank you."

"Hoorah, Marine."

Jack floated out of the hall with a rarely displayed smile.

* * *

Sunday dinners around Grandma Ethel's tiny table became an event Jack looked forward to all week. At Thanksgiving, Jack took Tray and his grandma to Columbia with him to meet the Millers and his mom. Ducky and Daisy filled him in on all the plans for their April 10 wedding. They'd chosen bright yellow and white for their wedding colors; fitting, considering their mutual fondness for ducks. Jack promised to get fitted for his tux before he headed back to the base.

Mawmaw Mabel fretted over his skinniness and caused him to add an extra mile onto his daily runs. She and Grandma Ethel conspired to fatten him up the best they could. Jack and Tray enjoyed military chats with Senior, though they drifted into serious territory as they discussed the news. Tray was inducted into the Hardy's Crap 'n' Coffee Club and quickly earned the moniker Checker King.

Jack and his mom poured over old pictures from his childhood and swapped book recommendations. She shared the good news that his financial gifts had allowed her to drop her second job and swap out the factory job she'd always loathed for one she'd always wanted—at the Bellum Library.

When it was time to say goodbye, it was with a sense of joyful normalcy that Jack couldn't remember experiencing before.

* * *

The new year brought new training. Both Jack and Tray earned spots in the Scout Sniper Course that Jack soon realized would be his toughest training yet. Sergeant Henry Thomson proved himself a no-nonsense trainer who ran his men hard and missed nothing. Even the tiniest errors couldn't slip past him. His Marines practically lived in the field throughout the course and then, well past exhausted, they trained behind the optics.

Early on, Jack learned that he could overcome any exhaustion-induced weakness by controlling his breathing. Like a piano teacher setting a metronome for his students, Thomson struck a breathing rhythm for the men under his instruction. Those who couldn't follow the beat, washed out.

Jack kept running. And breathing. Sighting-In on his targets. Hitting the bullseye. Running, running, breathing. Always breathing. Steady—in, out, in, out ...

Breathe in. Breathe out. Steady now. Deep breath. And hold.

Near the end of his training, Jack made an unpardonable mistake. He failed their hide construction exercise. A sniper's most important asset is his stealth. He must creep to the heart of his enemy's stronghold undetected and become one with the terrain. Once his task is realized, his extraction requires equal precision. Even the most miniscule indication of a sniper's presence can endanger his mission or his team's lives.

"Marines, today's exercise is simple." Thomson strode back and forth, hands behind his back, his unblinking gaze observing and assessing each man before him. "You must construct an ideal hide from which to observe your enemy. You will be given the tools you need and eight hours in which to complete your task. At that time, we will send observers out. They will observe from 300 yards and 150 yards before your instructors will narrow the field for them. You will then fire a blank. If your muzzle blast doesn't give you away, we will guide the observer to 25 yards. At any point you are spotted, your team fails."

The snipers-in-training chorused a "Hoorah!" as they grabbed picks, axes, shovels and sandbags. Jack and Tray had paired up enough to rarely need words to communicate. They chose an ideal location and set themselves to altering the earth's structure to look as if it had always contained two inhabitants with their gear and weapons.

Carefully, methodically, they removed patches of earth and set them aside until they'd dug their pit deep and wide enough. Jack moved on to dig and slope a sump, the vital drainage hole, while Tray began on the wall construction. Jack joined in to complete that and then cover it all with the grass clumps and other vegetation until only one exit remained.

After placing all their tools and gear neatly inside the hide, the Marines belly-crawled inside and barricaded themselves. Jack took up the sniper position and finished ensuring the camouflage of his rifle while Tray sat to his right, binoculars poised, ready to observe and calculate.

"Ten minutes to spare. Outstanding!" Tray fist bumped Jack as they settled in and prepared for the observer to enter the field.

In this elite class, each team passed the 300-yard observation. A couple got picked out at 150 yards. The observer's range was narrowed in on them then, and each sniper shot a blank in his direction. A couple muzzle blasts didn't stand up to close inspection.

Finally. 25 yards.

Jack felt his heartrate quicken. Out of the corner of his eye, he saw Tray clench his jaw. They were almost there. They may just pass this.

The observer pointed here, there, there. The hidden teams watched as those classmates were shown their mistakes.

Once more, the observer pointed.

Jack's heart sank into the cool earth beneath him.

When the pair exited to see what they had done wrong, Jack noticed it immediately. Sticking out of the midst of some pine needles shone a silver flash that may as well have been a giant white flag.

Never before had Jack failed a mission. This time, though, he failed hard. As he recalled how he had quickly shoved the gum wrapper in his pocket on the way to the exercise, Jack wanted to sink into the hide and never come out again. He knew better.

He'd gotten his team spotted, and they ended the training exercise KIA. Killed in Action.

"The Commandant extends his deepest sympathy to you and your family in your loss."

Jack looked at Tray. "I'm so sorry, man." They stood on the side of the field to await the conclusion of the exercises ... and Thomson's judgment. It fell with fury on Jack as soon as the instructor strode over.

"Calhoun! Was gum on your list of approved tools for the construction of a hide?"

"No, Sergeant."

"Maybe you thought you'd get bored or need a sticky substance to add some pinups to your wall in there. Whatever caused the cessation of intelligent thinking in your brain today gave away your position and led your team to slaughter."

Thomson stood squarely facing Jack. "You will not make this mistake again, Marine." He inched closer until Jack felt the heat of the instructor's condemning breath on his face. "When snipers make a mistake, Calhoun, they die. When they really screw up, they get other Marines killed. This will be the last mistake you make in my Course. Is that understood?"

"Yes, Sergeant."

Every error of this magnitude deserved punishment. Jack pulled on his full gear and ran—full out—until his calves ached, his thighs burned and his lungs flamed. Until his mind could no longer replay those words, *led your team to slaughter.* He'd led Steven to slaughter. The other kids that died senselessly that night. He'd caused it all.

Five hundred meters out and back. Jack was numb— inside and out.

"Now, shoot."

Jack watched himself lift his rifle in place and observed as his fingers found their proper spots, though he felt nothing. An echo pulsed in his brain—*led your team to slaughter.*

A tiny pixie face, frozen in pain forever.

Three shots. Three failures.

"Again, Marine."

Jack had never missed his target before. He ran—back and forth—the judgement pounding with each heartbeat and bootfall. *Led your team to slaughter.* This time, he saw a collage of faces as he ran.

Down. Set. Shoot, shoot, shoot. Too high.

Led your team to slaughter.

"Again."

Full out. Back. Forth. In. Out. Inhale. Exhale.

Lighten up. Breathe. One step at a time.

Like a dense fog dissipating before the sun's beams, Jack's head cleared; his thoughts crystallized.

You better live up to this title. Jack saw the Eagle, Globe and Anchor pressed into his palm.

Senior's lined face rose next in his mental vision. *Each piece gets sanded, shaped and stained to be the part it needs to be to make a finished product the craftsman can be proud of.*

Dawson's face filled with resolve flashed as Jack recalled the day he pushed his bunkmate to become a Marine.

Jack spoke his own advice. "Lighten up. Breathe. One step at a time." He shifted and straightened under his pack as he tightened his hold on the rifle in his hand. A surge of adrenaline shot through his system as Thomson called him in once more. "I am a Marine. I will not fail my brothers." Down. Set.

My rifle and I know that what counts in war

is not the rounds we fire,

the noise of our burst, nor the smoke we make.

We know that it is the hits that count. We will hit ...

Once more, Jack brought the scope to his eye. Finger on the trigger. Target lined up in his sight.

Breathe in. Breathe out. Steady now. Deep breath. And hold.

This time, Jack felt each bullet as his rifle spit them far and true. Three shots. One thousand yards. One hole.

My rifle and I are the defenders of my country.

We are the masters of our enemy.

We are the saviors of my life.

Had Jack glanced back at Thomson after he was dismissed, he would have seen a hint of a smile on the man's leathery face as he balled up the piece of trash and tossed it up and down in his hand. Truth was, it had almost not been found, but it led to Jack finding far more.

Tray jogged up to walk alongside Jack as they hiked back to their barracks. "How the heck did you do that back there? Three shots, one hole, a thousand yards? Yeah, that's gonna get passed down." He stared at his partner, eyes wide and smile wider.

"All that running loosened something in my brain. I will never lose another team to the enemy. I will be better. My focus firm. I will not be the reason the enemy wins." Jack had stared straight ahead the entire time he spoke. He stopped and turned to Tray. "I promise you. Never again."

Tray sobered up as he recognized the intensity in Jack's commitment. "Don't go makin' promises nobody can keep. What's this really about, Jack? I can see it in your eyes, man. You may be a heckuva hunter in the field, but you've got a whole host in your mind huntin' after you."

Faces flashed in Jack's mind as he stared back at the trees behind them—Steven, Leslee … little Abbie Mae. But more followed them. Every good person who'd shown him the right path, believed in him and pushed him to be better. His mom. Ben. Rachael. Senior. The entire Miller clan. Grandma Ethel. Tray.

Jack turned to his friend and poured it all out, filling in the rough outlines of a past he'd only partially revealed before then. The night in the Clearing; his first sip of alcohol and the slippery slope that caused; the mission and the light he found there; Rachael, her dad, his mom; that afternoon in his truck; the aftermath in the town; and his decision to take off and leave the ones he loved behind for their own good.

He rambled on through his time in Columbia and his decision to join the Corps. He told Tray about his communication with Ben and how he preached a sermon that left the town in a burst of revival. How he'd moved to South Carolina. And, how he didn't know where Rachael was and couldn't ask because he was afraid of the answer. He had left so she could move on and find someone more deserving of her. But that didn't mean he wanted to know she did.

"I just hope she's happy. That's all I ever wanted for her, even if I couldn't be the one to share it with her."

They began walking quietly again, letting the revelations sink into the atmosphere around them. Finally, Tray cleared his throat.

"Man, you've got more chasing after you than any dude should. But, I'm gonna tell you somethin' I know you've heard before. You can't hear it too much. God's way bigger than any demon lurkin' in your past." He paused until Jack met his gaze. "God's got the peace that passes all our earthly understandin'. We may not be able to comprehend how we can live through somethin' truly awful and keep it behind us so that it can't keep hurting us, but that's what peace does. It's inexplicable, man ... and only a prayer away."

Their eyes remained connected as Jack considered what his friend told him. He finally responded. "It's like I told Ben a few years back. When I see him and Rach—and now you and your grandma—I want to believe. But, then I see all the senseless tragedy. I think of all the hurt I brought on innocent people." He dropped his head for a moment. Shaking it hard, he looked back up. "No, I can't. I just can't believe in a God who would allow all these things or who would forgive me.

I'm not upset for what you said to me. Part of me wants to believe. I see what you've all got—the peace you shouldn't have with all that's happened to you—but I don't think that's meant for someone like me."

After a minute of fixation on the buildings and people all around them, he continued. "There's a difference between you and me. You had horrible things happen to you. I caused horrible things—inadvertently, but my actions resulted in tragedy and pain in people who deserved far better. I'm way past grace's reach."

Tray watched his friend run ahead across the parking lot to their barracks. As he did, he sent up a prayer for Jack to accept truth and its peace.

* * *

Toward the end of Scout Sniper, sunbeams danced atop the North Carolina swamp waters all around Jack and his fellow Marines. Noiselessly, they emerged from the glistening waters, rifles clutched tightly. As the light continued to rise, its warmth dried their uniforms to their skin, and sweat took the water's place. The Sergeant's signal alerted them to potential hostiles, so they dropped to snake through grass and chigger-filled brush. Mind over matter, Jack ignored the crawling creatures on his skin, the chafing beneath his clothes and the chilling trickle of sweat along his spine.

The mental fatigue combined with total physical exhaustion to make Jack question if he'd ever reach the end of the ten-week course. For the first time since joining the Corps, Jack found himself thoroughly worn from a training. He wasn't sure how he felt about that, but he leaned toward pride. Not only had he survived the grueling course and made a name for himself with his nearly flawless shooting, he stood down a beast in his mind—and won. Though the enemy in a training exercise was fictitious, he and every Marine knew the enemy in the not-so-distant desert was all too real. They'd all lost friends—brothers—and they knew there would be more. This was war. This was their near future. All they had to take up against the foe were their weapons and each other. He realized his completion and his mental victory were huge accomplishments and nothing to be taken lightly. He celebrated his new title—Marine Scout Sniper—on his twentieth birthday with his buddies at the rifle range.

After Ducky's wedding in Columbia, Jack and Tray furthered their skills with the Urban Sniper Course. At this point they knew without a doubt they would soon be heading to Iraq. As scout snipers, it would be up to them to watch over the Marines on the ground and to infiltrate ahead of them to take out known targets in the area or report back with accurate intel.

They learned more about planning and leading missions. They weren't just training in case; they were actively training for on-going war. Reality hung in the air like a storm cloud, but Jack faced it with confidence in his training and his ability to follow through with the "one shot, one kill" mindset instilled in all Marines.

In June, Jack dropped the *Lance* to his rank and added another chevron to his uniform. Thornton pinned him and the other promoted Marines during their monthly Battalion Formation. Jack continued to be on the early end of the promotion scale. He knew his future's options in his beloved Corps were wide open and couldn't imagine his life any other way.

Though he still missed Rachael, he decided he was better alone. A Marine without a reason to return home made for a more focused and fearless fighter. He did catch himself daydreaming about the future a few times, though. He decided he'd revisit the idea of a college degree. Perhaps he'd become an officer or instructor. Grow old and have a woodshop of his own. Who knew what his future could hold?

Seasons shifted again around Lejeune. Bright leaves brought beauty to daily training. They slowly sank to the ground and opened the door for brisk winds and temperature drops. Jack and Tray spent every moment of free time at Harvey's, the community center or Grandma Ethel's.

The holidays proved a bittersweet time for them, though. They received their deployment orders between Thanksgiving in Jacksonville with Grandma Ethel and Christmas with the Millers and Jack's mom in Columbia. In a few weeks, they'd be in the thick of the battles in Iraq.

XVII

Five Seconds

January through August 2005

An uncertain sun lurked behind billowy clouds above the runway in Cherry Point. The sprawling gray expanse had given flight to countless Marines on their way to the belly of the beast, many to return beneath a flag. New fighters gathered their supplies and filed inside the C-17s, gassed and ready for the more than 6,700-mile flight to Ali Al Salem Air Base in Kuwait. After a day or so there, the Marines would catch a KC-130 for the final leg of their trek to TQ—Al Taqaddum Air Base, Iraq.

Jack adjusted his gear and sucked in air to steady his nerves. The smell of jet fuel polluted the oxygen he inhaled. He'd come a long way from the kid who'd rarely left his tiny hometown three years ago, but planes sent his stomach reeling.

"Good to go, Marine?" Brighton barked.

"Hoorah, Gunny!" Jack responded. The question and response jarred his fears loose and sent them scattering on the wintry breeze as it whipped across the tarmac. He was ready to hit the streets and put his years of training to work—if he could just survive the trip ahead. The confidence he had in the skills he'd developed meant he had no reservations about running in to locate and identify insurgents, clear the way for his fellow Marines and take down any enemy targets that came into his sights. His certainty increased tenfold with the reminder that Tray had his back.

"Gotta be honest, man; I'm not a fan of these big birds." Tray shook his head as they approached the hatch. "Big as they are, I don't see how the heck they stay up at all. It's not natural."

Jack noticed Tray's leery glance from the giant plane ahead to the sky above and laughed. "Dude, I never thought I'd see a black guy turn green."

"Yeah, well, that friendly ghost called. Said he wants his shade of white back." Tray glared at his friend. "You know you're as scared as I am of this death trap."

"Fine. You caught me, but this stays between us. We're supposed to be the frickin' elite. No one else needs to know we're quakin' in our boots about this daggone flight."

"Deal."

They boarded—packs and gear on, rifles in hand—and harnessed themselves in for the bumpy flight ahead. Marines lined the sides of the C-17, vehicles and equipment strapped between them and a wide range of nerves displayed on their faces. Some more veteran guys joked and laughed about finding out just how good the new mechanics were. Younger seventeen- and eighteen-year-olds clutched helmets beneath their chins as their faces went through a variety of shades from yellow to purple. The deafening drone of the engines cut out any thought of small talk as they taxied down the runway, steadily gaining speed until they felt themselves lifting in a burst of power that propelled them toward the dangers ahead.

After a couple days in Kuwait, it was the next landing that Jack swore jarred every organ in his body loose. They had arrived in the heart of the giant beach with no water in sight. The hatch opened onto a blistering expanse of desolation. Even the distant sunrise appeared hopeless. Smell was the Marines' first sense to face assault.

"Man, what the heck is that?" Tray pressed his nose down to his shoulder as Jack copied him.

Brighton yelled over his shoulder, "Burning garbage. You get used to it."

Tray shook his head at Jack and spoke through the arm he pressed over his nostrils. "Nope. I'm gonna hafta disagree with the Gunny on this one."

The air that hit them was completely dry, nothing like the humidity back in Jacksonville. At least there they'd get an occasional redeeming breeze. Not so much in Iraq. This air turned their throats to sandpaper. They weren't without winds, of course. Those they had. Winds that slung grains of sand with the velocity of a speeding bullet.

War's reality had welcomed them to its home.

* * *

Jack and Tray found themselves on their way to Fallujah a couple days after their arrival in country. Once there, they met with teams whose places they were to take—Relief in Place, they called it. RIP made an ominous acronym for such a process. The men whose hands they shook—though many the same age as them—looked older, hardened, adjusted.

Adjusted to life in a brutal landscape with a violent enemy. On guard. Ready and willing to take any means necessary to neutralize dangerous targets. To their eyes, Jack and Tray looked like mere infants—as they had looked when they first landed.

After their initial week or so of soaking up all the knowledge their predecessors had to share, the team hit the ground running, literally. They had immediate orders to keep a watchful eye on polling locations. With upcoming elections, tensions heightened; and cast ballots could cost in blood. After that task, they spent the majority of the next several months assisting other Marines in gathering intelligence and watching out for insurgents crossing over from Syria. Most of their time was spent in hides across the northern part of the province. They rationed their MREs and rarely moved.

One March morning, Tray glanced over at his partner and handed him the MRE he'd just opened.

"Happy twenty-first, man. I'll get you a cake next year."

"Watch out! I may think you actually like me. Is this chili mac?"

"Yeah. You better eat that before I change my mind. This one looks suspiciously like a daggone veggie burger." Jack laughed at his friend's scrunched-up nose.

* * *

Life in Iraq was surprisingly predictable. Frequent bombs and shots rang out all around. The Marines carried out orders while battling the elements more than insurgents. Jack and Tray had spent a couple weeks holed up in an outstanding hide after his birthday. One afternoon, the sky to the north instantly darkened. Before they realized what the clouds meant—or registered that they weren't clouds at all—they were encased in a swift-moving curtain of dust. Wind swirled around them at more than seventy miles an hour and covered them, their equipment and everything around them with thick layers of sand and dirt.

It coated the backs of their throats as it irritated their eyes. Tears cleaned streaks down their cheeks. Blowing sand out of their noses and coughing it from their lungs while attempting to maintain their camouflage proved to be the one massive challenge training hadn't covered. They took solace in the fact that the same hellish winds tormented their enemies. That was the afternoon Jack made his first kill.

Tray kept watch as Jack rapidly cleaned his rifle. They had to be ready. Their purpose for being in this hole was to wait out an Iraqi sniper. Careful tracking had led them to fix sights on a spot directly across the desert from them.

"Got him!" Tray's voice trembled with the words. Jack clicked the last piece of his weapon back into place. Through the scope, Jack caught the glint of a lens. Tray whispered clear, quick calculations, from which Jack adjusted. He fingered the smooth curve of his trigger. Sure. True.

Inhale. Exhale. Release.

Time slowed. Jack watched the seconds pass until the spray filled his reticle.

Target eliminated.

The enemy was dead.

Jack held his reactions tight, like his breath when he squeezed the trigger. He and Tray didn't speak. Once they were able to safely extricate themselves from their temporary home, Jack released the captive thoughts. To his surprise, they weren't as jagged and raw as he had expected.

He evaluated each as it came and then shed it on the sand beneath his boots.

I intentionally killed a man. Shot him. He's dead ... from my bullet.

And unable to kill any more Marines or innocent civilians.

I took a life. Hunted and waited and killed. Like he was an animal.

He signed away his right to life—same as me. And, I've seen what they do to their own—and ours. He's not an animal; he's worse.

I'm stacking the death tower higher here, aren't I? Steven. Leslee. Bobby Lee. Susan. Abbie Mae. This man.

Those weren't intentional. That guilt's gotta die. Bury it in the sand. These killings, though—there's purpose.

Tray had tuned in to Jack's body language as they glided under the pseudo-protection of darkness. He could sense when Jack's thoughts had emptied.

"You okay?"

"Good to go."

That day wasn't the first time they'd experienced the powerful role wind played in the volatile Iraqi climate, nor would it be their last. They witnessed sandstorms enough to no longer stand open-mouthed at the light orange tinge which painted the desert. Their surroundings appeared like an ill-developed sepia photograph. For about six weeks between May and June, they learned to accept tropical depression-strength winds as just another part of life in the Sandbox.

Jack cursed the dirt and wind every day of their deployment as he guarded his weapon with every scrap of fabric he could find to form a makeshift cover. Dawson may have been impressed with the speed and meticulousness with which he'd cleaned his rifle in Boot Camp, but that was nothing compared to the detailed cleaning he did in the desert. As often as circumstances and surroundings allowed, Jack cleaned … obsessively.

He painstakingly applied lubricant to his weapon. Then, he wiped it down multiple times until he was positive none of the product remained. The last thing he wanted was to add to the danger of dust and dirt sticking to his weapon. His rifle equaled life for him and his fellow Marines. Keeping it functional was his top priority.

When they weren't cleaning or using their rifles, Jack and Tray kept them carefully sheathed in an unconventional, though effective, covering. Other Marines knew, should the need arise, they could always ask a sniper for a condom.

Orders came for a sniper team to assist fellow Marines with an attempt to take out insurgents smuggling weapons across the Syrian border. Jack and Tray geared up and spent the next six weeks embedded along the Syrian border. They gathered confirmations of dozens of known insurgents and their weapon caches and sent intel down the line so other sniper teams could take out more than half of them.

Jack didn't keep up with his number of kills, but he knew he never missed a target. After one especially active night with about a dozen insurgents engaged, the duo changed positions and hunkered down to rest for another busy night ahead.

"Each kill is eatin' away at me, man. I know they're the enemy; they do unspeakable things. We've seen that. God knows I'll never stop seeing that; but I just can't stop thinkin' of them as men ... like us," Tray confided to Jack in a whisper after an hour or so of silent reflection. "I have to think of them as human beings."

"I can't." Jack's voice toned low as a death knell. The thoughts that played after his first kill had replayed afresh with each additional bullet. "And, they're not men like us."

Jack lay back against his patrol pack. "You've got first watch." He slept dream-free until Tray woke him a few hours later.

Darkness draped him like a woolen blanket, oppressive as the summer heat. Jack's mind drifted to how he might feel back at home once they survived this hell on earth. The aftermath of the two car wrecks in his past flashed in a nightmarish mash-up with images of locals and fellow Marines dismembered and displayed and pink mist in his crosshairs. It was getting to Tray, that was obvious. Jack wanted to help him, but he couldn't even help himself. So, he suppressed his own thoughts again, burying them deep in some cavern of nightmares inside himself, and took a deep breath of the rancid air they hadn't gotten used to. If only they could cast all their thoughts in the sand and leave them there. He didn't think the MCI offered a course in Forgetting for returning veterans. Whatever a return to home brought, though, he and Tray would face it together. They had each other's backs.

* * *

Time in Camp Al Qaim rolled quickly with patrolling at night and passing out in their racks during the day. They put their know-how of digging catholes to use and adjusted to what they all called "piss tubes." While other Marines complained about the lack of variety in food, Jack and Tray declared the chicken enchilada T-rats good enough to eat three times a day. Jack hoped to never hear the hum of a generator again, though. The incessant droning often kept him up during their precious rest time.

Once things evened out along the Syrian border, Jack and Tray put their urban sniper skills to use as they stuck closer to Camp Baharia in Fallujah. Between the Exchange, the gym tent and the internet access, they decided they were living the high life. After a few weeks, they received orders to set up a hide and keep tabs on a suspected insurgent hotspot in the middle of the city.

The sun had long been asleep, though the air around the six-man fire team continued to squeeze the breath out of them. Jack swallowed down a packet of instant coffee and chased it with a bottle of water. He was ready. They piled in a Humvee and headed to the outskirts of Fallujah. As they rode, Jack understood the nickname "City of Mosques." It was easy to believe more than 200 existed within the city's boundaries when he counted a couple dozen along their brief trip before they stopped to continue on foot.

Still and seemingly deserted, the buildings' closed doors and empty windows didn't fool the Marines. Insurgents had eyes everywhere—hidden, easily bought or eventually broken. The chances of their sniper team inserting into an ideal hide without being spotted were about as good as them catching snowflakes on their tongues during this sweltering August. As they clung to the shadows and walked on high alert for block after block, they finally drew closer to their destination.

With only a few blocks left, they split into three teams. Each pair took a different route from that point on, wandering, backtracking and working their way back to rendezvous in front of the house they'd already chosen—a carefully choreographed dance around death.

"Good to go."

"Hoorah!" Jack thanked the other Marines who turned back the way they'd come as he and Tray prepared to enter the abandoned house. They would ascend to the roof to drill a few strategic holes for a lookout. Intel said three insurgents had moved in across the street.

Jack's hand gripped the doorknob. A feeling as shocking as cold water washed over him. He wasn't one to have "bad feelings" about things and shook his head as visions of the drag accident and then Abbie Mae's face flooded through his brain. *Of all the times.* He pushed open the door into the sudden brightness of a blinding flashlight.

Five seconds commenced.

Second one: eyes adjust.

Second two: outlines of men, weapons, and ...

Second three: in front, a woman holding a baby and a toddler in the arms of a man dressed in black.

Second four: more men dressed in black point rifles at them and the little family.

Second five: the toddler's huge eyes latch onto Jack's; she looks exactly like Abbie Mae ... with darker hair and eyes ... those big, bright eyes.

For the first time as a Marine, Jack froze—stuck in second five.

The insurgents did not. Something flew above the Marines' heads toward the rest of the fire team that had alerted to the sudden brightness and were running back to assist. As the grenade exploded, Tray reacted to the lineup of AK-47s aimed at them and threw himself and Jack to the ground.

Jack's world faded to black.

XVIII

In the Midst of the Urban Jungle

August 2005

Intense pressure flattened him to the earth. Oppressive heat surrounded him. Burned deep within. Jack couldn't move.

His eyelids finally formed two slits. Blinding brightness. The early sun bore down on him without mercy. He raised his left arm, slowly. Pain surged through it as his hand came into view, and he risked squinting into the sun again. Bits of metal shrapnel extended from his hand.

Jack's right side remained immovable. He turned his head ever so slightly and discovered why.

Tray lay across him, the back of his helmet facing Jack.

"No!" Jack summoned deeply reserved energy to sit up and roll his partner off to the dusty street next to him. Flames of white-hot pain shot through his abdomen, legs and right shoulder as he lifted Tray's face toward him. His partner's eyes flickered open in the shade of Jack's sagging form. For one breath their eyes locked. Jack's wide in painful terror; Tray's drooping with the weakness of a physical battle waged and its approaching end.

In that instant, the sun's light radiated off Tray's skin, grime and ever-present sand sticking to all the moisture caused by its overbearing heat. A shimmering halo enveloped him as he gulped his final breaths. Jack saw only peace in his friend's kind eyes—no fear of the journey ahead.

"Tray ..." Jack's emotion spilled onto his flak jacket. "Don't ... you can't leave me, man."

The Marine raised a shaking hand to grasp Jack's shoulder. "Don't you let this be another demon, Jack. Drive out the pain you got. Accept grace. Let in peace. Joy." His words slurred and came slower as his hand slid away. A small grin inched partway across his chapped and bleeding lips as two more words tumbled out. "Light. Glory."

With those final words, Trayvon Henry passed to his eternal reward and left Jack alone in his own mortal hell.

The world caved in on Jack as he wept and raged for the friend who had just slipped away. Time stood still or perhaps it spiraled on beyond his comprehension before he evaluated the situation around him. The grenade had instantly taken out the four Marines who ran directly into its blast. Shrapnel had sprayed from the explosion's center. Jack figured that's where he'd gotten his new jewelry. It wasn't what took Tray, though. His death came from the bullet holes dotting his body like a map of the insurgency.

Tray had shielded Jack from most of the gunshots, though several rounds had passed through him and lodged along Jack's body. As the reality of the night's horrors drifted across his mind, Jack felt heat flowing through him, seducing him down into unconsciousness again. But not before he recalled those final five seconds in the flashlight's beam … and his hesitation.

I'm the frickin' angel of death. I bring death to good people … great, innocent people.

Inner anguish depleted Jack's final store of adrenaline, and he hit the deck hard as a recovery convoy turned the corner.

"Got a live one still, Doc!" Staff Sergeant Davison's voice echoed in the midst of the urban jungle that housed too much death and destruction. "We've lost all the rest; we're sure as hell not losing this one."

XIX

Heart ... Soul ... Purpose

August 2005 through September 2006

Jack's unconsciousness held no peace. Flashes of battles, death, loss and destruction plagued him. He thrashed and cried out, so doctors kept him sedated. As a result, his early days in the hospital consisted of a blur of hazy images, a daily need to remember where he was and why ... and the searing pain that followed each recollection.

Commander Robert Matson sat beside Jack's hospital bed. Early afternoon sunlight streamed through the window behind him, illuminating his blond hair and giving him a celestial aura. Jack's initial thought was that God must exist, and here he was. The stethoscope resting around the neck surprised him, though. The doctor leaned forward with a cautious smile playing about his mouth.

"Sure is good to see those eyes fully open and focusing, Corporal Calhoun." His voice boomed more deeply than Jack expected to hear. "How's your pain this afternoon? On a scale of one to Fallujah."

Jack found himself nearly returning the grin. He relaxed and breathed deeply for what felt like the first time in a while. "More Al-Qa'im than Fallujah," he croaked out of a sandstorm-dry throat.

"Not sure if that's better or worse, Marine."

"De ... depends on the day of the week," Jack clarified as he cleared his throat and attempted to shift to a more comfortable position. A stabbing pain sent shocks down his right arm.

"Copy that." The glimpse of a twinkle in Matson's eyes faded as he sat straighter and lifted a chart that had been resting on the ankle atop his other knee. "Corporal, I'm not one to mince words; and I'm a pretty straight shooter. In my experience, that tends to be preferred by you Devil Dogs anyway."

"That'd be good to go, Doc. I'll be honest, I haven't got a clue where I am, when I am or what the hell happened."

"Understandable. You've been heavily sedated since the recovery team pulled you off the street in Iraq. It seems you have a predisposition to some night terrors." The doctor closed the chart and set it on the bed beside Jack's arm.

Matson paused to evaluate the effect of his words on the Marine in front of him. Encouraged by whatever he found, he continued. "Beginning today, we're weaning you off the sedatives you've been on since the field and then again in Germany. You're back in the States at Bethesda. Ever been to D.C.?"

"Never."

"Well, we're gonna make sure you see our nation's capital before we let you head home then." Matson smiled. "Now, let's talk reality. It's been a week since the attack. You've had a couple surgeries. According to your records, doctors in the field dug a bullet from your humerus before they packed you to fly to Landstuhl. Once you got there, they set that bone. You've got another bullet still lodged in your left arm, but it's harmless—a desert souvenir for you. A few more bullets cleared you through and through—easy enough to patch up.

"My current recommendation is that you remain here for a few more weeks of rehab. Today is Wednesday, so I'm gonna keep a close eye on you as we pull back these sedatives that have kept you calm in your travels. I am optimistic, though, that the process will go well. I want to move you to a less restricted wing as early as this weekend. My goal is to get you back on your feet and free as soon as possible, but we're going to take your speed with this. You're charting the course here. Once we have you a little less loopy, we're gonna start you on some good ol' PT.

"One of the perks of being a doctor—I get to check out your files. You've got a helluva PFT record, Marine. Your run times—impressive. Now, since I know what you're made of, we're gonna push you warrior style—head on and hard-driving. Hope you're okay with that."

"Hoorah!"

Matson smiled again with more confidence as he cleared his throat to finish his news. "You do have an uphill run ahead of you, though. You'll receive therapy for a traumatic brain injury. It wasn't a major event, so that's good. We just want to get you the help you need now to make sure you overcome any challenges that may pop up. The bigger hurdle lies with your right arm. Another bullet sliced through that shoulder and mostly transected your brachial plexus."

The gold flecks in Jack's hazel eyes darkened as he glanced down at the cast lying next to him. He realized he couldn't lift it and didn't hide his panic from the doctor.

"I'm not sure you'll regain full use of that arm; but," the doctor emphasized the conjunction and rushed ahead to calm his patient, "your history and strength and age are all in your favor. We've got some of the best physical therapists around, and they will work you as hard as they can to help you recover as much function as possible. From there, you need to continue rehab for another year or so. At that point, you'll know just how much use you'll have.

"Since I don't deal in best case scenarios, all I will say is I believe you will surprise me. I'll also say you need to begin thinking of ways to do everyday activities without that arm. If you were ambidextrous, that sure would come in handy for all the paperwork we've been stacking up for you."

Despite the horror that built up within him as the doctor spoke, Jack found himself chuckling at the corny joke. "Wish the Corps had taught a class in that."

The room stilled, and Jack's grin faded as truth settled around his shoulders. "I shoot right-handed."

Matson replied simply, "Not anymore."

The full truth landed on Jack's chest like a downed C-17, collapsing and crushing all his heart's desires. He was a Marine Scout Sniper to his very core. That was the title that taught him who he was. Who he had believed he was born to be. It brought him purpose and a vehicle for the leadership skills Boot Camp had woken within him.

How could he be anything less?

"We also have outstanding counselors on staff. They are here to listen when you're ready to talk."

Listen. Ready to talk. Talk about ... what? How I lost who I was? How I lost my best friend in the whole world? How I killed him?

No.

Jack didn't think so. That wasn't something he cared to talk about. Ever.

"I know you've got a lot to take in, but I have one more thing to tell you." Jack cast a look down the bed, searching the white blanket for two full ridges. He did still have all his limbs. That was something, wasn't it? The absurdity of being thankful he had limbs—whether or not they functioned—struck him and made him want to burst into unceasing laughter. What a ludicrous reality he'd woken up to.

"Typically, I like to keep visitors to immediate family, especially right after I've spoken with a patient about what he's facing, but you have a few visitors I think we need to make an exception for."

Rachael's face immediately filled Jack's mind. His emotions shifted rapidly from joy to panic. He didn't want her to see him like this. Not after so long.

"Your mom is here. She's quite a strong lady. Two of your friends came with her—Ben Burns and Ethel Henry. That's one fiery little lady. She insists I call her Grandma Ethel and brought sweet potato pies for the staff. I'm not sure I've ever had a pie as amazing as that one. I asked ..."

Matson stopped talking when Jack's ghostly pallor caught his attention. Jack felt the blood rush away from his face, from his fingers, toes, heart, brain, everything. He wasn't sure where it all went, but he wasn't sure he wanted any of it back.

His heart sped up, and he thought for sure it was going to leap out of his chest. He couldn't breathe, couldn't think, couldn't reason.

Grandma Ethel. She'd come all the way here. But, I saw Tray; watched him die. There was no way he could still be alive.

Was there?

Matson stood beside him, stethoscope pressed to his chest, concern flooding his expression.

"Trayvon Henry," Jack gasped out. "Did he ...?"

He could tell the doctor knew exactly what he was asking. "Let's get you a few deep breaths and get this heart calmed down before I answer that."

Jack shut his eyes, but he couldn't close out the images of the other Marines and Tray. Scattered pieces of the men he'd fought alongside. Blood trickling from the corner of Tray's mouth. Perfect peace falling all around him. Those final words.

His training rose up from somewhere deeper within. *Breathe in. Breathe out. Steady now. Deep breath. And hold.*

When Jack opened his eyes, Matson sat again, this time forward in the chair, his knees against the bed. "No. He didn't make it. Grandma Ethel wants to see you. She said you'd become as much a grandson to her as Trayvon was."

Jack clenched his eyes shut, squeezing them tight in a vain attempt to drive out the painful memories. To change the very past he longed only to run from—to forget. *Breathe in. Breathe out. Steady now. Deep breath. And hold.*

He lifted his head as he opened his eyes. He met the doctor's gaze and nodded. Barely a whisper, he responded, "Okay."

Matson kept his eyes fixed on the young Marine in front of him, gauging the depth of the pain he held. Finally, he nodded and rose. "I'm going to have her come in alone first, but I'll be right outside with one of our counselors. We're here for you, if you need us. We'll give you some time after you speak to her, but we'll be right there. All you have to do is call."

"Copy that."

Jack's voice sounded far, far away to his ears. Still back in the desert. Lost in a sandstorm. Carried off on the Shamal winds. Foreign to him. No longer his.

When he spotted Grandma Ethel in the doorway, Jack thought she looked simultaneously stronger and frailer than she had the last time he'd seen her before they headed to Iraq. She dabbed away a stray tear and rushed to his left side.

"My sweet, sweet Jack." She took his good bandaged hand in hers and kissed it. Her gray—more white—hair was pulled back in her signature tight bun. "It does this old heart so good to see your handsome face."

He looked up at her and didn't try to hide his tears. She stroked his hair and rested her hand on his cheek. "I miss him, too. But he's with Jesus and his grandpa and his parents now."

Jack's bloodshot eyes pled with her as he uttered the confession that shredded his soul. "It's all my fault. I killed him. Oh God, I killed him." He broke down as Grandma Ethel sat on the bed next to him and held his shaking form.

Once the sobs slowed, she spoke softly as she rested her wrinkled cheek against his bristly hair. "My Tray was ready to meet his Savior. And, his death was most definitely not your fault. He died doin' what he always wanted to do, and you couldn't have kept him from that."

Jack leaned against her shoulder and exhaled as she continued. "He loved you like the brother he never had. He wrote me about how brave you were, all the good you did. The strength you showed in takin' out those horrible people. You saved so many lives. He wrote that he just wanted to save one."

"How can you forgive me? I don't understand that. I don't understand how you can forgive the men who murdered your son and your daughter-in-law or the God who took away your husband or me who didn't save your only grandson. It was my fault. All my fault. I broke my promise to him. I opened that door and ... froze." Jack worked his jaw as he fought to control his emotions before he looked up at the woman who loved him despite everything he'd just told her. "How can you possibly forgive? You've had everything taken from you."

Tears flowed unhindered down Jack's cheeks. His face was a splotched canvas of guilt, sorrow and anger. Each emotion warred for his focus. Grandma Ethel breathed sympathy for the boy lying in the bed before her.

"Oh, my sweet Jack. Baby, you can't understand because you don't know my Jesus. He didn't take nothin' from me. He gave me gifts. Gifts to cherish and care for during a season. I'll be with them all again one day, but then I'll get an even better gift. I'll see my Jesus face to face. He's gonna take me by my hand and walk me up and down his streets of gold. We're gonna talk and laugh and sing and dance together. I'm gonna love dancin' with my Jesus."

Grandma Ethel's face glowed as she spoke about her eternity. Her warm chocolate eyes melted into tears of joy as she described her vision. "My honey and my babies are singin' praises round that throne already, but I'll join them one day when my time here is finished. I can forgive because I've been forgiven. I was a sinner. But, he didn't let me stay that way. No sir.

"The summer I turned sixteen I'd been chasin' the boys and livin' whichever way I saw fit, but my great-grandma drug me along to a revival beside this river. That preacher, he yelled and hollered 'bout hell and sin and death. He scared me 'bout crazy, but then another preacher got up. He was younger, softer spoken. He talked 'bout God's love and grace. He told us how he sent his only son, Jesus, to take our sins on him, get himself crucified—dead and buried—then raised up again on the third day. He took my sins on him then, thousands of years ago, cause he knew on that swelterin' summer day in 1929 I was gonna see his beauty and feel his forgiveness.

"He became my Jesus that day, and I ain't never looked back since I came up from gettin' baptized in that river bed. I went on to marry that soft-spoken preacher man, and he and I spent our lives together talkin' bout heaven and spendin' it praisin' Jesus for how he forgave and loved us."

Jack saw in Grandma Ethel's face something he'd seen before—peace in assurance. He'd seen it in his mom, Ben and Rachael, the Millers, Tray. He'd never felt it himself, though. How could he? He'd gone way further down the wrong path than this sweet lady in front of him ever could have. There was no forgiveness for someone like him. He swallowed back the tears and decided he'd find the solution somehow—a way to never hurt another person again.

Grandma Ethel gave Jack a final hug and kiss and left him with a prayer. "Lord, bless this lamb of yours and grant him peace."

He was no lamb, and peace was something he'd never earn. Head down, he fought to rein in his emotions. It was time to put on a brave front. He couldn't show the wreck he was.

When his mom walked in, Jack noticed new worry lines crisscrossing her still-beautiful face. Why should women like her and Grandma Ethel have to deal with so much crap in their lives? And, how on earth did they not throw in the towel?

"Oh, sweetie." Becky's drawn face softened as she looked at her son. No matter how many battles he fought, he'd always be her little boy. She slid onto the bed beside him, placed her hand on his cheek and faced him with a smile that echoed the relief in her golden eyes. "I'm so thankful I get to hold you again. Every day you were gone, I prayed. As soon as I got the call, I started praying even harder and haven't stopped."

Jack leaned in to his mom's hug and kissed her cheek. "I love you, Mama."

With those four words, the floodgates opened. She allowed her tears to flow freely. They were silent tears—not sad, simply a release. The salty current rushed away her months of worry and fear.

Jack told her everything the doctor had told him. He couldn't hide the twist in his insides when he revealed that his right arm may never function properly again. Becky saw it and kissed his forehead, wishing this simple endearment could still heal her boy's pain. She knew he contained injuries much deeper than in the nerves of his arm. Doctors didn't have medicine for those wounds. Neither did mothers.

"I'm here for you. Please let me help you through this." He heard a trembling in his mom's request, a fear he didn't entirely understand. He knew it hurt her when he'd left, but some pain runs deeper than others. How could he even ask for her help without hurting her again in the process? Plus, there was something about the way she'd worded her offer—like she'd held it out to someone before, but something was missing. A cloud of past despair drifted through his mom's expression, and he saw what she lacked—the hope of hearing the response she desired.

After a while, exhaustion claimed Jack, and he could no longer keep his eyes open. Before he fell asleep, he said, "Please tell Ben I want to see him now; I'm just so tired." Jack had barely finished the final word when he drifted off into a restless sleep.

*　*　*

The rattle of the evening food cart and an echoing crash jarred Jack awake. One of the trays didn't reach its destination. The deafening crash sent him right back to Iraq. He jolted upright and flailed for his weapon; but his arms remained useless, and his head was splitting from his sudden reaction. Slowly the hospital room replaced the desert sands of his mind, and he recovered from his first lesson in how the enemy was invisible to everyone else and felt only by him.

Jack forced himself to swallow one more bite of the tasteless hospital fare. It lodged in his throat, so he painfully inched a straw to his dry lips and washed the sustenance down to where it was required. A knock at the door prepared him for a new visitor. When Ben's head peered around the opening door, Jack managed a feeble smile, as his spirits lifted.

"That looks awful." Ben raised an eyebrow and shook his head at the remaining food.

"It is," Jack agreed. "You want the rest?"

"Not a chance," Ben laughed. "I finally herded your mom and Grandma Ethel to the hotel. They've been beside themselves, wanting to see you. I'm glad you got to spend some time with them earlier."

"Thanks for lookin' out for them."

"Matson said this is the first day you've been fully conscious, and your mom explained to me about your injuries. That's a lot to wake up to. How are you feeling about everything?"

"Yeah. I don't know. It's all ... so ..." Jack sought for the right words, sifting through a mass of inner turmoil to find some nugget of reality. "I don't know what I'll do without my arm."

"Therapy could prove effective, though, right?"

"Possibly." Jack turned toward the window and the dying day beyond it. "I'll give my all at rehab, but I'm not sure I'll get the reward I want."

He turned back to Ben who stood next to the spot where the two women had sat a few hours previously. "I can't be a Marine with one arm. And, I sure as hell can't be a sniper. Marine. Sniper. That's who I am. You wrote in that letter right before Boot Camp that I'd know God's plan when I saw it. Well, Marine Sniper was it, and I don't know how to be anything else."

"You will. If you have to."

Jack wanted to agree, but he wasn't so sure. He'd spent the last three years becoming a war machine. How could he revert to whatever he was before? The thought of before sucker-punched him. He recalled the hollow, lost kid he had been. It was the Corps where he'd finally found purpose, if not peace. Terror washed over him as questions rolled in and out.

"Sometimes God's got more than one life plan for us. Look at me. I thought I was supposed to be a preacher—and I was— but that wasn't all for me. Carolina tried to tell me that long ago, but I was too stubborn—or scared—to listen then. God's using me now to make a difference at the mission in Savannah. And, he's got something else planned for you, too. You'll see." Ben leaned down to squeeze Jack's uninjured shoulder. "I'll bring the ladies back in the morning. Tonight, I'll be praying you find restful slumber, undisturbed by any terrors."

"Thanks." Jack's response drifted away from him, wrapped in doubt at what he considered Ben's wishful thinking.

That night Ben's prayers received an affirmative response. Jack slept soundly without dreams of any kind for the first time since the terror on the streets of Fallujah.

***

A thunderstorm jolted Jack awake early the next morning and set the tone for the day. He met his physical therapy team mid-morning. By noon he was praying for Sergeant Marshall to walk through the door and start berating him about his big ears. At least the DI didn't tilt toward the torture side of things. The next three weeks improved, but only slightly. And very, very slowly.

By the time Matson sat beside Jack again, the Marine could raise the first two fingers of his right hand a full inch. The biggest progress was raising his entire arm level with the floor. Occupational therapy was better in some ways. Its practicality appealed to Jack. He had always preferred to focus his attentions on activities with a clear purpose in mind. In that respect, it was easier to face than PT. On the other hand, it left him depressed for the rest of the day. Managing to fumble a button through its hole after ten minutes of sweating and copious amounts of curse words sent the team around him applauding like he'd just won a gold medal.

A few short weeks earlier, his now-useless limb had taken down the enemy without fail with each squeeze of his trigger. That day, a button nearly defeated him.

"You've done outstanding in therapy. You exceeded my expectations for sure." Matson leaned back in the chair. It was the end of a long shift for him. The exhaustion darkened each valley on his forehead.

"But ...?" Jack prompted.

The doctor grinned and dropped his chin as he handpicked each word. "You've taken the strides to heal your body. More healing will come. With time and continued therapy, of course," he added. "I'm a firm believer in what I call the "-al" trifecta of healing—physical, emotional and spiritual. You can never achieve the fullest healing in one area without addressing all three. In your time here, you haven't spoken with anyone on our staff about your loss. About the nightmare you lived through and now live with. Ignoring it will not make it go away. Doesn't work like that."

He leaned forward as Jack's jaw hardened. "If you want to recover as much as you possibly can, you will not ignore the other two sides of this. You will get help. Counselors and chaplains are the healers you need now. I told you I'm not one to mince words or skirt around a hard issue. My abilities may be limited, and I may not know exactly what you're going through; but I've seen more guys than I can count who were just like you. Some worked the healing trifecta; and their lives are, in many ways, better than they were prior to whatever hell they endured. The others ... well, they're barely hanging on. Or, they let go."

Their eyes locked, and unspoken messages passed between them. "Don't let go, Jack."

Matson's pleading voice added to the chorus that had become the soundtrack for the reel that played nightly in Jack's dreams. The whoosh of a fire's flames as lighter fluid sends it skyward. The grinding crunch of metal. Screams of young lives snuffed out. A thump and jolt that causes him to break out in a cold sweat. The wounded animal cry of Hyram Cutter. The strangled pleas he hears only in his mind that signal the end of the many lives he took in war. The deafening silence of those five seconds in Fallujah. Tray's final words. The gurgle in his final breath. Like a choir of demons, the sounds of the horrors he caused clashed with one another and the pleas of Matson, his mom, Ben, Grandma Ethel. Their product became a grating dissonance that made Jack want to claw at his eardrums. A return to normalcy could perhaps cease the noise in his brain. Unfortunately, what passed as normalcy showed little resemblance to what he'd known pre-Iraq.

* * *

After his discharge from the hospital, Jack numbly attended a memorial for Tray. He held a weeping—but still smiling—Grandma Ethel. His mom had gone with him and then accompanied him to Columbia for a few days.

Mawmaw Mabel wrapped him up in a flour-coated hug as soon as she opened her front door. She stood speechless for the second time since Jack had known her. Senior stood behind his wife. The older Marine tipped a nod Jack's way. With it passed an understanding no one else had been able to share with him.

"Got a project I could use help with," Senior said as he turned toward the back of the house. Jack followed, thankful for a purpose for his hands—hand—once more. For the next couple of hours, Jack held pieces in place as Senior hammered and glued and formed a rocking horse for a new great-grandbaby. They didn't speak, but more passed between them during that time than ever before.

Back at Lejeune, Jack moved in to a new barracks. The following morning he reported to freshly promoted Sergeant Major Thornton.

"Good to see you back home, Marine."

"Thank you, Sergeant Major."

"Let's get right down to details. All the paperwork's completed for your promotion to Sergeant. Now, you've got just under a year left on your current enlistment. You've got time to think through what your future holds. For now, you have a place here as a Training NCO. I need you to make sure every Marine in your unit gets their PFTs, annual trainings and MCI courses completed and recorded. Sound good?"

"Can do, easy."

Jack appreciated the brevity of visits with Thornton. As he headed to his new duty station, he spotted the road to Scout Sniper School and felt a twinge. Like a phantom limb, his missing weapon left an ache on the shoulder where it should have hung. He drifted mindlessly into his new schedule and responsibilities—a passive existence, a mere state of being. Time didn't stand still, but it didn't clip along either. He couldn't bring himself to go back into Harvey's. He drove there and sat in the parking lot a few times. Memories of jokes and trash talk passing between him and Tray, rifles held easily in their shooting hands, replayed in his mind as he watched the door open and close on regulars whose names he knew and whose target groupings he could picture.

Instead of entering with them, Jack entertained the idea of a visit to the liquor store next door. On the third visit, he exited his car and reached the store's door. He grasped the handle and found his senses assaulted. Misty's abrasive laugh and strong perfume. Her sharp fingernails tracing down his arm before she took the money from his hand. The full coolness of the bottles on the counter. The unsteady feel of the weaving truck beneath his control and the terrifying lightness of no control over the roaring machine beneath him. The gut-wrenching pain and the stench of his own vomit.

Jack jerked his hand away as if the handle had been a lit burner and retreated to his car.

Grandma Ethel insisted he come for Sunday lunch each week. He dreaded each visit for the emptiness of that little table. He'd hit his rack as soon as he returned to the barracks. Sleep sometimes gave him a release; other times, it acted as an inhumane trap. For months after Iraq, his dreams contained repeated memories. His mind flashed back to replay the day in sniper training when Thomson sentenced him. *You gave away that position and led your team to slaughter.*

He'd promised himself something that day—a mission he'd failed: "I will never lose another team to the enemy."

Jack's mind carried him next to those five seconds in Iraq that led to his breaking that promise and killing his best friend.

* * *

Seasons came and went, but the broken promise remained at the forefront of Jack's thoughts to taunt him. He found himself facing Thornton once more.

"Sergeant Major, I am not the Marine I trained to be. I cannot shoot or PT the way a Marine should. Because of this, I cannot, in good conscience, remain in the Corps." Jack's words sounded rote and hollow, final. Thornton nodded and studied his desk for a moment before he responded.

"You're the finest sniper I've ever seen cross this base. You're also one of the best damn Marines I've passed anywhere. You would be a welcome addition to our instructors if you would reconsider your decision."

Jack knew compliments like that were far from standard issue and considered the offer for a moment, but his eyes held their resolve. "I appreciate that, sir. If I can't give 100% to my Corps, though, it's time for me to move on to something that doesn't deserve more than I have to give."

He kept his plans to himself. To Grandma Ethel, he said he'd be taking some leave time. To his mom, he said he'd be pretty busy in the upcoming weeks. But, to Ben, he sent another letter.

Ben,

I find myself facing yet another battle—one I have to take on my own. I've had any final checks routed directly to Mom. I will write to her, though. So, I'm not going entirely off the grid. Please check in on her and Grandma Ethel when you can. Don't tell her, of course, but I want you to know I never stopped loving Rachael. She was my guiding star so many times. I hope she's got the happiest life. She deserves it.

If I spoke to you about all this, I know what you'd say. Same as CDR Matson. Get help. Seek help. Talk. Well, I'm not much for talking. And I've figured something out on my own. I'm a frickin' poison. I don't want to spread that to anyone else, ever again. I made a promise to never lead a brother to harm. I broke that promise and won't risk breaking more.

This time I'm older and can do what I should have done four and a half years ago—go off completely on my own.

Thank you for all you've done for me and all you've meant to me. I don't have the right words to really express that as fully as I'd like, but I hope you'll understand and be able to read between these lines to my heart.

Jack

Uniforms found their way to the bottom of his seabag. Jack tossed in the little box he still carried and his Bible with the photos of happier times inside it. Out of habit, he slipped a couple extra pairs of socks on top before cinching it up and slinging it over his good shoulder. He looked around the room he'd called home for the past eleven months. Head bowed and eyes closed, Jack said his goodbyes to the life that had welcomed him and the Corps that had given him his first purpose. He looked straight ahead and marched forward all the way off the base before taking a full breath. Even then he didn't turn around for a final look at the man he left behind.

If he left his heart with a fiery redhead, his soul in the desert and his purpose at Lejeune, what was he carrying away with him?

XX

A Hide in the Midst of Raging Battles

September 2006 through March 2011

Marine survival training had prepared Jack to live off the land. Living with fellow humans presented a greater challenge. For that reason, Jack became one of those statistics to which no one can attach a firm number. Homeless Veteran. He decided to head west and see where the road led him. Along the way he found odd jobs he could do with his limitations, tucking away money. He didn't need much, of course. He'd come a long way from manger-crashing.

His first New Year's Eve on the road, Jack found himself in downtown Raleigh. He kept to the sides of the throng as each person jockeyed for the best spot to watch the acorn drop. He felt his heart pump faster, harder. Not enough air. Too many people. Lights. Sounds.

He had to escape the crush of bodies. Up ahead an alley beckoned. With any luck it would have an outlet on the other end. If not, at least he'd be out of the madness. As he approached his target, midnight merry-makers set off an arsenal of firecrackers that sent him spiraling into survival mode. With no weapon to draw, Jack instinctively grabbed the closest enemy around his neck.

Eyes wild, like a hunted creature's, Jack slowly came back to himself as the shouts of the teen's friends reached the part of his mind that knew he was no longer in Iraq's lawless desert. He dropped the kid. Hand up, Jack looked down at the wheezing boy. At what he'd almost done.

And so, Jack ran. He tore down the alley that did have an outlet. He ran out and across block after block until he was winded. Jack shook his head in a vain attempt to lose the image of the terror in the boy's eyes as he'd held a vice grip on his neck. No one rested safe from his toxic touch. He needed to steer clear of strangers as well as loved ones, it seemed.

Once he stopped running, Jack found himself lured by an old familiar resort. He walked straight into the beckoning liquor store without a single thought. He bought some golden relief and drank nearly the whole bottle as he walked along a railroad line. As he swayed along, Jack felt a rumble in the earth that had nothing to do with his drinking. He turned toward a light, growing ever larger. He thought again how sweet death's release must be. Just walk into the light and never hurt anyone again. Never again feel the searing pain of guilt. Jack smiled at the light and closed his eyes. Bright. Warm on his face. Flooding him with its shine.

Light.

Tray's final words. The beam of the flashlight in those five seconds. Two pairs of headlights soaring through the sky. One massive light barreling straight at him.

A sound pierced through the stillness around him, severing the liquor's hold on him with all the memories it exhumed. The blast rang out again, transporting him to the time his mom got off work just to take him a few towns over to wave to the President. A Whistle-stop Tour, they called it.

"Wave to the President, Jack!" Her smile outshone the sun that day.

Bright. Jack's eyes flew open. He took a step back, jerking back the bottle before he spiked it on the tracks just ahead of the train's mighty swoosh. Liquid and glass sprayed all around him. He felt the ripping of flesh across the top of his left cheek and let the blood fall unhindered.

Another scar. Another reminder.

This one that his mom deserved better than to have her son reported as rail kill. He would not do that to her. He would write to her, like he'd told Ben. He would also drift as long as it took to clear this fog in his head, break these panicked reactions and bad decisions.

The next day Jack wrote his mom a letter.

Mama,

I love you so much. Please know I'm going to be okay; at least I'm really trying. It's not good for me to be around people right now—for them or me, honestly. I promise to write often and send money when I can, but I don't know when I'll see you again. My head's not right. I'm not sure if it will get better, but I think being away from civilization's unexpected noises and pressures may be the best thing for me right now.

I love you and promise to come home if I can.

Love,

Jack

* * *

What Jack couldn't control were the nightmares. They'd returned. Every night he had at least one. It was all the old horrors, plus some. He saw the men he'd killed in Iraq. Whether he'd seen them in real life or not, he did now—each and every one.

In his latest recurring nightmare, Jack stood at the top of a mountain—nothing in sight as far as the eye could see. Behind him he felt the wraiths of his past creep upon him, slowly at first then faster and faster until they cast him over the edge. He fell longer than he could count. Instead of crashing into the valley below, though, he continued to pitch through total darkness. The entire time the air parted around him, he had only one thought. He was alone.

Alone in darkness.

At least he didn't wake up screaming from that one. He'd eventually jolt from the falling sensation. Sleep wouldn't return to him on those nights, so he'd stretch and do what exercises he could. He was up to a comfortable 300 sit-ups each day. Jumping jacks and knee raises warmed his blood in the colder months. He took care to exercise his gimpy arm as best he could. He never expected a miracle, but he didn't want to lose the few abilities he'd sweated for either. After a sufficient breakfast and enough water to keep himself well-hydrated, he'd hit the road again. He preferred cross country to roadside walking, though he liked to keep the main road in earshot.

Jack never had a destination in mind. He just kept moving. He saw the state as few had. As much as he walked, he never left North Carolina. For some reason it was home, but it wasn't the coastal breezes of Jacksonville that drew him. It was the mountains that sang to him. Once he reached the state's western side, he alternated among three sites where he felt most comfortable. Asheville, Black Mountain and

Burnsville created a triangle in which he existed. Seasons cycled. Citizens came and went around him, though they never noticed him. He made sure he never requested odd jobs from the same person. There were plenty of opportunities for him throughout the region. Jack was as much a part of the landscape as the trees, rocks, mountains and valleys he loved. He fell into a mutual understanding with the animals surrounding him. He learned the beauty of stillness and the peaceful cycle of nature as he lived within its simplicity.

He bathed in isolated mountain streams. Jack paused after coming up from a brisk dip under the water to examine himself in the clear liquid. He didn't recognize the reflection returning his gaze. The clean-cut, squared away Marine of more than a year ago had evolved into the epitome of a mountain man. Shaggy hair hung round his shoulders, and his beard covered his chest. Jack turned away from his image to revel in his surroundings. The mountains sustained him. He'd come to enjoy the trout he found in abundance in the many streams, and a gig in his left hand had become as deadly to the fish as a trigger squeezed in his right had been to insurgents.

Jack worked on other skills with his left hand. Thanks to his tasks during his final year in the Corps, he could write better left-handed than he ever did right-handed. So, he tried his hand at whittling a few things. He certainly had plenty of wood to choose from. At first, his frustration rose rapidly. During one of his early attempts, he sliced a gash in his leg when he tried to grip the wood between his knees. Writing with the wrong hand had felt awkward, but this seemed impossible.

One spring morning, the stream gurgled on its happy journey; and Jack sank back in the damp grass to listen to the water's song. A fluttering beneath a nearby pine stole his attention. A nest of baby birds had graduated to flying lessons. The smallest one struggled as he fell all over himself. His floundering lasted long past when his brothers and sisters had flown away. Even the mama bird had disappeared, given up hope on this final hatchling. As Jack watched, the bird's determination never wavered. The sun began to set; and, beneath its final rays, that tiny bird finally got it right. He soared off to begin a new life on his own.

Jack decided he would figure out a way to whittle again. His first passion had been building; and he'd be damned if he let Iraq take that, too. The following day—like the baby bird—Jack figured it out. His arm may have not been useful for much more than a paperweight, but it occurred to him that's all he needed. He found stumps on which to rest the fallen limbs and branches and then used his right arm to apply pressure as he whittled. He discovered ways to use other sticks to hold a project in place without having to bend over at awkward angles. He practiced over and over—every day— until he once again coaxed nature out of wood. He worked his way from simple pieces to more complex ones, eventually carving a family of bears like the ones with which he shared the mountainside.

Mama,

Are the hydrangeas blooming in Bellum? I remember how much you loved to see them each year at the park. Beautiful seems to be an awfully weak word to describe this part of the country. You would love it.

I've figured out a way to whittle again, even with this bum arm. My goal is to keep practicing until I can build furniture again. I sure miss Senior's woodshop. How are he and Mawmaw Mabel, Junior, Ducky, Daisy, Aunt E.? Ever hear from Ben and Grandma Ethel?

Even though you can't answer my questions, I like asking them. It just feels more like a conversation. I've been reading that Bible Senior gave me—some parts more than once. That almost feels like a conversation, too. Or maybe I've been alone for too long. Ha!

I think about you every day. I love you.

Love,

Jack

His confidence boosted, Jack entertained the idea of bigger wood-working projects. He bought a drawing pad and pencil set on one of his few trips into town. He sketched chairs and tables, stools and boxes. He even sketched some bed frames. One was an elaborate canopy-style bed complete with intricate carvings and delicate curves. He drew with a smile on his face. That night he dreamed of the look on Rachael's face if he could gift her such a bed.

Reading became another enjoyable time filler for Jack. He read cover to cover the little leather Bible the Millers had given him. Growing up, he watched his mama read it that way every year. As a boy, Jack couldn't understand reading at all. Reading the same book over and over? That was definitely beyond him. However, he found himself going back to some of the sections in this one more than once or twice.

* * *

Time wound itself around Jack as he lost track of ordered months and years. The seasons reminded him that somewhere people still flipped calendars. One sultry summer evening, Jack enjoyed the merriment and melody of the Shindig on the Green, a longstanding Asheville tradition. Local bluegrass bands and clog dancing groups entertained tourists and locals alike. He clung to the edges of the event under the shading comfort of a tree where he could safely observe the humanity around him. Carefree and laughing, families with children picnicked. Couples on their honeymoon danced or made out in their own little worlds. Groups of teenagers laughed and discussed unfolding futures. Odd that the world around him—the people he'd gone to war for—had carried on with their lives. Looking around, war seemed a distant whisper from this fairy tale realm. He supposed that's how it should be, though. That's why they went ... so lovers could meet and families could grow and friends could share.

Jack's throat tightened as he became conscious of an ever-present hollowness within. Eyes clenched tightly against the lively, spinning world around him, he envisioned a cavern—empty, save for the thick pitch of darkness—deep inside him where his heart had once beat.

This is what I want, though, right? To be alone? To stay far enough away from others to never hurt another soul?

Of course it was. He opened his vision again to the life around him. It had just been a long, long time since he'd immersed himself in this much civilization. He'd gotten temporarily overwhelmed.

Jack continued his stroll along the perimeter. He pondered how long it had been since he'd really spoken with anyone. Aside from asking for work and clarifying a job's requirements, his vocal cords didn't get much of a workout. He wondered, with an internal chuckle, if they could grow rusty and stop working altogether.

A girl with red hair twirled under the hand of a tall young man. Jack's smile was weighted with sadness. That could have been him and Rachael. Would have been. But he chose to leave. He walked away. He had turned his back on the love of his life.

His thoughts always circled back to her. He sighed as he wandered beneath the trees that encompassed the listeners. A bright paper tumbled past, carried by a rare June breeze. He retrieved it. Before tossing it in a nearby trash can, he gave it a read. Asheville did the Fourth of July right. Fireworks, music and food. He'd be sure to head higher into the mountains that holiday.

Warriors fought so people could remain unaware of how much like exploding grenades and bombs these spectacular light shows sounded. He'd stay as far away from people as he could then. He wouldn't risk an external casualty of his internal war. Just before he dropped the paper into the bin, the year caught his eye.

2009.

He'd been drifting for nearly three years. He was 25. A quarter of a century. How many more decades would he have to drift, dodging people and their celebrations?

Exhaustion rested heavy on his shoulders. Perhaps he could slip off to sleep one night and not wake up. It could all be over. No more wandering. No more waking from terrors of his dreams to the fear of his existence. He'd welcome the end like a long-awaited friend.

Something cold and wet interrupted his morbid musings as it pressed up into his limp appendage. Jack looked down—though not far—into warm brown eyes. An Irish wolfhound raised its head from its greeting to consider him, tongue hanging askew from a toothy grin.

"Well, hello there." Jack's voice surprised him. *Not rusted out yet.* "Who do you belong to?"

The dog's shaggy gray coat contained more than a few burrs, and he appeared thinner than Jack thought he should. "How could a good-lookin' guy like you be homeless?"

Although the dog followed him the rest of the evening, Jack figured he'd eventually wander off to whomever he came with. Instead, the massive dog stuck to Jack's heels as he crept along in the shadows of the mountain village. Jack figured once he hit the tree line on the outskirts, he'd surely lose his new shadow. The dog persisted. Thirty minutes later, Jack turned to evaluate his four-legged companion. The dog wagged its curved tail before sitting down expectantly.

"If you're expecting a home, you're gonna be disappointed." Jack shrugged as the dog grinned. He walked into his camp and busied himself with supper preparations. He pulled out some leftover fish, half a loaf of bread and some beans. "Lucky for you I've got two plates. A breakfast one and a supper one. Guess one's yours now, scout."

The tongue disappeared as the dog came to attention, cocking his head to one side.

"Scout?" The dog gave one sharp answering bark. "Okey-dokey. Scout, it is. Now, eat your supper and keep those barks to yourself."

The dog's grin returned as his tongue personally thanked Jack's beard before he set to work on the food placed before him. Jack shook his long unused smile at his guest. "You've got some charm for such a shaggy fellow."

Scout looked up with a burp as he licked up the bean sauce that had dripped into his beard. "Looks like we both have a problem with food gettin' in our beards. Guess we're not meant for polite society, huh, boy?"

He petted the dog for the first time and sealed their connection. That night Jack woke up screaming. Scout laid himself atop his new master's chest and licked his face and neck until the man's heartrate dropped back to normal. He nestled his furry chin into Jack's neck as they both drifted off into undisturbed sleep for the remainder of the night.

Early morning light and chirping birds woke Jack. Scout breathed softly in his ear, and the man smiled at the comfort the dog had brought him. "You're certainly bigger than Missy

Mee. You probably crap bigger than her, if we're bein' honest."

Scout answered with a lick that reached from Jack's chin to nose and all the way to his forehead. Jack led the way into the stream for a refreshing dip. He splashed his new friend and laughed at the surprise of massive paws returning the favor. Scout grinned his approval at their game. Sufficiently drenched, the pair clambered onto the bank and shook themselves. That's when Jack noticed the jagged scar on the dog's neck. It zagged from just above his front leg, across his shoulder and up his neck to disappear somewhere beneath his beard. It appeared to have healed naturally, despite the ill intention of the blade wielder.

"What happened to you, big guy? And, who on earth would do such a thing?" Scout whimpered his past pain until Jack rubbed his silky ears.

"I can't promise you won't meet a horrible fate if you choose to stick with me, boy—I'm kinda cursed—but I can promise I'll never do something like this to you."

Scout lifted a paw, and they shook on it.

The new team walked to nearby Weaverville. When he did go into towns, Jack did it sporadically and never to the same spots close together. He bought Scout a proper collar and leash and brush and replenished their bean supply. He wasn't sure how the dog would take to something around his neck, but he needed something he could snap to in case they encountered leash laws. Turned out, Scout was proud of his new leather accessory. When Jack buckled it on, the dog tucked in his tongue for only the second time since they'd met and examined his reflection in the window front. After a moment, his grin returned, and he leapt up to hug Jack. Jack's laugh surprised him, but the sight of the massive dog standing taller than him with paws resting on his shoulders proved more comical than anything he'd witnessed in a long while.

Mama,

You'll be happy to know I've got a companion. He's shaggy and sort of smelly—kind of like me. He also drools—also kind of like me.

Scout's an Irish wolfhound. He's huge! He just started tagging along after me one day and hasn't left. I guess he doesn't mind my grumpiness.

I love you and miss you.

Love,
Jack

* * *

Man and beast remained inseparable as they fell into the routine of life Jack had created for himself. Scout proved most helpful in the winter months. Jack discovered a cave on one of his hikes, but he slept in the open as long as he could. Being closed in made him feel claustrophobic—which did nothing to ease his nightmares. He'd been in the open air for too long to appreciate anything leaning toward indoors. On colder nights before ice and snow drove Jack to the cave's protection, Scout's warmth blanketed his master.

The following summer, Jack and Scout shifted over to a favorite site near Black Mountain. They settled across Flat Creek from a retreat. The families and groups that stayed there never noticed the mountain man and his giant dog keeping watch. On Sunday mornings, Jack heard hymns drifting on the wind from the nearby chapel. The words, though indiscernible from that distance, carried peace. He felt hope and passion on the breeze of their notes. It was on these mornings when he felt closest to Rachael. He envisioned her sitting in the church in Bellum, sunlight glistening around her and lighting on her captivating smile. She turned to send its rays his way as she sang one hymn or another. In his vision, though, she was older and even more beautiful than the last time he'd seen her. He ached to witness that smile, hear her laugh—a sound sweeter than all the choirs of angels could produce. At times his longing filled his chest so full, he could barely draw a breath.

And then reality would descend. He knew she surely belonged to another at this point. He hated whoever he was but shot out a plea to the universe that she had found true happiness even if it wasn't with him. He had thrown his chance away long ago.

On one of his early Sunday reflections, the chapel's music raised words in his mind.

Amazing grace, how sweet the sound,
That saved a wretch like me?

Yeah, he knew the words. Every Southerner did. He'd never really considered them, though. He was a wretch; that much rang true. But, grace? Saved? And then the whole lost and found thing popped up. He was lost all right.

"None of us deserves any good thing. So, when one does come—it's a gift. Accept it."

The gift of grace made sense for people like Rachael, his mom, Ben—good people. He was not good. He may be lost, but at least he knew it. He'd accepted his fate unlike the lost folks back in Bellum. God could keep his grace to himself and his special people. Jack didn't need any more reminders of the great God who let kids kill other kids and entire countries send people to end each others' lives in order to build some pseudo-peace. Jack wanted nothing to do with that God. He leapt to his feet, grabbing a nearby stone as he did. He tossed it up and down in his left hand a few times before calling on all the angry energy roiling within him to launch it as far toward the offensive music as he could. He felt its impact before he heard its thunk against a distant tree. He tripped back up the mountain, far away from the dying bars of the song that had lifted emotions he didn't know he carried. Words he didn't care to recall nearly caught him, hurrying his ascent.

> *... he will my shield and portion be,*
> *As long as life endures.*

Leaves burst with colors all around them as man and beast made their trek north toward a popular peak. Jack had rarely hiked the marked trails in that area. He lived in parts of the mountain still unspoiled by human carelessness; and, once someone experiences such raw beauty, heavily traveled paths can't hold much attraction. Jack continued his climb up the trail, Scout trotting along with his leash dutifully tucked into the pocket of Jack's cammies.

After a climb that couldn't break their even breathing, the scruffy pair reached a pinnacle that sucked out Jack's breath and left him stunned. It was the mountaintop from his dream; but, instead of vengeful corpses, he discovered only serenity. He gazed across at other mountain peaks and looked down on treetops. He sat, legs swinging over the valley far below. Scout sat at attention, panting his approval of their view.

The landscape before him carried Jack high in the elation of its majesty before casting him back into the valley of his corporeality—or lack thereof. He could slide off that ledge. Plummet into nothingness. End his painful existence.

At this point, of what use am I? I've done nothing beneficial for anyone in so long. Is a man without a purpose still a person?

Phrases flashed through Jack's mind.

Grandma Ethel's teary, cheerful voice explaining, *I'll be with them all again one day, but then I'll get an even better gift. I'll see my Jesus face to face. He's gonna take me by my hand and walk me up and down his streets of gold. We're gonna talk and laugh and sing and dance together. I'm gonna love dancin' with my Jesus.*

Tray, gasping for breath, pressing out commands: *Drive out the pain you got. Accept grace. Let in peace. Joy.*

Jack's hand reached up to his face. When was the last time he'd cried? How could this place—a spot where beauty found its very definition—bring him to tears?

The video in his mind played again. Rachael singing in church; her voice angelic as she turned back to him, a smile illuminated by a halo from the lucky sunbeam lighting on her hair.

"When we've been there ten *zillion* years,"—she always swapped out "thousand" for what she viewed a more fitting time period—"bright shining as the sun, we've no less days to sing God's praise than when we first begun."

Tray's last two words gave a lighter spot to Jack's regular dreams. There was something about the way he'd said them—like he was telling his buddy what he was observing. *Light. Glory.* He'd told him to "accept grace." Rachael had told him to accept the gifts. What did they even mean?

His mama. Rachael and Ben. Senior. Mawmaw Mabel. Ducky. Junior. Daisy. Tray and Grandma Ethel.

To them, grace was real. To them, God was real. And good. They'd say he created this beauty before Jack. And, they'd say he created the next life, too. It had to be better than this one, right?

Scout whimpered and nosed Jack's cheek before laying his head in his lap. His eyes searched Jack's face and cast a worried message to his master.

"I won't jump, boy. I'm staying right here with you." Jack sniffed, the scent of pine filling his lungs. "Maybe we need to venture toward a more inhabited area this winter. That cave may make me crazier than I already am."

Scout bounced up and trotted back toward the trail, urging his master to follow his beckoning bark. Jack laughed as he scrambled to his feet, wiping roughly at his dripping eyes, and followed the dog's shaggy form. "Some days I'm not sure which one of us is leading the way."

His dream on the ledge returned that night. Instead of darkness and death, though, light crept toward him. He turned to see Rachael gliding his way. She wore the sundress she'd worn the last time they picnicked together back in Bellum. Her smile warmed him to his core. Those beautiful red lips. He could still taste them, feel their softness against his lips. She floated on the beam of light that carried her slowly toward him. Before she reached his waiting arms, it enveloped her in its ethereal rays. Rachael would always be his love, his heart, his home—his hide in the midst of raging battles within and around him.

XXI

Family Portrait

Fall 2010 through March 2011

Wanderers from a myriad of backgrounds converged in downtown Durham. Some stayed there and, in their own way, labeled it home; others drifted through on their journey elsewhere. Jack found that the city, like the far more desolate mountains and forests, contained many nooks and crannies overlooked by the people who lived and worked around them. Abandoned warehouses, hidden alleys and shaded corners beneath bridges wore invisibility cloaks penetrable only by those who chose to see them.

Scout made hiding in plain sight slightly more challenging, but they soon blended in enough to deter locals from stopping to chat. Adjusting to life in a bustling city, however, took far longer for the veteran. Jack couldn't even consider sleep for the first seventy-two hours they were there. Constant traffic, train whistles, shouts and especially the gunshots they heard nearby on the second night filled his head with scenes of a waking nightmare. His brain played tricks on him, and he was back in Iraq. Every battle he and Tray faced in the desert replayed around him that night—a surround-sound experience he'd never wanted a ticket for.

Around the 48-hour mark of no sleep, the show became a multi-sensory experience. From then on, every bang, clatter, pop and crack plunged Jack to deeper levels of paranoia. His bloodshot eyes told him the enemy lurked behind dumpsters and in long-empty hotels and down every dark and dead-end alley.

Jack tasted salt and sand as his sweat ran into his gaping mouth. He tasted blood when he bit down on a scream after a truck backfired nearby. The stench of garbage and burning rubber combined with the irritation of every speck of grit he'd attracted since his last dip in a mountain stream. This amalgamation resulted in an immersion into a past that had exploded into his present. Toward the end of that third day, Jack's emotions escalated, his actions more erratic.

He claimed a vandalized building as his sniper hide. He picked a pipe up from the ground before they entered and held it awkwardly in his left hand, propped like a rifle on one of the pane-less windows. Scout sensed his master's panicked state. When Jack started chattering incessantly, the dog's eyebrows met in a concerned arch as his neck twisted right and left.

"Sand. Too much frickin' sand. Down in my sights. Have to clean it again." A garbage truck clanked into a dumpster a few blocks over. "No time. They're rollin' in. What's the dope?"

He turned toward Scout and asked again, "What's the dope, Tray?" The great dog gave a low grumble as he reached out a paw and laid it gently on Jack's thigh. That simple contact paused the widescreen action rolling before Jack and reminded him of what was real ... and what wasn't. Understanding registered. He twisted around to lean against the crumbling brick wall, the pipe clattering away from his surrendered hand. His face dropped onto his knees, and his shoulders shook with the realization that some part of his brain had been wounded in action. He may never be able to coexist with normal life—whatever *normal* even meant.

Scout burrowed his head between Jack's chest and knees, and Jack rested his forehead on the dog. Exhaustion finally claimed him, and he slept unhindered longer than he'd slept in years. His furry pillow didn't move until he slowly woke on his own. Once Jack's full consciousness returned, he sat up and petted his partner until the big oaf rolled over for a belly rub. Jack's laugh sounded creaky, like a door in a haunted house.

"What would I do without you?" Scout rolled onto his back while kicking out his hind legs and one of his front legs. He basked in the attention. "I'm really screwed up in my brain, aren't I?" The dog responded with a sneeze large enough to match its maker's size.

* * *

Jack backed away from bustling downtown life to reacquaint himself with society. He and his guardian headed closer to Duke University's campus. He found some seclusion there in the midst of the busyness. Carefully, strategically, he placed himself in more crowded, noisy situations. Each time he took it up another notch, it got a little easier to adjust and accept. Scout could sense when his master's heart began to race and would press himself closer. With a hand on the wolfhound, Jack would keep going, one step at a time. *Breathe in. Breathe out.*

Mama,

Scout and I are trying to rejoin society. Technically, Scout's fine with it. I'm taking a little longer, though. It's going to take longer for my mind to heal, but Scout is helping me do that.

I promise I'm trying. I love you.

Love,

Jack

* * *

The companions headed to the largely uninhabited stretch of nature to the east of the Bull City, while the rest of the world loudly ushered in 2011. When they returned, the pair settled in to more popular spots for the area's homeless. The community they found there had its downsides. After a few guys attempted to rob him and Jack put them down soundly, word circulated that he was no easy target and not someone to mess with. It also had benefits—the warmth of trash can fires was one. He looked at it, also, as an opportunity to reinsert himself with other people. He didn't sleep much the first few nights, but Scout placed a paw on him whenever Jack needed to shut off his brain and let go. He knew he had nothing to fear with his guardian watching over him.

Within a few days, the community welcomed him as one of their own. One man stood out as a leader of sorts. Tall, with graying hair that still held some of its blond strands and a face full of reddish stubble, Jay introduced himself to Jack and asked for his help on their daily food run. Area restaurants and groceries allowed them to pick up day-old items. It was an elaborate system with a dozen or so stops each day of the week. They brought it back and fairly divided the spoils. Jay made sure the older residents and those with little ones got first pick. Jack thought back to his life in Bellum and realized how oblivious he was to what really happened in the world. Bombings and hunger, shootings and homelessness. These weren't things he'd witnessed until he left the U.S. and then returned to drift through—and actually see—his own nation for the first time.

Jack looked around at the faces surrounding the food baskets. What were their stories? Why were they living on the streets? He looked at a family that typically huddled together away from everyone most of the time. The couple's names were Jed and Lana. Jed's empty sleeves were pinned up to his shoulders, and his face and neck were covered with bright white scars. He appeared to be not much older than Jack. Lana's strength and independence showed in the lift of her chin and reminded him of Rachael; but, unlike his love, this young woman had lost any of the hope that may have once sparkled in her eyes. Their two little ones were twins, as he discovered on his second day there.

Scout drew all the kids to him. Not at first, of course; he was the size of a small horse, after all. He grinned at the clusters hanging back from him as he twisted his neck from side to side. Tongue lolling, he bowed, lay down and showed his belly. One look at the silly dog's playful antics, and they forgot how huge he was. They ran over and rubbed him as he rolled around in the dirt. He'd twist up to give them each a lick. They were all best buddies from that point on. Since the dog belonged with the man in the camouflage pants, the children flocked to him as well. Jack soon discovered he had a knack for storytelling.

He told them tales of the desert and its sandstorms. In his stories the crazy winds weren't scary or dangerous or even aggravating. Instead, he created elaborate legends behind them and mythical creatures that sent them to drive out evil gods who sought to ruin the land with their trickery and deceit. He told stories of the mountains as well. Many of them centered around the bear family he lived near. He made them giggle whenever he talked about the silly bear cubs and how they played. He said their names were Travis and Jenna— which happened to be the names of the twins in the camp— and that they loved honey. Most of the stories centered around how they always stuck their noses in places they shouldn't, like the time they found a bee hive. Even the adults found themselves laughing until they cried as Jack described the way the cubs bounded down to the stream, a black buzzing cloud trailing them.

As he watched the people warm rapidly to this young man, Jay rubbed his hand absentmindedly over his bloated belly. He considered how Jack didn't look like he belonged there. He was haunted and battered but not broken. And, oddly familiar somehow.

After morning food collections, Jay disappeared into a bottle and withdrew from the rest of the camp unless an issue or disturbance arose. Jack recognized the lust for drink in the older man's eyes whenever they got close to the end of the distributions. Jay had offered to share, but Jack smiled and shook his head. "Been down that road. That's the one beast I seem to have slain."

"Good for you," Jay muttered as he took a long pull on the bottle of cheap whiskey and wiped his mouth on his jacket sleeve. "Long ago, I might have beat it. Had people who tried to help me. I decided I wanted the bottle more than I wanted them, so I walked away."

He sat silently and drank some more. The bottle was more than half empty when he continued. "Wish I'd let them help me. Used the excuse that I didn't want to hurt 'em, and they were better off without me. May have been true. 'Spose I'll never know."

The excuses from Jay's mouth pierced through Jack's heart. Those were the exact words he'd used to defend his own escape from those he claimed to love.

Jack missed his mom, his friends. More than that, he regretted all the time he'd lost. The time he could never get back with Rachael ate at him most. He had been a stupid kid when he turned his back on her. Jack began contemplating returning home. Would they forgive him and allow him back in their lives? He thought—knew—his mom would always welcome him back with open arms. He needed to work toward that, though. First step was learning to interact again with other humans. He had his mission set.

* * *

Jack settled in to a routine with this new community. Jay took a special interest in him, especially when he realized this kid could take leadership in the afternoons, allowing him the freedom of a second daily bottle.

"Never wanted the position," he slurred one evening to Jack. "Jus' kinda fell in my lap, like. Times got harder. Vets started wanderin'; families lost houses. None of 'em knew how to survive on the streets—or weren't quite able to go it alone. They started lookin' to me since I've been out and about for round a couple decades now. So, here we are."

Jay carelessly swung the near-empty bottle in a grand sweep of their little town beneath the abandoned train bridge. "'Spose I could name it 'Jay Town,' and they'd oblige me."

Coughing quickly choked out his mirth. When the man sat back up, Jack understood the cause of the rust-colored stains streaked across Jay's pants as the man rubbed a blood-covered hand down his thigh. Jay recognized the alarm on the face of the young man before him. "No one can help me." His smile stretched thinly on his sunken face. "I should've asked for help. Too late now."

Jack wasn't sure if Jay was referring to whatever illness he clearly had or something else.

"That's the thing 'bout time." Jay paused to drain the last of the bottle's contents. "It don't hang on for you to catch up. Jus' too late for my whole life now. Had a family once. I couldn't sit still and counted that a good 'nough reason to leave 'em. Seems the worst one possible, as I reflect. At the time I called it 'best for them.' I was a lousy husband and dad; they're better off."

Jack slid through a veil of helplessness as he witnessed the man's hopeless expression. "You never know. It may not be too late. I know my mom would love to see my dad again, no matter how long it's been. That's how she was with me the first time I struck out. She's the most forgiving woman I know."

"Sounds like a true prize of a lady." Jay's wistful smile told Jack he was drifting off to dream about whatever past he'd lost hope of ever redeeming. Jack leaned back against the abutment and pictured his mom's face. He needed to see her and maybe—just maybe—she needed to see him, too. Maybe he could help Jay find his way home, too. Jack had people believe in him and push him all along the way. Perhaps he could do that for Jay. Like Pete, his roommate at the mission, had told him, *You'll have people enter your life that'll be more of a support than you might think. Some are there for a few minutes; others decades. Each has a reason for meeting you when they do. Look for those reasons and thank God for 'em.*

Mama,

Scout and I have joined a little community here. See, he really is helping me! There's this guy who's kind of the accepted leader—Jay. He talked to me yesterday about how he missed his life and lost all the people who loved him. He says it's too late for him. I don't want to believe that. And, I don't want to be him one day.

I think I'm almost ready to come home. But first I want to work on getting Jay back to his.

I'll be in touch. I love you. Thank you for loving me and being patient with me.

Love,

Jack

***

The next afternoon, the children surrounded Jack with a chorus of "One more story! One more!"

Jack quieted them and kicked over an egg crate with his worn boot. The children formed a seated semicircle around him while Scout bounded in front and lay down where they could all lean on or pet him as they listened.

"Long, long ago," Jack began and then whispered, "I was your age." Gasps and giggles rose from his group of listeners. "I grew up in a tiny town in Northeast Georgia called Bellum."

A crash of bread baskets and shattering of a liquor bottle jolted all attentions away from the story, including Jack's, as he instinctively reached for his phantom weapon. Jay mumbled an apology. He stumbled over a few baskets in a futile attempt at gathering bits of broken glass. The children's attention returned to the story before Jack's did.

"Tell you what, guys, let's hold onto that story for around the fire tonight, okay?" He didn't stick around to hear the begging that followed. When he reached down to help Jay pick up some of the longer glass shards, the man quickly turned away but not before Jack noticed a haunted look pressing moisture from his eyes. He asked the older man, "You okay?"

"Yeah. That'll teach me to try to drink and balance crates at the same time." His half-hearted attempt at humor only further convinced Jack something was wrong. Jay remained with his back to the younger man but began talking in a sober near-whisper.

"I don't know what you're runnin' from, but you're young enough to go home. Make amends. Let your family and friends help you. Comes a time when a man draws close to his end days, and he looks back and sees things more clearly. Don't you make my same mistakes. I know everything could've been so different if I hadn't been too proud to open myself up to the love and support offered ... especially from my Becky." He set down a worn and faded open wallet on a teetering stack of crates before walking away.

He called back, "Goodbye, Jack. It was an honor to get to meet you, son."

Jack's gaze locked on the wallet. Disbelief and denial held him rooted to the spot. Finally, he fingered the soft leather framing a single photograph. All the air escaped Jack's lungs, as he accepted the truth before sinking to the ground, clutching the family portrait—the same one that sat on his nightstand throughout his childhood. He was only two or three. His mom's bangs were higher, and she wore a bright pink jacket with shoulder pads. Behind them both stood a much younger Jay. His father.

Act IV

Instauration

XXII

Running Toward Something

March 2011

Once Jack recovered from having his world tilted on its axis, evening was approaching. Jay had not returned, so Jack and the other men in the community spread out to search. Jack and Jed teamed up to hit nearby shelters, Scout trotting along between them. The whole time he walked, Jack replayed the conversations they'd had. He couldn't believe he'd lived with his own father for weeks without noticing the similarities between their faces. Or the resemblance to the man in the photo he'd stared at every night until he had stopped wishing that man would return.

By the time they neared their final stop before heading back to rejoin the rest of the search party, Jack had run through his entire range of emotions—denial, anger, fear ... sorrow.

Jay believed he was doing right for his family by leaving them, but the whole time he was running from himself and his inability to ask for the help he so clearly needed. Jack's anger returned as he kicked a rock at a chain link fence. *Why couldn't he have been stronger ... just taken the help my mom tried so hard to give him.*

Mom. Tears stung Jack's eyes as he thought of what she would do if she got to see her husband again. She still wore her wedding band on a chain around her neck. Maybe he should tell Jay that. Tell ... his dad.

Jack still couldn't believe it. He had so many questions. Where had Jay been all these years? What was wrong with him? Was he dying? Maybe he just needed medical attention. Jack felt his eyes grow heavy as they dammed up his emotions. He had been heading along the same path as his father, but it wasn't too late—not for him. And not for Jay.

He would get them both home—back to his mom. No man left behind.

As they turned the corner across from the soup kitchen, bright lights met their eyes. Police cruisers, a fire truck and an ambulance had the usually quiet area in a whirlwind of sights and sounds.

Jack took in the scene in a single sweep and felt the pendulum on time snap.

"No. No ... no ... no!" Jack sprinted across the road toward the stretcher and the body bag strapped to it.

Officers attempted to hold him back; but, before Scout's growls could escalate to a sharper defense, the manager of the kitchen came to Jack's rescue. "He's from the community."

"Sir, do you know Mr. Jay? Could you positively ID his body?"

Jack nodded numbly as he shook away the sobs simmering within him. The coroner unzipped the bag to reveal the resting face of Jack's father, Jack Calhoun Sr. What had been only an initial had become a name to the community he cared for, while his real name had passed down to the son he'd left behind.

After confirming his father's identity, Jack accepted a detective's card before sinking to the curb where he watched them cart away the man he'd made up hero stories about when he was a kid. Scout rested his head in Jack's lap as the whirlwind of a single afternoon's events raged within the young man's mind and heart.

The next morning, Jack contacted the detective and found out where his father's body had been taken. He paid for a proper, though simple, burial for his father. The doctor who regularly visited the shelter told Jack the cancer had begun in Jay's liver, but his body was likely full of it at this point. It had only been a matter of time, he said.

As Jack tossed a spade full of dirt atop the rude box, he resolved not to meet the same end. He also decided his mom needed closure, the truth … and her son. It was time for an instauration for them both—a restoration of their relationship and a re-establishment of his place back in society.

Jack finally recognized his self-proclaimed "best-thing-for-everyone" as what it was—a selfish denial of something he was running from. He gifted himself a birthday present that year. Jack headed home.

* * *

Before Jack hoisted his pack to head out, he handed a piece of paper to Jed. "Here's the number to a great friend of mine—Ducky. His dad's construction company built a community of houses for families with kids in Columbia, S.C. Give him a shout, and he'll help y'all get down there. Tell him I sent you."

"Thanks, man." Jed's green eyes misted as he clutched the scrap of paper. "All I need is a leg up to get my family back in the kind of life they deserve."

"Ducky's definitely your guy. You just take care of your family." The two young men bumped shoulders in farewell. Jack thought again of Pete's words. *Some are there for a few minutes; others decades.*

"And each one means something, don't they?" Jack tousled Scout's ears as they walked past a post office box where Jack dropped off a final letter.

Mama,

In a few days—maybe before you even get this—I'm going to call you. I'm finally on my way home—home to family and friends. I've got Ben's address down in Savannah, and that's where I'm going first. As soon as I can, though, I'm bringing you over. We've got so much to catch up on, and I have a lot to tell you.

Scout's looking forward to meeting you.
I love you. I'll see you soon.

Love,
Jack

Scout eagerly trotted alongside Jack as they struck out beneath the sun's watchful rays toward the interstate where they did something out of their ordinary. Jack stuck out a thumb and prayed for a ride. His resolve was strong and walking too slow. Twenty minutes later an 18-wheeler slowed down and finally halted about 300 yards away. The travelers jogged up to the passenger side and opened the door. Inside, a man with a bushy brown mustache, plaid shirt with rolled sleeves and dark jeans nodded toward him and asked, "Where you headed?"

"Final destination's Savannah, but I'd be thankful for as far as I can get in that direction."

"Luck's smilin' on you today, kid. I'm headin' down 95 to Florida, passin' right through Savannah. Let Big Shaggy there take a leak, cause we ain't stoppin'. I run fast and full out."

"Copy that. Thank you, sir."

Jack walked Scout down the bank and let him relieve himself before they loaded up into the cab.

"Let me guess—Marine?"

"Yes, sir."

"That's good to go. I was in the Army. I'm Burt, by the way." He held out a tattooed arm that Jack accepted with his good hand.

"Jack. This is Scout. He keeps me sane."

"Sometimes, I think God gave animals bigger hearts and better understandin' than most people he created."

They passed the morning swapping war stories. Jack thought about the men who gathered every morning at Hardy's and how he'd listened to them telling tales and shooting the bull. He never thought back then he'd be one of those guys.

Jack's stomach began to rumble sometime before noon.

"I'm feelin' mighty hungry here," Burt said. "Open up that fridge back there and pull us out some sandwiches. My wife makes the best finger sandwiches, but when I'm out on the road I like to take advantage of eatin' all the fried food I can. She likes to limit that on me. Anyway, Jacksonville's my home stop, so I need to get rid of these sandwiches ... make her think I ate 'em all. You and Big Boy can help me clear out the container."

They ate in silence and cleaned out every last crumb. They washed them down with some sodas Burt directed Jack to in the little fridge.

"Do you like driving?" Jack asked.

Burt nodded before elaborating. "Sittin' still don't agree with me, but sittin' still at seventy miles per hour works. Plus, I get to see the country, meet some int'restin' folks and don't have to sit around twiddlin' my thumbs."

An hour after devouring the sandwiches, they pulled off the interstate into Savannah. Jack offered to buy Burt a cup of coffee or pay him for his trouble.

"Nah! Just glad I was headin' your way."

Man and dog climbed out of the cab before turning to say thank you again.

"I hope you find it."

Jack paused, uncertain of Burt's meaning. "What's that?"

"Whatever it is you're runnin' to. I hope you find it."

"Thank you, sir." Jack chuckled. He'd never been accused of running *toward* something before. "So do I."

XXIII

Searching

March 20-21, 2011

Jack pondered Burt's last words as he watched the rig inch out of the travel center's parking lot and on to the last stretch of its homeward journey. What exactly *was* he running toward? He needed to make sure it wasn't Rachael. She was probably chasing a passel of kids around a park … with a husband she'd kiss before they hopped in their minivan to head home. He shook the image from his mind as he pulled a wrinkled letter from his seabag. No, he was here to see Ben. He had questions—about life … about death and peace. About God. He'd read that Bible the Millers had given him.

Today was about getting to Ben; tomorrow he'd head to Columbia. After that, he needed to decide where his future lay so he could bring his mom to him and care for her the way she had for him for so many painfilled years. It all began with directions, though.

"Excuse me." Jack stepped toward an employee who walked out of the center's sliding glass doors. "Could you point me toward Danberry Lane?"

"Sure. My folks live near there. It's about five miles away. Do you have a map?" The young blonde flashed him a smile that was a little too trusting, Jack thought. He would expect a girl to be more cautious when approached by a grubby drifter with a horse of a dog.

"I don't. Can I get one inside?"

"You can, but I'm happy to just draw you one to where you're goin'." She wound a strand of hair around her finger and popped a bubble onto her bright red lips as she added, "Unless you're gonna be stayin' around here for a while and want to know where to get other places in the city."

Her flirting caught Jack off guard, and his jaw dropped for a moment. Scout sneezed and lifted a paw to rub his snout. The sound brought the young man back to reality and the task at hand. "Just the directions to Danberry, please."

Disappointment at his lack of interest darkened her face as she reached out a hand for the letter he held. "Want me to draw it on there?"

"No, if you could just tell me, I'd really appreciate it." As a storm cloud crossed her face, he tapped his temple and added, "Excellent memory."

Her seductive smile returned as she translated his words to some sort of flirtatious message. She gave him a string of directions involving salons, boutiques, a water tower and an uncertain number of stop signs. When she'd finished, she asked, "Sure you don't want me to write anything down for you?"

"That's quite all right, ma'am. You've been very helpful." His manners brought a deeper color to her cheeks and a twinkle to her light blue eyes.

"No problem … 'excellent memory,'" she responded with a tap of a fake nail to her own temple. As she walked backward, she recited a phone number, twice. "In case you decide to stick around. Ask for Bethany." With a wink, she twirled around and sashayed across the lot.

"I think I'd rather call up a host of insurgents," Jack muttered. Scout let out an agreeing bark as his master slung the pack onto his shoulder again.

Despite the vague directions, the companions arrived on Danberry Lane mid-afternoon. No car rested in the driveway of 2200, but Jack knocked anyway. He wasn't surprised with a response, so they meandered across the street to a shady vacant lot. They did what they did best and blended in with their surroundings. The last thing he needed was to have worried neighbors call the police to handle a vagrant situation. The travelers shared the last of the water in Jack's canteen and dozed beneath the shade of a massive oak tree in the late afternoon haze.

Traffic increased on the idyllic street as families returned from weekend activities to prepare for another week of work and school. Jack's heart raced at the absurd normality of the life unfolding before him. To calm himself, he pulled out Scout's brush and groomed him as meticulously as he had always cleaned his weapon. Not like the dog needed it. He was already the most stately homeless dog in history.

The sun had long since dropped from sight, and spring's chill crept along Jack's spine. Headlights appeared, slowing and turning into the driveway they'd watched all afternoon. "Sure hope it's still his house," Jack mumbled. Scout uttered a worried whine. He wasn't used to missing many meals.

Jack breathed a sigh of relief as a familiar figure stepped out of a time-worn SUV. The pair crossed the lot and street then. Jack called out, "Don't you think it's about time you traded this heap in for somethin' that may not leave you stranded?"

Ben turned as the voice of a ghost reached his ears. He smiled and shook his head as recognition rose in his face. "You are one unpredictable young man." He greeted Jack with open arms. "How the heck are you? And, who is this big guy?"

"This is Scout. He's a big reason I'm finally doing okay."

"Well, then, you're most welcome, Scout!" Ben stooped to pet the wolfhound and received a sloppy kiss in return. "I'm sure you two are starving. I'm not much of a cook, but I could probably rustle up something that doesn't require much culinary ability."

"Before we go in ... Rach isn't ..." Jack couldn't finish the question that had gnawed his gut all afternoon.

The preacher shook his head back at the new man before him. "No. She's here in Savannah now, but she's on her own. I'm not usually this late, but she cooks for me on Sunday evenings."

Jack nodded, head down, as he followed Ben up the steps to his front door. His heart tightened and twisted in his chest as he realized how close he was to Rachael—to seeing her in her new life. His breathing came harder as he tried to decide how he felt about that. Ben led the way into his home without offering further information. "How about some soup? I'm pretty sure I can warm that up without burning anything."

"Sounds great."

"Bathroom's down that hall to the right if you want to wash up. Back yard's fenced, too, if he wants to explore. Leave the sliding door open so he can come and go as he pleases." Ben watched Jack kneel down beside his friend and give him a playful ear scratching before opening the door. "And, Jack? Happy birthday, son."

Jack's surprise at the man's recognition of the day flashed in his eyes as he reflected on the birthday they'd celebrated together nine years earlier. His future had still spread ahead of him then, rosy and untarnished.

The soothing talk and warm soup filled Jack more completely than he'd been in many years. "Thank you," Jack said after he'd dried the last dish. "For opening your home to me. For not forgetting me ... or giving up on me."

"Never." Ben's genuine smile wrapped itself around Jack's heart.

"I've got questions—about life and ... about death."

Ben nodded. "Consider tomorrow our catchup day. I don't have any pressing appointments at the mission. The weather's supposed to be beautiful, and I think it's time we introduce this fine fellow to the best dog park Savannah's got to offer." He patted Scout's head as they bid each other goodnight and turned in to opposite rooms.

It didn't take Jack long to realize he would be sleeping in Rachael's room. Everywhere he turned, there she was. In her portraits from high school, the poster and photographs she'd chosen to decorate her space and the books that lined bookshelves and dresser tops.

On her nightstand lay *Jane Eyre* and *Wuthering Heights*. He remembered they were her favorites. He sure would love to know why. Too bad he'd missed his chance to ask.

A beach photo caught his eye. He recognized Rachael with Anna Claire and Shannon. A boy and a girl built a sandcastle in the background. Jack decided they must belong to the other two girls. Other photos showed Rachael hang gliding off a cliff and ziplining through a forest. One more showed her surrounded by children, all half-naked with the distended bellies of poor nutrition. Despite their circumstances, their smiles were wide. Rachael looked right at home in their midst, a young Mother Teresa.

He picked up a heart-shaped pillow from her bed. Feeling its softness tugged at that connection deep within him. When he lifted it to his face and breathed her in, he knew he was playing with fire and would emerge with only ashes left of the heart he'd willingly sacrifice for her.

The poster over Rachael's bed held Jack's gaze the longest. The photo showed a mare with her head nuzzling a spindly-legged foal. The words were a Bible verse—Rachael's favorite.

"You will keep him in perfect peace, whose mind is stayed on You, because he trusts in You." Isaiah 26:3

A lightbulb went off, and Jack recalled the little watercolor painting Rachael had tried to gift him back in high school. He cringed at the way he'd dismissed her talents and this verse. He chewed over its message and wondered what it could mean and if it could ever apply to him. He looked back at Rachael's face in the photo with the children. Perfect peace radiated from her.

He examined himself in the mirror and decided if he was going to rejoin society, he'd need to look less wild. It took him an hour to trim his beard and hair and take the first shower he'd had in longer than he could remember. He'd forgotten how incredible warm water could feel on his skin. When Jack returned to Rachael's room, he stood for a moment looking at the soft bed in front of him. He sat down on it and, again, felt her all around him. He stood back up and crossed to Scout who lay near the low window. Sleeping in her bed seemed wrong somehow. Sleeping in any bed felt foreign. He had been without one for so long, he wondered if he'd ever be able to sleep in one again.

Jack lay against his faithful companion, grabbed a blanket from Rachael's chair and draped her scent around his shoulders. He drifted off into a marathon of dreams filled with light and softness and hope, pictures in which Rachael played every leading role.

***

The following morning, Ben peered through the open doorway to his daughter's room. He smiled at the boy lying on the floor with his dog. What this kid had been through, he didn't know, but he was pretty sure none of his journeys had included a bed, a shower or a hot meal. He thought back to the day he received that final letter. He'd prayed that God would save and rescue this lost lamb and stay his hand from any desperate action. Becky had let him know each time she received a letter. They were surprised the postmarks remained in one state. They were pleased at the slow but noticeable growth and change each delivery revealed. Gazing at Jack, Ben breathed a thank you and sent up another request. This one for wisdom. Wisdom in his words as Jack had clearly come to him for guidance. And wisdom on what to share—and what to withhold—between his daughter and the boy who'd broken her heart.

Ben might be one of the world's worst cooks, but pancakes he could make. He was determined this boy wouldn't have cold cereal or cold anything for a meal if he could help it. Breakfast was nearly ready, and coffee was brewing when Jack staggered down the hall, sleep-tousled and groggy. He wore ripped camouflage pants and no shirt. His defined chest bore bullet scars from the war; a cut peeked out from his beard, a reminder of his battle with alcohol; and scratches from life in the mountains marked the rest of him.

"Mornin'! You're in luck because pancakes are my one culinary ability." Ben chuckled. "Hope you're hungry. I only know how to make them for an army."

Jack's eyes lit up at the tower of pancakes his host had stacked on the counter by the griddle. Scout trotted past his master and nudged Ben's hip for attention. He was rewarded with a pet and a pancake. He grinned up at the chef as soon as he gulped it down.

"Well, Scout approves. And, he's surprisingly picky for a dog on the drift." Jack ran a hand through his sun-lightened hair. It hung just beneath his ears and felt oddly light after years of it covering his shoulders.

It didn't take the three long to work their way down the giant stack. They cleaned up the kitchen in silence and then dressed for the day. Scout paced by the front door, urging them to hurry up. "I swear that dog knows everything we say."

"You better believe it." Jack grinned. "So, don't mention a steak unless you're prepared to deliver."

"Right back at you. I'm pretty sure he just looked at me and saw a cartoon S-T-E-A-K."

Scout's booming bark filled the entryway.

"Oh, yeah. He can also spell." Jack clapped his host on the shoulder as they followed the bounding dog down the front steps.

Savannah's Paws & Claws Pet Park spread out across six acres near Ben's house. The early Monday morning turned out to be the perfect time to enjoy the park. They had it to themselves. Scout ran nonstop, chasing squirrels and birds and butterflies and the wind. The two men sat on a bench and talked—small talk and weather at first. From there, they discussed Ben's job at the Genesis Mission. The men whose lives he'd impacted over the years—many became preachers or counselors or businessmen. So many lives rocked to the core and transformed for futures abounding where before they held no hope. Jack talked about his time on the mountain peak and in the mirage hide where his PTSD raked him. He described the homeless camp and how he met his father. And lost him.

"The war shook stuff up in my brain. I've had to relearn how to live with people. I'm still learnin'." Jack squinted out toward Scout who was nosing around the ground, on the trail of something that had passed earlier.

"I'm not sure I can ultimately beat this. Every time I think I've conquered one demon, five more appear. What can I do? And how can I stop bringing my crap back on you and mom and all the others?" Jack's emotion showed as he turned to his lifelong mentor. "I don't want to be a burden to you or anyone else anymore, but I realize I used that as an excuse for far too long. Just like my dad did. I don't want it to be too late for me, too."

Ben's smile radiated love, comfort and peace to his young friend. "You are no burden to me. God gave us family and friends to carry us when we need it. To walk alongside us when we may stumble. To run behind us when we spread our wings to soar. You have to let us do that, though."

"I think my dad finally understood that." As Jack spoke more about his dad, Ben heard the wistfulness in his words. "I saw the regret etched in every line of his face. As I reflect on my time with him, I pick up more hints at that—things he'd say, a look in his eye I didn't quite understand in the moment. I do now, and I don't want to end up like him—full of regrets."

"We're here. We've always been here. Ready to carry, steady or cheer you along your way. As for how you can win the war you've been waging all these years, I don't have the answer you think you want. I do have the only true answer to every question, though. Jesus."

Jack nodded as the answer settled into his soul. "I knew that would be your answer. Senior gave me a Bible, and I've been reading it. I have questions about that, too. But, I'm not sure yet how to ask them. I'm getting there, though."

"When you're ready, I'm right here." Ben's smile filled Jack with a hint of hope.

Scout ran up to them, grinning around a tennis ball. It was coated in dirt, a clear sign he had uncovered another dog's treasure. The men took turns throwing it for him.

"I don't want to take advantage of your hospitality. I need to get to Columbia to see the Millers and apologize to them for my lack of goodbye. Plus, there's Grandma Ethel, unless … "

Ben answered the unfinished question with a shake of his head. "The year after you left. Actually, I'm glad you mentioned her. She left you a box. Remind me to give you that when we get back to the house."

"I'm so sorry I missed saying goodbye to her." After his recent caress of encouragement, Jack felt the weight of guilt to be far more heavy than in years past. "Do you ever talk to mom?"

"Every few weeks, we touch base. She's shared your letters the past few years. Those meant so much to her. She misses you like crazy, and she's never stopped praying for you." Ben tossed the tennis ball up in the air a few times before lobbing it across the park. "She's still in Bellum, as you know. That's a totally different place from when you and I left. Even with the positive changes, though, I think she'd rather be somewhere else."

"I can make that happen." Jack nodded as a look of determination settled across his brow. "This arm's pretty useless, so I've got to find a way to put all my monetary needs into this one." He flung the ball a little farther than Ben had.

"Not bad." Ben nodded his approval. "Well, I definitely want you to go to your mom and the Millers, but my home is yours for as long as you need it."

Jack sat back on the bench and studied his hands. "There's one other thing. I'm scared to death to see Rachael after all this time. After the way I left. How do I apologize for that? 'I'm sorry' seems so inadequate."

Her father slid beside the young man and waited for him to continue.

"It goes a little deeper." Jack leaned forward, his good arm resting on his leg, his head down. "Her face, her voice—the connection I still feel to her—they carried me through and gave me strength in the battles, in the desert and on my Peak. I'm sure she's got a great life—the future I always knew she deserved. It's just ... in my heart, she's still my future. I never stopped loving her. Not once."

Ben began answering Jack's unspoken questions. "Rachael attended Georgia Southern University over in Statesboro to study Nutrition and Food Science and Exercise Science. She had a job lined up for herself at a gym here when she graduated—wanted to be near her old man, apparently."

Every time his daughter had tried to move on from the boy next to him, Ben had been there to see the heartache and pain. He had watched her love for Jack pull her away each time. He also saw the love that burned undiminished in Jack's eyes. If God had carried them this far for each other, he could get them that last little distance.

Ben breathed deeply as he looked straight into Jack's searching eyes. "She's never given her heart to another."

XXIV

Life Won't Ever Be the Same

March 21-27, 2011

Jack felt like an overfilled blender had turned on inside him, and he knew the lid would soar off at any moment. A mixture of joy, terror, uncertainty and shock pulsed through him each time he thought about how Rachael had not settled down. He fought any trust in the shimmers of hope that shone through the muddied mess.

He spent that week with Ben, though he called his mom and Mawmaw Mabel after their outing to the dog park. They made plans for Becky to meet him in Columbia the following week. Jack had no doubt Mawmaw Mabel and Aunt E. would spend the time until his arrival cooking and baking in preparation of all the "fattening up" they would insist upon as soon as they choked him with hugs and coated him with kisses. His mom's voice held a lightness and joy he didn't remember her having. She'd sold their house and moved to a smaller place in town where she could walk to work at the library. He knew she loved literature, but she'd never had much time to read as a single mom with two jobs. He remembered how she and Rachael's mom carried on an unofficial book club that gave him and Rachael extra-long playdates when they were young.

That Tuesday, Jack accompanied Ben to the mission. He sat in on a discipleship group for that week's graduates and found himself encouraged by the men who'd slayed their own demons during their time in the program. Their courage was contagious, and their certainty in a Savior they couldn't see fanned the flames of a desire he'd felt slowly growing within himself since his time on the mountain peak.

Afterward, he ate lunch with one of the men from the group. Randy Stillman, a former Army Ranger, understood Jack's haunted expressions and shared similar nightmares. Throughout their conversation, the words *peace* and *grace* kept popping up.

"Honestly, it's only God who keeps me from going off the deep end. When I take my eyes off him, that's when the nightmares and the panic threaten to drown me. By God's amazing grace, I keep going each day. He doesn't make life easy, but he makes it a *life*."

Through Randy's words and the earlier group conversation, Jack began to comprehend how this grace truly was a free gift. And, with it, came the peace in Rachael's painting.

***

Over that week, Jack worked around Ben's house for him, cleaning gutters and painting the outside trim. He smiled at the recollection of the time they'd shared paintbrushes. Ben had been there for him through so much—put up with an awful lot, too. On Saturday evening, the bachelors tucked away a couple large pizzas and a two-liter while watching spring training baseball games and speculating about the Braves' chances for that season. Ben had always been a die-hard Braves fan, so Jack ragged him about that and cast his speculation toward the Cardinals taking the whole enchilada.

"LaRussa's got the hunger for one final ring; I'm tellin' you!" Jack laughed at his friend's stubborn devotion to his team.

Before heading to their rooms, Ben asked, "Wanna go to church tomorrow? I'm preaching to the guys at the mission."

Jack hesitated. "Will …" He hadn't been able to say her name out loud since Ben revealed the truth about Rachael.

Ben shook his head. He hadn't pushed Jack for his reaction to his daughter's feelings and prayed he hadn't spoken out of turn.

"Okay … yeah." Jack's hand turned the knob to Rachael's room before he paused to add, "I'm not sure yet what I'd say to her."

***

The next morning dawned chilly, but the sun soon thawed the earth. Jack leaned against the brick side of the house as Scout lapped the backyard, inspecting the perimeter before taking care of his business.

Jack felt restless. He propped a foot up against the wall behind him and shook it in his agitation. No … not restless, exactly. He'd been restless—that's why he drifted around for so long. It's part of why he joined the Corps and left Bellum to begin with. Restless. Uncertain. Seeking purpose.

This feeling made him want to stand still instead. He was missing—something. He had an inexplicable desire to be still and listen. To what, he wasn't sure.

Scout's nose flicked up his master's hand in a not-so-subtle plea for attention, and Jack welcomed the contact to distract him from his foreign musings. Ben found them, foreheads together, when he poked his head out the door. "Ready?"

"I think so." Jack stood and followed.

***

Ben preached about how the sufferings in this life are only temporary, because this isn't all there is. Eternity lasts forever, he said. As Jack listened, he felt that desire take shape within him until he felt a tugging, not toward something, but Someone. Ben spoke with more certainty than Jack had ever held about anything in his life.

"Randy asked me this morning if he could say a few words." Ben said before he sat down on the front pew.

"Thanks, Ben." The soon-to-be graduate Jack had met earlier that week cleared his throat. "This morning I was sitting out by the pond spending time in God's word, and I knew I should share my story. I'm not a big talker, so this is a new one for me."

He cleared his throat and set a tattered Bible on the pulpit. "Army Ranger defined me, and I didn't need more. This old book here ..." He pointed to the Bible in front of him. "It was just the 'good book,' something my Grandpa carried around with him. Nothing more. Certainly nothing living or real or beneficial to me. When I came back to the States from Afghanistan, I was a mess. My brain'd been fried. I couldn't sleep, eat, function in real life. All I saw every time I shut my eyes were the faces of each kid I'd sent to his death and every enemy whose life I'd ended."

Jack leaned forward, his eyes leaking unchecked.

"We buried my Grandpa soon after I got back stateside. He'd been a preacher for sixty years, and this was his favorite Bible. He left it to me. At first, I tossed it in a drawer and forgot about it. I kept trying to drown out the pain and the voices and the images. But then, I started recalling lines from this book—most my Grandpa had taught me when I was a kid. Finally, I opened it. The words read like a mystery at first, some weird code I couldn't decipher. Over time, I began to break through some of the pieces of the message."

Randy opened it up then and moved the burgundy ribbon marking his place. "I got here to Romans 8 and camped out for a few weeks. Thought it was pretty cool that's where you preached from this morning, Ben." He raised the Bible toward the preacher before continuing. "Anyway, I just kept reading it, day after day. Each time I did, I learned something else. When I read about a 'bondage to fear,' I realized that was me. My fears, demons—beasts, Ben calls them—they consumed me. But there was hope in this chapter, too. God isn't some way-out-there being that may or may not even exist. He's real and he's here. He's got a purpose for each of us here today; it's already figured out in his mind, we just need to lay back and trust him to get us there. It's the whole grace thing—it's really free, even for someone as screwed up as I was.

"As I read more in this one little book, I understood for the first time ever that I'm a sinner. I can't do anything good on my own—which I pretty much knew. What I didn't know was there was someone who came to save me. Someone perfect who could take on the punishment I deserved. Perfection's not in my skill set, but God sent his son Jesus to be that for me. He let himself be put up on that cross—like the one out by the pond—and his father turned his back on him because he took my sin ... he took your sin ... he took it all on him, so we don't have to.

"Like we've all heard Ben say, 'We can't ever do more bad than God's willing and able to forgive.' More than that, we don't ever have to be separated from God. I've felt that separation; and I know you guys have, too. It's dark. Lonely. Terrifying.

"With God, though, there's peace. He doesn't promise a life of ease; he doesn't even promise to take away the struggles or the fears completely. We're still human. We're going to have to keep fighting beasts along the way." Randy's face shone then, like it was lit from within. "Difference for me now is, I'm not fighting alone."

Ben walked to in front of the stage. "Many of you guys have stories similar to Randy's. You were lost, now found; blind, now you see. We're going to sing that song, and I'm going to invite any of you who've got questions about what it means to have this peace, to be saved, to serve God ... come on down, and I'll do my best to answer your questions. I'll pray with you if you're ready to turn those burdens over to God. He can lift them right now and lead you on a brand-new path today."

A hundred gruff voices, moist with emotions, chimed in with the guitar chords that had been strumming from the stage. "Amazing grace, how sweet the sound ..."

Jack didn't hesitate. He walked to Ben, good arm outstretched, and said, "Now I'm ready."

Ben grasped him by the shoulder and arm as he shared words of encouragement and answered and asked questions.

"Salvation—being saved from our sins—it's a gift. You don't have to do a thing but open your hands to receive it. Believe his promise and lift your heart up to God in prayer.

Admit to him your desperate need for a Savior from your sins and confess your belief in his gift and your desire to serve only him."

Jack's tears continued to pour as he felt peace, true and strong, for the first time in his life. "Dear God, you know where I've been, what I've done; but I believe you sent your son to pay for all those mistakes, those sins. Like Rach said all those years ago—'none of us deserves any good thing.' For too long I ignored the second part of what she said about accepting the gifts you give us. You've given me the greatest gift now. I don't expect to never struggle with the nightmares or doubts or guilt, but I know you'll walk with me and you'll help me face down my beasts. I'm not going into battle alone anymore. Thank you. In Jesus' name, amen."

He looked up into Ben's watery eyes and witnessed true joy. Jack smiled and said, "My life won't ever be the same, will it?"

"No, it sure won't." Ben laughed as he hugged the kid he'd wanted to shoo away from his daughter with a shotgun.

XXV

Be Worthy

March 27 to April 3, 2011

Although Jack's drive to Columbia that afternoon turned overcast and rainy, heavenly light flooded his soul. He had rented a car, and Scout happily rode shotgun. The canine adapted more quickly to the new mode of transportation than his master. Jack had to relearn the multitasking of driving while reminding himself of laws he hadn't used in a long time. The two-and-a-half-hour trip provided him a helpful re-immersion. When they reached their destination, the travelers found the Millers' house overflowing with family and friends.

"Did the entire city show up?" he asked as he found himself passed from one pair of arms to the next. A few moments of smothering anxiety gripped him in the midst of the throng around him. Scout pressed himself against Jack's leg or nuzzled his hand, and Jack reminded himself he was back amongst friends.

Senior recognized the panic cascading over the young Marine and aided him in reaching the backyard's fresh air. "They get too clingy, you just go on in the shop. Nobody's allowed in there, unless they belong." Senior waggled his eyebrows to emphasize his point and squeezed Jack's shoulder.

The evening was a blur of conversations, updates and food. His prediction was accurate. Mawmaw Mabel and Aunt E. had pulled out all the stops and spared neither sugar nor butter. Scout fit right in to all the festivities and discovered he didn't have to beg too hard to acquire all the free samples he could gulp down.

After everyone had eaten seconds and thirds and rolled back for dessert, each person found somewhere to recover. Jack sat next to Ducky and Daisy as Scout dropped his head in his master's lap and promptly fell into a food-induced coma. "It sure is good to see you two."

"Us? It's good to see you! We were so worried and scared when we didn't hear from you. Ben shared your final vague message and updates from your mom, but those just weren't enough." Daisy's scolding reminded Jack that he had a whole community of people who loved and cared for him and wanted to support him. Why he'd never accepted that before, he wasn't sure.

"We got to meet your friends this morning at church." At the sight of Jack's quizzical look, Daisy explained. "Jed and Lana and their two adorable kids. He called Ducky last week."

"I'm so glad you gave them my number," Ducky added. "We just had one of our houses at the Tucker Complex open up. Perfect timing!"

Daisy smiled and said, "There's a lady in town who's working with Jed to determine what kind of work he can do.

In the meantime, they've got a home for as long as they need it."

"Thank you for helping them. They're a pretty great family. I may have to head out there and say hello. The kids would probably love to see Scout." Jack laughed as the hound lifted his head and grinned, his beard askew.

"Who wouldn't love to see Scout?" Daisy scratched the dog's ears as she stood up. "Now, you boys catch up while I help Mawmaw Mabel with the dishes since we all know she won't ask for help."

Ducky kissed her hand as she turned to smile back at him. Jack grinned at the color on his friend's cheeks. "I see you two haven't lost that newlywed glow. How're y'all doing?"

"We're really great." Ducky's smile said it all. "Marriage is hard work. Sometimes we get frustrated with each other. But, at the end of the day, we still love each other."

Jack returned the smile. "I'm so happy for you guys."

"What about you? Have you seen your Rachael yet?"

The question caught Jack off guard.

"I know she's not attached. Of course she was going to wait."

Jack's surprise grew to shock at Ducky's matter-of-fact statement.

Ducky's laugh broke his friend's stalled thoughts. "I could tell when you talked about her. You two had a connection. That's something I understand. Love like that, it doesn't take no for an answer."

Jack shook his head at Ducky's insight.

"So, you gonna go see her when you get back to Savannah?"

Jack studied the shag carpet beneath him as he thought about his answer. "I'm not sure. It's not that I don't want to. I love her more today than I did when we were dating in high school, but I'm scared to death. Of hurting her. Of disappointing her. Of ... I don't know what all, honestly."

"I can understand all that." Ducky nodded as he considered Jack's response. "Ask yourself something. If you don't go to her, will you regret it?"

"Every day of my life." Jack's quick response surprised him ... but not Ducky.

"Exactly." Ducky patted Jack's shoulder as he got up to join his wife in the kitchen. "Just go to her, Jack."

Later that evening Jack found himself finally alone with the couple who'd welcomed him into their home and hearts long ago. The years apart showed in a few more lines on their faces, slower movements and the absence of a white fluff ball. Missy had passed away while Jack was in Iraq. Her absence had weighed heavy when he'd last visited Columbia, and he breathed a prayer of thanks for another canine companion.

Jack knelt in front of their recliners. "I'm sorry I didn't let you guys know where I was or how I was or even say goodbye before I took off. I've got a track record of running, but that's all in the past. My life's going to be very different from now on—full of time with all of you, if you'll have me."

"Oh! Get over here, you!" Mawmaw Mabel pulled him in for another hug. "We wouldn't have it any other way, and this is as much your home as ours."

Senior rocked a little harder to shake the emotion from his face.

* * *

The next day Jack and the wolfhound walked with Senior to the American Legion for a morning cup of coffee. When they entered, a chorus of greetings bombarded them. Jack's left hand shot out to his faithful companion already pressing against him. He carefully skirted the group as he headed straight for the coffee pot. His breathing had just steadied when he felt a hand on his shoulder. Elmer's eyes played a reel of nightmares as Jack understood he wasn't alone with the torments of battles. Each member found a chance to lay a hand on him and pass on a silent story of pain ... and of survival.

Jack was welcomed as a brother by the group of men who'd last seen him as a naïve kid trying to figure out what life was all about. That day, he wore the mantle of veteran alongside them.

"Good night, son! D'you walk around with this horse all the time?" Murphy asked. Scout trotted over and leapt up on the former detective, a paw on either shoulder. The men clapped and laughed as the dog's giant tongue gave Murphy's red face and spectacles a proper washing. Glasses askew and fluffy white tufts of hair on either side of his face damp, Murphy muttered an incoherent message as he patted the dog's head and accepted a hand washing for his attention.

Once coffee cups were drained, Senior and Jack continued to the hardware store. Like their first Memorial Day together, Senior made coffee while Jack went to work dusting and re-shelving items that had been misplaced. They worked side by side in silence until members of the Hardy's Crap 'n' Coffee Club jangled the bell.

"Stale coffee again? I'm gonna start bringin' you new bags down here, so we don't have to keep drinkin' this galldurn tar, Pat."

"I've told you every day for goin' on three decades now, Gene, you're welcome to take your lack of business elsewhere. Course, we both know no one else'll put up with your mouth."

Jack chuckled. With all that had changed in the world since he'd tried to disappear from it, Hardy's remained the land time could not touch.

The stories began then, but today they leaned more serious than jesting. He quickly learned that every branch and every war had its own form of ongoing battles. It wasn't something they spoke about often, but when they did, tears flowed and grief was shouldered equally amongst them. Brothers in arms across generations, the bond of battle united them. As true warriors, they spoke of war as a loathsome evil and of peace as their purpose in taking up arms. They closed the morning together with a coffee toast to the brothers they'd lost and ended it in honor of Tray with a chorus of "To the Checker King!"

***

After a lunch to rival the dinner from the night before, Jack and Senior headed to the woodshop. "What you plannin' on doin' now, son?"

Jack had been asking himself that same question. "I'm not sure. I don't know what I can do with my bum arm."

"What do you want to do, bum arm aside?"

"I'd like to build. I've been able to do some whittling, despite my arm. But, I want to build furniture and I can't quite figure out how to handle all the big pieces I plan to do." He handed Senior the tattered notebook he carried with him. The older man flipped slowly through it, his expressions ranging from approval to amazement. As he did, Jack walked around the shop, running his stronger hand over the varying wood grains stocked and awaiting their purposes. He stopped and lifted a cedar plank to his nose. He'd missed the feel and smells of this place. Senior had once declared, "A woodshop's a healin' place for the creative soul." Jack agreed.

"Let's get started." Senior blurted out. His eyebrows may have thinned a little over the years, but they could still send his points straight home without a single spoken word. "Where there's a will, you've gotta make your way."

Senior went into motion then, pulling out bench vises of all shapes and sizes. "You can use these to lock in what you're working on. Some of the more delicate details—you can use a rotary tool 'stead of doing it all by hand."

Scout settled in at his master's feet, content and at home. Jack allowed hope to grow within him and envisioned his sketches coming to life. Maybe—just maybe—he could follow this new dream after all.

Becky arrived in town the next day, and Jack spent the rest of the week getting to know his mom all over again. She declared his beard and longer hair handsome. Scout followed her like a little puppy and tried to climb in her lap every chance he got. Even though Jack had been through a war the last time he'd seen her, he found their conversation this time to be different. He'd grown up. Matured. So, as they talked, it was as two adults—still mother and son, but in similar seasons of life.

On their first evening reunited, Jack knelt before his mom and held her hands. "Mama, I've got something to tell you, and this isn't going to be easy for either of us, I suppose. Do you remember me writing you about Jay—the man who led the homeless community I lived with?" When Becky nodded, Jack continued. "Turns out, that wasn't his name; it was his initial. Mama, he was dad."

Becky's jaw dropped, but her shock shored up the tears welling behind her eyes. She shook her head as she grasped her son's hands, holding on to them for the support she needed to hear the rest.

"I didn't know it. The whole time. We talked. I wrote you how he told me he regretted so much; talked about lost time and it being too late for him." Jack was crying as he pressed on to get the full story out. "He figured it out one day when I mentioned Bellum. Told me he was sorry and to go home. He talked about how he'd messed up not going back to you and he was glad to meet me."

Jack's shoulders shook with his emotion as his mom slid from the recliner to crumple against him. "He left his wallet with one picture—our family portrait." Jack wiped at his eyes as he put an arm around his mom. "I tried to find him. I'm so sorry, Mama. So sorry."

"Oh, sweetie!" It was Becky's turn to comfort her son. She kissed his forehead and then pressed her cheek against his until he was ready to finish.

"He was sick—cancer, the doctor at the shelter said. His body just gave out." Jack shrugged and whispered, "He ran out of time. We ran out of time."

They sat in silence for a while. Sorrow, anger, grief, confusion and loss filled the air around them. Finally, Becky leaned back against the recliner and wiped away as many of the tears as she could. "Your father just couldn't accept my help. It went against his nature, I suppose. I am so glad you got to see him, to find out ..." Her smile rose, tired and worn. "I'm thankful to know. And, I'm most thankful that you came back. Please, please always ask for my help. I'm right here, holding it out, anxious to give it to you."

"I know that, Mama. Thank you for loving me through all of this. I really am trying to figure things out. Make sense of it all. It's just ... soon as I think I almost do, something else happens."

"My sweet boy, your life has been quite the roller coaster." Becky cupped her son's cheek as she smiled at him.

"I'm glad I got to meet him, too. He taught me that I don't want to end up like him. He also showed me how selfish I'd been all those years and how I can help others who are lost—

like I wanted to do for him. He made me a better man, even though I didn't know who he was."

"He always was my one true love, but I knew—even before he did—that he wasn't going to stick around for me. His spirit was restless, unsettled." Becky sighed. "I'm thankful for how he influenced you, despite all that."

Jack and Becky stayed up chatting each night and visited museums together or parks with Scout during the days. During the course of their conversations, Jack learned that all his mom had ever wanted to do was work in a bookstore. Bellum didn't have one of those, and she never had the revenue to open one. The passion she shared for her dream was contagious; and, by the end of their time together, they decided they wanted to open a shop—Becky & Jack's. They would sell books and custom furniture and decided Savannah would be the perfect location.

They remained in Columbia through the weekend to attend Sovereign Grace where everyone rejoiced over Jack's acceptance of Christ the week before. Becky beamed at her son through tears of joy and thankfulness for the answer to a prayer she'd repeated his entire life.

After another feast prepared by Mawmaw Mabel, Jack and Becky sat in the rocking chairs he'd made for the Millers. Jack told his mom what he'd learned about Rachael and said, "I love her, always have. Her dad says she never gave her heart to anyone else, even after all this time. I feel too unworthy to go to her. I mean, I abandoned her. Like dad did to us." Jack's cheeks flushed as anger at his father—but mostly at himself—coursed through his veins to recirculate as shame. "Ducky said I just need to go after her."

"Ducky's a wise man," his mom said with a smile. After a moment, she added, "You do need to go to her. Go and then *be* worthy."

XXVI

Not Going Anywhere Without You

April 4, 2011

See You Soons replaced Goodbyes that Monday morning as Jack and Scout headed south and Becky drove west. She would put her house up for sale in a few months, while Jack followed some leads on jobs in Savannah and looked for the right spot for their shop.

Jack stopped by the grocery on his way back to Ben's since he knew he wouldn't find any actual food there. He wasn't sure how good of a cook he could be, but he'd grown up watching his mom and then Mawmaw Mabel and Grandma Ethel. At the very least he couldn't be as bad as his host. Since Ben had left a key to the house, Jack entered and started preparing chicken parmesan. If all else failed, they'd have the salad and bread. He shouldn't mess up those.

Everything was nearly ready when the phone rang. Ben was calling from the mission. "Hey! Are you almost home? I decided to cook you supper since, you know, you burn toast and …"

Ben interrupted. "Jack, I need to tell you something; and I hope you won't be mad. Your mom told me you're finally ready to talk to Rachael."

"Well, I mean, we talked about it, but I wanted to talk to you first. I'm just not sure and I don't want to …"

"What's your heart say?"

"Rachael is the only woman for me. Always has been."

"Okay then. She's on her way there now. She thinks I'm cooking her dinner. So, honestly, she probably already ate."

"But …"

Ben cut him off with a command. "Shut your mouth and go run a comb through that hippie hair of yours."

"Wait, Ben! Are you sure? I mean, I don't want to pursue anything with your daughter without your blessing."

Ben laughed at his worry. "Son, I sent her to you, so what do you think? If a war and almost a decade can't keep you two apart, I sure as heck won't try. Have a good night … not too good, of course. An appropriate amount of good will do."

Jack stared at the then-silent phone. The roar of a motorcycle engine turning in to rest in the driveway revved him back to reality. He quickly turned off the oven and burners and dashed down the hall. The comb idea was probably a good one.

"Daddy? It's me. Please tell me you didn't actually cook the food. I didn't eat this time, and I'm st …"

Jack emerged from the hall, drawn by the lyrical sound of her voice. The voice he'd never stopped hearing.

"Hey there." His words tumbled out. Simple. Inadequate. He felt the color rise beneath his beard as he watched tears form in her eyes—those bright, beautiful, guiding blue eyes. This was all wrong. This was his chance to start fresh with the woman of his dreams, and he'd already screwed it up.

And then, Rachael smiled.

She dropped her helmet, ran and leapt into his arms. He caught her weight with his left arm and rested his right on the leg that wrapped possessively around his waist, as it had beside the creek in Bellum. He buried his face in her long, red hair. He drank in her essence, her strength, her love.

"Oh, crap! Am I hurting you? Was it an arm or a shoulder?"

Her questions confused him. Ben had said he hadn't told her, right?

"Right. Stop. Back up." She hopped down, tucking her hair behind her ears, and looked back into his eyes. "I found all the letters. My dad may think he's slick and a good liar, but he's been a preacher too long. I've kept up with everything. Also, I knew you'd been here. In my room. I could smell you."

"Smell me? But, I showered, and I didn't sleep in your bed. It felt … wrong, somehow. I …"

"Oh, just shut up. I could never forget the smell of you. It's as much a part of me as your voice, your touch … your lips." She raised her hand to his reddish beard. "I like this look on you."

Her voice had softened as her hand rested on his face and her thumb traced the scar there. His breath flew away under her touch, and all he could do was admire her beauty. This was his Rachael, all grown up. Grown and spectacularly breathtaking. Gazing into her eyes, Jack discovered he'd come home.

He rediscovered his voice. "I never stopped loving you. You've been my girl since we were babies. I didn't understand our connection back then; I still don't. It's hard to explain.

The whole time I was in the desert. When I was wandering and trying to find peace—or whatever it was I was searching for. On all my very worst days—in my lowest moments—I still felt that bridge to you. It stayed unbroken despite the miles, the mistakes, the depths of hell and it—you—guided me on the path that led back here. You've always been my crystal clear scope through which I see the world, Rach."

"I never stopped loving you, Jack. I couldn't. I was meant for you, and you were meant for me like the birds in the trees and the fish in the stream." Rachael gave a cheesy grin to match her goofy line as Jack raised her hand to his lips.

At that moment, a booming bark rang out, and the two turned to face Scout, his head tilted, eyebrows furrowed, as he requested an introduction.

"Who's this big stud?" Rachael laughed as Scout trotted over.

"This is Scout." Jack nodded toward the dog and finished with deeper emotion. "Scout, this is my Rachael."

Scout politely offered a yip along with his raised paw. Rachael's laugh rang out as she shook the shaggy paw only to receive a face full of kisses. "Hey there, Scout!" she said. "I sure am glad to know my Marine wasn't alone."

Jack smiled at the two most important helpers in his life. When Rachael stood up, he asked, "Could I interest you in dinner? I'm not sure how it'll be, but I'm pretty sure the bread didn't burn."

Rachael's laugh melted his heart again. "You sure know how to sell yourself, don't you? I'm starving, so it better be good. Dad's invite was kind of last-minute, and I didn't have time to stop for fast food."

"Geez, no pressure, right?"

They fixed plates and sat down. Jack took her hand and bowed his head. "Father God, thank you for this gift. Guide us and our conversation. In Jesus' name, amen."

When he opened his eyes, Jack caught Rachael staring at him, open-mouthed. He laughed and asked, "You didn't magically know I gave my life to Christ, huh?"

Tears glistened on her lashes as she laughed. "I didn't."

"I told your dad I want to get baptized, and we chose next Saturday at the mission. Will you be there?"

Rachael's smile covered a multitude of lonely nights and dashed dreams and filled him with the desire to be the best he could for her. "I wouldn't miss that for anything in the world."

"Why do you have to be so dang perfect? It's downright terrifying."

Rachael snorted at Jack's words. When she saw the seriousness on his face, her eyes widened. "You really believe I'm perfect. How far from the truth you are." Clouds rolled across the darkening sky of her eyes. "I tried to take that love I held for you and fling it as far away as I could. I cursed you and told myself I hated you. I tried to drown in bottles, like you did. I tried to lose you in others' arms. The love and curses were boomerangs that always returned to knock me down. I cried myself to sleep every night at the lie of hating you. After an entire weekend drinking and passing out, waking up and drinking some more, I woke up loving you even more. It made no sense and hurt so deep."

It was Jack's turn to caress her cheek as she continued. "The thing was, I couldn't run away like you could. And, yes, I was furious at you for running. I wanted to scream at you for it, shake you. Despite all that, I still loved you. And, the other guys? Oh, there were so many; I lost count. So many *first* dates. Every single time I couldn't continue. They'd go to kiss me goodnight, and my heart would scream at me, 'He's not Jack!' I wanted to forget you so very much, but all the things this world does so easily to run away or forget, I couldn't do. I even said yes to another man and nearly tricked myself into walking all the way to 'I do,' but I couldn't in the end.

"So, then I screamed at God—night after dark night. When I had no clue where you were or if you were even still alive, my heart broke. Not all at once. I died a little more inside each day; but still I loved you. And then, I understood you'd been broken, completely. I finally saw that, and I stopped screaming. I stopped crying. And, I started to heal. Slowly, microscopic bit by bit. Peace came for me from God. I knew true contentment in him for the first time in my life, and I was still, calm. And, yeah, I still loved you; but it no longer consumed me. My contentment and purpose rested in God, not you—that's what I had to learn. I didn't think you'd come back into my life. I really didn't, but the peace I experienced meant I didn't need to know or expect anything. So, no, I'm not perfect. Far from it, in fact. But, I'm finally content."

"I don't want to wreck that for you, Rach. I really wasn't sure I should see you. But I definitely wanted to apologize— for leaving you, for hurting you, for turning away from us." He dropped his gaze and continued. "It feels selfish to apologize, to be here—just like the reason I ran was selfishness."

"Running may have been selfish, but you couldn't see another option then. You had a lot to learn about yourself, our world and God. Those were things you had to do on your own, in your own way. I get that, Jack. And, I forgave you long ago." Rachael smiled and placed a hand on Jack's chest. "Apologizing's never selfish when it comes from your heart."

They ate in silence as they relished being together again. Jack watched her as she dabbed the napkin on her pink lips. She caught his gaze, and her cheeks matched her hair.

Jack cleared his throat, his voice serious. "I'm terrified of messing up again and hurting you somehow."

Rachael tilted her head as she asked, "Do you plan to hurt me?"

"Never. But, I also never intended to hurt you before—in school and when I ran from Bellum. I'm afraid of not being good enough for you, of the beasts returning, of not being able to fight them again." Jack lowered his head as he cursed the thought that he could cause her pain again.

"What makes you think I won't hurt you?" Rachael's question caught Jack off guard, and she saw the questions in his creased forehead. She grabbed his hand and led him to the sofa. She nestled in, legs crossed, and pulled a pillow to her chest as she pieced together her thoughts.

"Every relationship launches when both people decide to risk it all for a chance at love. Risk being hurt. Risk losing everything or coming out the other side with half a heart." Rachael looked down at her hands. "I hurt Tyler. I hurt him in the most public way possible."

She looked back into Jack's eyes as he waited for her to gather her story.

"It was right after that last letter you wrote my dad. I was low, so low. The words you wrote … I just wasn't sure what you were going to do." Jack reached up and caught her tear on his thumb. He cupped her cheek and then took her hand as she inhaled deeply.

"Tyler had started working at my gym a few months before. I hadn't paid much attention to him because I figured he was like most of the other juiced-out iron pumpers. Anyway, we both had personal trains cancel at the same time—though I still think he passed his client off to one of the other guys when he saw me head into the break area. We got to talking and found out we had a bunch of stuff in common. I finally agreed to a second date and just kept pushing myself ahead. He was so patient with me. And, he really and truly loved me. I mean, he had to with all I put him through. He told me he was ready to marry me two months after we started dating in October 2006. Our wedding wasn't until last year. That should show you how patient he was."

She swallowed and pieced together the end of the story for him. "I faked it for a long time. I got so good at that, I believed it myself. So, I nodded yes, wore the diamond, put on the white dress and stood at the back of the church. I was ready to walk down the aisle. When those doors opened, though, I couldn't breathe. All the air had been sucked right out of my lungs. I fell to my knees. The last thing I saw before I blacked out was your face.

"Even after all that time, you were still the only one for me." Her tears dripped down onto their hands. "And then I had to hurt Tyler and explain that my heart had never belonged to him. It had always been someone else's. Someone who may be dead for all I knew.

"My point in telling you that is this." Rachael paused, closed her eyes and gathered her thoughts. She laced her fingers into Jack's and took a deep breath. "A relationship is jumping off a cliff with no promise the wingsuit you've pulled on will help you soar. With my hand in yours, though, I'm ready to leap."

Jack pulled her to his chest and counted. "1-2-3."

Foreheads touching, the couple closed their eyes as their lips connected. In that moment, they both felt whole again.

He smiled down at her and said, "I'm not going anywhere without you—ever again."

XXVII

The Man He'd Become

April through August 2011

Summer dipped its toes into April's early days and spiked Saturday's high above 90 degrees. Jack's nerves jittered and shook like he'd had too much espresso. After prayer with Ben and Randy in the mission's chapel, they walked out to the pond where a crowd waited. Scout ran ahead to greet everyone. Jack's smile widened with each person he recognized. His mom. Ducky and Daisy—who had decided to spend their anniversary weekend in Savannah. And, Rachael. Jack decided she would never stop taking his breath away. He aimed his smile in her direction as he followed Ben into the water. Despite the heat beating down, the pond held winter's chill.

"Jack has given his life to Christ and wanted you all to join him today as he makes that public. His baptism is a symbol of what God's already done inside him. In a moment, Jack's going down in this water—this ice-cold water." He waited for the crowd's laughter to subside before continuing. "When he comes back up, it will be a reminder that he was washed clean long ago by Jesus on the cross."

Ben nodded to Jack and then said, "In the name of the Father, the Son and the Holy Spirit, I baptize you ... my brother."

Thankfulness coursed with the cold through Jack's veins. He had a brand-new life stretching out before him, and he couldn't wait to see what it held in store for him. He emerged from the water to barking, cheers and applause. No one seemed to mind getting wet, either, as everyone hugged him. Becky gave him a kiss and said, "I'm so thankful."

"Me too, Mama."

Jack introduced Rachael to Ducky and Daisy, and the four planned some double dates in Savannah and Columbia. They would start there the following weekend, so Jack could introduce her to the rest of the Millers and to his woodworking skills. He gave her a rose he had whittled the summer he first learned. It was her face he had envisioned as he coaxed it from the block of wood. She stared wide-eyed and speechless at the intricate design he'd created that made wood appear as delicate as a flower's petal.

Though Jack and Rachael shared unified roots, they had to get to know the adults they'd each become. The car ride home allowed them the perfect opportunity to discuss their dreams.

"I can't believe I never knew how long my mom had dreamed of opening a book store," Jack said soon after they got on the road south to Savannah. "Of course, I was a self-involved jerk when I lived in Bellum and I haven't been much better since."

Rachael let out a snort that resulted in a vigorous licking from Scout and uncontrollable laughter from the couple. She finally calmed down and wiped the moisture from her eyes. "I'm so glad I hadn't just taken a big sip of my drink. You would've had sweet tea all over you."

"Scout would have been confused about which of us to lick first, I'm afraid." Jack grinned at Rachael as she held the hand he had propped on the armrest. Most of their outings included Scout. He and Rachael had bonded right away, and he often spent more time with her than Jack when they were together.

"I am beyond excited about y'all's store. What all do you plan to sell?"

Jack's face glowed with the excitement of all the possibilities the shop promised for him and his mom. "I'll have mostly small items, like the flowers, in the shop. Those will be easiest to display, but I'll have some larger pieces as well—chairs, rocking horses, chests. Maybe some smaller tables. My plan is to take custom orders as well. I've been working on improving some of the furniture sketches I did on the mountain. I'll put them in a binder people can flip through as they think about what they want. I think I'm most excited about building unique bedframes."

"They're going to be amazing!" Rachael's smile shone on Jack. She lifted the flower he'd given her and examined it. "You know, while I love this exactly the way it is with just a light stain, I bet some people would like to have theirs painted. I could do that for you on some, if you want to have colorful options."

"That's a great idea. We make a pretty incredible team." Jack's eyebrows rose as he returned her excitement. "Now, it's your turn. Tell me your dreams."

"Other than you?" Rachael leaned over and planted a kiss on Jack's cheek. "Well, you asked, so here it is. I would love to own a fitness and nutrition gym for women. I want to have all the regular gym equipment and rooms for classes and personal sessions, but I also want a huge kitchen. Women could learn how to prep food for a month, how to choose healthy foods and how to properly portion it all. We could have meal prep parties. Maybe I could even have an herb garden, so we can use fresh flavorings as we cook."

Jack didn't hide his pride as he beamed at her. "I love how passionate you are about your career and, even more, about people and their health."

Rachael blushed. "It's a massive dream, so I doubt it'll ever happen."

"I have to disagree with you because you have got all the skills to make it happen. I believe in you and want to make sure your dream becomes a reality."

Rachael whispered "thank you" in his ear as she kissed his cheek again and leaned her head on his shoulder for the remainder of the ride.

✳✳✳

Back in Savannah Jack and Rachael spent as much time as they could together at Ben's house, filling in the gaps in their missing decade. Jack answered Rachael's questions about what happened between each letter she'd found. He told her all his struggles after Iraq and about his time drifting across North Carolina.

Ben had given Jack the box from Grandma Ethel, so he shared its contents with Rachael—Tray's dog tags, several photos of the two of them, the hummingbird his dad had carved and his Purple Heart. Rachael asked about their training and his time as a scout sniper in Iraq. She saw the passion in his eyes, but she also glimpsed pain in the longing glances he gave the rifles in the photos of Tray and him. He missed who he had been nearly as much as who had been by his side.

"Tray would call me out on my crap quicker than he and I could take down one of Grandma Ethel's pies." Jack looked wistfully at one of the pictures. "One time while we were in Iraq, we'd been in this one tiny hide for almost a week. I was a little grumpy by that point because I thought we'd gotten bad intel and were wastin' our time. Anyway, I'm complaining about anything and everything except what I'm really ticked off about. I'm takin' it out on the sand, the winds, the air. Once I resorted to blamin' how he'd dug out his side of the hide and accused him of stealin' my coffee packet—which I'd actually dropped and set my pack on—he'd had enough. Tray pulls ear plugs out of his pack, holds them in my face and says, 'Until you finish your toddler tantrum. Tap my shoulder when you're ready to be a Marine again.'"

Rachael laughed at the stories Jack recounted about his friend and their time together. She found herself missing a man she never got to meet. At the bottom of the box, Jack found an envelope. It had been Tray's just-in-case letter. They'd all written them before shipping out and carried one copy on their bodies and left a second in their stateside lockers. One paragraph mentioned Jack.

He won't agree, but Jack will need some looking after. The weight of the world rests on his shoulders, but it doesn't have to. He just won't accept help unless it's pushed on him. I believe God's got a plan for him, so I just keep praying for him. I hope I'm around to see it. Of course, if you're reading this, I'm not.

Rachael finished reading Tray's letter and dried her face. She handed it back to Jack and asked, "Did you write one of those to your mom?"

He nodded as he tucked the letter back in the box. "I wrote several others, too. One to the Millers, Ducky and Daisy, your dad. And you."

She clutched his hand as he explained. "I figured I'd put it in with your dad's and let him decide. I wanted you to know, regardless of all the crap and my poor decisions, I died loving you." His voice trailed off as he traced each finger on her hands. "God's got other plans, it seems. Now I get to live loving you."

He pulled her into his chest as his lips sought hers. He both lost and found himself in her. Where she began and he ended, he wasn't sure, but he knew she completed him. All he wanted was to find ways each day to be worthy of her love.

They talked about Bellum. She filled him in on Anna Claire and Shannon and their families.

"Anna Claire's clothing line, Stevie G. Fashions, is in all the major boutiques in the South. She's even been approached by some big names in New York, so she'll be heading there for Fashion Week in September. And, little Stevie's almost twelve!"

"It's hard to believe it's been that long since … everything." They held hands as visions from That Night rose in their minds.

"Shannon's in Augusta now. Married a golf pro there. Her little girl Laylah's the cutest nine-year-old ever. Shannon's got her own photography business, too. You remember how amazing her photos are?" she asked.

He smiled and replied, "Of course. I carried that photo she took of us to Iraq and back."

"I didn't think you'd still have it." Rachael's smile stole his breath as he remembered that day at the picnic and how he'd known then she was the only girl for him.

***

Rachael asked Jack to go to church with her, so the following Sunday the couple walked up the steps of Peace Presbyterian. Jack turned to smile at the glowing woman beside him. He'd been to church with her many times before. This time was different. They were there for the same reason. When they sang the songs together, they both meant the words. When they recited the Lord's Prayer, they were both praying to their heavenly Father. The ache in Jack's heart was a joyful one.

Jack cooked lunch for Rachael every Sunday after church. On one of those occasions, once he had everything ready, he found her curled up with Scout on the couch, both of them sound asleep. He chuckled at the sight of the giant hound tucked against her. Later that afternoon, he got to snuggle with her—to Scout's annoyance. After a long and easy silence, Rachael asked, "Would you ever go back? To Bellum?"

Jack stared off as he considered her question. "You know, I think I would, but it would have to be for a good reason; something I could do to pay it back a little. I do owe a lot to parts of that area and to some of the people. I know your dad said many of the people there have changed—like I have; and I've forgiven everyone—even Mr. Cutter—but that doesn't mean I want to travel all the way there to sit down and sing 'Kum Ba Yah.'"

Rachael laughed at the mental image. Jack continued, "Besides, with mom moving here and us opening up a store, I don't know any reason I'd need to go back. Though, your dad did mention how sharing my story at the mission there might be helpful. Maybe I should start using that to help others. I wandered without a purpose for so long. I don't want to do that anymore."

***

One weekend Rachael took Jack to Statesboro to visit Georgia Southern's campus and shared with him about her time there. She led him to the creek where she had fled in the middle of a rainstorm the night her dad told her he was on his way to Washington, D.C. She knew why, but she couldn't tell anyone and had no way of knowing how bad it was. She had raged at the night around her as she screamed Jack's name into the soggy ground she collapsed onto.

As much as Jack hated hearing of Rachael's pain—the pain he had put her through—he was thankful for all she was sharing with him about her life since he'd left. He was so proud of her job and the passion she had for it. He could see it radiating from her whenever she talked about it. She was a registered dietician in addition to being a certified fitness instructor. She explained how this allowed her to treat the health of the whole person. He could always tell when she was excited about something, because her words bounced like overflowing bubbles.

"What so many people don't get is you can run around the track a few times every day or even go to a couple classes a week, but if you eat nothing but fatty foods, you're gonna be a fatty. And, if you starve yourself, but never get off the couch, you're gonna be a grumpy fatty." She rolled her eyes and continued her rant. "Of course, eating healthy is never about starving yourself. But, you know, I hate the term 'cheat meals.' It makes it feel like a cop out. Instead of practicing good food choices and then moderation in portioning when you go out to eat, people toss out that ridiculous moniker and let it be a free-for-all. Then, next thing you know, they're 'accidentally' going out to eat four times a week and eating the entire excessive American-sized portions of food they ordered."

Jack laughed at the way her cheeks darkened whenever she got fired up over something and at the way she rolled her eyes at the masses of people who just didn't *get it*. When she realized he was laughing at her, Rachael swatted his arm with a stretch band and said, "Hey! Don't you laugh at me. If people called your sniper rifle a gun, what would you do?"

"Shoot 'em for their stupidity, ma'am." His straight face elicited another eye roll from her.

Rachael showed him photos of her daredevil antics and travels over the past several years. She had a fondness for dangerous activities—BASE jumping and skydiving topped the list. Bungee jumping wasn't as exciting, but she'd done that as well. She loved ropes and challenge courses, rock and mountain climbing and hiking—and considered ziplining relaxing. She had traveled to Peru and Nigeria many times in the past few years to assist missionaries with nutrition education in remote areas. When Jack saw her riding her cherry red motorcycle for the first time, he did the impossible and fell even more in love. Despite all the pain he'd caused her, Rachael had *lived*. His thrill was being part of that life.

* * *

Jack had just missed Rachael's birthday in April, but he bought her a gift later in the summer—a 9mm pistol for protection. He worried about her leaving the gym alone, often late at night, and wanted her to be safe. They went a couple nights a week to a nearby range where he taught her how to shoot. He had missed the interwoven scents of a recently-fired weapon's heat and the various lubes and cleaners used by experienced shooters. It had been a long time since he'd been around weapons with their sounds and memories, so he made sure the range would allow Scout to stick by him. The first time was the hardest, but having Scout and Rachael with him calmed him quickly so he could focus on his breathing and clear the ghosts from his mind.

He may no longer be able to shoot with his right arm, but Jack could press his body against Rachael's and guide her with his voice as she did. She turned out to be an accurate shot, and he enjoyed the pleasure of teaching her something he loved.

* * *

One Saturday, Jack cooked all day for supper with Ben and Rachael. He lifted the pulled pork out of the oven. He'd already burned the buns three times when Ben emerged after a shower. He'd come home from the Mission's work day covered in grass clippings, dirt and briers.

"I'm glad you're out. There's something I want to ask you before Rach gets here." Jack poured a glass of water and slid it to Ben before continuing with his request. "I love your daughter more than life. She's the best part of me. I know you know all this and I'm rambling, but … I want to ask her to be my wife. Will you give us your blessing?"

"It's about time, son!" Ben met him with a bear hug. "Are you gonna ask her tonight?"

"No sir, but I do want to ask her to go back to the mountains with me, near where I lived for so long. There's this ledge … my Peak, remember?" Ben nodded. "That's where I want to ask her."

"So, you'll be going off for a long weekend?"

"Yes, and before you object, I've got us a cabin with two bedrooms, sir."

Ben laughed. "Very well. Seems you've thought of everything. I'm excited for you two, and I can't wait to officially call you my son."

Jack reflected on how many times they'd shared emotional moments. He hadn't compared notes with other guys, but he was pretty sure this wasn't standard father/son-in-law procedure.

Rachael burst in then with a case of Cheerwine. Scout beat Jack to the first hug, as he typically did.

"Hello, my sweetie!" Rachael crooned to the dog towering over her. "I'm starving, so supper better be ready … and taste dang good."

"Sheesh, you're demanding today." Jack gave her a quick kiss as he took the drinks. "How'd your classes go?"

"Awesome sauce!" She popped up on her tiptoes to plant a kiss on her dad's cheek. "Have you three boys behaved today?"

"Don't we always?" Jack's question held a tone of astonishment.

"Only Scout." Her quick response earned a pop with a dish towel from Jack and a tug at her ponytail from her dad. Scout, however, sat gazing up at her adoringly until she rewarded his devotion with a kiss on his giant snout.

After a downhome dinner of pulled pork sandwiches, jalapeño mac 'n' cheese and baked beans, the couple went into the backyard and sat in a swing covered with intricate patterns carved across the back and arm rests. Jack had made it for Ben as a thank you for letting him live with him. It was the first big piece he'd made without full use of his arm and confirmed his decision to open the shop.

"Got a question for you," Jack announced. "I've been thinking it would be fun to take a road trip together. If you're up for it, I'd love to take you back to Asheville. We can do some hiking, and I can show you where I made my home for a while. And where I met Scout."

The hound sat at attention as Rachael's eyes lit up. "I'd love that! When d'you want to go?"

"I was thinkin' September—maybe Labor Day weekend? Would you be able to get off work?"

"Absolutely! I've always wanted to visit there. I've heard it's beautiful."

"It really is, and you'll love it. I've already scoped out the ziplining, hiking and mountain climbing. We can do it all if you want." Scout barked his approval, and Jack's laugh rolled over Rachael.

She discovered a sense of security and belonging in his arms that she'd never experienced with anyone else. As fiercely independent as she was, Rachael realized she'd be content letting him plan the rest of her life. Her heart skipped, and she wondered if he may have a bigger question to ask her soon. She knew her answer and would have given it then had he asked her. She'd waited this long for the man he'd become ... the man she'd known he would be. She could wait a little longer.

XXVIII

More Than Worth the Wait

September 2, 2011

The dog days of summer, the old timers would call it. Rachael declared it *balmy*, but Jack just called it hot. The couple hit the road bright and early for their weekend in the mountains with Scout sitting expectantly in the back seat. He loved car rides and looked like an eager kid with his big eyes taking in everything they passed. They arrived in Asheville at lunchtime. Instead of getting a reprieve from the heat, they'd driven into rain coupled with high temperatures.

Cabin check-in times weren't until mid-afternoon, so they spent a soggy couple of hours browsing Asheville's quaint shops. Jack felt odd experiencing the town as part of it instead of as a shadow lurking around it. His focus was Rachael and her delight at each shop and café they visited. The cloudy day didn't bother him. All the light he needed stood directly in front of him, and he couldn't wait to spend the rest of his life with her shining all around him.

Once they checked in to their cabin, they changed into hiking clothes; and Jack slung a picnic supper on his back. He prayed God would smile down on them and clear the rain. They should hit his Peak well ahead of sunset, with plenty of time to take in the view and enjoy their supper. The rain cleared by the time they arrived at the park. Scout trotted beside them, a grin firmly planted on his shaggy face. He clearly knew where he was.

As they climbed, the light peered from behind dispersing clouds; and, once they reached the crest, the last of the clouds dissipated. Jack breathed a prayer of thanks and found his hands sweaty and shaky, but not from the climb. He wasn't so much nervous as he was emotionally raw. He was about to drop down on one knee before the woman he'd been in love with for most of his life … with the ring he had carried for nearly a decade.

Rachael thought how stunningly handsome Jack was. As they reached the top and the sun finally burst through, she looked—not at the breathtaking view around them—but at the man she adored. He was looking back at her. It did seem a shame to waste the scenery, but love alters perspective.

She felt Jack take her hand and followed his lead to the ledge. The wolfhound leaned against his master's leg and lay down with his paws dangling over the edge like he'd done the previous year. Looking at the valley far below and feeling the rush of having nothing between them and the drop, Rachael discovered that holding the hand of the man next to her was far more exhilarating than if she were to launch herself off in her wingsuit.

Jack put his arm around his love and kissed her forehead. He led her to a spot back from the ledge where they could still see the sights. Together they spread a blanket, and Rachael sat down while he unpacked their supper. Chicken salad, croissants, cheese and crackers with Cheerwine to wash it down.

"Best picnic supper ever!" Rachael declared. Jack had planned their entire trip, and she was perfectly content to follow along and roll with each surprise as it came. He had chosen her favorites, though. She marveled at how he always thought about her. She had told him once she wanted to choose his favorite things so it wasn't always about her. He had smiled and replied, "Then we'll always do what makes you happiest and brings that beautiful smile to your lips."

After they'd cleaned away the food, she leaned against him. He rested his cheek on her silky hair. They didn't talk; their contented silence spoke volumes. As sunset began, Jack kissed the top of her head and then stood up. He held out a hand.

"Let's get a little closer for this show God's puttin' on for us." She returned his smile. "Stay, Scout." The dog obeyed, and the couple returned to the ledge to stand hand-in-hand for a few more minutes.

"A rainbow!" Rachael pointed out the colors right as Jack noticed them.

"Stunning … like you." Rachael realized he had turned toward her and dropped her hand. He was pulling something out of his pocket and lowering himself onto one knee. Her hands flew to her mouth as she realized how this perfect day was about to end for them—with an even more perfect beginning.

"Rachael Jane Burns, you're the one I want by my side for every sunset and sunrise from here on out. I fall more in love with you every day, and I can't imagine a moment without you. Will you be my partner for life, my lover, my wife? Will you marry me?" He opened the box to her in anticipation of the one word he'd yearned to hear.

"Forever … my answer is yes!"

Jack rewarded her affirmation by sliding the ring onto her finger and lifting her into his arms. The sun made its final descent, and they lost themselves in each other as their lips fit together. When they resurfaced, she whispered in his ear, "I love you, Jack Calhoun; and I can't wait to be your wife."

She threw her head back and laughed the sun away as he twirled her around. A dozen strangers applauded and cheered, surprising the oblivious couple who hadn't noticed anyone but each other. Scout jogged up and hugged them both. One man with a camera slipped a business card into Jack's hand. "I happened to snap at the right time. Shoot me a message, and I'll send you some pictures."

"Thanks, man!"

Rachael showed off her ring and blushed as well wishes drifted around them.

"You ready?" Jack asked.

"Absolutely."

He slung their bag and blanket on his shoulder, pulled out a flashlight and handed it to her so he could hold her hand on the way down. He planned to hold that hand every day for the rest of their lives.

Halfway down the trail, Jack stopped and pulled her into him. "I love you so much it hurts." He pressed his lips to hers. Time stood still as the darkness swirled around them. He cupped her chin and said, "You've always been my true north. When I drifted down a windy path so far I had no clue where I was, how I got there or if I'd ever make it back, I always knew you could point me straight. You are my one for all time."

Rachael wrapped her arms around his neck and whispered, "You're my only for always."

They held each other tightly as the world around them fell out of their sight and hearing. All they knew was each other and the unified beating of their hearts to the melody of their love.

When they parted slightly, Jack said, "With the store about to open, it may take a while before we can get married. I want to provide for you as you deserve. Maybe even have a house for you other than your dad's." Their laugh stilled as their lips brushed together again.

"I don't care about any of that, but I will wait as long as you ask me to." She looked up at him, her gaze glistening with her love. "You're more than worth the wait."

Act V

Inquest

XXIX

We've Got This ... Together

December 2011 to August 18, 2012

Becky and Jack spent their holidays viewing potential store locations in Savannah, but none felt right. After Becky closed on her house in Bellum on February 1, their agent found a spot that hadn't hit the market yet. The two-story building seemed far too big from the outside, but Raymond declared it a gem.

"Trust me. You will love me forever for snagging you a showing on this one," he promised. "Every dream you've ever had but didn't think you could ask for is waiting right inside."

The shop had two distinct sections. One was perfect for displaying larger pieces of furniture. As he imagined the space as theirs, Jack drew plans in his head for custom bookshelves throughout his mom's side. He even envisioned carving intricate scrollwork into them. Watching his mom's eyes light up as she talked about showcasing local authors' books and hosting children's story times, Jack sent a prayer of thanks heavenward for this new opportunity.

Behind the shops lay a long-forgotten courtyard. Its overgrowth and tumble-down appearance didn't deter Becky and Jack. They saw beyond the disarray to its potential. Their words flowed endlessly as they discussed how they could spruce it up to match their visions.

The large lot beyond housed a spacious outer building Jack could easily convert into his woodshop, with plenty of space inside for classes on rainy days. A new worry crept into their minds, though—the cost for a place that had everything.

"Don't think about that yet," Raymond scolded them. "I've saved the best surprise for last ... and then we'll talk numbers."

He led them to one of two wooden staircases just inside the back doors of the main building. They had overlooked them in their earlier excitement. "Follow me." His look was one of combined mystery and giddiness. They followed one another up the narrow, creaky stairs. Jack admired the banister's craftsmanship. He pictured himself sanding and re-staining it to capture its original glory. Ahead, a door inlaid with a glowing stained-glass window greeted them. Light poured through the panes, casting a rainbow of impressions on the paneled walls and stained stairs stretching toward them. Raymond unlocked and opened the door, welcoming them with a dramatic sweep of his arm.

Becky and Jack entered a bright and cozy apartment. It wasn't huge, but it was full of natural light and had all Becky could desire. Jack smiled at the twinkle in his mom's eyes. She mentally arranged her furniture and memories within the walls around her. Raymond waited by another door and used one more key.

"This can also be accessed from the matching staircase on the other side of the shop."

Through the doorway, they found another apartment, this one more spacious with two bedrooms, an open kitchen and living area. Beneath the large window overlooking the street stretched a spacious window seat. Jack pictured Scout sprawled out in the morning sunlight streaming across the floor. In the master bedroom, they found a balcony overlooking the back courtyard.

"This will be perfect for you and Rachael." Becky squeezed her son's arm as he pictured bringing his soon-to-be wife into this quaint home.

"It's more than perfect," Jack breathed, contentment holding his smile. His gaze lingered on the window seat.

Raymond took his cue and clapped his hands. "Let's talk numbers. Since this contains everything you're looking for—two living areas, two shops and a woodworking space—I think you'll find it quite reasonable. Plus, as it hasn't hit the market yet, the current owner would love to make a deal for a quick sale."

* * *

Before they placed an offer, Jack took Rachael and Scout to see their new home. They examined every inch of the downstairs and outside.

"Ready to see what I think will be our perfect home?" Jack wrapped his arm around Rachael's waist, pressing her against him and brushing his lips along her cheek.

"As long as you're there, it could be a cardboard box for all I care."

"Tried that," Jack joked. "Didn't work out so well in a rainstorm. Ask Scout." He jerked his head in the dog's direction. Always part of the conversation, the hound barked his agreement.

She buried her laughter in Jack's chest. He slung her up with his strong arm and carried her up the stairs to their little home.

"You'll have to open the door for us, I'm afraid. Bum arm and all." She rolled her eyes at him as she fingered the prismatic stained glass before twisting the antique knob to their future.

The door swung ahead of them as Jack carried his love across the threshold of their dreams. Rachael's eyes widened as they drifted from the bright yellow cheeriness of the kitchen to the flood of sunlight from the over-sized windows. When they landed on the window seat, she gasped. Jack smiled at her reaction. As he carried her toward the seat, he whispered, "Once upon a time, there lived this red-headed princess. On the bank of an enchanted creek one day, she turned to the dashingly handsome prince lying beside her and whispered a wish. That wish was for a home full of sun and a seat beneath a picture window where she could gaze on her kingdom and dream the loveliest of dreams."

He set her down on the seat and faced her on his knees. "She also wanted to make out with the prince on that seat. Or maybe that was his wish." Rachael blushed as she rubbed her hands on either side of his face and spoke an entire conversation from her eyes and heart to his. She pulled his face to hers and fulfilled the prince's wish, even as he had done for her. Jack's lips traced the outline of her jaw and worked their way down to her shoulder. "I can't believe you remember that day," she breathed in his ear. "We were only, like ..."

"We were twelve," he spoke against her cheek. "How could I forget the wishes of my princess? It's the prince's job, after all, to make them all come true."

She wrapped her arms around his neck and pressed her laughter into his hair. Scout joined in the merriment with sloppy kisses for both. They discussed their new home together, making plans to paint and redo a few details. Mostly they planned their lives together and how they would fill those walls with love and laughter and memories. Rachael added with a whisper, "And babies."

Jack leaned into her and rested his chin atop her head as fear bubbled within him and threatened to overflow into panic. Of course, people get married and have babies, but he hadn't thought of their children. Of him as a father.

Suddenly images of little Abbie Mae flooded through his mind and made him want to scream. *Why is this happening?* Jack's brain had been calm for so long, since he and Rachael had reunited. With these thoughts, if someone held an inquest for his mind, he'd surely be sent away. For a long time.

Why is all of this surging up in me right now? Of course Rach wants to have kids. I used to want the same. I can push past this, right?

"Jack?" Rachael's brow furrowed. She saw the faraway, haunted look in his eyes and felt her heart drop. "Jack?"

"Yeah, sorry ... my mind drifted around there for a minute. I'm fine. Too many paint color choices swirling in my head." He played it off with a smile and hugged her to his side as they sat in the middle of their living room. The seed of worry rooted itself in Rachael's mind, even though she tried to forget the look of terror that had covered her fiancé's face.

* * *

After a couple days of offers and counters, Becky, Jack and Rachael added final signatures to their purchase agreement and opened the gates for countless more x-marked lines. By early March, they closed on their new property. While Becky loved her apartment exactly as it was, Jack convinced her to let him spruce up the paint and build some sturdy built-in shelves in her pantry. Once those improvements were done, she had her items delivered in the storage container they'd been kept in since she sold her house in Bellum. Ben and Jack unloaded her furniture and boxes while Rachael helped her unpack and set up her kitchen.

"I know I told him not to, but I sure do love these shelves Jack built." Becky pulled out one of her custom spice racks while Rachael filled it.

As she bent down for another armful, Rachael's smile widened. "He said he'd make some for ours as well. I can't wait to set up our home with him."

"It really is perfect for you two." Becky beamed at her future daughter-in-law. "And, once you fill that side up, I'll have Junior's crew come build me a mother-in-law suite out back so you can keep on growing your family." Her wink triggered a giggle from Rachael, until the younger woman recalled Jack's expression following her comment about babies. "I'm not sure how Jack feels about kids. When I mentioned them, he looked terrified. I've never seen him like that. I mean, he's told me how much he struggled with fear and flashbacks and all, especially before Scout; but this was different. This was definitely fear, and it was when I mentioned starting a family."

Becky set down the can she'd been holding. "Did you ask him about it?"

"Well, kind of; but he brushed it off and tried to act like nothing had happened."

"You need to talk to him. Jack's been through several lifetimes of trauma, and I can't begin to understand the damage inside him." Becky paused as she studied the box at her feet. "I've been wondering if perhaps Jack needs more help than he's had so far. Help that goes beyond anything you or I—or even your dad—can give."

Rachael nodded. "When he first told me about everything, I asked if he could get some help at the VA. He just laughed. He said reactions like he has to noises like backfiring cars aren't really talked about." She dropped her expression as she leaned against the counter. "He did tell me meeting with the guys at Senior's hardware store and other veterans like Randy really helps, though. Maybe I need to encourage him to drive to Columbia more often."

"That's a good idea." Becky considered Rachael's evaluation. "I'll talk to your dad, too. If I've learned anything over the years, it's that Jack likely won't ask for help when he needs it. We may have to be a bit more proactive for him."

Rachael reached for a box of spaghetti and smiled. "Remember when you asked if Jack was good for me and said that was something I had to answer?" Becky's nod encouraged her to continue. "He gives me freedom to rest. I'm such a take-charge person, but I trust Jack completely. I'm okay letting him lead and guide. Some people think it sounds naïve, given his past, but I've always known him—the him he hadn't met yet. And—the funny thing is—resting in him makes me better at trusting God. I don't know all our future holds; but I trust that God's plan is perfect, and he will guide us through whatever comes our way."

Becky gave Rachael a hug as they shared the burden of worry and the blessing of love for the man they both loved.

Even as the ladies contemplated how they could help him, Jack approached Ben with his own worries. As they unstacked towers of boxes in the storage container in front of the shop, Jack cleared his throat.

"There's something I've been wanting to ask you about." He grimaced under the weight of another box labeled Books. "I'm new to this whole Christian thing and I'm starting to understand it's kind of a big deal for me to lead my wife in studying the Bible and praying and all that. But, well, Rach is your daughter ... and I'm me ... and, well, how on earth am I gonna lead her when I can't remember where to even find that famous chapter on love."

Ben's chuckle echoed in the storage unit before he replied, "It's okay, son; those are things you'll learn the more time you spend in God's word. Leading doesn't mean knowing it all. It doesn't even mean knowing more than the other person." Ben rested an elbow on a dresser as he continued. "Christian leadership is all about loving another more than yourself and finding ways to encourage that person in her own journey with Jesus. It's also about being an example."

Jack hung his head, and Ben read a new concern in the frown on his face, so he added, "Being an example doesn't mean being perfect. Trust me, that little hot-tempered girl up there isn't perfect either. You'll be an example in your good actions and in all the many mistakes you're going to make. Because, regardless of what happens in a day, you've got to keep God at the center of what you're doing; so that when you hit rocky patches—because you will—you'll still stand firm on him."

"But, what does that mean? How do we make God the foundation of our marriage?"

"Every day you pray—together and separately. You read God's word. You talk and share. Be honest—with yourselves, each other and with God."

Jack studied the moving blanket he'd been folding. He rubbed his hand along the rough blue fabric as he formed his next phrases. "I've screwed up so bad in the past. I've hurt her so much, and I'm always going to be trying to make up for all that crap. The last thing I want to do is fail and hurt her again."

Ben stepped toward Jack and laid a hand on his shoulder. "Son, first off, you've got to forgive yourself. She's forgiven you. God's forgiven you. No reason for you to clutch that guilt. It's gone. Breathe free without its crippling weight." Jack met his smile and felt a flicker of hope light his heart.

"Beyond that, you're going to screw up. Accept that and know that you two are in this together; but you're not the only ones. God's there to guide you—when you listen for him by doing all those things I mentioned." Ben clapped him on the back as they got back to hoisting boxes and furniture. "Plus, you've got your mom and me. We've been through a thing or two over the years and may have some wisdom to share. Of course, you've got to ask for it."

Jack laughed. "I get it. Asking for help is another thing I'm working on."

Ben's smile revealed a greater depth than his earlier joking. "I know you are. And, that's going to take time and practice, too. You'll get there. And, we're here for you as you work through all these things."

The next day was Jack's twenty-eighth birthday, so Becky rewarded them all with a celebratory homecooked meal. Her new home swelled with cheer as they made their first memories around her round wooden table. Jack took Rachael's hand and studied her joy-filled face. He remembered his eighteenth birthday around this same table with these same people. Time and space had changed, but the love that fused them together had only strengthened and deepened. His heart tightened under a rush of thankfulness.

Jack considered how the past year had been full of grace, love, forgiveness and—for the first time—peace. One year ago, he had slept in a house for the first time in more than four years. Tonight, he sat near a home he'd bought to share with his soon-to-be wife above a business he was about to open. He'd accepted Christ as his Savior and found himself speaking hope to the residents of the local mission who had been through many of the same battles he had. He'd visit with the men at Hardy's every so often and always leave with a deeper sense of camaraderie and a reminder that he wasn't alone. They filled the void left by more official channels.

* * *

The spring and summer months flew past as Becky and Jack painted and redesigned their store spaces. He worked for a local builder friend of the Millers each day and then updated the shops in the evenings. Some weekends he arranged his woodshop or added to his basic inventory of furniture and décor. On others, he and Rachael would work in their apartment or the courtyard together.

One Saturday morning, they hacked through some overgrown vines and low-hanging branches in a back corner of the yard. Rachael made the discovery first. Beneath a tangled bunch of bramble stood a stately arbor. It needed a fresh coat of paint and a few minor repairs, but it was largely intact and resolute.

"Didn't see that comin'." Jack whistled once they'd pulled away the last of the mess.

"It's perfect," Rachael breathed. She spun around to face Jack, excitement illuminating her face. "Can we get married back here? Please?"

Jack's laugh rolled over her as he pulled her against his chest. "Could I ever say no to you?"

Rachael peered up from beneath his beard. "So, is that a yes?"

He tucked her head back beneath his chin as he said, "Of course it's a yes. This is the perfect spot for us." He planted a kiss atop her head and asked, "What do you think about keeping it small?"

Rachael leaned back, her arms around his waist. "I like that. I'd already thought about who I really want there, and it's a tiny list. Shannon and Anna Claire and their families. Daddy. Your mom. Ducky and Daisy."

Jack nodded. "I'd add Senior and Mawmaw Mabel, Junior, Aunt E. and Randy. I think that's it."

"Sounds perfect." Rachael smiled at her lifetime love before falling back into his embrace.

"Like you," he spoke into her silky hair.

They planned their wedding as they continued to clear and clean the venue. Picturing their happy day in the cobbled courtyard lightened the work.

* * *

The shops were ready. Boxes of books and other inventory began arriving every day. Jack smiled at his mom's excitement over each book she unwrapped and placed on the shelves he'd built her. She decided to offer a small section of classic used books along with new books of all genres. Setting up the children's section brought her the most joy. She scoured garage sales for the perfect kid-size table and chair set that she and Rachael painted and decorated with favorite children's book covers. Jack loved watching them work together. They had a bond that warmed his heart.

He brought some completed furniture pieces to his side of the store. He had made custom displays for all his flowers, animals and other figures. Rachael painted some of the figurines in addition to some flowers, so customers would have plenty of options.

They set August 22 as the Grand Opening of Becky & Jack's and passed out flyers throughout the community. Becky had a few local authors lined up for readings and book signings throughout their opening weekend. Jack set woodworking demo times each day and offered a discount on his Beginning Whittling classes that he'd start after Labor Day.

The weekend before the big event, Becky tweaked displays and rearranged books she'd already moved a dozen times.

"Mama." Jack took her hand. "It looks amazing. You have done an incredible job putting every bit of this together, from the overall concept to the tiny details."

She let her son's words sink in and then exhaled all the stress she'd held since they signed the contract on the property. "Thank you, sweetie. I just ... I don't want to fail and mess this up for all of us."

Jack hugged his mom as she put her head on his shoulder and allowed herself to release pent-up tears. "You could never fail. Sure, this is a business, and nothing's ever guaranteed there; but we're in this together. We've got this ... together."

He bent down until she returned his nod and smile and then he kissed the top of her head.

XXX

You Don't Have to Fight Alone

August 22, 2012

Music from the bluegrass band in the courtyard drifted to the balcony where Jack and Rachael held each other. They smelled the food trucks lined up out front and felt excitement in the air. The Grand Opening had arrived.

"I'm so proud of you," Rachael said as she rose into his lips. The intensity of his kiss expressed his thanks for her encouragement. Jack had been his mom's rock and put on a calm front for her; but, the truth was, he was nervous.

Jack loved building. It had grown to be a deeper passion than shooting ever could. This was life-giving in its creativity, not destructive. Nine times out of ten, he really loved the way his pieces turned out. But, like any artisan, he always had that nagging prickling in the back of his mind:

what if no one else does? He kept a positive confidence about him most of the time. When he was with Rachael, though, he could open up and let his insecurities show. He knew she supported him no matter what and loved him even when he worried and stressed about their future. She was his rock.

"I should probably get down there. I'm sure Mom's moving stuff around again. I swear she's gonna wear a hole in all those shelves I made." They descended the stairs, Scout bounding dutifully behind. Becky was, as Jack predicted, rearranging things "just one more time."

"Ready?" he asked her.

She nodded and kissed his cheek. "Thank you."

"No ..." He shook his head as he kissed her forehead. "Thank *you*." Their words extended beyond that night and the building around them. That opening celebrated a survival from the demons of Jack's past as well as from the grief and hurt they shared from losing the man who should have been their support system.

Hand in hand they walked out of their shop's front doors to something they weren't prepared to see. Nearly two hundred people lined the sidewalks and spilled out into the street in front of their store. Becky's face lit up as tears flooded her vision. She mouthed, "Thank you" to Ben. He had spread the word to everyone he knew and nodded in return as the crowd burst into applause. The mayor held a special pair of giant scissors the city loaned to new businesses for such events. Rachael had chosen a red velvet ribbon and bow to tie across the front columns. It popped against the massive wooden double doors that Jack had refinished and stained. Everyone's eyes fixed on the mayor as she welcomed them and congratulated the mother-son team.

Rachael and Scout, though, focused solely on the man beside them. As Jack faced an unexpected battle, they fought together for him.

When Jack had stepped into the orange sunset haze and faced the massive boisterous crowd before him, panic flared. Instantly, he stood on the streets of Iraq and felt for his weapon ... in vain.

To his left, a woman dropped to the ground. Like a tiger eyeing its prey, Jack felt every muscle in his body crouch, ready to spring himself onto her. Before she stood, she handed a dropped toy to the toddler in the stroller beside her.

Further back in the crowd, a man slid his hand inside his coat pocket. Jack shifted to take him down until the man revealed a handkerchief for his wife.

A sneeze and two loud coughs triggered more rifle reflexes.

To the right of the building, a group of children huddled around a dirt pit. Jack leaned toward them when he momentarily mistook one child's spade for an IED about to be buried.

The scenes around him flashed vividly, as if he were back in Iraq. A forced blink and shake of his head briefly reminded him where he really stood and why these people were here. But the smell, the feel of war wrapped itself around him. Tighter, tighter it coiled. A cold sweat slithered over Jack's body from head to toes, crawling along his skin.

His breathing grew shallow; his glimpses of reality, shorter and weaker. The din around him droned like the silent roar under water. Every sense told him he was drowning, until ...

Rachael pressed her hand to Jack's chest. He grasped it, as a drowning man would a life preserver. Scout positioned himself in front of his master and leaned into him. Jack dropped his hand to the dog's head and stroked it, forcing himself to focus on the dog's breathing, his warm breath against his leg. He closed his eyes tightly and returned to his sniper training.

Breathe in. Breathe out. Steady now. Deep breath. And hold.

His heart rate eased. Panic's flames faded to embers. He opened his eyes, took in the crowd again and reminded himself he was in Savannah, Georgia. Iraq was long ago, far away. These people were here to celebrate with them. These were friends. He patted Scout once more before raising his hand to gently squeeze Rachael's, still resting on his chest.

The mayor was giving her welcome speech. "Savannah has the honor of being home to many small businesses like the one behind me. I encourage you all to shop local whenever you can. Enjoy the handmade craftsmanship and the personal shopping experience you will receive here at Becky & Jack's. Becky has quickly become a precious and dear friend to me. If you need a great book recommendation, here's your lady. Jack is a talented craftsman. I was actually speechless the first time I saw his work—and you all know it's next to impossible to keep me from talking." The crowd rewarded her humor as she continued. "Plus, Jack is an Iraq veteran. I always think it's a bonus when we can support our military personnel who've given so much for us. So, it is my honor to welcome you all to the Grand Opening of Becky & Jack's."

Becky took the scissors and cut the ribbon. The crowd erupted in cheers and applause, Scout leapt up to give his master a hug, helping him get through the next few moments of camera flashes and echoing noise. The crowd ate up what they considered the dog's goofy antics and didn't notice the wild fear pulsing in the eyes of the man behind the giant furry body. Jack managed to help his mom open the double doors as she called, "Welcome to our store!"

The new owners led the way for their guests, but Jack and Scout didn't stop. They continued straight back as Rachael whispered an explanation to Becky before following her fiancé upstairs.

She found him curled up in a corner with Scout resting his massive head on his side and paw on his thigh. Rachael crossed and knelt beside Jack. His hand felt clammy in hers.

"I'm sorry. Didn't see that comin'. I'm okay. Help Mom." He looked up then, pleading. "Please, she needs you. I've got him."

Rachael didn't want to leave Jack, but she knew he was right. She petted Scout's gray head and kissed his nose before brushing a kiss on Jack's temple.

"I love you, and I'm right here. I'll check back as often as I can."

She checked on Jack a few times. Once he was outstretched on the floor with Scout laying chest-to-chest on him. Later he sat on the window seat with the dog's head in his lap.

"I'm sorry." His words dripped with bitterness and disappointment in himself. Rachael knelt next to him and turned his head toward her.

"Don't you ever say that to me. Not about this." Jack tried to drop his head from her gaze, but she cupped his beard and tipped his face back up. "This is a horrendous battle; but you don't have to fight alone. I am here, and I want to help. Maybe I don't know how, but I want to. And, we've got God to guide us both. I love you."

Rachael's final three words brimmed with commitment to the man before her. Jack lifted his streaming eyes to hers and whispered, "Thank you."

XXXI

All I Want or Need

August 23, 2012 to January 2013

Jack paced himself through the remainder of the week's festivities and worked behind the scenes to make things as smooth as possible for his mom. He kept apologizing for abandoning her on that first night until she grabbed his arms and turned him to face her.

"You listen to me, son. You don't have anything to apologize for. We are all here to support and love you. We may not always know when you're going to have these attacks or what to do for you, but we're learning as we go. So, we'll be better prepared next time." She searched his face before continuing. "I was worried and nervous about the opening, but I learned something. I can do this—even the hosting and speaking. If you ever need to back away from the public side of things, I know now that I can handle it. I didn't know that before. You helped me discover I can be more than I ever believed I could. Thank you for that gift."

Jack hugged his mom. He didn't want to fail her or Rachael. Maybe this venture was a mistake for him, though this opening was a one-time deal. They'd have other events, but those shouldn't draw such a large crowd. He'd have to accept the fact that this was a part of his life and prepare for unexpected issues as best he could. He hated the thought of disappointing his family by not being there when they needed him. He was thankful for Scout and knew God sent this special creature to him on the mountain for a great purpose—to bring him back down to live, even in the valleys.

***

The woodshop became Jack's retreat. The smells, sounds and textures mixed into a soothing sensory blend. His excitement with a new project or the fulfillment of a completed one motivated him. Jack pulled out a plank of cedar to begin a chest for his bride. While his hands stayed busy, his mind considered the incidents during the grand opening.

His "old nature," as Ben would call it—who he was before he surrendered his life to God—would have had him scrawling a letter and grabbing his duffle; but he had a new nature. God had set up camp in his life. Jack's daily routine had drastically changed, especially since his discussion with Ben as they moved his mom into her apartment. Each morning, he would read his Bible and pray for wisdom and guidance to carry him through the day. That worn book Senior gave him sat on his work table. Jack kept it nearby for whenever he wanted to reread a verse or two. He brushed cedar shavings off the board he was sanding before turning it over.

The Bible held a central spot for Rachael and him as well since they read it together on most of their dates. They prayed with and for each other. God's place in his life had filled Jack with a peace he never knew he could have. So, even when these episodes occurred, he had a solid rock to lean on.

Jack thought of his favorite of Jesus' twelve disciples, Peter. Peter was rash, emotional and headstrong. He didn't always think before he spoke or acted. Perhaps Jack liked him most because he was like him; he chuckled to himself before sanding a rough corner.

During a recent sermon at the mission, Ben had focused on one event where Peter and the other disciples were in a boat. Jesus had stayed behind that day. Suddenly, they looked up and saw a man walking toward them ... on the water. Their first reaction was to totally freak out; which made sense, Jack thought. A sight like that would've had him wishing for a modern-day boat motor. Jack shook his head and reached for another panel.

The water-walker turned out to be Jesus. He was ready to hang out with his disciples; and, when you're the God of the universe who created all the laws of nature, you can override them.

As soon as Peter realized who it was, he told Jesus he was going to walk on out to meet him. So, impetuous Peter hikes up his robes and clambers over the boat's side to walk ... on water. No fear. No second thoughts ... until ...

A few steps into his endeavor, Peter remembered he was on water. The waves caught his eye, and he started watching them crash all around him. That's when he began to sink— and freak out again.

Jack had finished sanding each panel. He surveyed his work and pulled out a sketch of a detailed design for the lid. As he mentally carved the pattern, he realized he was even more like Peter than he thought. When Peter took his eyes off Jesus and focused instead on the waves crashing against him, that's when things went south. Jack was the same way.

He rubbed the hand that still occasionally tingled and looked out the double doors at birds pecking the ground in the courtyard. When Jack forgot to spend time praying or reading God's word, he felt off ... like each strand of his life would unravel in his helpless hand. Focusing on his inner demons instead of all God had saved him from kicked that feeling up a notch. He rubbed the back of his neck as he pondered how his anxiety and flashbacks required his attention, but there had to be balance in the help he sought. He needed to spend time with other veterans for earthly support and ask for help, but he also had to keep his eyes on God and his Peace.

It reminded him of his missions. He had trained himself to keep both eyes open. That way he could see potential dangers around him while still focusing his sightline on the target. He needed to remain vigilant as he continued through this war of life.

"Thank you, God, for this lesson today." Jack thought of the guys at the mission and wondered if these thoughts could help them, too. Randy's words sure helped Jack. God never promised an easy life but gifts peace when the waves get rough. Perhaps he'd talk with Ben about starting special meetings at the mission for guys who come home with this same battlefield in their brains. Jack wasn't ready to lead anything this important on his own, but Randy could help. Of course, he'd just started seminary in Due West and would be making a four-hour commute a few times a week. Maybe in a few months.

***

The shops maintained steady business that skyrocketed closer to the holidays. Jack's classes turned out to be popular, so he sold gift certificates. He kept classes small—only a few people at a time—and discovered he enjoyed teaching. He also taught at the mission several times a week and featured his students' work in his shop. All proceeds from those sales went to the craftsmen and the mission.

In the midst of the holiday bustle, Jack and Rachael set a wedding date for the following spring—April 6. Shannon came for an extended girls' weekend with Rachael and shot their engagement photos at Forsyth Park. They ended at a fountain where Rachael pushed Jack in. She didn't anticipate how he would read her like a book, though. He pulled her into the freezing water with him. Shannon was ready, though, and those photos ended up their favorites.

The couple planned every detail of their wedding together. Jack didn't get bored with flowers and dresses and details. He'd longed for this wedding, and he wasn't going to miss any of it.

* * *

One Saturday in January the couple tucked away from the biting cold as they painted their master bathroom.

Jack mentioned, "You know, I've got to book our honeymoon; so, where would you like to go?" He stopped and set down the paintbrush before turning to her with a deeper question. "Are you going to want to work in BASE jumping off the Eiffel Tower or skydiving over Iraq. Because, honestly, I could've done that last one. Personally, I didn't see the thrill."

She dabbed his nose with the tip of her brush before responding. "No, silly. I don't need that kind of stuff anymore.

You're the greatest thrill of my life. Why do you think I traded my motorcycle for the Jeep?"

"Look at you being sweet." Jack kissed her and then rubbed his nose on hers to return the paint favor. "So, what do you want to do on our honeymoon?"

"You." She winked before rising on her tiptoes to kiss his forehead. "I want a quiet place where we can be just us, together at last. You're all I want or need."

XXXII

Accept My Gift

January 2013 to April 6, 2013

Slowly the second house above the shops transformed into almost a home. Jack and Rachael began filling it with furniture and photos and other touches, though neither would move in until their wedding day. They wanted to begin this new season together.

Jack built much of their furniture, including a round wooden table similar to his mom's. This one came with two leaves they could add if they hosted a big dinner party. As in his mom's apartment, Jack built shelves in their pantry and added custom cabinets to their bathrooms. Together they made a table and chair set for their balcony. Rachael sewed cushions for the chairs and window treatments for each room. She had an eye for design and surprised Jack with her ability to choose a few colorful items to transform a space.

They spent Jack's birthday putting up finishing touches, including the hand-carved rods and finials he'd designed to hold Rachael's draperies. "When will you stop surprising me?" Jack stood speechless as he examined the intricate pleating of the satin panels framing the window and the seat they loved. Rachael had cut and sewn the fabric before hand-embroidering a trim along the sides and across the bottom. The combination of their creative skills made their humble house magazine ready and, more importantly, a home.

The only room they hadn't finished was their bedroom. Jack was building their bed, like he'd done for the guest room; but he insisted this one be a surprise.

They completed their work for the evening and celebrated with pizza and triple chocolate cupcakes.

"Your gift was made especially for you, and I assembled it." Rachael's sly smile made Jack laugh. She handed him a large wrapped package. "Oh, and don't tilt it," she added.

He eyed her and the package with suspicion as he tore the top off the paper, careful not to tip the contents. Inside he recognized a deep frame. A lightbulb went off.

"You were that weird call for a deep frame with a shelf! Who was that on the phone?"

Rachael giggled. "Mary, from work. It was hilarious when you ranted to me for a full hour about the inconsiderate jerk who placed a custom order and never picked it up."

"Well, I was upset. I worked hard on ... my gift." Jack defended himself with a smile as he tore the rest of the paper away. What he discovered brought mist into his eyes.

Rachael had copied the photos of Jack and Tray to make a wallpaper for the back of the case. On the bottom rested the life-like hummingbird Tray's dad had carved. It looked ready to fly away at any moment on its paper-thin wings. Hanging from the top were Tray's dog tags; and on the little shelf rested his Purple Heart in its open case.

"It's to hang over the counter in your store because I knew you wouldn't make it on your own. I know you think of your shop as a tribute to him. Now, other people will know, too."

Jack pulled her into his arms; his heart too full to verbalize his gratitude.

"I've got one more thing to pass on to you." Rachael pulled back from Jack's embrace and squeezed his hand. She retrieved an envelope from her bag and returned with a smile. "Remember all the letters my mom wrote me? Well, she wrote one to me on my wedding day. And, she wrote one for my groom, too."

As she placed it in Jack's outstretched hand, a teardrop fell, smearing the handwritten words, ***Rachael's Intended.***

She nodded toward it as she said, "That letter was how I knew I made the right decision in not walking down the aisle before. I couldn't bring myself to give him this. I packed it for the honeymoon, but her letters to me about knowing I had "the one" and about my wedding day just didn't fit. That letter was never meant for him."

Rachael raised one hand to Jack's cheek and covered the letter in his hand with the other. Her smile radiated her joy. "I couldn't wait any longer to give you this, because it's belonged to you our whole lives. I have zero doubts about you ... about us."

Jack's look and kiss gave her all the response she needed.

* * *

Later that night, Jack leaned against his mom's couch, Scout's snoring head resting in his lap. He stared at the sealed envelope and envisioned the woman who had written it. Carolina had been like a second mom to him. He wondered what she'd say if she were here, if it would be any different than what she'd written. Would she be happy with her daughter's choice? With a deep breath, Jack stilled his inexplicable nerves and opened her message.

Dear Son,

Congratulations! My heart is so full right now thinking about you and Rachael getting married. I feel like it may just beat out of my chest. I suppose it could be the meds I'm on, but let's stick with the first reason—it's much more poetic, don't you think?

First off, I want you to know how happy I am for you and Rachael and how proud I am of you. You've obviously gotten past the force that is Benjamin Burns in full "protector Daddy" mode. That's no small feat, so I tip my bonnet to you, good sir.

Second, though I cannot put a name or face to the other side of our conversation, I can confidently say I love you. If Rachael chose you, then you must be special. If you chose Rachael, then you are also wise and value a "virtuous wife," whose "worth is far above rubies." [You can find those words—and many more to describe your bride—in Proverbs 31.] I also feel as though I know you. I've prayed for you since long before you were even born. When I was still a star-crossed teen, I started praying for my future husband and our future kids and their future spouses and kids and on and on. Some kids count sheep; I prayed for descendants. Anyway, the point is, when someone's been in your daily prayers as long as you've been in mine ... well ... I feel a certain bond.

Third, you're beginning an incredible journey together. It won't be easy. It won't ever after be "happily." She's going to yell at you about your dirty socks, and you're going to yell at her about the makeup she leaves scattered across your bathroom sink. You're going to disagree about way bigger things than socks and makeup, too. At the end of the day, you still have the "ever after;" and, son, let me tell you ... that's a precious, precious gift. Cherish every moment—whether it's nowhere near long enough or seventy-five years of Mr. and Mrs.

Fourth, cherish my Rachael. Love her. Guard her. Guide her. Support her. The Bible calls you to love her like Jesus loves his church. Do you love Rachael to the point of sacrificing yourself for her and taking all her burdens upon yourself? Because that, my son, is forever love.

Finally, though really this falls first in importance; follow God. Lead your family in His word. Make Him the cornerstone of your marriage, and He will give you strength to withstand the countless storms of life.

Congratulations and welcome to the family, Son!

Love,

Mom

Jack carefully refolded the letter. He missed Carolina, but he knew his sorrow was nothing compared to his mom's and especially Rachael's. He remembered a time when their class went on a field trip to Atlanta. Carolina usually chaperoned, but this was at the beginning of her treatments. She pulled him aside and said, "I'm counting on you to watch out for my Rachael, okay?"

"I promise to watch out for her," Jack had solemnly responded.

He took his vow seriously, sticking by Rachael's side the entire day. He held her hand up and down stairs, pulled out her chair at lunch and even held her purse when she went to the bathroom.

Jack smiled at the memory as he looked heavenward and whispered, "I promise to watch out for her."

***

The night before their wedding finally arrived. Jack set up heaters in the courtyard and helped Ben arrange chairs and tables for their barbecue dinner. The rain had stopped in time, and the next day's forecast promised clear skies. All their wedding guests arrived that night to celebrate. Rachael rode with her friends and their families. They were all staying in Ben's house, where Rachael had been living since her apartment lease ended in January.

Jack turned in time to watch Rachael exit the back door, and he forgot to breathe. She was laughing at Shannon's story, and her eyes shone in the lights strung across the courtyard. She wore an emerald green jumpsuit and ivory wrap. Her red hair, usually up in a ponytail, swayed beneath her shoulders. He wanted to run his hands through those long, thick curls. When she saw him smiling at her, she felt the heat rise in her cheeks. He wore khakis and the emerald cashmere sweater she'd bought him for Christmas. It clung to his body, showing off the strength in his chest and arms. He crossed to her and lifted her hand to his lips. "You're stunning, as always."

In the emotion of the moment, Rachael's voice failed her, so she hoped her eyes communicated well enough. They spent the evening, hand-in-hand, catching up with all their guests. Scout trotted around greeting everyone and receiving samples in return.

Once everyone finished their banana pudding, Jack stood up. Clinking glasses and calls of "Speech! Speech!" greeted him.

"Rachael and I would like to thank you for being here this weekend. You are the most important people to us, and we couldn't imagine celebrating this event without each of you. This wedding's a long time coming. For me, anyway, tomorrow can't get here fast enough." He smiled and turned to Rachael as he raised his glass of lemonade. "Tomorrow I marry my best friend and the love—quite literally—of my life. We've overcome a whole lot of crap—entirely my fault, by the way—to get here. Despite all my screw-ups, this incredible woman chose to wait for me. And, I'm ready to spend the rest of my life waiting on her. To Rachael!"

"To Rachael!"

The bride dabbed away tears as she stood to kiss the man who would be her husband in a few brief hours. Their guests clapped while the couple kissed. They broke apart to laugh at the applause, and she nestled her cheek against his. "I sure am glad I wore waterproof mascara," she whispered in his ear.

"I'd still love you if you had black streaks down your face."

"Thanks." She winked at him.

They reminisced with their guests. Ben and Shannon chatted with Jack about other group members from the mission. They talked about the influence Pete had been on thousands of people across the South during his time as a traveling preacher before his death a couple years back. Jaida Masters and her husband had a couple more kids after the mission graduation. She traveled across the country, speaking to women about how to cast away the masks they wear.

After a couple more hours of stories and jokes, the time came to part ways and rest for the busy day ahead. Ben and Rachael returned to his house with their guests. The Millers headed upstairs with Jack and his mom. While everyone else parted to prepare for bed, Senior motioned for Jack to stay downstairs.

"I've got somethin' for you. It's not so much a gift as a return." He reached behind Jack's counter and pulled out the wooden box Jack had crafted years earlier, the knot's patterns still as eye-catching as before. "I'm proud as I can be of the way you've embraced the rough times from your past and made them part of who you are and who you're growin' to be."

Senior flicked his hand to dismiss Jack's emotional attempts to thank him. "It's time this box held some real store files anyway. No sense keepin' all my coffee receipts anyway." He clapped Jack on the shoulder as he returned to the stairs. Senior was more stooped than when Jack first met him, but the Marine in him still showed in his sure footsteps and lifted chin. The light reflected on his Marine Corps ring as he slid his hand along the banister. Jack was proud to be part of the same latticework as the man before him.

* * *

Jack and Scout sacked out on his mom's sofa for the night. It took him a while to get to sleep. He thought of all the people in his life who had supported him through so much. He thought of Rachael and their life together. Tomorrow he'd finally sleep in their new home ... in a bed. He had graduated from the floor to a creaky cot in Ben's house to his mom's sofa. He thought he was finally ready to sleep in a bed again—as long as Rachael lay beside him.

Their wedding day dawned clear but chilly. Jack checked the heaters while he prayed for accuracy in the forecast that it would warm up by noon. He recruited some help from Junior and Ducky to transport the bed he'd made for his wife to their new bedroom. Once they had it all set up, everyone started getting dressed for pictures. The rest of the party would be there soon, and Shannon had warned Jack that he better be ready to smile as soon as they arrived.

He stole a few more minutes before he slipped into his dress blues. Jack opened the package of bedding he and Rachael had chosen and their parents had bought them. His Boot Camp training proved useful as he tightly tucked each corner. There were a few more layers than the DIs had prepared him for, but the picture on the bag clarified any uncertainties. He slid a cedar chest from the closet and centered it at the bottom of the bed. He had made this as Rachael's actual wedding gift. She knew nothing about it … or the bundle of letters he'd written her during his time in Parris Island to the sands of Iraq through his journey into the mountains.

Jack opened the chest's lid and pulled out a plastic bag with candles and a package of rose petals. He arranged the candles on the chest, the dresser and the nightstands. He smelled the petals. Their scent reminded him of Rachael and of their first kiss in her mom's garden, surrounded by blossoming rose bushes. He sprinkled the memory all over their bed and made a trail to the doors. He couldn't wait to witness her reaction when she saw this room tonight.

Tonight, Rachael would be his wife.

Jack knelt by their bed and asked God to help him live well for the name Christian and the woman who was about to take his name. He never stopped feeling unworthy, but he tried to follow his mom's advice to *be* worthy.

He entered the courtyard a couple minutes before Ben and Shannon turned the corner.

"Good! You're here and ready. Now, get that smile on, and let's do this." Shannon was all business as she directed the men in various poses.

"Living up to that new last name, aren't you, Mrs. Savage?" Jack joked, as he straightened the bow tie around

Scout's neck. He had chosen his protector, Senior and Ducky as his best men.

"First time I've come in second to a dog." Senior noted. "S'pose I don't mind so much for this fella." Scout rewarded him with a slightly sloppy kiss that triggered an unusual full smile. Shannon didn't miss a snap of the exchange.

The guys went around to the front of the store once Shannon finished with them so the girls could take their photos. Jack heard Rachael's laugh, melodic and sweet, as it drifted around the building. His heart missed a beat or two as he counted the minutes until he finally saw her.

Ben called them back twenty minutes later. He had set up a wooden divider from the shop. The couple had decided they wanted a few photos with it between them before they spent a moment alone.

"Okay, groom, back against that divider."

"Aye, Aye, Ma'am!" Jack saluted. Then he teased, "Seriously, if you get bored of snapping photos of people far less attractive than me, Parris Island could always use new drill instructors."

She rolled her eyes at him before firing back, "Just remember, mister, I edit my images and can do so for good ... or evil."

"Well-played." Rachael piped up.

"Hey, pretty lady." Jack reached behind him around the divider. Her hand met his, and she asked, "How's my handsome prince today?"

"About to be the luckiest man in the universe, so I'm pretty daggone outstanding."

"Got it!" Shannon said. "We're all getting out now. You have exactly five minutes." She shooed everyone inside and called over her shoulder, "Keep the tears to a minimum."

Jack pulled Rachael around the divider for his first view. She stopped time. Her hair hung around her shoulders like it had the night before, but with a pearl clip on one side this time. She wore a simple ivory mermaid-style gown with an emerald wrap around her shoulders. Neither spoke. They were captivated by each other. Words could come later; that was time to capture memories they would recall for the rest of their lives.

No sooner had their lips met then Shannon and the rest of the party burst through the doors. "Y'all get to do that all night. Right now, I need a bride who's got some lipstick left."

For the next thirty minutes they took turns laughing, talking and smiling while they finished their photos. It was almost noon, and the sun had covered the courtyard with a pleasant warmth. Jack pushed the heaters away and pulled chairs out for everyone not standing with the bride and groom. They fashioned an aisle for the bride. Jack and his best men—and dog—stood before everyone while Becky started the music CD. Anna Claire came first, followed by Shannon, in their emerald mermaid-style gowns and ivory wraps. Then came Rachael on her father's arm. Joy bubbled inside Jack as he watched his bride float toward him and their life together.

Randy began the ceremony. "We are gathered here today to join this man and this woman in holy matrimony. This is a sacred covenant before the Lord God and will be entered into with the highest reverence. Who gives this woman to this man?"

"I do," Ben responded, emotion tinging his voice. He kissed his daughter's cheek and passed her hand to Jack's before taking Randy's spot beneath the flower-draped arbor to continue the ceremony.

For his part, Scout had been the ideal best man. He sat at attention next to Jack the entire time. He grinned up at Ben as the preacher led the couple in their vows and ring exchange. Once they were pledged to one another and everyone had said all the right things in all the right places, Ben declared, "You may now kiss your bride."

The couple smiled at one another. Rachael framed Jack's face with her hands as he slid his around to the small of her back. Their family and friends applauded and whistled as they sealed their vows.

"I now present to you—Mr. and Mrs. Jack Calhoun!"

The caterer arrived as the men pulled out tables. Everyone laughed and talked as they filled and refilled their plates with simple southern comfort food that even Mawmaw Mabel and Aunt E. blessed with their approval. Once they were all stuffed, the couple cut their wedding cakes.

While the older members of the wedding party kept the bride and groom occupied, the younger ones decorated Rachael's red Jeep. Each window had streamers dangling from it. The bumper displayed a classic string of tin cans, and the back window declared the occupants Just Married. The couple's getaway vehicle would be ready and waiting for them when they headed to the mountains the next day. Their wedding night would be spent secluded in their home upstairs.

Becky and the other women packed leftover food and cake for the couple and lugged it up to their fridge. When they returned, the wedding party lined up with packets of birdseed to toss on the happy couple. They hugged and thanked everyone for celebrating with them. Ducky, Junior and Ben waited at the end. Jack realized halfway down the line that they were up to something. Sure enough, when they got closer, he spotted the buckets, tugged Rachael's hand and yelled, "Run!"

Despite their best efforts, they ended up with all three buckets of birdseed dumped directly above their heads. Scout waited inside at the bottom of the stairs and followed them as Jack carried Rachael for the second time into their home—this time as his wife.

Jack nodded toward the guest bedroom. "How about you change in there? I've got a surprise for you in our room when you're ready."

"I like surprises," she called over her shoulder.

Jack slipped into their room to light all the candles and change into fleece pants and a white shirt, carefully hanging his uniform back in their closet. He returned to sit on their sofa with Scout as he waited. A few minutes later, Rachael appeared in a short white satin gown that had Jack gripping the edge of the couch.

"So, what's the surprise?" she asked.

"Let's find out." He crossed to her and led her to the French doors. Scout started to follow, but Jack held up his hand and commanded, "Stay. Not this time, buddy." They laughed as the hound grumbled his complaints before hopping back up onto the couch and plopping down with a sigh.

"Close your eyes," he instructed. He opened their doors, guided her through and then closed them behind her before whispering, "Now."

She opened her eyes to a dream. Jack had built a canopy bed fit for his princess. The curves of the base flowed upward through its slender arches to the crowning point on top. It was the bed he had sketched for her on the mountain.

"It's a fairy tale. Your talent amazes me more with everything you create."

"So, you like it?"

"No." She shook her head in wonder as she padded in bare feet across velvet petals to her husband's waiting arms. "I adore it. And, I love you."

He lifted her and placed her gently on their bed. She breathed in the roses around them as she ran her fingers through his hair and eagerly pressed her lips to his.

Jack's teeth gently scraped her shoulder as his lips lowered the silky strap of her gown. She shivered beneath him, and he rose up on one arm to gaze into her eyes. "You okay?"

"Better than okay." She smiled and bit her lip as she lowered her lashes. "I'm just nervous."

Jack buried his laugh in the warmth of her neck as he breathed her in, finding a high in her intoxicating scent. She lifted his face to hers as she ran her fingers through each side of his beard, pulling his lips to hers. Her kiss breathed life into his heart with the passion she spread throughout his body. Her arms wrapped around his neck as she whispered in his ear, "You're my only."

He tensed, inching back as the depth of her softly spoken words sank into his soul.

"I don't deserve that. After all the times I ... purposely hurt you? The way I ran from you?"

"'None of us deserves any good thing,' remember? This is simply my gift to you." She pulled him back to her arms and smiled as she caressed his lips with hers, barely touching him before she breathed, "Now, accept my gift."

And he did.

XXXIII

Your Turn

Mid-February to April 6, 2014

"Life's just too good." Jack spoke the words early one Saturday as he and Rachael enjoyed an unusual morning away from both shop and gym. He caressed her slender fingers with his otherwise useless ones. She lifted her head off his shoulder to read his face.

"Too good? Really. That's your complaint?" She laughed.

He smiled and pressed his lips to her brow. "Not complaining. We're about to celebrate our anniversary, and this past year as your husband has been more than incredible. I certainly don't deserve it ... or you."

Rachael raised herself up on an elbow and stroked the scar that covered the bullet Jack still carried in his arm. "'None of us ...'"

"… deserves any good thing.'" Jack joined her in a duet that ended in laughter.

"Okay, smart aleck. The point is, I think you still forget that we're sometimes given gifts—good ones. Instead of questioning them, accept them with gratitude and enjoy their beauty." She got up and crossed to their doors, closing them before turning around with a smile. "How about I give you a gift right now?"

"Pretty sure I'll like unwrapping this one." Jack smiled as she jumped back into bed with him. "How'd you get so wisdomous?" he whispered as he nibbled her ear, before laying her down and covering her with his passion.

***

The lovers drifted back asleep in each other's arms. Their lives had become busier over the last several months. They woke early and returned home late. Some of the habits they made in the beginning of their marriage had fallen to the side in their new routine—daily runs, date nights, weekend getaways and Bible time together. It was just a busy season, they had decided.

So, on this unusual morning of leisure, they slept soundly. Neither heard Scout scratching at their door.

Jack's eyelids fluttered. He was back in Fallujah on that final day in country. This time when he opened the door, he didn't hesitate. No five seconds. He simply attacked and lunged straight at the man holding the child.

A woman screamed.

A dog's rumbling growl followed an echoing bark.

The crash of a splintering door preceded a barreling weight against Jack's chest.

From across the room, a groan rose.

Jack woke as he tumbled backward from the bed following the massive impact. He turned to face a growling Scout inching closer, his breath a furnace against Jack's skin. Jack saw justice in the brown eyes boring through him.

Rachael lay sprawled against the wall ... where Jack had thrown her.

His lungs deflated, and his heart stopped beating. It was Iraq all over. And the air wouldn't come. He was gasping, drowning on land. He flailed for something to grasp until reality stopped spinning. A gentle pressure rested on his chest—hot breath, but no growling. Scout's eyes had returned to normal. He eyed his master for a sign of relief—of returned breath. With a ragged inhalation came words—forced and strained.

"Thank you, boy. I understand your scar now." Jack pressed his face into the dog's warm fur before Scout slowly padded backward off his master's chest.

"Rachael?" He scrambled up and across the bed until he knelt beside his wife. She pressed her hand to his throbbing chest. "I'm fine. It's okay. Just a little bump." Her eyes opened, and she flashed him a wobbly grin. "You've got a mean left hook."

He pressed his forehead to hers and shook his head. "I'm so sor ..."

She lifted her hand to his lips. "What did I say about you telling me that?" She sat herself up and moved her hand to his cheek. "I'm fine. Really. Are you okay, though?"

"I guess not." Rachael held her warrior as he wept on her shoulder, while their guardian lay across their laps.

* * *

Fear darkened Jack's days. Rachael urged him to visit his buddies in Columbia. She knew they helped. As solid and strong as he appeared, he still had nightmares. They didn't usually wake him, and he'd never reacted like he had that morning. Scout would always jump up at the first twitch or moan and rest his head and paw on him. Rachael would lay on his other side until a steady rhythm returned to his chest and lulled her back to sleep.

"So, we don't close the door," she told him. "Scout's pretty good about turning his back whenever we're gettin' busy anyway."

He had laughed with her, but he couldn't shake the terror that gripped him when he woke to what this demon had done through him. After a few nights without sleep, he waited for her breathing to even out before he escaped to the sofa. He set his alarm so he could slip back to bed before she woke. Rachael knew, though. Tears dripped on her pillow as she begged God for wisdom. How could they fight a foe they could neither see nor predict?

One night she stopped him. "Please sleep with me. I'm fine, and Scout's right here. Please."

He lay down beside her, his arms around her. "I love you, Rach. I'm so sorry for the mess I am."

"You're my mess, and I love every part of you." She kissed his cheeks, his nose, his eyelids; each temple and, finally, his lips. "Take some time. Go to Columbia. Spend time with Randy—he knows exactly what you're going through. You cannot fix this on your own."

Jack nodded as Rachael lay on his shoulder. He stroked her satiny hair and inhaled its coconut scent until she fell asleep. He resolved to do better, be better. First, he had to put his sightline back where it belonged—on God. And, Rachael was right; he needed help. After their anniversary, he'd plan a trip to Columbia. Randy would be less busy in the summer between semesters at the seminary. He could wait a few more months.

* * *

The couple decided a quiet first anniversary—away from phones and demands—was just what they needed. Their festivities began with a picnic like the one they shared the night Jack proposed. They spread a blanket in the living room. Jack set the photo of him down on one knee next to the blanket. "Who says we can't have the same view, too?"

Rachael laughed and kissed him. "Great idea. That was a perfect night."

After lunch, the couple spent the afternoon in bed. They talked about their past, their present and their future. They talked through Rachael's business plan for the fitness center she would open soon.

Raymond had tipped them off about the building next door before it hit the market. It contained plenty of space for an open equipment area downstairs and smaller rooms for classes or personal training upstairs. A half dozen offices in the back could be converted into a spacious kitchen to host meals-for-a-month sessions. It was perfect, plus it was right across the alley from their home.

She and Jack loved to work in their kitchen together. They spent their anniversary evening chopping veggies for the red sauce and mixing meatballs that they'd pan sear before finishing in the oven. Rachael dropped the angel hair into boiling water as Jack mixed up the salad. It was a meal that brought comfort and warmth in its simplicity. Jack watched his wife's contented face and felt a pang of love shoot from his heart. Rachael may not be perfect, but she was perfect for him.

After dinner, they each pulled gifts out from different hiding spots in their little home. "I thought we said, 'No gifts,'" Rachael reminded him.

"Looks like someone didn't get that memo." He pointed to the rectangular box she held. It was wrapped in camouflage paper with one of his smaller wooden roses on top. She'd painted it to blend in with the paper.

"You're one to talk!" She laughed as she traded him for a black box.

"I want you to open yours first. My original plan was to hold onto this until the day you open your new studio, but I suck at waiting."

She snapped open the lid and gasped at what he had commissioned for her—a silver necklace with two crossed dumbbells, each with shimmering emeralds coating the ends. "It's the most beautiful thing I've ever seen."

"Then it should look okay around the neck of the most beautiful woman I've ever seen." He smiled as he clasped it behind her and left a trail of kisses from her shoulder to her temple. "I'm so proud of you and how you've taken your passion and used it to help others."

"Thank you for believing in me and my dream." Her words floated back to him on her smile. She nodded to the wrapped gift resting in his lap. "Your turn."

Jack carefully set the wooden rose aside as he ripped off the paper and lifted the lid. Inside lay a tiny camouflage onesie sporting the words Future Marine with a white stick on top that unmistakably read Pregnant.

XXXIV

Gone

April 6–7, 2014

"**Y**ou're going to be the best Daddy ever," Rachael said when Jack looked up from the gift lying in his lap, mouth gaping his shock. She threw her arms around him. "I found the little onesie a while back and tucked it away for … whenever. I took the test over the weekend but wanted to surprise you tonight."

Jack's head rested heavily against his wife's shoulder. He longed to share her happiness, but all he could do was see Abbie Mae, the child in Iraq, that kid's shovel that looked like an IED and Rachael crumpled against the wall in their bedroom.

I can't do this. I can't be a father. What if I lose control and strike my own kid? What if I can't attend birthday parties or graduations because there are too many people?

The storm of what ifs poured down upon Jack as he fought to keep his breathing even and his heart rate steady. He couldn't tell Rachael this. No way was he going to ruin this beautiful moment she'd planned for them. This memory.

It hit him that the woman before him was pregnant, and it was his job to care for her. He pulled back.

"Are you okay? Do you feel sick? Should I go to the store for pickles and ice cream or something weird like that?"

Her laughter soothed his raging soul. "I haven't felt super sick yet. It's still kind of early. I went online and found one of those pregnancy tracker things. Our baby should be here by the end of November." Her joy coated the jagged edges of hearing "our baby," and Jack returned her smile. "As far as cravings, I'll be sure to let you know. I plan to milk your willingness to run out and fetch me food at all hours." Her wink pulled a chuckle out of him.

"I almost forgot. My mom wrote letters to each of us for when we find out we're going to be parents. It's under the onesie." Jack pulled out an envelope with familiar handwriting. He slid it in his pocket and kissed Rachael's forehead. Jack held her close again as he battled rising demons.

This beautiful woman has done nothing but love me despite myself and now carries life within her—life we made together—and all I can do is think about myself and how I will face and handle these changes. I've proven myself thoroughly unworthy, yet again.

* * *

That night he poured his heart into his love for her and held her tightly afterward. She slept peacefully in his arms. Memories rose then with pain and panic, scrambling his thoughts. Mixed messages from years ago joined with his current situation to produce an incoherent jumble.

Jack whispered to his sleeping bride, "You deserve better. So does our child. How can I tell you I'm too scared—terrified—to be a father to the child you're already carrying? I promised you I'd do better, be better; but I haven't. I could lose control at any time—hurt you again. Hurt our baby."

Self-loathing consumed him as Jack considered all the dangers and uncertainties ahead. "I've failed you, Rach. Like I failed Tray and broke my promise to him."

Jack pictured Rachael crumpled against their wall and realized he would likely lead his team to slaughter again. This time, though, the team was his wife and child. And, he'd be the one to pull the trigger.

Rachael's hair billowed across Jack's bare chest. He looked down at the curve of the nose he loved to kiss and then to the lips he could still taste. She was his dream come true, a shining light in the darkness of his nights, his constant compass and the sight through which he clearly saw life around him. He could not bear failing her again.

He gently shifted her down onto the bed and softly kissed her lips as his tears dampened her cheeks. He got up and slipped on his jeans from earlier and a hoodie. Scout sat up, ready to follow, but Jack commanded, "Stay. Take care of our girl."

Jack pulled on his shoes, grabbed his wallet from the dresser and picked up one other item from their closet. He slipped out the bedroom door and grabbed his keys on the way to his pickup.

Scout's scratching at their door summoned Rachael from a deep sleep. Sleep-confused, she felt for Jack in the void beside her. Terror jolted her awake. She flung open the double doors to their room as her eyes darted around their home. Scout dashed to the front door, frantically pawing beneath the door, as Rachael returned to the bedroom and ran onto the balcony.

Jack's truck was gone.

She returned to the counter where she'd left her phone the day before. As she walked to their closet, she tapped a recent number. Her father's voice broke the third ring.

"Jack's gone." Rachael's stretched voice nearly cracked as she continued. "And, Daddy, so is my gun."

XXXV

Sacrifice

April 7, 2014

Jack cut his headlights before turning into the vacant lot on Ben's street. He recalled how he and Scout had found shade under that oak. He never should have come here.

He slid out of the truck; the 9mm cold and live in his palm. Jack was a trained killer; it seemed fitting he'd be his own executioner. Memories rose as he approached the tree. The liquor's seduction. The train's blinding light. The breeze blowing beneath the rock ledge. Each time he had feared eternity. Jack had certainty in his end this time and accepted that he must sacrifice himself for his family. His foggy mind blinded him to any alternative. No more swinging like a wrecking ball into his loved ones' lives. He could control this and finally fix his destruction.

The dampness between the oak's roots soaked his jeans as Jack knelt beneath its watchful limbs. He looked up and cried out to God, praying for forgiveness, for his family's protection, for their comfort. He poured out his sins and cursed his demons as he slid the barrel into his mouth. The roughness of the grip awoke other memories—the bad of his past; the good of his present. The icy metal burned his mouth as he sealed his lips around it and ran his thumb along the trigger's smooth curve. He wouldn't have to shoot clean; he only had to squeeze. The bullet couldn't fail.

Jack sat back on his heels and heard a crinkle. Confused, he put off his intention and reached into his jeans' pocket. It was the letter from Rachael's mom. He removed the note from its envelope as he returned to his truck's light.

Hi there, Dad-to-Be!

If you're reading this, then I've got a grandbaby on the way. How exciting! If I were there, Rachael can tell you I'd be fussing over her and shopping for impossibly tiny shoes and clothes and hats.

So, let's see … words of wisdom: parenting doesn't come with a guide.

You will always feel lost and entirely inadequate and uncertain about this whole parenting thing. Get used to it. You'll make a million mistakes and worry and fret all hours of the day or night over food choices, teething, school, friends, rules, discipline and so much more.

You need help to be a godly father. That's the first and only thing you've got to know. And, you've got to admit it and ask for it because, buddy, you are this kid's daddy; and being a dad is the most important thing you can do for him or her. The good news is, being a dad is fairly simple. It's all about sacrifice. To sacrifice for your child, you just need to show up.

Be there. Listen. Love. Lead.

You've got plenty of help all around you. Rachael, of course—you're a team in this and don't forget it! Grandpa Ben [moment for me to chuckle at that one, please]. Your parents. Your church family. So many places to turn for help, so DO IT! Ask for help. Ask for prayer.

Because the second you think you can take it into your own hands and handle all the fears, uncertainties and challenges of parenthood by yourself, you will fall.

At the end of the day, you've got to run back to the foundation of your family I mentioned in our last letter conversation—the cornerstone of Christ. In Him lies the greatest help of all. So, on the days when you're feeling like the least of the dads, check yourself. Have you been spending time with God—reading His word, praying? Are your eyes focused on Him or on something or someone else? Have you been leading your wife and little one to Him? If the answers are no, then race to Him in prayer and say, "I need help. I cannot do this on my own."

Because you can't. Repeat after me: I can't. Say it out loud. I can't. Now, accept it. You cannot do this in your own power.

Please kiss my girl for me, kiss her belly and kiss that baby when he or she is born—and every day after that. Soak up each and every moment.

Also—and, this is extra important—don't call me Grandma. I'm currently much too young and spry to be okay with that. You and Rachael come up with something cute and fun for this little bundle to call me when it's time for first words. Oh, and definitely, definitely use "Grandpa Ben." Make sure he doesn't get a choice!

Love,

Mom

Jack dried his eyes as he exited his truck once more. He carefully folded the paper and returned it to its envelope. He walked straight and sure to his spot beneath the tree. Again, he knelt; his face lifted to the heavens.

Jack closed his eyes, as his future flashed all around him.

***

June 22, 2016

Ben scanned the broken faces before him. Every pair of eyes shimmered with the emotions stirred by each act of Jack's story.

"After I got off the phone with my little girl that night," Ben continued. "I threw on a pair of shoes and hit my front door. The last sight I expected was a man, walking up my driveway and beaming with a radiance I'd only seen on him a few times."

A collective gasp rippled through the listeners. A man with shoulder-length dirty blond hair and a reddish beard emerged with his arm around a smiling redhead. She carried a toddler with his daddy's hair and his mama's fierce blue eyes. Along the man's other side trotted a shaggy beast of a dog with a goofy grin and a scar.

"Jack ran up that driveway to me and wrapped me in a bear hug. He told me I was gonna be a grandpa and that he couldn't wait to be a dad, but that he needed help—a whole lot of it."

Jack kissed his wife's temple before accepting the microphone from his father-in-law. "A few lifetimes ago, I sat where you do today; so, I can stand here and tell you life won't be easy. If you're in this room, it means you're battling a fiercer foe than others might. The thing is, the war's only lost if we stop fighting or if we give up when we're too tired to continue alone.

"Our demons will continue to rise. We still have battles to fight. I said I knew life wouldn't be easy, but part of me believed the lie. That lie introduced hopelessness, fear and despair; and they nearly swallowed me whole. When the gifts come, ... and they will ..." Jack smiled at his wife as she moved beside him. Their son reached a chubby hand to Jack's shoulder. "We have to accept them, embrace them and remember we don't have to fight alone. That night I destroyed my flimsy excuses instead of myself. All the procrastination on getting help, on helping others like me—I buried them beneath the oak. Once I called and apologized—again—to Rachael, Ben and I put on a pot of coffee and talked. We called Randy over and started a plan. We made time to get together and we set in motion a support group for PTSD warriors that's grown to stretch across several states.

"The final night I almost ended the life God gifted me, I forgot the truth that we weren't made to walk alone. I was too proud to ask for help, and I pulled a Peter. I took my eyes off my target, off Jesus. The waves beat at me, and I nearly drowned. Worst of all, I misused my confidence in eternity and totally butchered the concept of sacrifice. It's true that, in Christ, there's no fear in death; but there's also responsibility in life.

"I spent all those years running because I thought it was best for others. Fact is, that was nothing but selfishness and pride in thinking I could control something. I let my eyes lead me astray, heard the train whistle blow, looked down on the valley and tasted the metallic bitterness of a bullet. Every ridiculous excuse I waved like a white flag held me back from getting help—and from helping others. Turns out, I can't fix anything. And, sacrifice and leadership? Like my mother-in-law wrote, they begin with simply showing up. Being there to listen and love—even with our imperfections, inadequacies and battles—is the best gift we can give. As I look back, I realize how most of my life has been spent searching for purpose in something or someone, but I never put all my focus on the *right* Someone.

"I hope you learn these lessons quicker than I did. If you're not sure where to start your search for help, that's where."

Jack nodded to a roughly hewn cross covering the back wall of the chapel. A cloud shifted, allowing a sunbeam to illuminate its center.

"Look to the symbol of true Sacrifice. Sacrifice that created abundant life on this earth, eternal life to come and perfect peace throughout for those who simply accept that greatest gift and keep their eyes fixed on Him above all else."

§

RESOURCES

Within the pages of this fictional account, you'll find much truth in the pain and struggles of our main character. For that reason, we have included a list with some resources in the United States for your own battles and beasts. For more local guidance and assistance, contact a church near you. Help awaits, friend. Accept it!

SUICIDE PREVENTION: 1-800-273-8255
suicidepreventionlifeline.org

SUBSTANCE ABUSE: 1-888-633-3239
http://drughelpline.org

HOMELESSNESS: 211
www.211.org/services/housing-and-utilities

PTSD & OTHER VETERAN-SPECIFIC CHALLENGES: 211
www.woundedwarriorproject.org

CREDITS & PERMISSIONS

The hymn "AMAZING GRACE" is public domain.

"THE MARINE RIFLEMAN'S CREED" was written by Major General William Rupertus following the 1941 attack on Pearl Harbor. Since that time, countless Marines have memorized it. It's only fitting to include parts of it here in a fictional account of a young man whose first purpose came with the title United States Marine. Thank you to KAREN JENSEN, editor for WWII Magazine, and MICHAEL HASKEW, editor for WWII History Magazine, for their advice on providing proper credit for this iconic poem.

Use of the trademarked name CHEERWINE comes with gracious permission by the soft drink makers and Carolina Beverage Corp. No story set in the southeastern United States is complete without inclusion of "the South's unique cherry soft drink."

ACKNOWLEDGMENTS

While the seed of a story is first planted by the MASTER STORYTELLER where it grows in the heart and soul of a writer, a multitude of gardeners assist in its weeding, tending and watering.

First, to my husband TONY, thank you for reading my book, for guiding my red pen to make it better and for giving me the courage to start and the confidence to end.

To MY CHILDREN, thank you for enduring my impatience and exhaustion and understanding my many deadlines. This is the first book of many, and one of which I hope you'll be proud. Thank you for giving feedback on the cover design, helping with my logo and always being there with tiny shots of encouragement.

To my sister JANE SIMS, you always knew I'd be writing this page, even when I didn't. Thank you for believing in me and in Jack. Thanks for brainstorming with me about everything from his motivations to marketing his story. And, thank you for inspiring Rachael's passions and helping me design jewelry in my imagination.

To each of my SUBSCRIBERS AND FOLLOWERS, thank you for believing in me before I had my name on a book cover. For that faith, I'll be forever grateful. You motivated me more than you know and showed me the joy of writing for readers.

To my many READERS, thank you for choosing to give your precious reading time to Jack's story. I hope you found it worthy. A special note of thanks to you. Yes, you—reading this page. I do that, too. To the last word, my fierce reader friend!

To MEA SMITH, you are my first reader, editor, critique partner, writing partner-in-crime, biggest fan, better half of the QWERTYs and incredible friend. Your critique and edit turned my fledging tale into a full-feathered bird who learned to soar. Thank you for making me so much better than I was, all while telling me I would be.

To my critique partners, KELSEY ATKINS, TAURI COX and DEVON HARRY, what would I do without you ladies? You drive me to be better, help me see scenes from a different point of view and show me how to improve. You encourage me, motivate me and send the best GIFs at just the right times.

To my expert readers and sources, you are why there's truth in my fiction; and any lingering inaccuracies are certainly my own errors. Thank you for taking the time to answer endless questions, even when they probably didn't make much sense. For those who gave your time to read as well, thank you for your willingness to read passages, even in their roughest conditions.

Thank you to Rev. Dr. JUSTIN B. STODGHILL, Capt/USMC (ret.); BEN RINGVELSKI, Col/USMC; and JAKE HUNT, MSgt/USMC (ret.), for helping me honor THE FEW. THE PROUD.

Thank you to JOHN W. STODGHILL, MSM/HRM, BSN, BA, RN, and DR. JOSHUA STODGHILL, D.O., for evaluating my many medical tragedies while you flew across the ocean and at least a couple continents together.

Thank you to TONY RANCATORE, SR., CW2/Army (ret.), for answering my many, many questions about building, woodworking, whittling, carving, tools and so much more. Thank you also for letting me turn your shop into a photo studio.

Thank you to PAUL DUTSCH for your mechanical expertise and helping me make my tragedies realistic, despite my "writer-ease."

Thank you to ALYCIA LONG for your real estate knowledge and suggestions and your excitement to share them.

Thank you to Officer ERIC DEMMER, NOPD, for your law enforcement guidance and for asking about word counts and being excited to hold the first manuscript.

To KEN STUMPF JR.—your vast knowledge of all things pinball saved my story. Thank you!

Thank you to BJ BOURG who took time out from packing for a much-deserved vacation to answer my sniper mantra question.

And, a special thank you to DIANNE BAHAM for your sensitive reading and for your love for and approval of our friend, Ducky.

To my BETA READERS who willingly took a chance on me and my story. You gave incredible feedback that helped me put the finishing touches on this manuscript. Beyond that, you gave me the push I needed to turn that manuscript into the book we're all holding. So, from the bottom of my heart, thank you, BRIAN J. CASE, ANNIE HENDRICKS, ADAM HENDRICKS, GABRIELLE HILL, OSCAR SHOEMAKER, KATIE HOLLIER, DOMINICK RANCATORE, ERIC DEMMER, AMY DUTSCH and MIKE DORAN.

A published book requires more than just the words inside. Thank you to RACHAEL RITCHEY for your incredible design work on this cover. I am still amazed at how you took my initial explanation of my book and a few vague thoughts of mine and turned it into exactly what I wanted. It's perfect. Thank you for all your advice and assistance in how to publish in the first place. You've been a mentor, a colleague and, now, a dear friend. And, thank you to AMY DUTSCH who graciously loaned me your camera baby so I could finish up the photos for the cover. That's true friendship right there!

Every writer should have a writing community behind him or her. I'm blessed with many. They encourage and drive me, pick me up when I'm down and forgive me when I disappear for a couple weeks when deadlines are looming. So, thank you to WRITER MOMS INC., WRITER MOM LIFE, TURKEY ON WRITE—which morphed into our NINJAS, the CRUX CREW, #WRITERSCHEER, MOTIVATED WRITER, my BLOGBATTLE buddies and, of course, my ACOWAR girls. Plus, a special thank you to my in-person community, CREATIVE MINDS WRITERS GROUP in Ponchatoula. Thank you for welcoming me and my kids and for sharing in my excitement over each and every step of the journey.

To the ST. TAMMANY PARISH LIBRARY system, especially my two Slidell branches: thank you for getting excited with me and embracing my cheesiness when I take weird selfies where my books will one day live. Also, thank you for the massive tables I can spread my work out on, the wi-fi and my most comfy chair back in that corner. When I sell millions of books, I'll bring you a plaque to put above it.

To the T.A.R.D.I.S. LITTLE FREE LIBRARY OF SLIDELL (AKA the best LFL ever), keep being nerdy and promoting the joy of reading in our community!

To my church family at NORTHSIDE BAPTIST CHURCH, thank you for your support and for always asking when you can buy my books and attend book signings.

What writer doesn't have a faithful companion or two or more? To BENTLEY, ROMY and—of course—TOLKIEN CAT, thank you for the snuggles, the nudges, the licks and even the drool on my pages. Oh, and the CHICKENS. We survived your bathtub days; and, despite your mess, you're five pretty cool chicks and one studly rooster.

And last, but not least, to my CHARACTERS—thank you for making yourselves real to me. Some of you appeared, larger than life and wrote your own lines—looking at you, Ducky. Others took time, patience and getting blindsided when I least expected it … and rarely had a pen. Either way, I love you all and couldn't have dreamed up a better cast for my debut. Go forth and live on in more imaginations, my babies!

Photo: Casie Jones Photography

Legacy and identity, founded on hope-filled faith, infuse the tales of the soul written from the heart of **JOY E. RANCATORE.** Her Carolina's Legacy Collection embraces everyday moments that constitute a lifetime and its heritage. Told around multiple related characters, this collection explores faith, life, death and the demons within through four mediums—novel, novella, short stories and epistolary.

An avid reader, student of human behaviors and unwitting empath, Joy absorbs emotions and spills them onto the pages of her work. Joy's technical background includes more than two decades of professional writing and editing. Ongoing training in writing, publishing, business and counseling enables her to package soul-filled stories for her readers. An award-winning, multi-genre Indie Author, Joy believes extraordinary things await her characters and their tales.

Despite a fondness for her roles as author, editor, podcaster and speaker, Joy is a hobbit at heart with Bilbo's zeal for mountains. She enjoys a life of quiet stillness with her husband, two children, dog and cat and more books than she's willing to count. When daily homeschool lessons are complete, she eagerly prepares for teatime before writing your next favorite story.

Visit Joy for Book News, Free Stories,
Book Club Kits and More:
www.joyerancatore.com/links

HAVE A BOOK CLUB?

READ:
Any Good Thing
(or any book in Carolina's Legacy Collection)
together.

REQUEST:
- a Book Club Kit
- a virtual or in-person chat with the author

VISIT:
www.joyerancatore.com/book-clubs

COLOPHON

The typeface used with gracious permission in the cover design and throughout the book is Bentham, created by designer and developer, Ben Weiner. Interior formatting is primarily 12 point sizing. Headings and subheads fluctuate between 16 and 34 point sizing. For more on this typeface, read the creator's description:

"I like the lettering on nineteenth-century maps, on gravestones and on the maker's plates of cast-iron machinery. It is characterised by expressive flowing and bulging curves, mannered awkwardness and the bobbles on the terminals of its characters. The letterform conventionally called 'modern face' is the typographical equivalent, and it can be found in books printed throughout the nineteenth century. Its descendants survived into educational textbooks produced into the late twentieth century, and it is preserved in computer science as the style which Donald Knuth adopted for his TeX typesetting system.

"Bentham is a half-way design; it's true neither to the type produced during the nineteenth century, nor to the letterforms of cartographers, stonecutters, or engravers. It's really a sort of examination of the characteristics these letters share, coloured by my approach to type drawing."

WANT MORE?

For more information on upcoming releases from
LOGOS & MYTHOS PRESS

Visit logosandmythospress.com/links and subscribe to their
email list.

Thank you for reading!

LOGOS & MYTHOS PRESS

SLIDELL, LA, USA